HIGH Stakes

A Deal with the Devil

Nicola Jane

Copyright © 2020 – Original by Nicola Jane under the title A Deal with the Devil.

Copyright © 2024 by Nicola Jane Under the title High Stakes.

All rights reserved.

No portion of this book may be reproduced in any form without written permission from the publisher or author, except as permitted by U.K. copyright law.

Cover Designer: Wingfield Designs

SPELLING NOTE

Please note, this author resides in the United Kingdom and is using British English. Therefore, some words may be viewed as incorrect or spelled incorrectly, however, they are not.

This book is a work of fiction. The names, characters, places, and incidents are all products of the author's imagination and are not to be construed as real. Any similarities are entirely coincidental.

NICOLA JANE

HIGH STAKES

Trigger Warning

This book contains betrayal, miscarriage and situations that people may find triggering.

contents

Playlist	X
CHAPTER ONE	1
CHAPTER TWO	10
CHAPTER THREE	20
CHAPTER FOUR	31
CHAPTER FIVE	40
CHAPTER SIX	50
CHAPTER SEVEN	62
CHAPTER EIGHT	74
CHAPTER NINE	89
CHAPTER TEN	109
CHAPTER ELEVEN	127

CHAPTER TWELVE	137
CHAPTER THIRTEEN	147
CHAPTER FOURTEEN	156
CHAPTER FIFTEEN	169
CHAPTER SIXTEEN	188
CHAPTER SEVENTEEN	205
CHAPTER EIGHTEEN	216
CHAPTER NINETEEN	232
CHAPTER TWENTY	242
CHAPTER TWENTY-ONE	260
CHAPTER TWENTY-TWO	282
CHAPTER TWENTY-THREE	293
CHAPTER TWENTY-FOUR	305
CHAPTER TWENTY-FIVE	318
CHAPTER TWENTY-SIX	336
CHAPTER TWENTY-SEVEN	352
CHAPTER TWENTY-EIGHT	367
CHAPTER TWENTY-NINE	387
CHAPTER THIRTY	404
CHAPTER THIRTY-ONE	417

CHAPTER THIRTY-TWO	432
CHAPTER THIRTY-THREE	443
CHAPTER THIRTY-FOUR	451
EPILOGUE	460
A Note Before You Go	462
About The Author	463
Social Media	465

PLaYLIST

I Hate You, I Love You – gnash ft. Olivia O'Brien
I Don't Wanna Live Forever – Zayn ft. Taylor Swift
Be Alright – Dean Lewis
Bruises – Lewis Capaldi
Let Me Down Slowly – Alec Benjamin ft. Alessia Cara
If We Had Each Other – Alec Benjamin
Brother – Kodaline
Train Wreck – James Arthur
you broke me first – Tate McRae
that way – Tate McRae

rumours – gnash ft. Mark Johns
the broken hearts club – gnash
One Last Breath – Creed
Hide & Seek – Stormzy
Love The way You Lie – Rhianna ft. Eminem
Strip That Down – Liam Payne ft. Quavo
For You – Liam Payne ft. Rite Ora

CHAPTER ONE

Bella

I close my eyes and put my head back letting the rain splash against my face. It's been weeks since we've had a good down pour, and it feels good against my clammy skin. I press the volume button on my headphones, blasting Drake into my ears. I can't wait to get in and shower. As much as I love my job, I hate being covered in sticky cake mix and icing sugar.

As I approach the small semi-detached house, which I share with my dad, I notice the black pick-up parked outside. It looks out of place in our run-down area, but it must be a visitor for the neighbour. The new girl that has moved in next door seems to have a lot of male callers and most look suspiciously loaded, not that I'm judging.

I open the front door and fight with my bag. Why can I never just stick my hand in and find my phone? It's literally like Narnia in there with wrappers, deodorant, pens, my kindle, amongst other stuff and all I want to do is turn the music off.

I come to an abrupt stop; Standing in front of me is the biggest guy I have ever seen. For a second, I wonder if he's a statue because he doesn't move, he doesn't speak; he just stands there looking completely cool, rocking a black suit and shades, blocking my entrance to the kitchen.

"Erm, hey." I smile nervously.

He doesn't speak but gives a slight nod of his head to acknowledge that he's heard me.

"Dad?" I call out, not taking my eyes off mister muscle mountain.

"He's in the kitchen," he says, making me jump. He's got such a deep voice, it rumbles through me, and I shiver. He notices my reaction because he sniggers, giving a knowing nod. He isn't bad looking so I'm sure he's used to getting that kind of reaction from women.

He moves to one side and points in the direction of the kitchen, like I don't know where the hell my own kitchen is. I slowly edge past, keeping my eyes on him for any sudden movements. Not that I would do much if he suddenly made a grab for me, my height stands at just five-five, and I have a tiny, slim frame. It's nothing compared to his large, well-built, mountain of a body. He clearly works out...a lot.

I open the kitchen door to find Dad sitting at the kitchen table looking glum. "Dad, who the hell is that man mountain in the hall?" I ask in a hushed tone, hoping the beastly guy doesn't hear me, "I literally almost screamed the house down. And why is he just standing there not doing anything, it's weird. What's going on?"

I place my bag on the table and look up. My dad is staring past me, so I follow his line of vision and then let out a little yelp when I notice another huge guy. He's stood at the far end of the kitchen, leaning against the wall and watching me with amusement.

"Oh dear god," I squeak.

"Bella, this is Aiden Tremos." I don't miss the guilty look that crosses my dad's face. I glance again at the stranger. He is so completely gorgeous that I daren't look him full in the eye in case I make a complete idiot out of myself. He's well-built, like the man mountain guarding the hall, but taller, with the brightest blue eyes I've ever seen. Tattoos crawl across his arms and up his neck and he's dressed well, in navy suit trousers with a white shirt, the sleeves are rolled up, giving him a casual, yet dangerous look.

Aiden gives me a cocky grin and folds his arms across his broad chest. "Have you finished?" he asks, humour lacing his words.

I feel my face burn with embarrassment, *he caught me ogling*. I turn back to dad, who still isn't meeting my eye. "Please tell me you don't owe money again, Dad?"

He looks at Mr. Tremos who moves towards me, "Maybe you'd like to sit down?" he offers, pulling out a chair.

I take a step back, "No, I want to know what the hell's going on?"

He grips the back of the chair and bites his lower lip, "Sit, Isabella." The way he commands leaves no room for argument and I find myself lowering into the chair. I don't think I should piss this guy off; he's come with backup and who knows what they are into. *Drugs, gambling?* I've recently read that the numbers are on the rise for human trafficking.

"I own a few nightclubs and bars in the area," he explains, sitting across from me. He looks too big to be at this table, in this kitchen. "Your dad was in one of my bars last night." I look over at dad; I feel disappointment start to creep in.

He's been battling an alcohol addiction for as long as I can remember. Mum died ten years ago, but it started way before then. I've spent most of my twenty-three years looking after him. Putting him to bed whenever he is too intoxicated and working extra hard to keep this roof over our heads. Lately, things have improved. Dad got a job at the local fish market, and for the last two months, he hasn't drunk a drop. Stupid me for thinking we had turned a corner.

"Whatever he's done, I'm sorry okay," I say, "He isn't well. If its money, I can pay you back, I just need time."

He puts his hand up, effectively shutting me up. I bite my lower lip to stop me calling him out on that, I hate rudeness. "Your dad doesn't owe me anything, but he was spouting some crazy stuff and I'm here because I'm worried he's put you in danger."

Relief floods me for a second, knowing that I won't have to pay off another debt. My wage is only just covering everything as it is. But then the words sink in, *he's put me in danger*. I glare at Dad, who grabs my hand, I pull it away before he gets chance to beg my forgiveness. "What kind of danger?"

"He offered to sell you, Bella." I inhale sharply. Of all the things I was expecting, that definitely wasn't one of them.

"He what?" I gasp, convinced I misheard.

"Bella, I can explain," rambles dad, tears forming in his eyes.

"Then please start," I stand up and begin pacing the floor.

"I was stupidly drunk; I don't remember much apart from waking up in Mr. Tremos' office. But I've received texts from some nasty pieces of work telling me I owe them."

The words are taking a while to penetrate my slow, tired brain.

I look at Mr. Tremos, whose watching our interaction with interest. I put my head in my hands, the reality of what is happening making me feel nauseous. "My god Dad, just when I think you can't possibly fuck up anymore," I mutter quietly. "When you say sell, what do you mean exactly? For work?" I ask, looking directly at Mr. Tremos.

He glances at my dad; then back to me. "No Bella, your virginity."

I freeze, open mouthed, looking from him to my dad. It's like a story from one of those stupid books I've been reading.

People tell me it's something I should be proud of, my virginity, but I'm not. It's like a bad omen, always hanging over me. It brings me stress whenever I meet someone new and becomes some big deal, and then before I know it, everything becomes about that instead of me.

"I don't know what I was thinking, Bells, I'm so sorry," says dad, interrupting my thoughts.

When I look at him, really look, I see the desperately sad old man he's become. I was kidding myself he'd change. "You need to go, Dad. This is the final straw," I whisper, hurt evident in my voice. I've spent most of my life caring for this waste of space and he repays me with this.

He looks at me confused. "It's not safe for you to stay here, sweetheart, not on your own. What if these guys come looking for you?"

"And where the hell am I supposed to go?"

He rubs my arms, sheer panic on his face, "Go back to Carl, just for a bit."

I shove him away and he falls back, landing on his backside. "Go back to Carl. Are you serious right now? You think I'm safer with that maniac. Have you forgotten what he did to me? I hate him, more than I hate you right now, and that's saying something."

"Bella, he's a copper. He'll keep you safe. Who's going to come after a cop's girl?" he asks, trying to convince himself more than me. "Besides, he's expecting you."

I glare at him. "You just went ahead and sorted that; you didn't even talk to me about it?" I shake my head in annoyance, adding, "First you sell me, and then you dump me on the biggest arsehole you can find."

"Well, when I realised what I'd done, Mr. Tremos suggested I find you somewhere safe to stop, I didn't know where else was safe. I didn't want to put Aria in any danger. I just thought Carl owes you one and he said he'd be happy to help out."

Of course he would, he's been trying to get in my knickers from the second he realised I was still a virgin. *Creep.*

Mr. Tremos stands, pulling my attention to him. He makes a show of refolding his shirt sleeves. "I'm sorry we met like this Bella. Good luck with..." he pauses, glancing at me, "everything."

I place my hands on my hips. "Really, that's all you've got?"

He stops at the door and turns back to face me. "Sorry?" he asks, confused.

"You come in here with that scary gorilla out there and you get all like; *'Hey Bella your dads sold your ass to some dodgy bastards'* and then you just get up and go. I thought you were concerned for my safety."

He gives a laugh. "I really don't sound like that."

"Did you buy me?"

He laughs again and shakes his head. "No, I turned the offer down."

I arch a brow, folding my arms over my chest. "Why, am I not good enough?" I can't believe I've just said that exact sentence out loud like some offended bitch, and I inwardly cringe.

He begins to walk towards the door again and I feel panic, like if he leaves, something bad will happen. Surely, I'm safer with him and his gorilla.

"What shall I do?" I ask.

He shrugs, pats the man mountain on the back and they leave. I stand there like a goldfish, my mouth opening and closing.

What the actual fuck just happened? This stuff doesn't happen in real life, in MY life!

CHAPTER TWO

Aiden

I did the right thing. I went and told the girl what her dumbass dad was doing, but then he mentioned the damn copper and that was my cue to leave.

Fuck. I run my hands through my hair. Raff said it would be easy, that she would be putty in my hands, but she really doesn't seem like the putty kind.

Her dad had told me previously about an ex-boyfriend that Isabella could stay with, one that she had no interest in any longer. But he failed to mention it was the copper, one I know very well. I'm going to kick Raff's dumb arse when I get back to the club. What's the point in having him do background checks and research, if he misses huge details like that.

"Thought she was coming with, Boss?" asks JP.

"Yeah, me too. Raff's an idiot. She's the Ex of Carl, as in Cop Carl."

"Oh. That's not good. Do we have a plan B?"

"Who knows what Raff's come up with for plan B, he couldn't even get plan fuckin' A right."

※

We arrive at Tremos, my nightclub. I shove open the club door in frustration and it bangs back against the wall, the hinges creaking in protest.

"Raff, you dumb fuck, where the hell are you?"

He appears from behind the bar, topless and pulling up his jeans with a wide grin across his face. I roll my eyes. I'm out pulling in the girl, and he's fucking about without a care in the world.

"Aid, where's the girl?" he asks, pulling a blond to her feet. She wipes her mouth then totters off towards the bathroom, butt naked. We all watch her tiny ass before I turn back to him.

"Cop Carl's ex missus, you mean?" I ask, chucking my suit jacket on the nearest bar stool.

"What? No way, I checked her out, man; she's never been with anyone. Jake was very clear about her."

"Then tell me why she's heading there right now?" I grab a glass and pour a shot of whiskey. I knock the amber liquid back, wincing as it burns, and then I slam the glass on the bar. "I'm running out of time, jackass!"

He buckles his belt. "Her hospital records did show an assault about a month ago, it's how I know she was still a virgin, cos they checked she hadn't been raped. Just cuts, bruises and a broken wrist. You reckon that was Carl's work?"

I shrug my shoulders. "Possibly, she did say he had done something to her."

"Then that's it, big man," smiles Raff, slapping my back, "Swoop in there, rescue the chick from the big bad ex, and she'll come running willingly."

I drop my head to the bar and groan. "This is why I don't do this shit, too much hard work."

Bella

Carl sits back on the sofa with a huge smug grin across his face. "I knew you'd be back."

"You're a police officer; you protect people, and right now, I need protecting. But please don't get it twisted, Carl, we're not a thing anymore so let's call this your apology for landing me in hospital."

"Call it what you want, Bella. Go and unpack your shit."

I sit on the edge of the double bed, looking around the room in disgust. It's a typical bachelor pad with black silk sheets on the huge bed, but not much in the way of furniture. There's a mirror on the opposite wall to the bed and I can only imagine the reason Carl would have it positioned there.

How the hell did I end up back here? Surely, I'd be just as safe with Aria. We grew up together; she owns the bakery where I work and lives above it in a cosy little apartment.

She's petite like me, standing at just five foot two, but she's fiery and I reckon she could keep me safe. I smile at the thought. She's going to screw when she knows I'm staying here with Carl, she hates him.

I met him a few months ago; he was on duty and looked fit in his uniform. We got chatting in Costa and I agreed to go out for a real drink with him. He was charming and funny and the fact he had a great body and a gorgeous face to match, helped. We began seeing each other but Carl got fed up with taking things slow. Three months into the relationship we began arguing, a lot, so I ended things. He became obsessed with getting me into bed and it was such a turn off.

Last month I bumped into him on a night out, things got ugly fast, and he hit me. I ended up in hospital with a broken wrist. Don't get me wrong, I'm no damsel in distress. I didn't sit sobbing whilst he hit me; I fought him with everything I had which is probably the reason I came off worse. Luckily, some security guys from a nearby club broke it all up.

I didn't press charges, Aria was so mad at me, but I didn't see the point. Carl is a slippery little fucker; he would have gotten off the charges somehow and I didn't want the stress of a court hearing with everything I had going on with dad. The thought of standing up in court and explaining that he was pissed off because I wouldn't give him my virginity, gives me hives. The fact that I'm still a virgin at the ripe old age of twenty-three is embarrassing enough.

I decided cutting contact was the best way. Carl came to see me in hospital and apologised. He loves his job and agreed to stay away from me, and up until this point, he's stuck to his word.

Aiden

I flick through the pictures of Bella. She really is stunning. Long brown hair going all the way down to her rounded backside. A tiny, slim waist and c cup perky tits. Blue eyes and a perfect smile with lips begging to be kissed. If I were the kind of person to feel, I'd definitely feel something for this beauty.

I drop the pictures back into the file and pick up the paperwork. I stare at my brother's signature at the bottom and shake my head. That son of a bitch must have thought he was so funny drawing up these papers.

I'm interrupted by a knock on the door.

"Enter."

JP appears. "Hey Boss, just thought you would want to know that the girl is queuing to get in." My head snaps up, "What?" He nods and points to one of the CCTV monitors on the wall opposite me, "See." Sure enough, Bella is in the queue, and she's dressed to impress in a dress that's barely there, with a group of females.

"Go get her in, JP. And try not to scare the shit out of her this time." He nods and disappears.

Bella

"I feel like it's too short, Ari." I tug the bottom of the dress that just about covers my backside. She knows I hate revealing clothes; it makes me uncomfortable to be on show.

"Jesus, Bells, chill out will yah, it's a night out. Besides, you're out to impress, aren't you?"

"Impress who? In case you have forgotten, I'm back staying with Carl," I remind her, she rolls her eyes. She wasn't impressed when I relayed my recent events, but I distracted her with the night out.

"A relationship of convenience doesn't count."

"I feel like Carl won't agree with that statement." I laugh, but it soon fades when I notice the man mountain from earlier, heading towards us.

He stops in front of me. "Follow me," he orders.

I glance at Aria warily who shrugs and rushes to follow him. I groan and follow. He takes us up a flight of stairs and opens a door. "Tonight, you are all VIP guests to Mr. Tremos."

I stare around the crowded room, full of sparkling golds and silvers. I've never been in a VIP area before and I have to admit, I'm excited. "Wow," I mutter, "thanks." He nods his head once and leaves.

Aria gives a little squeal. "Is that the guy?"

"One of them. Mr. Tremos must own this place. I never connected the name," I reply, looking around at the huge chandeliers hanging low above the bar. The place is amazing and way better than the main bar downstairs.

Four Porn Star Martinis later and I'm feeling the buzz. The bar man is amazing, not only is he stunning to look at, but he makes the best drinks.

"So, Raff," slurs Aria. "Tell us more about Mr. Tremos."

He grins, "Why don't you go over and ask him what you want to know?"

I freeze and glance over to the spot he's nodding towards. Aiden is sat in a booth with two blondes either side of him, talking to another man in a suit. He suddenly looks at me and I look away, embarrassed he caught me staring.

"Fuck." I mutter.

"Fuck indeed," says Aria with a slight smirk crossing her face.

"What?" I ask in a panic. I daren't look back in case he catches me again, but curiosity is getting the better of me, and then I feel him. My skin prickles and I know he's there.

"Bella, what are you doing here?" His deep voice makes me shiver. I take a deep breath and turn to face him.

"Mr. Tremos, thank you for the VIP treatment."

"Well, as it's not safe for you to be out and about, I thought it better you be where I can keep an eye on you." His voice is stern and suddenly, I feel like I'm a naughty child.

He presses a finger to his ear and then says something into his wrist. I want to laugh at the James Bond style gadgets but the serious look on his face tells me I shouldn't.

"I am quite capable of looking after myself, but thanks again." I say, bringing his attention back to me.

I smile and turn my back on him. He leans in, and when I feel his front press against my back, I stiffen slightly.

"Do not turn your back on me, Isabella." He uses that growly voice again and I fidget against him. "If you keep pressing your backside against my cock like that, I may just have to take your father up on his offer."

I hold my breath, hearing him laugh as he moves away. No one's ever spoken to me like that, and I can't deny that his choice of words sends sparks straight to my core.

"Bella?" My heart drops at the sound of Carl's voice.

"Oh great," Aria says on a sigh.

Carl grabs my arm and spins me to face him. "What the fuck are you doing in here, I told you to stay at home." He's in my face before I can react. "How can I keep you safe if you're out here whilst I'm at work?"

Coming to my senses, I shove him from me, and he stumbles back. "How did you even get in here?" I rub my arm where he grabbed me, noting there's already a red mark.

"The door staff asked my permission to let him up," Aiden says, approaching again. "I thought he was your boyfriend, aren't you staying with him?"

"Well thanks for your help," I say sarcastically, "And for the record, he's my ex."

CHAPTER THREE

Aiden

She's pretty. Even when she's mad and her gorgeous, flawless face is all screwed up in anger. And my god does she smell good, all vanilla and fresh. Being so close to her makes me want to drag her off and lock her away, only letting her out to pleasure me with those plump lips.

I continue to watch this creep yelling at her, and notice JP glaring at me. "What?" I mouth, shrugging.

He points to Bella, who I note is giving as good as she gets. "Save her," he mouths, and I laugh. *I will, just not yet.*

Bella's friend nudges her arm against mine. "Hey, fancy a drink?" She gives me a cute smile. "We could be waiting for this to die down for a while," she adds, nodding to Bella and her boyfriend.

I indicate to JP to get us a drink and guide her over to my booth. "Is your friend always like this with her fella?"

"He's her ex. Bella hates him, but she needs a place to stop."

"Can't she stop with you?" I nod a thanks at JP, as he places our drinks down on the table.

"The plan," he whispers in my ear, but I shoe him away, much to his annoyance.

"She doesn't want to bring trouble to my shop," she explains.

I figure this must be Aria, the cake shop owner and Bella's best friend. She's pretty, in an English rose kind of way. Pale skin but rosy cheeks and large brown eyes. Her brown hair is cut short, and it suits her small oval face. She's petite and if I didn't have my sights set on her friend, I'd consider seducing her. "She must have other friends she can stay with?"

"There's Jack, but he just moved his boyfriend in, so she doesn't want to put on him. She's spent so much time looking after her dad, she's kept her circle small."

I watch Carl grab Bella and try to drag her from the club. I guess this is where I swoop in to save the girl. I stand and fasten my suit jacket as I head over. "Let her go." I say it firmly, I hold all the authority in this club, and I don't appreciate this idiot causing a scene in my VIP area where some of the top socialites hang out, including the top dogs that sign his pay check.

"Who the hell are you to tell me what to do, Tremos. This is my girl and I'm taking her home."

"She doesn't want to go with you, Harris. I suggest you let her go before I call DCI Caine and tell him what a fuss you're causing in my club."

He lets go of her arm, shoving her towards me. I catch her. "Keep her, she's too much trouble anyway," he spits, "-and don't get your hopes up, she doesn't put out." He storms off and I roll my eyes at his childish behaviour.

"Are you okay?" I ask, turning to Bella, but she doesn't look happy at all. In fact, she looks like she's about to explode.

"Why do you keep jumping in to defend my honour, I can look after myself."

I watch in confusion as she stomps away towards Aria. *"Win her over they said, it'd be easy, they said."* I scoff, shaking my head. I catch sight of Raff and JP laughing from behind the bar. Jake's probably up there with the big man and killing himself laughing. *Bastard.*

I join the two women, much to Bella's disgust, but they're sitting in my private booth and I'm not one to waste a perfectly good opportunity to get what I want. "So," smiles Aria, staring back and forth between me and Bella. "That went well." Bella throws a peanut at Aria's head, and she dodges it, laughing.

I wave my hand in Raff's direction, indicating that I need more drinks.

"Does everyone just serve you when you wave your hand like that?" asks Aria, arching a brow.

I shrug, "Usually. What's the point in owning a club if you have to serve yourself?"

Bella

I swallow my drink in one go because I feel uncomfortable. Carl's completely ruined my night and now I'm stressing about where I'm going to stay. If I was a normal girl of my age, I would probably hook up with some random guy and spend the night with him, only I'm not normal. I'm starting to feel like holding on to my virginity for the right one has become a hindrance.

It's not like I woke up one day and decided I was going to save myself, it just kind of happened. I haven't met a man that I've wanted to go that far with. The thought brings my attention back to the gorgeous God, sitting opposite me.

"Do you own this club?" Aria is quizzing him.

"Sort of." He finishes another drink and indicates to the bar that he needs a refill. It must be nice to hold that much power, and boy can he drink a lot.

"How can you sort of own a bar? You either do, or you don't. Why did you turn up at Bella's today?"

He shifts in his seat looking uncomfortable. "She already knows why."

"No, I want the real reason," insists Aria, "Why would some hot, club owning man, with people that run around after him, just turn up and pre-warn a girl about that. Why would it bother you what happens to her?"

I feel like I should jump in and rescue him from her never-ending questions, but I want to know the answer to this one, Arias got a point. Suddenly I'm shoved along the booth by the bar man. He grins at me as I squash up next to Aiden.

"Hey gorgeous ladies, your night doesn't look very fun from where I was standing."

"We were trying to get to know this mysterious man here, but he's not giving much up." says Aria.

Raff gives me a mischievous grin. "You want to get to know my man here, Bella?"

I feel myself redden with embarrassment, and I stare down at my drink. "It's Aria that wants to know him, not me." I'm mumble before kicking Aria under the table.

She laughs, "I just find it odd that he keeps popping up to rescue Bella, are you even single?"

Aiden gives Raff a warning glance, and when he notices I've witnessed it, he stands abruptly. "If Bella wants to ask me shit, then she can do it herself, we aren't in school."

We watch in surprise as he stomps away. Raff shakes his head, still grinning. "Don't mind him, he gets moody quicker than a woman. No offence."

♡

We carry on our night. Shots and various cocktails are constantly being brought to the table, all compliments of Mr. Tremos. Aiden occasionally appears, chatting to various people, before disappearing again. It just adds to his mystery.

It's not long before I'm starting to feel sick, and I realise I haven't been this drunk in a long time. I look around and notice the other girls we arrived with are nowhere to be seen. I get to my feet, grabbing on to the table for support because my head is seriously spinning but I need to pee. "Toilet," I explain, when Aria and Raff stop their conversation to look at me.

I stumble my way to the bathroom and stand in the queue, wondering why the hell we have to wait when this is supposed to be VIP treatment.

I pull out my phone and notice I have fifteen missed calls from Carl. "Wanker," I mutter, deleting them.

"Charming," rumbles a deep voice from behind me. I jump in fright, dropping my phone.

"Shit." I bend to get it, and lose my balance, falling on my backside. I look up at Aiden, who doesn't look amused by my stumbling, drunken self.

Sighing heavily, he swoops down and grabs my hands, tugging me back onto my feet. "Come, you can use my bathroom."

I rub my backside, then shove my phone back in my clutch bag. How many times can I possibly embarrass myself in front of him?

Aiden leads me back through the club, his huge hand encasing mine. He stops by the booth and says something to Raff and Aria. I notice how cosy they're looking together and make a mental note to ask her about it.

We continue on and into an office. It's huge and there's an entire wall off books which impresses me slightly. Before I can question him, he draws my attention to an elevator by pressing the call button. The doors open and he waits for me to step in, before entering himself and punching a code into the panel. The minute the doors close, I inhale and hold my breath. Anticipation pours from me, and I can't stop the slideshow of possible scenarios playing through my imagination. Him kissing me or pushing me against this elevator wall and demanding I fuck him. I shudder and press my thighs together, trying to ease the ache that he's unaware of.

The doors open into a lobby. It reminds me of a hotel. There's a large white door directly in front of us and he leads toward it, opening it and pulling me inside. My mouth falls open. The place is luxurious with a minimalist look and floor to ceiling windows that I'm sure have a fantastic view over London. "Wow, you're like Christian Grey," I blurt out without thinking. He rolls his eyes in amusement. "But you look like that actor, the one from Game of Thrones, Drogo." He leads me to the kitchen area and sits me on a stool. "Oh my god, you really do, what's his name?" I say it more to myself than to him.

He sighs and hands me a glass of water, "Jason Momoa."

"Yes, that's him," I say with glee, clapping my hands together. "You look just like him, only without all the hair. I really need to pee."

He takes me back through the apartment and to his bedroom. "Are you going to seduce me?" I ask with a giggle. He shoves me through another door and I'm in a bathroom. The lights flick on, and I'm temporarily blinded by the brightness.

"Hilarious," he huffs "Now pee."

I wait for him to leave before fumbling about to lift my dress. The relief is instant, and I groan in pleasure. Once I've finished, I open his bathroom cabinet and peer inside. Aria reckons you can tell a lot about a man from what he keeps in here. It's all very neat and tidy, with bottles of expensive looking aftershave all lined up. Painkillers, a razor and a comb, nothing exciting.

I wander back through to his bedroom. It's clean and bright. Nothing like Carl's. The sheets are white cotton, not a crease in them. I run my hand over them, loving the feel of the cool cotton against my hot skin. It's so inviting, I can't stop myself as I slip out of the dress and climb onto it, allowing my head to sink into the fluffy pillow, closing my eyes.

Aiden

"I'm serious, JP, it's not funny," I whisper yell into the phone. "She's completely naked and lying on my bed. What am I supposed to do?" His laughter rings out. I knew

I shouldn't have rung him, the useless bastard. I left her for five minutes and when I went back, she was lying on top of my bed, fast asleep.

"Bet she as the most gorgeous pair of tits," he muses, "Is she tanned everywhere?" When I don't respond, he calm's himself down. "Okay, just chuck a blanket over her. I'm sure she'll be mortified when she wakes up. But see this as a great opportunity. She'll respect that you didn't try it on with her, and that you took care of her while she was wasted and vulnerable. Girls love that shit."

I disconnect the call and quietly creep back in to where she's curled up on my bed. She is tanned everywhere, I note, as I pull a blanket from my built-in wardrobe.

I freeze when I hear her moan. *"I'm sorry, please don't."* She's clearly having some kind of nightmare. I feel like I'm intruding so I start to back out, she suddenly cries out. I place the blanket over her quickly so that I can make my escape, but she grabs my arm. I'm frozen to the spot, staring at her tiny hand gripping my thick, tattooed wrist.

"Stay," she whispers, and I can't tell if she's still dreaming. She gives me a gentle tug. "Please Aiden, stay with me." She shuffles over and gently tugs me until I lay down.

Well, this is an unexpected turn, I didn't even have to make an effort, I muse.

I lay on my back and hold my breath as she crawls against my side and snuggles down, burying her face against my bicep.

"Thank you," she murmurs, and I hear her light snores a second later. I lay wide awake for some time, trying not to notice the heat of her warm, naked body, pressing into my side.

CHAPTER FOUR

Bella

Oh gosh, my head. I groan before stretching out and I freeze as memories of last night flood my mind. *Oh god, oh god, oh god.* I squeeze my eyes tight. *Please don't let it be real.* I slowly open one eye but soon squeeze it shut again. Yep, that confirms it, the memories are real. *Crap, crap, crap.* A cough makes me jump in fright and my eyes shoot open.

"Morning sunshine." Aiden's smirking, and I want to slap it off his gorgeous face.

"Why am I naked?" My voice is croaky, dry from all the alcohol, and I pull the blanket tighter around me.

He grins wider. "You called me Khal Drogo."

I throw my forearm over my eyes, "No I didn't."

"Oh you did. Do you often play out fantasies, Bella? Or should I say, Daenerys." I can hear his sniggers. I pull the pillow over my head and hold it there to hide my embarrassed, crimson coloured face. I'm sure I would remember saying that, but he does look a bit like him, it was my first thought when I saw him at my dad's house. "Your phone's been ringing non-stop; I think Carl's getting annoyed." I peek out from under the pillow and see he's holding my phone and flicking through it. "Call me before I track your mobile and come and find you." He reads it with a smugness in his tone, "He really isn't a nice guy, is he? So clingy and desperate."

I sit bolt upright. "Shit, where're my clothes?"

He shrugs his large shoulders. "You took them off."

"Aiden help me, if he comes here, he'll go mad. I don't need his stress today, I feel like crap," I say, desperately.

He holds out my phone so I can see it. "Can I post this on your Facebook?" It's a selfie of me and him. I'm passed out and he's grinning up at the camera, doing a thumbs up.

"Delete that right now. Do you not understand my current situation or are you trying to ruin my life?"

I climb from the bed, keeping the sheet wrapped around me as I stomp into the bathroom, relieved to see my dress just inside the door. I dress quickly and proceed to go through his drawers until I find some toothpaste, alongside several unopened toothbrushes. I arch a judgmental brow, wondering if he has a lot of unexpected, overnight visitors. The thought niggles me.

Aiden

I click 'add photo' and upload the image of me and Bella to my social media. I don't often use it, but if I want to have this woman for myself, I need to start stirring up some shit between her and lover boy.

She appears in the kitchen doorway looking dis-shelved, but still beautiful. I mentally slap myself. *Since when do I see anyone as beautiful?* Fuckable, *yes,* but never beautiful.

"I've deleted the pic from your phone . . . after I sent it to mine."

She glares at me, "Why would you send it to yourself?"

"Memories, Bells," I tease, "Not often I role play. Although, many girls have compared me to Drogo." I say it proudly.

Her phone lights up and she sighs before accepting the incoming call and pressing the device to her ear. "Hi Carl, so sorry. I passed out at Aria's place." She lies easily, but her expression shows she's uncomfortable doing it. I hear him yelling and she moves the phone away from her ear slightly. "Don't be like that, I'm sorry I worried you. I'll make it up to you," she soothes, glancing at me.

I role my eyes and pour a coffee, setting it down in front of her. "Well, maybe not that. I thought we agreed you were just helping me out." She whispers her words, trying to prevent me from hearing. He yells some more. "I'm not teasing you, Carl. Look, I don't want to talk about this over the phone, I'll see you after your shift." She disconnects the call, looking annoyed.

"Lover boy getting fed up with waiting?" I smirk. She sits opposite me at the large island in the middle of my kitchen. "What are you waiting for anyway? Marriage?"

She blushes, "No, I just don't feel it with him."

"Feel what? Please don't tell me you're a fairy tale kind of girl cos if you're waiting to be struck with cupid's arrow, you're gonna to be very disappointed. All you're going to feel is pain, and then relief that it's over."

She glares at me, "I just want to feel comfortable with the person I'm with, and Carl is not that person."

"Then stop using the guy."

She looks annoyed again. "My Dad didn't give me much choice."

I shake my head. "Don't use excuses, Bella. Your dad fucked up, but surely you have other people you can run to? I feel for this guy, he's holding out for your cherry, and you have no intention of giving it to him. No wonder he's frustrated and pissed at the world, holding out can send a guy nuts."

"Maybe I should just do it, just to get rid of it. That'll solve all my problems. My Dad can't sell what I don't have."

Her words instantly piss me off. "No," I grit out, clenching my teeth in agitation.

She looks confused. "You said I was teasing him."

I take a deep breath, knowing I've got to keep my shit together or risk everything. I need her virginity, but I can't make it obvious. "Look, not to be rude, but I have stuff to do."

She quickly stands. "Of course. I'm sorry." She grabs her clutch. "And I'm sorry if I made a fool of myself last night. I haven't been that drunk in . . . well, ever."

I give a stiff nod. "JP is waiting in the lobby to take you wherever you need to go." She heads for the door. "And Bella," She glances back. "If you need anything, I'm here."

She leaves just as Raff enters, giving her a slight smile as they pass one another. He waits for the door to close before fixing me with narrowed, suspicious eyes, "Tell me you didn't fuck her yet?"

"No, I didn't sleep with her, I'm not stupid."

He helps himself to coffee. "You need to play the long game with this one, or you're going to lose the lot."

"Don't you think I know what's at risk, Raff? I just don't know how to do all this. You know what I'm like, I need rules, I need control and knowing that I can't just go in there and claim her is too hard. All this work bores me."

It's a running joke. I don't settle down, which is why Jake's done what he's done.

Me, Jake, JP and Raff have always been close. Jake, my non-identical twin, died a few months ago, up until that point we were all inseparable, right from school. We were pranksters, always playing tricks on one another and never taking life too seriously. None of us had settled down, although at some point or another, we've all been in a serious relationship. It's how I know relationships aren't for me.

When I met Laurie, I was just twenty. I loved her fiercely, and soon became possessive and obsessed, until I pushed her away. Losing her tore me apart, and I refuse to put myself, or any other girl through that again. I still see her. She's married now, and every time she hits a rough patch, she turns to me. It's not healthy, but I can never find it in me to turn her away.

Her husband is a rich prick, he owns a massive hotel chain and most of the time he treats Laurie like shit, but she insists she's happy.

"Did you get anywhere with her friend?" I ask.

"No, I'm a gentleman." He grins. "She wants the chase; I can't be bothered with that shit. I fucked some random out in the alleyway instead."

"Classy. Aria's nice, if I wasn't chasing Bella, I would definitely have a go at her. But you're right, they both seem to be hard work, cracking Bella is going to take weeks. No wonder Jake gave me two months."

"Look man, whose to say we haven't planned this all wrong. Go in there as you, stop keeping that beast under lock and key, maybe she'll like your dominant, bossy arse to take charge."

Bella

Carl storms across the room and pins me to the wall, I don't even have time to register what's happening before he slaps me hard across the face. Tears rush to my eyes as my vision blurs. He holds his phone next to my face. "What the fuck is this?" I side glance, seeing it's the picture that Aiden took. His hand goes to my throat, clamping around it tightly, almost cutting off my airway.

"Carl." It's barely there as he squeezes harder, pure determination on his face.

"Six months, Bella, and you give it to this bastard." He shoves me to the floor and lands a punch to my stomach, making me double over.

"I didn't," I cry, rubbing my neck. My throat is sore, and my brain is having trouble keeping up with what's happening. "I didn't. I was drunk and slept there, that's all."

"Prove it," he sneers. I frown, and as he crouches down and takes a hold of my skirt, pushing it up, I realise what he's implying.

I try to scramble away, kicking out, but he's too quick. "Don't do this Carl, please don't do this."

His fingers grip my knickers, "You know he's a player right? A fuck em and chuck em kind of guy. Did you fancy a bit of rough, Bella? Cos trust me, I can play rough too." He laughs to himself, and I notice his dark eyes look even darker as he tugs my knickers down my thighs. I kick out, flailing around to make it difficult for him, but he hits me full force in the face and I still, gasping in shock. A warmth trickles from my nose, and I touch the blood and stare at my fingers in bewilderment. *How can this be happening?*

There's a loud bang, distracting Carl, but before he can get off me, he's pulled back. I stare open mouthed as JP punches Carl hard in the face. He falls back and JP stands over him, hitting him repeatedly in the face. Coming to my senses, I pull my underwear up and scramble towards the pair. "Stop," I cry, grabbing JP's arm midair. He pauses to look back at me and I note Carl's bloodied face. "He's a copper," I remind him.

JP shoves Carl away and stands, holding out a hand for me to take, which I do, and he tugs me to my feet. "Get your stuff," he orders. I grab the bag I hadn't yet unpacked, and he takes me by the hand. "Let's get out of here."

CHAPTER FIVE

Aiden

I allow my head to fall back as my hands glide down the woman's thighs. The perks of owning clubs, is I can pick up random women whenever I want to. I gently squeeze them as she rubs her backside against me. My cock strains in my trousers, desperate for some action but as I close my eyes, it's Isabella I see. Her smile. Her plump lips. *Fuck*. I can't get her out my head. I slide my hands around the woman's front, cupping her breasts. She moans, low and sexy in the back of her throat and grinds harder. She leans back so her body is perfectly against mine. Her back to my front. She tips her neck slightly and I nip the skin there whilst rolling her nipples between my thumb and finger. It's sending her wild as she reaches between us and rubs my cock through my trousers.

JP barges in looking pissed. His eyes land on me and he groans, "We have company," he hisses.

I grin, wondering why he's not rushing over here to join us. "Good, let's get this party started."

"Not the right time," he mutters, stepping to one side to reveal Bella. Her head is lowered and she's wearing what I think is JP's hoody. It buries her and I'm momentarily jealous. I don't like seeing her in another man's clothes but before I can analyse that too much, she slowly raises her head. I see blood and dive from the couch, practically shoving the woman from me. "What the hell happened?" I reach for her, the urge to cup her face and examine every bruised inch of it, but she steps back from me and moves closer to JP.

"Carl saw your photo," she says, her voice laced with hurt. "Thanks for that."

The reality of what I've done hits me hard and I wince. It was obvious he'd see it; I have lots of police on my socials, they like to keep tabs on me, and I entertain it because I'm not stupid enough to alert them to anything I'm doing that breaks the law. "Bella, I am so sorry," I say as sincerely as I can muster. "I didn't think he'd do this." The woman is getting dressed and I glance back before turning to JP. "Can you show her out, I'll take care of Bella."

I hold out my hand for her to take and she stares at it for a few seconds before eventually slipping hers into it and allowing me to lead her through to the kitchen.

I get the first aid box from the cupboard and tap the worktop, indicating for her to sit on it. She pulls herself up and I lay the box next to her, opening it. I rip open a couple of antiseptic wipes and then step between her legs. As I raise it to her face, she leans back slightly, "I can do it," she mutters.

I give my head a shake and begin to wipe the small cut on the bridge of her nose. "This is my fault, let me clean it up."

Bella

I sit quietly while Aiden cleans my cut and then he passes me an ice pack which I hold to my throbbing cheek. My mind has turned from thinking about what Carl's just done to me, to how Aiden had his hands all over some woman when we arrived. I didn't like it. "You can stay here," he says, breaking my thoughts.

"I can't; I don't even know you."

"I caused this latest problem," he tells me, gently pulling my hand away from my cheek to check it. "Longer," he adds, pressing it back. "I have space, and you need somewhere to stay where that fucker can't get to you. Stay, please."

My heart thumps faster in my chest. I've never done anything so careless before and staying with a stranger . . . a sexy stranger, is exciting. I give a nod, and he smiles, "Great, I'll get the spare room set up." He proceeds to send off a text then goes over to the kitchen island where he gets out bread and begins to slice it. I watch with a frown as the first slice comes off too thin and he picks it up to examine it. "I don't really do this," he says with a smirk.

"Murder bread?" I tease, jumping off the side and going to help him.

I slice the loaf while he gets butter and some cheese from the fridge. "I usually order lunch," he explains, "I'm normally at the office. I think my housekeeper gets this stuff in for show." I grin, watching as he attempts to butter the bread. Eventually he gives up and I take over that too. "See, this is already working out well," he says, watching as I make us both a sandwich. "I tend to go to the club in the evenings, especially at weekends. Tonight, I have to go to one of my bars across town, I was thinking you could come tonight, maybe invite your friends?"

I shrug, "I'm not sure I'm in the mood."

"It might take your mind off what's happened today. Besides, I hate the thought of you sitting around here alone on your first night."

I offer a small smile, "I imagine I look a mess," I mutter, "I don't want to cramp your style."

"Firstly, it takes a lot to cramp my style," he says in a teasing tone. I grin wider. "Everyone knows I don't settle down so no one will think we're together." My heart sinks a little. I inwardly scold myself. He's being nice and I'm planning a fucking wedding. Of course he doesn't settle down, he must have women throwing themselves at him. "And you look beautiful, even with the bruises," he adds, making my heart swell again.

I bite on my lower lip, trying to hide my smile. "Fine, I'll call the girls and see if they're free."

Aiden

I sit at my desk staring at the CCTV camera's. I left Bella home to get ready, although lord knows why she's taking so long.

"What's the plan now?" asks JP, interrupting my thoughts.

"I'm playing it cool," I say with a shrug. "She likes danger and excitement, I think if I play the bad boy, she'll be eating out my hand."

"Play the bad boy," he repeats, sounding amused, "You've had enough practise."

"Right now, I'm playing the friendship card. She needs to feel protected from that prick."

"Yeah, it took everything I had not to end the fucker. He was gonna . . ." he shakes his head like that'll clear the images, "Anyway, she's away from him now and that's the main thing. It's worked out well for you, given you a way in."

"Exactly," I say with a smirk. "Now she'll be putty in my experienced hands."

I finally spot her entering the VIP lounge and I instantly relax. She's looks amazing and JP leans closer. "Damn, she's fine." I arch a brow, and he holds his hands up defensively, "Hey, we all know you ain't gonna keep her around. Maybe I can swoop to the rescue when you've fucked her over." His laughter rings out as he leaves.

♡

When I eventually go down to the lounge, I spot Bella and Aria sitting at the bar. As if she senses my arrival, she turns, scanning the room until her eyes land on me. Two women immediately take a place either side of me, tucking themselves under my arms and I grin. I won't ever tire of this sort of attention, and it helps my plan with Bella if she thinks I'm not interested in her. One of the women runs her hand over my chest, tipping her head back to make eye contact. She runs her tongue over her lower lip, eyeing me in a way that suggests she wants me to kiss her. I inch closer and she smiles, closing the gap and sealing her lips against mine. Her friend clears her throat, and we pull apart. My eyes fall to where she's caressing her friend's breast, and I arch a brow. "Shall we go somewhere quieter?" I suggest and they giggle as I head for the office. I catch Bella's eye and wink; she turns away abruptly.

Bella

"Wow, Bells, what I wouldn't give to be one of those bitches right now." Aria sighs.

"Eww Ari, please don't lower yourself. Why would you want to sleep with him? Who knows what diseases he carries." I take a sip of my drink before adding, "He was with a different woman earlier."

"When you've lost that cherry, you come back and tell me you wouldn't ride that beast."

I laugh, shoving her playfully. "I'm not saying he isn't hot. Of course he is. But he's a player."

"I'm not after a relationship," she states.

"Still . . . don't you want him to be a little less . . . used?"

"You see used, I see experienced," she says with a smirk.

I roll my eyes. "Well personally, I wouldn't touch his dangly bits with a ten-foot pole."

Aria looks past me and jumps up excitedly. I turn to see Jack and his handsome partner, Beck. We all take turns to hug one another before ordering another round of drinks and heading over to one of the free booths.

Once we're comfortable, Jack stares at me with raised brows, "What the hell is going on with you? Aria said you were split from Carl, then you move back. And now this?" He indicates to my face, and I feel myself blush. "Again," he adds.

"I needed a place," I mutter feebly with a shrug.

"And of course he's the only one with a spare bed, right? Did you forget about me and Aria."

Aria leans closer, "Don't worry, she's found somewhere now, haven't you?" And she grins wide.

"Argh, yes, you must be talking about the God like hero that managed to swoop in and rescue you?" he asks, smirking.

I glare at Aria, "You've been busy gossiping."

"Of course I have, he's way too hot not to gossip about."

"Is he another wanker that just wants to get in those knickers?" asks Jack.

I scoff. "No, he's not interested in me. And trust me, I'm not interested in him."

"Bullshit," exclaims Aria.

"I'm not," I argue.

She rolls her eyes, "Wait until you see him, you two will see exactly what I mean."

"Men don't help a woman for no reason," says Beck, looking concerned.

I smile gratefully. "Trust me, he isn't short of women. And he isn't interested in me."

"So, what's his motive for helping a woman he doesn't even know?" he asks.

I shrug, "Right now I'm just grateful for a place to stay. I have his address, his name and his place of work. He's hardly going to do anything. He's openly invited you guys here tonight, hardly the moves of a killer."

"Or he's playing the long game and wanting your V card?" suggests Jack.

I shake my head. "Definitely not, he's in his office with two women right now, he wouldn't flaunt it if he wanted to get me into bed." I finish my drink, "Now, can we stop talking about my shit show of a life and dance?"

We dance until my feet ache and my cheeks hurt from laughing. It's almost enough to make me forget about everything that's happened in the last few days.

JP approaches me, gently placing a hand on my waist and leaning so his mouth is positioned at my ear. "The boss is wondering where you are," he says. His deep voice rumbles through me and I shiver. He looks up and I follow his gaze to where Aiden is staring down from the balcony. I offer a wide smile and a thumbs up. "Well now he knows."

"He thinks it would be better if you were to stay in the VIP section . . . where he knows you're safe."

I turn in his arm and slide my arms around his neck, standing up on my tiptoes. "You could stay here and keep me safe," I suggest, pressing myself against his hard body.

He grins, placing both hands on my hips and holding me at arms length. "Are you trying to get my backside kicked?"

"Aiden?" I ask, laughing, "He has no interest in me, you're safe."

He shakes his head looking amused, "If only you knew."

CHAPTER SIX

Aiden

I haven't been able to take my eyes from her. The way she lights up the room has me transfixed, the fact she doesn't even realise it, adds to her appeal. She dances with a sexy edge, carefree and relaxed. And she laughs with her friends hard, making me long to be a part of their circle.

Despite her attempts to drag JP off to dance with her, he backs away, glancing up and me and giving his head a slight shake. I don't want to come over all alpha, but I want her up here with me. Down there, she's getting way too much attention from other men. And as predicted, the second JP walks away, she turns to a man who's been trying to grab her attention for at least ten minutes. I ball my fists in anger the second she engages with him, laughing at something he says. He slides his hands to her waist, and she slips hers around his neck, they begin to sway to the music. He gently presses his nose to hers and I lose it, slamming my glass on the table behind me and heading for the stairs. She shouldn't even be down there, not when she suspects men are after her.

JP blocks my path on the stairs, his face full of concern. "Where's the fire?"

"She's about to kiss someone," I snap.

"What happened to playing it cool?" he asks with a grin.

"We're moving to stage two of the plan," I grit out, continuing down the stairs.

I hear him laughing, "What's stage two, possessive, psycho, dickhead?"

The guy she's dancing with sees me coming, and whether it's my demeanor or the fact he recognises me, he steps back, letting her arms fall away from him. I slam against her, pulling her against my front, "Are you trying to piss me off?" I growl in her ear.

"Why would I be pissing you off, Aiden?" she asks innocently, and I'm not sure if she's playing her own game.

I feel her backside pressing against me and I inhale sharply. "I warned you what would happen if you kept rubbing against me," I whisper, grabbing her hand and dragging her towards the stairs.

As we get towards the VIP area, I begin to calm down. Having her where I know she's safe, feels better and all thoughts of dragging her to my office and fucking her over my desk, fade away.

Bella

I'm sightly disappointed when his march slows down to a casual stroll over to the bar area. For a minute there, I thought he was going to drag me off to his office. I give my head a shake, *what the hell am I thinking?*

He gets us both a drink and we sit in his usual booth. After a few silent minutes, I clear my throat, bringing his attention to me. "Where did your two friends go?"

"They got what they wanted and moved on," he says bluntly. "Mutually beneficial."

His words confuse me. One minute he's acting crazy jealous, and the next he's making it very clear he's not looking for anything. "Doesn't that get boring?"

"Why would I get bored of women throwing themselves at me?" He looks smug and it annoys me.

"There's no affection," I state, shrugging. "No tenderness. Don't you crave a connection?"

He eyes me like I've lost my mind and scoffs, "I'm not into that fairytale bullshit, Bella. My current situation suits me just fine."

"Have you ever had a relationship?"

"I realised pretty quickly that relationships don't work for me. First of all, I love sex way too much and relationships tend to be more about date nights and effort. Shit I don't have time for. Secondly, I'm too fucked up. I get jealous and possessive, I get crazy."

I want to point out what he just did by dragging me from that guy, seemed jealous and possessive. Instead, I analyse him. "Love sends you crazy and you hate to be out of control," I surmise.

"I like an easy life. I have friends, male and female, and I have women I have sex with. The two are separate to keep feelings out of it. No one gets confused that way. You won't see me hanging out with a woman I have sex with."

I've officially been friend zoned. I don't know why I feel disappointed when he's admitted that he runs from everything that I run towards. "JP and Raff seem nice."

He gives a boy like grin, and I realise they mean something to him. "They've known me my whole life. My mum said it felt like she had four kids instead of two."

"You have a brother or a sister?" I ask, unsure of why I sound so surprised.

His smile fades and he stares down at his drink, "I had a brother, he died."

I instinctively reach for his hand and place mine over it. "I'm so sorry, that must be hard, especially when you were all so close."

He takes a deep breath before knocking his drink back and signalling to the bar staff for more. I sense the subject is over and he confirms it when he asks, "So, how did you end up with Carl?"

"I met him in Costa, he asked me out. I thought it was love at first sight, but he turned out to be a dick. So, here I am." I tell him the quick version to make me look less pathetic.

"Did he make a habit of hitting you?"

"Two times this bad," I admit, fidgeting uncomfortably. I always feel stupid when people ask about it because I should have stood up to him. I should have left and never gone back. "We were always a fiery couple," I add, like that explains it. "We would get into the worst fights and friends would have to separate us," I give a sad laugh. "I'm addicted to drama, I swear. Anyway, the last time was about a month ago and I ended up in hospital."

"Was that time over you sleeping in a stranger's bed too?" he asks in a teasing tone.

I shake my head, "Believe it or not, I don't make a habit of that. No, it was because he wanted to have sex, and I refused . . . again."

"How come?"

"Because . . ." I sigh, "He comes on too strong. The harder he pushes me, the more I step away." I shudder. "And I don't think I like him," I admit and Aiden laughs.

"You don't like the man you were in a relationship with?"

"I did, in the beginning, but as time passed, he did things that gave me the ick. But the thought of living back with dad full time made me try and at least make it work."

The barman brings over a bottle of Sambuca and two shot glasses. Aiden opens it and pours us both a shot, sliding the nearest one to me. "I admire you. Not many women get to your age and are still virgins, it must takes some will power to hold out until twenty-three."

"How do you know my age?" I ask, knocking the shot back and wincing at the taste.

"You told me," he says, drinking his own. I narrow my eyes, I'm certain I didn't. "Shall we head home?" he asks, pulling his phone out and swiping the screen and staring hard at whatever's grabbed his attention.

I push to stand, "I'll let Aria and Jack know," I tell him, but he doesn't look up, so I go off to find them.

When I get back to the booth, Aiden's nowhere to be seen, but Raff is leaning against the table speaking into his phone. He doesn't spot me as he spits, "You're gonna fuck this up." He disconnects and looks up. He forces a smile, "Sorry to disappoint, Bella, but Aiden had something he needed to sort out. He asked me to drop you off."

I frown, wondering what could have popped up that required his immediate attention at this time of night. I smile, "It's fine, Raff, I can make my own way back." I head for the stairs.

"Actually," he calls out and I slow down to look back at him, "He was very insistent I take you. Besides, I get paid for this sort of thing."

I wonder if he means to drive for Aiden or drive his women around. It makes me shudder and I continue to the stairs. "I need the air to sober me up. Thanks though."

Raff follows me, I know this because people are staring as I pass and that never happens when I'm alone, which means the six foot something giant is chasing me down.

Outside, he catches my arm, halting me. "Bella, make this easier on me will yah. Let me take you."

"Call him" I say, and Raff looks taken back.

"What?" he asks.

"I don't have his number, ring him and give me your phone."

"That's not a good idea."

"Because he might fuck it up?" I ask, repeating his earlier words and arching a brow.

His expression confirms he was probably talking to Aiden, and maybe about me. Raff sighs and pulls out his mobile. Before he can press it to his ear, I snatch it and take a few steps away.

"Raff, this better be good," snaps Aiden when he answers.

"If you're going to ditch me then at least stick around to say goodbye, and for the record I don't need chaperoning anywhere so please tell your bulldog to back the fuck off." I hand the phone back to Raff who almost looks impressed, and then I stomp off.

I'm not sure where that outburst came from. I guess I'm disappointed. We were having a nice talk back there, and he'd shown he was jealous which means he might like me, even if he isn't planning on crossing the friendship line. The fact he'd let me say goodbye to my friends because he'd decided to call it a night, pissed me off. I could have continued my night if I'd have known he was going to dump me on Raff.

I spot a quiet little bar, the kind with low lighting and a soul singer in the corner and decide to hide in there just in case Raff is on the warpath.

I order a glass of wine and take a seat at the back of the bar. Pulling out my phone, I spend some time catching up on my socials. I search Aiden's name, and his profile pops up right as my phone rings out, causing me to almost throw it in fright. "Shit," I mutter, cancelling the call. It was from a number I don't recognise.

His social media profile is set to private, and the only picture that comes up, is the one of him and I in bed, the one Carl saw. The fact he set it to open, annoys me. *Did he mean for Carl to see it?* Or was he just trying to show off?

There are ten comments on the picture, and I open them up, scrolling through them. Most are from men telling him that he's punching. I laugh to myself wondering what they see, because Aiden is definitely way too good for me in the looks department.

I stare at the last comment, it's from a woman, Lauren Casey. I study the tiny profile picture, she's pretty with long blonde hair and I just know by the way she's dressed, she's loaded. Her comment reads, *I hope this isn't your way of announcing you're in a new relationship, plastering it across your socials like a teenager. Classy!*

I smirk and notice there's a response, so I click on it to see Aiden's reply. *Call me.*

Did she call him? Is that why he rushed off tonight, to appease Lauren. Maybe she is one of the women that he has sex with, and if she is, it seems like she's into him.

My phone lights up again with the same number that just called me. I answer, pressing it to my ear. "Where the fuck are you?" snaps Aiden.

I disconnect, wondering how he got my number.

Aiden

I run my hands through my hair in anger. How dare she hang up on me. Who the hell does she think she is?

I call Raff again, "Aid, I don't get why you're stressing, we know she isn't in danger, no one paid her dad, remember?" he says, sounding annoyed. I know he's talking sense, but I can't explain the sudden need to know where she is, or what she's doing. "Boss," he adds, sounding hesitant. "I'm worried you're going to that dark place again, maybe this wasn't such a good idea." I disconnect because anything I say right now will only confirm what he's thinking.

I approach the front door and knock once, and Laurie opens it in nothing but her silk slip.

"Thought you'd never get here," she mutters, opening the door wider for me to step inside. My heart sinks a little, this isn't where I want to be right now.

I look around the hotel room, noticing she's already ordered me a bottle of my favourite whiskey. She sits on the edge of the bed. "Who is she?"

I bite my tongue in annoyance, "Nobody important, Laurie."

"You never post pictures of other women on socials," she points out with a pout.

I roll my eyes as I crawl onto the bed, placing my hands either side of her. She lays back.

"Are we really going to waste time talking about unimportant shit, or are we gonna fuck?" She places her hands above her head, and I pull my tie off and use it to bind them. "And stop stalking me on socials, you're married." I nip the top of her breast, and she arches her back off the bed, smiling.

"Don't post pictures of you in bed with other women. How would you feel if I posted pictures of me and other men?"

I crawl over her body until I'm sat over her chest and flick open my button, pulling out my cock. I lift her head, lining her mouth up with my erection. "It doesn't bother me, and you shouldn't care what I think, worry about what your husband thinks."

When she opens her mouth to speak, I press forward, my cock filling her mouth and touching the back of her throat. She takes it all, her eyes watering as I fuck her mouth. It doesn't take me long before I'm almost ready to release into her, all the build up with Bella has me in knots. I pull out and Laurie gasps for breath. "Fuck, what's gotten into you Aiden?" she snaps.

"Don't pretend you don't like how I give it, Laurie," I grin, tapping her backside so she'll turn over. She does so without protest, sticking her arse up in the air. "It's the reason you call, so I can use you, fuck you," I push in to her tight pussy, "Do all the things that he doesn't do, the things you don't tell him you like in case he dumps your trashy arse." I coat my cock in her juices and then line it with her puckered backside. I push forward and she lets out a deep, low moan.

"And does she let you do all this shit to her, Aiden?" she pants, looking back at me over her shoulder. I grip the back of her neck, forcing her head to look forward before I push her face into the pillows, holding her down whilst I fuck her hard and fast.

"You just concentrate on pleasing me, don't worry about what anyone else does for me."

CHAPTER SEVEN

Bella

I finally stumble my way into Tremos, the nightclub that Aiden lives above. JP is behind the main bar, and I lean over, so he can hear me. "Large white wine please, JP." He places a large wine glass on the bar top and takes a bottle from the fridge. "Where's Aiden?" he asks.

"I'm not his keeper," I mutter, and he frowns, filling my glass to halfway and sliding it towards me. I go to pay but he waves me away. I glance to my left and a man is staring at me. He smiles and I return it before sliding closer and taking the vacant seat beside him. "Hi, I'm Luke," he says, offering his hand.

"Bella," I say, slipping my hand into his. He kisses the back and I swoon a little. I love a gentleman.

We chat and he tells me he's a university lecturer. He amuses me with stories of his own student days, comparing them to his students now. I missed out on those options because of dad, I was too scared to leave him alone. My grades were outstanding, I could have easily gone off to Uni, but I was desperate to keep the roof over our heads so had to get a job instead. Time passes quickly as we chat, and it isn't until the doorman steps over to ask us to drink up, I realise the lights have come on. I glance at my watch and I'm disappointed to see it's almost three in the morning. I'm not ready to leave, I like Luke, so I ask, "Why don't we grab a coffee? I know a little all-night café just around the corner."

To my relief, he smiles, "Sounds like a plan, lead the way."

"Bells where are you off?"

JP heads over, throwing a cloth over his shoulder, "Where you off, Bella?"

I frown, "I didn't realise I had to give you a run down, JP?" I add an amused laugh to hide my embarrassment. Luke must be wondering what the hell is going on.

"Perhaps you should call it a night?" he suggests. I scoff, grabbing Luke's hand and leaving.

We get into the café and order two coffees before taking a seat. "Who was that guy, your brother?" Luke asks.

I laugh, "Would you believe me if I said I hardly know him at all?"

"He seemed pretty concerned about you."

"I'm staying with his friend for a few days, he's helping me out. I think his friends seem to have taken on some kind of protection role." I roll my eyes. "It's been a mad few days."

"Are they anything to do with the . . ." he trails off, pointing to my face.

"No," I rush to say, "Nothing to do with any of them."

"It's just he was a big guy; I don't want him doing that to my face."

"The guy I'm staying with is saving me from the ex that did this," I tell him. "Long story. Boring really. But I am free and single, trust me."

"Good, because I'd like to go out with you again some time, if you're available?"

"I am definitely available." I hand him my phone, "Put your number in and I'll miss call you, so you have my number."

Once he hands my phone back, it lights up with Aiden's number. I ignore it, I really don't want to hear his yelling. I miss call Luke, and he saves my number.

Once we've finished our coffee, he walks me back to the club and gives me a light kiss on the cheek. I like him, and I like that he doesn't try and stick his tongue down my throat.

I'm smiling as I enter the side door that leads into the club. The place is now empty of party revellers, and I pass some of the bar staff that are heading home. I head to the bar where JP and Raff are chatting, whilst JP restocks the fridges. Raff sees me and whistles loud, I realise why, when Aiden storms from his office straight towards me. He looks so angry that my step falters. "Where the fuck have you been?" he snaps, not stopping until he's right in my face. He reminds me of Carl, and I instantly step back, but I square my shoulders, trying to give the impression I'm not terrified. At least with Carl, I could read him well enough to know when it was coming, but with Aiden, I don't even know him.

I inhale, to steady my breathing. "I've been out, Aiden. What's the problem?" He throws his hands in the air and turns to Raff and JP. "Is she for real?" he asks them, and then turns back to me. "The problem is, Bella, your dad tried to fucking sell you to some nut jobs and then you stroll around like that's not an issue, not only that, but you left with some jumped up twat that you don't even know."

"I don't know you," I'm yelling with outrage, "I don't know Raff or JP."

"Then maybe you should get your head out of your arse and sort your life out. You're gullible, and too trusting. I know all that, and I've only known you a few days so if I've picked it up, other men will. You're screaming vulnerability and men will prey on you. No wonder you end up with arseholes that beat you up."

I break eye contact, scared he'll see the tears that are threatening to fall. I clench my fists, digging my nails into my palms to distract myself. I chose not to answer, my voice will crack, and they'll all hear the hurt, so instead, I walk over the elevator and press the call button. It open's a second later, and I step inside and stare blankly at the keypad. *Fuck*. I have no idea what the code is. All three men are watching me expectantly. "Will someone give me the damn code," I yell, taking them by surprise.

Aiden heads over and I move to the far corner of the elevator as he steps inside. "Bella, I'm sorry, I was out of order," he mutters.

"The code," I say coldly, folding my arms over my chest and avoiding looking at him.

He punches the code in, and the doors slide shut to my relief. At least the other two can't watch the shit show. "I'm going home," I say, and he turns to me. "I don't care if these men come for me, I'll call the police."

"I said I'm sorry," he begins, and I hold a hand up to shut him down.

"I've been here before, Aiden. The arguing, the getting all up in my face, it was always followed with sorry, and I don't like how you just made me feel down there. So, I'm going home. Thank you for everything you've done."

He sighs heavily, "At least wait until the morning when it's light. I'll take you myself." I give a stiff nod, and he smiles. I can't help but think I've let him win.

Aiden

"Why don't you take a seat," I say once we're in the apartment. I point to the couch. "I'll get you some water and a couple of painkillers."

She does so without argument, and I head into the kitchen and grab the water, taking a minute to get my head straight. I owe this to JP and Raff; we've worked too hard for me to mess everything up. Damn Jake and his stupid games, even in death he haunts us.

I quickly slip out of my shirt, throwing it in the basket and go back to the living room where Bella is curled up on the couch, looking like she's always belonged here. I like how that feels, and as I place the water on the table, I notice the way her eyes scan my body.

"You have a lot of tattoos" she observes, taking her water and opening the cap.

"My brother designed them all, there's pretty much one for anything big that's happened in our life." I glance down at my chest, smiling at the memories etched on my skin forever. Since his death, I haven't been able to add to it, it's all too painful.

"Did he own the club with you?" she asks.

"Yeah, we were partners in all the businesses."

"You must miss him so much, having the clubs being a constant reminder," she says sadly.

"I know I've said it, but I really am sorry for what I said back there," I repeat, "I'm not like Carl though, I'd never hurt you."

She picks at the label on her bottle. "Mentally or physically?"

She's asking me outright if I intend to break her heart, and I can't answer, so I hit her with another line. "There's something about you, Bella. I can't get you out of my head."

"You're good," she says with a smirk, and I realise she hasn't fallen for my charm. *Usually, women eat that shit up.* "Let's just be friends, save us both the hassle. Maybe you can teach me to be a little less . . . gullible."

I roll my eyes, "I didn't mean all that."

"I'm not a one-night stand type of girl, Aiden. I won't fall into your bed when you throw me a scrappy line you've probably used over and over. Save yourself the work."

I give a stiff nod. *Fuck. Now what?*

Bella

"I should go to bed, I'm shattered," I announce.

Aiden also stands, looking uneasy, "Yeah about that. The spare room is a little empty right now."

"Empty how?"

"Like a blank canvas," he says wincing.

I frown, "So why did you offer to let me stay?"

"I plan on furnishing it, I just haven't had time. Look, take my bed, I'll have the couch."

I narrow my eyes, "Did you plan on getting me into your bed tonight?"

"No," he says, following it with a smirk.

"Oh my god," I mutter, shaking my head but trying hard not to smile. "I'll take the couch," I add, "It's comfortable."

He hands me a blanket and pillow, arguing constantly that he should take the couch, until I have to shove him from the room. I lie down and check my phone, smiling when I see a message from Luke.

> **Luke: Thanks for tonight, I really enjoyed myself. Can we do it again soon?**

> **Me: Me too. I'd love to meet up. Monday, after work?**

> **Luke: Great. 5p.m. Outside the bakery?**

> **Me: Yeah, see you then.**

I wake with a start, groaning when my head pounds from the hangover.

"Sorry did I wake you?" whispers Aiden and I open one eye to see him in his running gear.

"It's your house, make as much noise as you want."

He pulls his leg to stretch the muscles, and I run my eyes over his sweating body, noting how his shirt clings to his muscled abs. He smirks, catching me and I groan, pulling the pillow over my head. "It should be illegal to look that good on a Sunday morning."

He laughs, "It takes a lot of hard work to look like this. Early morning runs are not fun on a Sunday morning when most of the world are sleeping off hangovers. What are your plans today?" he asks, taking off his shirt and using it to wipe his chest.

"You're doing that on purpose," I accuse, causing him to laugh again. "My friend owns her own salon, and she opens up on Sundays exclusively for family and friends, I might pop over and get a wax."

"Wax?" He wiggles his eyebrows suggestively.

"Well, I have a date tomorrow, and I don't want hairy legs scaring him away."

His smile fades. "A date?" he repeats.

"Yeah, the guy I met last night. Only for a drink after work, but still, I have to make a bit of an effort don't I."

He gives a stiff nod before heading down the hall towards his bedroom.

Aiden

I thought this would be easier than it's proving to be. I'm supposed to be consuming her head, not some fucking mug she met when she was pissed. I groan, I'm playing the game all wrong. I put some calls in so I can at least try and turn her head in my direction.

When I go back into the living room, Bella is smiling at her mobile and I instantly feel a pang of jealousy. *Is she talking to him?* "Get dressed we're going out." I announce.

She glances up, "Huh?"

"I know someone that owns a furniture shop, she's waiting for us to go and choose some stuff for your bedroom."

She stands, shaking her head, "No, please don't go to any trouble. Besides, I told you last night, I'm going home."

"I need to decorate it anyway; it's been empty for too long. And at least spend the day with me before you make any rash decisions, I could actually turn out to be nice." I give a wide smile, and she rolls her eyes.

"Fine, but I'm making no promises."

I can feel her looking at me nervously as I swing the car into Bond Street. I pull up outside Harpers store. Her furniture is exclusive and costs a fortune, but I know Bella will love it.

She gets out of the car warily and looks around at all the expensive shops surrounding us.

"Aiden, It's so expensive here." I take her hand and pull her into the shop.

Harper greets us with a huge smile. She is stunning and was madly in love with my brother, Jake. He met her after his diagnosis so refused to get involved with her, he didn't want to make her fall in love with him; only to leave her behind. She fell anyway, and she is still very much heartbroken.

"Aiden." She smiles kissing each cheek, "and this must be Isabella?" she adds kissing her too.

"Take your time, give me a shout if you see anything you like. My guy already has his van out the back with the bed, so we can just add to that." She wanders off and I risk a glance at Bella who looks like a deer caught in headlights.

"You're doing me a favour here," I tell her, hoping she'll relax. "I need a woman's touch in my apartment, let's start with the spare room that you happen to be staying in."

CHAPTER EIGHT

Aiden

Bella is hesitant at first, until I pick up a gold eagle lamp. She stares wide eyed, "No," she says simply.

"No?" I ask, taking a good look at the ugly lamp.

"It's awful," she whispers, glancing around to check Harper isn't within ear shot.

"It's one of a kind," I argue.

She reaches for a simple glass feature where the bulb is extra-large. "Modern," she says, shrugging, "And it fits with the décor in your apartment."

I give a nod, "I like it." And I place it to one side.

Bella's eyes light up, "Cushions," she says, heading off to where there's a huge display. She selects some, holding each up for my approval, which I give because I have no idea about any of this. I usually pay someone to sort the décor. Who even has the time these days? But as I watch Bella select things, I realise that most men probably go with their women, just for this. To see their face's light up at bright fabrics, or to hear them passionately discuss artwork and why they love it.

When she's selected practically half the shop, I hand over my card while Harper's assistants take it all out to the delivery van. I lean closer so Bella doesn't overhear the amount, and then I hand over my spare key so that everything can be taken up to the apartment.

We step outside and I take her hand, ignoring the way she glances down at it in confusion. "I'd love to take you to lunch," I say.

"Why?" she asks, as I lead her in the direction of a nice restaurant I know around the corner.

"To thank you for your help."

She smiles, "Well, as long as you know this isn't a date, Aiden Tremos."

I scoff playfully, "Like I'd date you."

She giggles as we cross the street, and I push the door open to the little Italian I've been coming to for years.

Lucas, the owner, greets us warmly and leads us to a spot by the window. It's busy and has a long waiting list, but me and Lucas have an arrangement which means I can walk in here any time I want.

I pull out Bella's chair and she lowers gracefully. Once I take my own, she smiles coyly. "I'm almost impressed," she admits, "Shop's that open for you on Bond Street, whipping out a card and putting almost eight grand on it to furnish a room you don't even sleep in, and now this," she says, looking around, "A table in a restaurant that I know is always fully booked and has weeks of waiting lists."

"It's not what you know-"

"But who you know," she finishes for me, and we both laugh. "Why are you single?"

Lucas brings us a bottle of white wine, pouring me a small amount and waiting for me to taste it. I take a sip and give a nod. Once he's poured us both a glass, he leaves the bottle and disappears again. "Because I choose to be," I reply.

"I think you're wasted," she remarks, "But I get it. I'm thinking of taking up the single life myself."

I grin, "Does your date know that?"

She shrugs, "Luke seems nice, but they always do in the beginning. Once I tell him about . . . yah know, he'll change. Maybe I should just do it, get rid of it so it's not a big thing anymore."

I swallow a mouthful of wine, my eyes widening. "Get rid of what?" I ask, even though I know exactly what she means.

"My virginity," she whispers.

"You've held on to it for twenty-three years, why suddenly give it up to a stranger that doesn't deserve it?"

"Because I never meant to hold on to it for this long."

The waiter comes over and places olives, bread and oils on the table. "The usual Mister Tremos?" he asks. I give a nod, and he leaves us.

"Jesus, how many times do you come here?" she asks, laughing.

"Often."

"Always with women?" she asks, popping an olive in her mouth.

"I don't think you should rush into a decision," I say, taking us back to the conversation.

"Oh god, I bet they think I'm one of your conquests," she adds, glancing around.

"I haven't known you long, but I know you'll regret just giving it away."

"Do you remember your first?" she asks.

"Not really," I mutter.

"Exactly, it wasn't special. And this won't be either. Yah know, I read somewhere about a woman that sold hers on the internet. She made a million."

I roll my eyes, "That's not true."

"How do you know? There are people out there that pay good money for feet pictures."

I laugh, "Ridiculous."

"Would you pay?" she asks.

I raise my brows, "For your virginity?" *Unfortunately, that's not a part of the rules or I would.*

"God no, not for mine, just in general. Would you sleep with a virgin and pay for the privilege?"

The waiter arrives with our food, and I sag in relief. Bella stares down at the juicy steak. "Oh shit, you're not a vegetarian, are you?"

"No, this looks amazing. I've just never had a man order my food before."

I smile, "All part of the service."

She looks troubled as she picks up her cutlery. "Maybe that's why you're single?" she suggests.

I roll my eyes, "Because I know what's good in a restaurant I often frequent?"

"Some women don't like that. It's a little . . . controlling."

"Or it's thoughtful depending on your mindset."

She smirks, "You have an answer for everything." She pops the piece of steak into her mouth and closes her eyes in delight. Once she's swallowed it, she says, "Oh lord, that is amazing."

"Told you." I can't keep the smugness from my voice.

Bella

When we arrive back to the apartment after the best meal I've ever eaten, there are boxes everywhere. "Luckily, I have people that do this," says Aiden, pulling out his mobile.

Less than half an hour later, JP, Raff and Aria turn up.

We all get stuck in, unpacking items and placing them around the room. The guys set the brand-new oak bed up and once the new sheets and cushions are placed on it, it looks amazing. We're sorting the last few bits when Aiden comes in with a bag of Chinese food, "Thought we needed fuel after all that work," he says, and we eagerly follow him to the kitchen where he sets out various container on the center island so we can all dip in. I check my watch, noting it took us almost four hours to work on the bedroom. "It looks like a hotel room," gushes Aria, "I'm so jealous right now," she adds, looking in my direction.

"Apparently, she isn't staying," says Aiden and all eyes turn to me. "She wants to go back home."

"It's not safe," Aria and JP say in unison.

I laugh, "I can't impose on Aiden."

"Don't put this on me," he argues, "I want you to stay here."

I smile, "You do?"

He looks away like he's embarrassed. "It's safer," he mutters.

"We just worked our backsides off to set your room up," snaps Aria, "You're staying, no argument."

I can't stop the smile as I nod and watch as everyone relaxes and goes back to helping themselves to food. I haven't known the guys long, but right now, I feel like they're all in my corner and it feels good.

❧

The next morning, I arrive at the shop ready to bake my happy heart out. Aria is already there whipping up some muffins and I join her at the counter, tying my apron.

"I think I'm totally in love with Raff. He's the perfect guy for me," she tells me dreamily.

I roll my eyes, laughing. "You've said that about almost every man you've ever met."

"Don't roll your eyes, Bells. He was made for me; he just doesn't know it yet."

"Um, then I suggest you make it a priority to tell him, so he's on the same page."

She begins to spoon the thick mixture into bun cases. "And don't think I don't see the way you and lover boy look at one other."

I scoff. "We're just friends. He's a one-night stand type of guy, and I . . . well, I'm not that sort of girl so," I shrug.

"I vote you give him just one night, he'll be begging for more."

"It's a good job I haven't put it out for vote," I say, arching a brow. "Besides, I have a date after work with Luke. He's nice, friendly, funny, reliable."

She drops the spoon in her bowl of mixture. "Well, he sounds delightful," she says, her tone mocking. "Boring but delightful."

"I think he's exactly what I'm looking for, actually. And he's really nice looking."

"But does he set you on fire with one look?" she asks, "Does his touch awaken something deep inside you? Do you wanna rip his clothes off?"

I throw my cloth at her and she catches it, laughing. "Not everything is about sex, Ari. The sooner you realise that the quicker you'll find Mr. Right."

It's been a busy day and I'm dead on my feet, but I smile when the bell rings and I see Luke walking through the door.

"Mr. boring has arrived," whispers Aria in my ear. I elbow her, and she giggles handing me my jacket.

"Hey," he greets, his green eyes twinkling.

"Aria, meet Luke. Luke this is my very annoying friend, and boss, Aria."

He shakes her hand, then turns away to go and look in the cake stands. Aria's hand is still in the air and she's staring at it in bewilderment. I nudge her and she drops its before mouthing, "He shook my hand?"

"He's a gentleman," I hiss, rounding the counter right as Aiden enters the shop. I freeze mid-step but he's too busy glaring at Luke to notice.

"Aiden?"

He brings his eyes to me and forces a smile, "I know you have plans tonight, but I really need you." There's something different about him, and the way his eyes are pleading silently with me, twists my heart.

I step closer, "What's happened?"

"You know I wouldn't ask unless it was really important."

I glance at Luke who's watching the exchange carefully. He smiles, "It's fine, Bella, we can meet another night. Just text me when you're free."

"Are you sure, I feel terrible."

He gently rubs my arm, "Honestly, it's fine. Your friend needs you." He gives a nod to Aiden who doesn't return it, and he leaves.

Aiden rolls his eyes and Aria shakes her head. I frown, "What?"

"He's too nice," says Aria, and Aiden nods in agreement.

"How can someone be too nice? He's a gentleman."

"All I know, is that if some guy came and interrupted my date with you, I wouldn't have been the one leaving," Aiden chips in.

"He was being nice," I snap.

Aiden shrugs, then takes my hand. "Night Aria," he calls as he leads me out to his car.

Ten minutes later, we stop outside a bar. It's busy inside and Aiden twists in his seat to face me. "I want you to pretend to be my date."

I notice he doesn't look so upset now and I frown. What are you talking about?"

"There's a change of clothes on the backseat." He twists back to face the front. "I won't look."

I glance back. The windows are blacked out so it's not like anyone can see. "Why didn't you call and ask me to do this?" I ask, climbing into the back.

"Because you'd have said no."

"For good reason. I can't help but feel you've ruined my date on purpose."

"You owe me," he complains, and I sigh heavily. He has been good to me, and I guess one favour isn't too much to ask. Plus, he's paid for the outfit and I'm a sucker for new clothes.

"Keep your eyes forward," I mutter, wriggling out of my tights.

"I've already seen you naked," he reminds me.

"I cannot be responsible for what the drunk me does, Aiden. It's something you need to know if you're going to continue to be my friend."

I lift the lid on the Selfridges box and lift out the black dress. "Did you pick this?"

"Just put it on," he says with a grin.

"Who does all this stuff for you?" I ask, slipping the dress up my legs and over my thighs. "Can you do anything yourself?"

"I wipe my own backside," he jokes.

"Really? That surprises me." I take a mascara from my bag and apply it, followed by lip gloss. I slip my feet into the heels he's also brought. "Okay, I'm ready." He gets out the car and rounds my side, opening the door and offering me his hand which I take. "What exactly do I have to do?" I add.

"Just be my date for the evening. If anyone asks, tell them it's early days but we're happy. And do not tell anyone you're in my spare room."

"Why would anyone ask that?"

"Oh, trust me, they will," he mutters, leading me inside.

The room is impressive with large chandeliers and shimmering crystals dotted around. There are a lot of important looking people in suits and nice dresses, and I'm thankful Aiden brought me a black dress, it seems to be the most popular colour theme of the evening. He takes my hand and hooks it through his arm. "It's going to be boring and for that, I apologise."

He wasn't kidding. Aiden is popular, with men constantly wanting his attention so they can talk business. I zone out after the third conversation about investment, slipping away to use the bathroom.

I'm topping up my lip-gloss when the blond I recognise from Aiden's social media appears beside me. She sets about topping her own lipstick, occasionally flicking her eyes my way in the reflection. Eventually she smiles, but it's not kind or friendly, and instead comes across colder and bitchier. "So, you and Aiden?"

"Yes." I run my fingers through my hair, trying to ignore the feeling of dread in my stomach.

"Funny, he never mentioned you."

"Should he have?"

She slowly pops her things back in her clutch bag, sniggering, "It depends how long you've been together. I'm a girl's girl," she states, and I almost laugh. "So, you should know he was with me on Saturday night . . . having sex." She smirks before leaving me.

I brace myself against the sink unit and stare at my reflection in the mirror. I don't know why her words affect me, but right now, as I think about her and Aiden together, my heart aches and my stomach twists into knots. I feel like she's just thrown ice water over me, waking me up. Despite my protests to Aria, and even myself, I've been enjoying Aiden's attention. He's unobtainable, yet he was starting to convince me that wasn't true. And she's reminded me it is. Aiden is a player, and he will break my heart.

"He's no good for you, Bella," I tell myself out loud. "So, stop dreaming he'll change for you. It's never going to happen."

When I step out of the bathroom, Aiden is waiting for me, leaning casually on the wall. He pushes off and steps closer, "Are you okay? You've been ages." I nod, not trusting myself to speak. "I want to introduce you to a solicitor." It's an odd thing to say and I wonder who this guy is and why Aiden wants me to meet him so badly. "It's important he thinks we're together," he adds, not quite meeting my eye.

I force a smile, "Show me the way."

He looks relieved as he grabs my hand and takes me back into the room. I can't help but scan it for his blonde bombshell. "Isabella, this is a good friend of mine, Drake."

I bring my attention back the tall gentleman before me. "Hi," I say.

He holds out his hand and we shake, "It's nice to meet you, Aiden's told me so much about you."

I narrow my eyes with confusion, "All good things I hope?"

"Of course. He tells me you work in a bakery?"

I open my mouth to answer when the blond bitch taps Aiden on the shoulder, he glances back, and I feel him stiffen. She hooks her arm through his, "Walk with me, Aiden."

He immediately drops my hand and allows her to lead him away, throwing an apologetic smile our way before adding, "I'll be right back." Blondie smiles smugly and I watch them disappear into the crowd, leaving me alone with Drake, the solicitor I don't know, yet am expected to lie to.

I offer Drake a small smile, "It must be important," I say, "Shall we get a drink?"

CHAPTER NINE

Aiden

Laurie leads me upstairs towards the toilets. We bypass them, heading straight up to the terrace which is closed to the public tonight due to the event. She makes sure to close the doors behind us and we make our way to the wall, looking down at the busy streets below. "What's so urgent, you have to fuck up my plans?"

"I text you yesterday and you didn't reply." She pouts before adding, "I think he's having an affair."

I roll my eyes in annoyance. "So are you, Laurie."

"That doesn't mean he gets to. I'm sick of it. Besides, if he wasn't busy shagging his side whores, I wouldn't need to look elsewhere."

"You interrupted me for this?" I snap. "I'm not your fucking agony aunt, Laurie. What happens in your messed up marriage is nothing to do with me."

Her bottom lip protrudes slightly. "Don't be cross with me, baby." She gently places a hand to my cheek, kissing the other. I stare straight ahead, not daring to run my eyes over her body. She's wearing red, my favourite colour.

"Look at me, Aiden," she whispers, and I turn my head slightly.

She kisses the corner of my mouth, and I don't move away, giving her the green light to take the kiss deeper. Her fingers rake through my hair, and she places herself between me and the wall. "I'm wearing red especially for you," she whispers, pressing herself against my erection. "And I forgot my underwear," she adds between kisses.

I lift her long red dress, bunching it around her waist. It's an automatic action, like my hands have a mind of their own whenever she is around me.

I groan, hating how weak I am as I slide her dress up to her waist. She grins, running her hand over the bulge in my trousers. "I'm so wet for you," she pants, tugging my button open, followed by my zipper. She pulls my cock free, and it stands proudly between us. I lift her onto the wall and press my erection to her opening. She's so wet, I slip right in, and *fuck*, it feels good.

I pull the top of her dress down, exposing the perfectly perky tits her husband paid for, and tease her nipples as I slam into her. She runs her fingers under my shirt, raking her nails down my back. The sting adds to my pleasure, and I tug her head back by her hair and nip at her neck. She shudders, coming apart and I follow seconds later, growling as my body stiffens.

I press my face to her neck, taking a minute to get my breath back. She drops her legs back to the ground and tucks me back into my trousers, fastening my zipper and button.

"I think she likes to watch," she whispers in my ear, slowly running her tongue up my neck. It takes a second to realise what she said, but when it clicks, my head shoots up and Bella is standing at the doors, glaring back at me.

"Fuck!"

Bella

"Fuck," I hear him yell, as I turn and run back towards the stairs.

Tears trickle down my cheeks and it's from the anger I have coursing through my body right now. How dare he mess up my date so he could bring me here, leave me, and fuck her. And yes, maybe a small piece of my heart is breaking. *Just a small piece.*

I shove the doors open, almost knocking into a doorman, and head for the tube. It begins to rain. "Marvelous," I shout up towards the sky. I don't even have my jacket, it's in his car.

My phone buzzes in my bag and I stop to pull it out. Of course it's Aiden, so I cancel the call, but it immediately lights up again. I shove it back in my bag and look around at my surroundings. I decide to go into a busy bar to get out of the rain, and once inside, I head straight for the bathroom. I pull out my phone to see five missed calls from Aiden and I snigger, he's acting like a damn boyfriend who got caught cheating. It rings again and I sigh, connecting it.

"Bella, where are you? It's raining, you don't have a coat, let me come and get you." He's shouting to be heard over the sound of the rain and passing cars, which means he's out there looking for me.

"Why did you do that to me tonight, Aiden?" I ask, hurt evident in my voice, "Why did you make me cancel on my date?"

He groans, "I'm a prick," he yells, "I always fuck shit up. It's what I do. Please let's talk face to face, Bella. I'm sorry."

"I don't want to see you right now," I snap. "You humiliated me tonight and ruined my date with Luke."

I notice he's gone quiet, and I pull the mobile back to check we're still connected. The bathroom door opens, slamming back against the wall. I stare open mouthed, surprised he found me. He's still holding his mobile to his ear and he's dripping wet from the rain, it's hot as hell. We stare at one another in silence. There's pain behind his eyes, which only confuses me more. "I'm sorry," he whispers into the phone. His eyes still fixed to mine.

I cancel the call without breaking the contact. "You hurt my feelings tonight, don't ever do that again."

He stuffs his phone in his pocket holds his hand out to me. "Let's go home."

I cross my arms over my chest, marching past him. "I'm not touching you when you've been touching her." I head out into the rain with him hot on my heels.

Aiden

We get back to Tremos and Bella marches straight for the elevator to the apartment. She didn't speak a word all the way back, and for the first time in a long time, I feel guilty which is ridiculous when we're not even a thing.

I head for the bar, noting how quiet the place is, probably due to it being a Monday. JP fixes me with a glare,

"What did you do now?" Raff also comes over and I fill them in on the disastrous night.

"Jesus Aiden, what is it with you and that stuck up bitch?" snaps JP, slamming his hands on the bar.

"I fucked up, what do you want me to say?" I ask, grabbing a bottle of Jack and unscrewing the cap. I take a large gulp and relax slightly. Tonight was supposed to be about Drake meeting Bella, and I completed that task.

"Did you at least convince Drake you're making progress?" asks Raff.

I nod, "Yeah, he met her but then Laurie interrupted us, and I left them to talk."

"Wait," snaps JP, "So you left her with him? What if she told him you've only just met and it's all bullshit?"

"Yeah," agrees Raff looking equally concerned. "I had a job convincing him you'd moved so fast."

"Relax, Bella knew it was important she lie for me."

JP frowns, "You told her?"

"Of course I didn't," I snap, tired of him assuming I'm so stupid. "I got her there on the pretence she pretended we were dating. I told her she owed me one."

"And she didn't think that was weird?" asks Raff.

"Probably but she didn't object so who cares. I got the job done."

"No," snaps JP, "You left the job half done so you could fuck that bitch. You're gonna blow this if you don't start acting like Bella is the only damn thing you see, Aiden."

"He's right," Raff agrees. "Laurie is in the past, leave her there. She made her choice the second she left you for that rich fucker.

I take another gulp. "This is all Jakes fault," I hiss angrily. "The entire thing is fucked up. I don't know if I can do it."

"Give up then," says JP, shrugging, "Prove him right. You've always been a selfish bastard, why should we expect anything different?" He throws his cloth on the bar top and storms into the back office, slamming the door.

"It's not hard, Aiden. Just fuck the virgin. Most men would kill for that challenge," mutters Raff in annoyance.

"But it's not that simple. She's hard work and how the fuck will I get proof. This whole thing feels like it's set up to fail. And why her? Why did Jake specifically pick Bella? I can't even ask her if she knew him because of his stupid fucking rules."

"There's no obvious connection between them," admits Raff. "I've asked myself the same questions over, but it makes no difference. The deal is you take her virginity. So, take it and we can all move on."

Bella

Aria glances back from where she's perched in the window to fill the display cabinets of this morning's bakes. "I don't see the problem, Bells. You aren't together," she states matter of fact.

She's right and I can't even explain why I feel so gutted by the entire thing. I've avoided Aiden since we got home last night. I even got up earlier and came to work at five a.m. just so I didn't risk bumping into him going for his early morning run.

"I guess I just feel disappointed," I mutter with a shrug.

"That it wasn't you he had up against the wall?" she asks, smirking.

I narrow my eyes, "No, of course not. But he made me cancel my date. Why didn't he just take her as his date? It makes no sense."

"Have you asked him?"

"No. I've been avoiding him."

She laughs, climbing from the window and turning to me. "Seriously, you can't be a weirdo about this, he'll run a mile."

"I don't care. I'm not trying to catch him."

"Sure," she says, her voice full of sarcasm.

"I'm not," I cry, annoyed she'd think differently. "Especially now I've seen what a whore he is."

"You can't comment because you've never had sex. He's free and single, he can shag whoever he wants."

"I know that, but he can't ruin my plans."

She sighs, placing her hands on the counter and fixing me with a stern stare. "Just fuck him."

"God no," I screech.

"He's not going to turn you down is he. Get him out your system."

"I don't want to sleep with him."

"Then stop freaking out when he's with other women. It's none of your business."

I roll my eyes and begin to rearrange the cakes in the counter. "Was it hot?" she adds, and I glance up to see her smirk firmly in place.

"You are disgusting."

"It was, wasn't it." I bite my lip to stop the smile threatening to break through. She laughs, "I knew it. He's way too hot to be a crap lay."

♡

When I get home, the apartment is quiet. There're candles on the dining table and flowers. *Oh great*, just what I need. Trapped in my room all night listening to his bloody date night.

I kick off my shoes and drop my bag and as I shrug out of my jacket, Aiden comes through holding a bottle of wine. I scan my eyes over the jeans and t-shirt he's wearing. It's the most casual I've seen him so far but it's sexy as hell.

"Good day?" he asks. I nod. "Great. I hope you haven't eaten."

I stare at the table, realising this is all for me. I'm part relieved, at least I don't have to listen to him shmoozing some woman, or worse, the blond from last night. "I haven't," I confirm.

"I thought I could at least try and make up for ruining your date night."

"Is Luke here?" I tease and he rolls his eyes. "Look, you really have nothing to make up for. I overreacted."

"You didn't. I was out of order, and it was disrespectful. Please let me say sorry and eat with me." He lifts the lid on the pot in the center of the table. Steam billows out and I peer closer. "It's homemade soup," he tells me. "I can't take the credit; my mum helped me out."

I smile, lowering into my seat. "I love leek and potato, it's one of my favourites."

"My mum is the best cook," he says, sitting opposite me and using the ladle to scoop the soup up before pouring some into my bowl.

I inhale deeply, closing my eyes in appreciation. "You can't beat homemade." I open my eyes, and Aiden is staring at me. I smile and it breaks his trance. He gives his head a shake and pour some soup into his own bowl.

"Go ahead," he encourages, nodding at my bowl. "Try it, I want to know what you think."

I take a mouthful and groan in pleasure. "Oh my god, that's amazing."

He smiles, almost looking proud. "I'll let her know." He shifts nervously. "This might surprise you," he begins. "But I've never taken a woman on a date."

I laugh, easing any tension. "That really doesn't surprise me, Aiden." I take another scoop of soup. "Not even the blond from last night?" I ask, trying to sound as casual as possible.

"Laurie," he tells me. "And no, we haven't been on an actual date."

I arch a brow. "Wow, aren't you lucky to have women like her that will just drop their knickers for you wherever they are, and you haven't even had to pay for a date."

A serious expression replaces the smirk, and he sits straighter. "I loved Laurie," he announces, and the sentence surprises me. "From the beginning she intrigued me. We were fire together and in case you didn't know, that's never a good thing." He sighs, "We would fight so bad, and she'd purposely do shit to bring out my jealous side, which wasn't hard to be honest. At first, I loved that. The chemistry we had was the best high I'd ever experienced. But the lows," he gives his head a shake, "The lows were depressing and consuming. And then she left me for someone richer," he adds a laugh, "Married him too."

"Is she divorced now?"

He laughs again and gives his head a slight shake. "On her wedding day, I fucked her ten minutes before she walked down the aisle. I went there to ask her not to do it, but then I saw her in her fancy dress, and I couldn't bring myself to be a selfish prick. The next thing I know, she's got me pressed up against the wall and we're kissing . . ." He scrubs his hands over his face, and I get the impression this is the most he's ever told anyone. I like he's confiding in me. He scoffs, "And then I sat in the church and watched her promise to love him forever." He slides his bowl away despite hardly touching it. "And the worst part is, I didn't feel remorse," he admits, "It turned me on to know I'd fucked her, that she's been screaming my name on her wedding day. How messed up is that?"

"Sounds toxic," I mutter.

"That was just one of the many fucked up things I've done involving Laurie. Jake hated her. He said she had too much of a hold over me," he looks me in the eye, "I guess she still does."

"You just have to say no," I tell him, and a smile spreads over his face.

"You're right."

"I know it's not that simple," I add. "Not when feelings are involved."

"I think she's just a bad habit I'm struggling to break."

"Every time she calls, think about Jake and what he'd say," I suggest.

His smile fades again and pain shines through. "Good idea," he almost whispers.

"I think the best medicine would be finish this delicious soup and watch a movie?"

He groans playfully. "The last movie you made me watch, made me sick."

"Love Actually is a classic," I argue.

"No, Bells, The Goonies is a classic. Back to the Future is a classic. Love Actually is trash."

※

We're halfway through an action that Aiden insisted on, when his mobile phone lights up, buzzing on the coffee table with Laurie's name as the caller id. He glances at me, smirks, then goes back to watching the film. She instantly calls back twice more. "She doesn't take a hint," I mutter.

"This is what she does. She'll get more and more persistent."

"Stalker much."

He snatches it up, sighing heavily. "Maybe you could answer it?"

I laugh, "No way. She already hates me."

"She doesn't know you."

"I'm on her radar, Aiden. She followed me into the bathroom last night, making sure to stamp her territory."

He frowns, "She did?"

"Just tell her you can't talk right now."

He stares at her name flashing on the screen for the fourth time. "She'll sweet talk me."

I shake my head in exasperation, snatching his mobile. "You're weak," I whisper hiss, accepting the call.

"Hello?"

"Put him on," she snaps.

"Aiden's busy."

"Does he know you're screening his calls?"

"I'll let him know you called."

"Listen to me," she hisses angrily, "If he finds out I called and you didn't get him, he'll be pissed. I'm saving you from a dressing down."

Her rudeness only annoys me, and I give Aiden a wicked smile. "He's currently in the shower waiting for me to join him," I say smugly. "And it was him that asked me to answer your call and get rid of you because he's occupied with me. So, stop with the constant calls and go fuck your husband." I disconnect, letting out a small gleeful giggle. "Holy shit, I can't believe I just said all that."

Aiden

Bella throws the phone at me, and I catch it with one hand, making sure the call has been disconnected before laughing with her. I'm so hard for her right now that I have to sit forward to hide the evidence. "She's so rude," she adds, "What the hell do you see in her."

"I think she's just rude to you," I tell her, smirking. "Jealousy can do that to a person."

She leans a little closer, her hand on my chest, "Seriously, you can do better."

"Yeah?"

"One hundred percent."

I kiss her. Gently to the side of her mouth, lingering to gage her reaction. She's surprised, her eyes are wide with shock but as my hand glides along her jaw, I feel her relax a little. "Do you want me to stop?" I whisper against her lips. She gives a slight headshake, and it's all the permission

I need to kiss her properly. She tastes sweet and fresh, and my cock strains in my jeans. Her eyes flutter closed, and her hands grip my t-shirt, tugging me closer. I pull back slightly, still cupping her face in my hands. I study her for a second, her blue eyes are shining, and her cheeks are flushed. "Sorry, I couldn't help it," I whisper.

Bella's mobile phone begins to ring, and she inhales sharply, dragging her eyes from me to reach for it. She accepts the call, clearing her throat before saying, "Hey, Luke."

My eyes widen in shock. *She fucking answered his call after what just happened.* "Really?" I hiss.

She turns slightly to avoid my glare. "Yes, that'd be great. See you then." The she disconnects.

"You're seeing him?" I ask, clenching my jaw in irritation.

"Yes, tomorrow," she mutters.

"But we just kissed," I snap.

"I know," she almost whispers, "And we shouldn't have. We're friends, Aiden, and friends don't do that."

I roll my eyes and push to my feet. "Fuck you, Bella," I spit. Humiliation burns me as I grab my car keys.

"Where are you going?" she asks, also standing and following me to the door. "Aiden?"

"To see Laurie," I hiss.

I arrive at the hotel and approach the desk. The maître d' gives me a nod, which means she's alone. I slip him a twenty and head straight up to her room. I know I shouldn't be here and ignoring Laurie's calls felt good. *Being with Bella felt good.* I groan, raising my hand and knocking once. At least Laurie can calm the rage within me.

The door swings open and Laurie glares at me with her hands on her hips. I smirk, wrapping my hand around her throat loosely and pushing her further inside before kicking the door closed. Her eyes narrow in that way they do right before she tries to piss me off, "Don't think you can have me after leaving her bed."

I scoff, "We both know that isn't true." My head is full of Bella, *damn it*. She's all I can see. I give it a shake and focus on Laurie. I grip her silk nightdress and tug it hard, letting it pool to her feet.

"Are you serious about her, Aiden?" she demands. I lean in, trying to kiss her but she turns her head, shoving me back.

"Why do you care, Laurie?" I snap, "I'm here, aren't I? That should tell you all you need to know." I take her hands, pinning them above her head. "Besides, I don't fuck virgins, I like my women with a little more experience."

"Bullshit," she spits, cupping my chin tightly and forcing eye contact. "I see it," she adds, digging her nails into my skin. "You want her so badly it's killing you."

I force a grin, "You think you know me so well." I wrap her hair around my fist and tip her head back, kissing along her jaw and down her neck. "Now, you called me several times today and I know it wasn't to talk about Isabella."

She smirks, gripping onto my shoulders and forcing me to my knees. "We have the entire night," she says, raising her leg and slipping it over my broad shoulder.

I grin as her scent consumes me. "We'd better make the most of it."

❧

I pull my jeans up, hardly able to look Laurie in the eye. She steps in front of me and places her hand against my face, pulling it away to show me blood where she'd dug her nails into my chin. "Opps." She smirks. It's not the first time either of us have come away with injuries. We fight and fuck, loving the adrenaline it gives us. It's unhealthy and toxic, but somehow, I can't walk away.

I go into the bathroom, taking a breath before staring at my reflection in the mirror. It's the first time I've felt weird about fucking Laurie, like I'm ashamed of myself. *Bella's got into my head.* I touch the scratches and then notice marks on my neck where she's sucked too hard on my skin. I have no doubt that was done on purpose.

I groan out loud then splash my face with cold water. I've got to get Bella out of my head. The sooner this is all over, the sooner I can go back to my normal life. Fucking Laurie and anyone else I want, without feeling guilty.

There's a tap on the door and Laurie enters, still naked. She has red marks around her neck and bruises to her hips where I gripped her too hard. She stands in front of me so that she's leaning against the sink and hands me a bottle of whisky and places my mobile phone on the countertop. She watches me carefully as I swig straight from the bottle.

"I haven't seen you this distracted in a while," she muses running her fingernail down my front. I take another swig. "Who is this girl, anyway?" she asks, licking up the side of my neck seductively.

She rubs her hand over my cock, through my jeans. "I'm helping her out with a place to stay."

"She's living with you?" she queries, halting her movements. I cover her hand with my own and encourage her to continue.

"It's not a permanent thing, she's in the spare room." I groan, my cock stiffening again.

"And she's a virgin?" she asks. I nod, rubbing my hands across her breasts.

"Why haven't you fucked her?"

"Long story," I mutter.

"I wanna know," she pushes.

I have no intention of telling Laurie the truth, so I shrug, "Cos' I want a woman that can handle me, not some virgin that has this ridiculous notion of love and saving herself. She's just after a free ride."

CHAPTER TEN

Bella

I replay the message, gripping my phone so tightly, it hurts my hand. "Cos' I want a woman that can handle me, not some virgin that has this ridiculous notion of love and saving herself. She's just after a free ride." I can't help thinking Aiden sounds smug.

When I woke this morning to a missed call from him, I assumed he was apologising. When I'd pressed play on his voicemail, my blood had run cold. The entire conversation played out, and before it had cut out, the moans from the pair were audible.

Aria arrives and I tuck my phone into my pocket. She takes in the filled cabinets then checks her watch, "Another early start? What's going on with you."

I shrug, "I'm in my organised era."

She takes off her jacket and disappears into the back room to hang it up. "Or Aiden's annoyed you?" she guesses.

I groan, "Why am I letting this man affect me so much when we're not even together?"

She returns, rubbing a sympathetic hand down my back. "What happened?"

"He kissed me."

Her eyes widen, "You lucky cow."

"And then I messed it up."

She winces, "What did you do?"

"Luke called, like right after the kiss."

"Oh lord, tell me you didn't answer it?"

"Of course I did," I wail, "I wasn't thinking straight. I was in shock he kissed me and then the phone rang, and I just picked it up. I agreed to another date."

"And it didn't go down well?"

"Of course it didn't." I bury my face in my hands. "His eyes were so full of hope, Ari, and the second he heard Luke's name, they just changed. Then he left in a huff."

"Well just explain you weren't thinking straight."

I shake my head, "It's too late for that. He went to Laurie's." I pull out my phone and replay the message.

Aria listens with her mouth slightly open in shock. She waits for it to end before exhaling, "Shit, that was savage."

"Yeah, he went right for the jugular. The worst thing is, before we kissed, we'd talked about her, and he'd said how he'd loved her, and she broke his heart. Now, she keeps him dangling even though she's married. I really felt like he'd opened up to me. I even cancelled my date with Luke."

"Oh, Bells," she mutters, rubbing my arm. "I'm so sorry."

I shrug. "I fucked up, but he handled the whole thing so badly. I can't help but feel like I've had a lucky escape."

"Do you think he called you on purpose?"

I shake my head, "I think he probably butt-dialled." She doesn't look convinced. "If he did, then it only confirms what I already thought, he's not for me."

"Do you know what you need?"

"Do not say a night out."

"It's the answer for everything bad in the world. Alcohol and friends. I'll get Jack on board."

When I get in from work, Aiden is sitting at the kitchen table working away on his laptop. He glances up and I notice the marks on his neck, but neither of us speak as I march past and head to my room.

Once I'm showered, I apply some light make-up to brighten my dark undereye circles, add a little mascara, then slip into a cute, white summer dress. It clings to my curves in all the right places, flaring at the bottom.

When I go back through the lounge, Aiden is staring blankly at the television. He glances my way, letting his eyes run down my body. "Enjoy your date," he mutters.

I roll my eyes at how childish he's being. "Actually, I cancelled my date after you stormed out last night." I slip my sandals on.

Aiden stands, closing the gap between us and I stare into his relieved eyes, "That's great, do you want to do something?" My eyes fall to the marks on his neck, and he shifts uncomfortably, tugging his collar up on his t-shirt to try and hide them. "Cinema perhaps, somewhere dark?" he adds a small laugh to lighten the mood.

"I have plans," I mutter.

"Please, Bella. Just give me a chance."

"What for?" I demand.

"We were getting on yesterday, right?"

"You threw a tantrum because I spoke to another man, Aiden. And whilst I realise, what I did wasn't great timing, you handled it by going to fuck another woman to spite me. It's not the sort of situationship I need in my life."

"I didn't fuck her," he lies, and my mouth falls open in shock.

"I should go," I mutter, heading for the door.

He chases me down, trying to block my path. "You know it's not safe to be out alone."

I reach for the door, tugging it open and he steps to the side. "I'm not going out alone. I'll be with my friends, and JP is coming too."

"He is?"

"And he doesn't seem to think the threat is that bad, so hopefully, I'll be out of your hair in no time."

His eyes narrow, "JP actually said that?"

"I've also left some rent money on the side, I wouldn't want you thinking I was taking you for a *free ride,*" I say, smiling wide. "Have a good evening." And I leave, making sure to slam the door closed.

Aiden

As soon as the door closes, I call JP. "Yeah, man?" he answers.

"Why the fuck are you telling Bella the threat is almost over?"

"Because you're fucking it all up, Aiden. I like the girl, and I can't stand the way you're going about this. I mean, going off with Laurie like that, it's causing unnecessary hurt."

"She was always going to get hurt, JP. It's not like I'm going to marry her."

"I just don't think this was what Jake meant when he came up with this idea. He chose Bella for a reason, and I can't help thinking he was giving you a shot as happiness. You're blowing it."

"No JP, you're blowing it for me, because you want to bang her friend. If you mess this up, I'll tell Sara what you're up to, whilst she's looking after your baby."

He scoffs, "Fuck you, Aiden." Then he disconnects.

"Fuck," I mutter out loud. It's not like I'd actually tell Sara anything, she thinks the sun shines out of his backside. But she doesn't want to be with him, she made that perfectly clear after she fell pregnant with his kid. Although, I suspect they still sleep together.

Bella

I stare at Aria and JP longingly. They look cute together as they flirt like they're the only two people in this packed-out club. The minute Raff didn't fall at her feet, she set her sights on JP, and I don't blame her, he's equally as hot.

Jack sighs heavily, bringing my attention back to him. "It sounds like a bad romance, or it at least has the potential to be. He's going to break your heart and stomp all over it."

I nod in agreement. "I know. That's why I'm going to move out. I've been flat hunting on-line. Aria's going to lend me a deposit."

"You should go and kick your dad out of the house, you've paid so much into it. Have you heard from him?"

I shake my head and stir my cocktail with my straw. "No. And I've seen no dodgy men hanging round. Maybe it's all sorted. JP seems to think the threat isn't that real if we haven't heard anything." I smirk, "Maybe if the men he sold me too are fit, I could role with it."

He laughs, "What are the chances of that?"

JP leans on the table with Aria holding onto his arm. We were thinking of heading back to Tremos?"

"Only if you want to," adds Aria, her face full of sympathy.

I give a nod. I'm still mad with Aiden, but I can't deny I love being around him, even if we're not speaking right now.

꒰ღ꒱

Aiden is behind the bar when we arrive, which is odd, and he looks out of place, but I guess he sometimes has to help out in his own place. He stares past me to JP. "Sorry about earlier," he says, and it's the sincerest I've ever seen him as JP fist bumps him.

"Already forgotten," he replies.

"What happened to your face?" asks Aria smirking.

"Yeah, looks nasty," adds Jake.

Aiden runs his hand over the scratches on his chin. "It was a . . . cat." He winces.

I scoff, placing my mobile on the bar. He stares down at it. "Press play," I tell him.

He eyes it warily. "Why?"

"It's okay," says Aria, leaning over. "I've got this." And she presses play on the recording.

I let the recording play out, including the moans and groans that continue after his statement. The way his jaw is clenched, and his eyes narrowed, makes me think he's angry. I take my phone back, feeling smug in my drunken haze.

"I'd say those scratches were from a dog, not a cat," says Aria, laughing.

"You didn't need to lie, Aiden," I say, disappointment lacing my words. "And I'm so sorry you feel I'm just after a free ride. But you offered me a place to stay. You furnished it, even when I said it wasn't necessary."

"I'm sorry," he mutters, staring down to avoid looking at me.

I roll my eyes, "It's just a word," I say, turning from the bar and heading for the dancefloor.

We spend another hour dancing, chatting, laughing, and it's not until JP throws Aria over his shoulder, that I realise it's almost one a.m.. Aria screeches with laughter as he slaps her backside. "I'm taking this woman home," he informs us. "Jack, you want to share a cab?" he asks.

Jack nods, finishing his drink, "Will you be okay, Bells?" he asks. "Yah now you can stop on my couch, Beck won't mind."

I shake my head, offering a reassuring smile. "I'm fine. Thanks for a good night."

I watch them leave; thankful I have such amazing friends. Aiden stomps past me, acting like I'm not even there, and somehow it only adds to the pain currently twisting my heart. I don't want us to be mad with one another but after everything he said, I think I have the moral high ground here. I sit at the bar, knowing he's in the apartment, makes me want to avoid it. Hopefully, if I give it ten minutes, he'll be in his bedroom, and I won't have to face him.

Unfortunately, he's in the kitchen by the time I get up there. He's topless and I run my eyes over the scratches across his back, rolling my eyes.

I might not have had sex, but I've never known anyone to come away looking like they've wrestled with a tiger. *She clearly marked him for my benefit.*

He turns to face me, folding his arms. "It was Laurie," he states, and I stare blankly until he adds, "The call you got last night. She called you from my phone and led me to have that conversation knowing it was recording to your voicemail."

"But she didn't force you to cuss me out like that," I point out.

"No," he admits, staring at the floor. "That was me being a prick."

"Glad we cleared that up," I mutter, heading on towards my room.

"I'm sorry," he calls out and I turn back to find him in the doorway. "Again."

"Me too," I say, "Sorry I ever thought we could be friends."

"We are friends," he argues.

I smirk, continuing to my room, "Not anymore, Aiden. I'm moving out." And I slam my door.

Aiden

I groan, burying my head in my hands and scrubbing them down my exhausted face. "Fuck you, Jake," I say out loud. "I bet you're loving this."

The deal was I spend two months getting to know her. *Two fucking months.* I can't even manage a few weeks. She's tying me up in knots and making me think and feel shit I haven't had to deal with for so long. Like guilt. Why the hell do I feel guilty about last night? Laurie is what I know. She grounds me. Yet I spent the night fucking her and thinking of Bella. Yet my guilt is all with Bella. I fucked someone else, knowing it would upset her. Knowing it would push her further away, when it's the last thing I need to be doing. And every second we spend fighting, is more time wasted. Time I could be spending having her fall in love with me, so she hands over the v-card, because if there's one thing I've learned about Bella, it's that she won't part with that, unless she's in love.

Before I can talk myself out of it, I'm heading after her. I shove her bedroom door open, and she spins to face me. I take in her white laced underwear, letting it momentarily steal my breath. I wasn't prepared to walk in and find her half naked.

"What the hell are you doing?" she demands.

"I don't know," I mutter, frowning. "Following my heart for once?" And I close the gap between us. She tips her head back to look at me and I run my fingers through her hair and slam my lips to hers. The kiss is bruising, desperate even, as I sweep my tongue into her mouth. *Fuck she tastes good.*

Bella

I hold onto his broad shoulders to stop myself from collapsing. The kiss is rough and demanding and it sends shock waves through my body. He grips my neck with one hand and his other is in my hair, gently tugging at the roots and causing a delicious sting. He trails wet kisses along my jaw line and down my neck, before resting his forehead against mine and looking me in the eye. "My favourite view," he almost whispers, "Is that cute pink flush on your cheeks and your swollen lips, right after I've kissed you." He adds another chaste kiss on my lips. "I want you to stay while we figure this out," he adds. "Please." And then he releases me and leaves.

I stare wide eyed at the closed door, frozen there for at least a minute before I carefully raise my hand to my face and tentatively run my fingers over my lips. He's right, they are swollen.

I fall into a restless sleep. Aiden fills my dreams and at one point, I even feel like he's here, in my room.

I wake with a start, and the sunshine blinds me as it streams through a gap in the curtains. I sit slightly, looking around in confusion. *This isn't my room.* I glance to my left and almost jump from the bed when I see Aiden fast asleep beside me.

I carefully lift the sheet, wincing when I realise, I'm just in a t-shirt. But in my defence, I didn't expect to be carried into Aiden's bed in the middle of the night. I slide to the edge of the bed, trying not to wake him.

"Where are you going?" he asks, and I jump in fright as his deep voice rumbles through me. I glance back and see his eyes remain closed.

"How did I get in here?"

"I carried you."

I frown, "I thought I was dreaming," I mutter.

He sniggers, "At least you didn't think it was a nightmare."

"Why, Aiden?" I ask, my voice exasperated.

"I needed to see if it felt right." When I don't reply, he sighs, "Having you in my bed."

I scoff, "Like a fucking interview?"

"Like a trial," he says, opening one eye. "Now, can we enjoy the last five minutes in peace before my alarm goes off, I don't do talking first thing."

I open my mouth to set him straight, tell him he can't just drag me from my own bed and force me to sleep in is. But he wraps a strong arm around me, tugging me back into bed and almost wrapping himself around me. My backside is pressed firmly against his crotch, and I am so aware, that each wriggle makes me blush deeper. "You keep moving like that and I'm gonna have a premature accident in my shorts," he murmurs.

"This is not appropriate," I whisper, stilling as his erection pushes against me.

"Don't pretend we weren't on the same page, Bella."

"You know this isn't normal, right? Your behaviour is so frustrating."

"Being around you is frustrating," he mutters. "I'm certain I asked for peace."

"Let me leave and you can have your damn peace."

"I prefer you next to me."

I sigh, "Where's this going, Aiden?"

"One day at a time, Bells." His alarm sounds and he groans, pressing a kiss to the side of my head before unwrapping his arms from around me and jumping out of bed. He stretches, not bothering to hide the bulge in his shorts. "Shower," he tells me, "I have meetings this morning, I'll drop you to work."

"I can make my own way," I say, training my eyes to his face rather than them travelling to his cock.

He smirks like he knows just where I want to look, "Now, Bella," he says firmly.

I roll my eyes and get up from the bed, stomping to the door. "Not your shower," he says, and I freeze. "My shower."

"Absolutely not."

"Walk or I'll carry you," he tells me, shrugging. When I don't move, he closes the gap, "Suit yourself."

"Okay, okay," I say, before he can grab me. "Whatever you say."

I step into his en-suite, closing the door. I lift the t-shirt, dropping it to the floor and step into the shower. Steam billows out the second I turn it on, and I groan as the hot water relaxes my muscles. My mind is racing, wondering what the hell Aiden is playing at. One minute we're fighting and now we're... well, I don't know what we're doing. We need to talk, that's for sure.

The door opens and Aiden steps in. "Jesus," I hiss, using my arms to cover myself best I can.

He ignores me, stepping into the shower. I automatically step to the side, and he steps under the spray, closing his eyes as the water hits his face. I watch mesmerised. His cock is standing proudly. "Aiden, what are you doing?" I manage to croak the words out. I could easily get out of the shower. I could tell him this isn't happening and pack up my stuff, but instead, I wait for his answer because as shocked as I am at this turn around in behaviour, I'm also intrigued. *Where could this lead if I allow it?*

"Are we going to analyse everything from now on?" he asks, turning to face me.

"I feel like I missed the conversation where you asked me if any of this was okay?"

He pushes the water from his face, slicking his wet hair back, before fixing me with those gorgeous blue eyes. He takes my hand, and I let him. Then he tugs me closer and slides a hand along my jaw, cupping my cheek. "Conversations are so over-rated," he says, tipping my head back slightly and placing his lips to mine. The kiss is soft and gentle, and all I can think about, is how his cock is pressed against my stomach. When he pulls back, his eyes are full of lust. I run my hands over his broad chest, my own breathing coming out ragged. I glance down, biting on my lower lip whilst contemplating my next move. Before I can talk myself out of it, I reach for his cock, taking the thick length in my hand. Aiden inhales sharply, also looking down between us. "Show me how you like it," I whisper. It's not like I haven't ever touched a man before, I've fooled around. But I've never been confident at taking the lead.

Aiden places his own hand over mine, squeezing it so I'm gripping it tighter. Then we begin to move back and forth, slowly at first. Aiden closes his eyes, letting his head fall back. It's empowering to know I'm making this man feel a certain way and I lean closer, placing kisses along his chest. He speeds up his hand, then uses his free hand to grip my hair, tipping my head back and kissing me again. He stiffens, groaning deep from somewhere in the back of his throat, before coming hard. Hot spurts of liquid hit my stomach, and he stares at it, shuddering, while the rest drips over our joined hands.

"You're going to make me late." He smiles against my lips. He releases my hand, holding it under the spray and washing his come from me. Then he turns me away from him, pressing his front to my back, and running his hands down my body, over my breasts and down my stomach, rubbing his release into my skin. The entire encounter is hot and if he was to press his hand between my legs, he'd feel just how much I want him right now. I've never met a man that's made me want him like this.

As if he can read my thoughts, he presses a kiss to my head and steps away, getting out of the shower and grabbing a towel. I risk a glance his way and he offers a small smile, "If I stay in there a second longer, I'm gonna lose control." And he goes back into the bedroom.

I release a long breath, switching the shower to cool and letting the water run over my face and down my body. I have to be stronger than this. He's a walking red flag and I'm literally ready to fall to his mercy.

We drive to work in silence. It's exactly how we got ready too, moving around one another in the kitchen in silence as we filled our coffee cups to go. I want to talk. I need to ask him what the hell is going on. If this is real and he's told Laurie he can't see her again. But instead, I sit in the silence, enjoying whatever this is and pretending there aren't a thousand questions buzzing around my head. Ones that could potentially ruin it all.

CHAPTER ELEVEN

Aiden

I feel like I'm back in control. Like I have this handled, and Jakes stupid game is a done deal. Bella was practically on her knees for me this morning and I didn't even touch her. A few more weeks and I'll do what needs to be done and walk away. It'll be easy. *Right?*

I scrub my hands over my face, I want to believe that, but I've spent the entire morning focused more on her than my damn meetings.

I head out to the waiting car, climbing in. JP gives me the side eye before starting the engine and pulling out into traffic. "You're distracted," he notes.

"You'd be distracted if you had the shitty deal hanging over your head."

"I do," he says, arching a brow. "We all need to make this happen with as much damage limitation as possible."

"I'm working on it," I say, pulling out my mobile and calling the local florist. I order fifty red roses to be delivered to the bakery.

JP waits for me to hang up before asking, "You made progress?"

"Raff was right, I needed to take control. And actually, it worked."

JP's head whips round, "You've fucked her?"

"No, not yet. I thought I'd do it at the end," I say, my voice slightly lower as guilt eats at me. "It'll hurt less."

"And now you're just kidding yourself."

"I could sleep with her now, drag it out into what she sees as a full-on relationship. Or I can play the long game and wait for the two months to be up, shag her at the end and leave."

"Both ways will break her heart. Besides, what if she asks you to sleep with her? She'll think it's odd if you tell her you want to wait."

"Or she'll respect me for respecting her? I have to make her believe I'm worth giving her virginity to. She's not the sort of girl that'll jus fall into my bed without my effort." My mind flashes back to this morning, wondering if I could have taken things further.

"Has Raff sorted the end game, like, how is this going to play out?" he asks.

"Jake sorted the doctor out. I just have to convince her to go for a check-up after the deed. Fuck knows how I'll do that."

"Unless someone walks in on you, confirming you were fucking?" suggests JP and I know he's back on side and all that bullshit about trying not to hurt Bella, is past him.

"Maybe, we'll cross that bridge when we come to it. How was Aria, did you get her home safe?" I ask, smirking.

He grins, "Wild! I've never met anyone like her. We had a crazy night. She showed me moves that I've never seen before, and you know how many tricks I've learnt along the way. But this morning, she practically kicked me out of there. It was weird." I smirk again, "You sound like a hormonal woman right now, JP. Replay those words in our head then go and wash your mouth out with soap."

He laughs, "I just didn't get her reluctance this morning. I thought she enjoyed the night too."

"Did she come?" I ask, and he laughs harder.

"Of course she did." He groans, "So many times. And now I feel like she's got me by the balls with her name tattooed all over them. I can't get her out my head."

I slap him upside the head, "Pull yourself together would yah. A month and a half left, and we can tag team a whole bunch of girls at the click of our fingers, now get a grip."

Bella

"If you like him, I don't understand the issue?" I ask Aria who's going through the accounts while I stand in the office door.

"He's keen," she says, referring to JP. "But I like to keep him on his toes."

"Ah, he's keen and that's why you're backing off?" I smirk, knowing this is always the moment in any kind of 'situationship' where she panics.

"It's not that," she argues, even though we both know it is. "I like him."

"So, what's your problem."

She sighs heavily and wraps a handful of receipts into a rubber band. "I just don't want him to think I'm falling hook, line and sinker. It's only been a couple of weeks and he's already texting me at least five times a day."

"He's attentive."

"Needy," she counters.

"It wouldn't hurt to see where it goes," I add.

"I will," she says, "Just at my own pace."

I arch a brow, "I can see this going horribly wrong." She'll push him away and he'll find someone else, then she'll be heartbroken, and we'll end up picking her up off the floor again. Although Jack tends to be better at that part than me.

"What about you and Aiden? Did he say anything about the voicemail?" I turn away slightly, feeling my cheeks blushing. "What?" she asks, suspiciously.

"He blamed it on Laurie."

Aria rolls her eyes, "Of course he did."

I shrug, "It seems like something she would do."

"Regardless of who sent it, what was his excuse for being with her in the first place?"

"He didn't give me one," I say, "But wasn't it you that said we're not together, so I have no right to be pissed?"

"Don't listen to me, I'm blagging life right now."

"But something weird happened last night." She eyes me, waiting for me to continue. "We slept in the same bed."

Her eyes widen, "How come?"

"That's the weird part, Ari. He kissed me mid argument before stomping out. Then he waited until I was asleep and carried me into his bed. When I asked him what he was playing at, he said he wanted to see how it felt to sleep beside me."

"Oh," she says with a thoughtful expression.

"And then he demanded I shower in his bathroom."

"Oh," she repeats, smirking. "And how did that go?"

I groan, burying my face in my hands. "Well for him."

She laughs, "Again?"

"I'm weak," I wail. "I wanted to be mad with him. I even told him last night that we were no longer friends."

"I hate to be the bearer of bad news, Bells, but you're giving the guy mixed signals."

"I know," I cry. "He just has this way of getting out of shit and worming his way into my good books."

"The way I see it, you can just relax and enjoy whatever this is between you, or you can sit him down and talk about it. But something tells me he won't like that option."

"Yeah," I agree, "He isn't the talking kind."

"Would it be so bad to just enjoy it then?"

"Whilst it lasts," I add.

"Exactly."

We're closing up when Aiden arrives. "You don't look like the type of guy to purchase a sweet treat," remarks Aria as he leans casually in the doorway with his eyes fixed on me.

"Depends how it's served," he says with a smirk.

Aria rolls her eyes, "Let me guess, you're a whipped cream fan?"

He smiles wider, "Too messy, I prefer to eat straight from the source."

My cheeks burn, "Are you here for any particular reason?"

"I was passing," he replies, biting on his lower lip briefly before adding, "Thought I'd drive you home."

"Cute," Aria remarks, grabbing my bag and jacket from the chair behind the counter and passing it over to me. "See you tomorrow."

I follow him out onto the street, pulling on my jacket. Aiden takes my bag before slipping his hand in mine. "Have you eaten?" I shake my head, and he continues walking on past the car. "Me either. Let's grab something now."

It's on the tip of my tongue to question him further, but the words die on my lips. Aria is right, I just need to relax and see where this leads.

Aiden

I order two steaks the second we're seated. I have another meeting in an hour and then I'll be at the club until the early hours, but the need to see Bella was overwhelming and I found myself driving to the bakery without giving it much thought.

"Did you have a good day?" I ask, shaking my head at the waiter when he approaches with a bottle of wine. "Just water today, please," I tell him.

Bella frowns slightly, "It was busy. You?"

"Same. Although I was extremely distracted all day."

"With what?" she asks innocently and thoughts of our morning shower flick through my mind for the thousandth time. I shift uncomfortably as my cock stirs to life. I've already had to relieve myself twice already, I can't do a third.

"Oh, business stuff."

"Are things harder now without your brother?" she asks.

"Not really, Jake was the clown. He was great at promotion and advertising, but I've always ran the business side of things. Do you miss seeing your dad?"

She stares down at her hands, "Sometimes. I'm so used to looking out for him, it feels weird not checking in."

"It shouldn't ever be like that," I say bitterly. "He's supposed to look after you, Bella."

"He's not well," she defends sadly, "But he does love me."

I want to scoff out loud. The man is a waste of space and how she can think he gives two shits about her is laughable.

The steak arrives and I dive into mine, checking my watch. Bella eyes it and after a few seconds, she says, "You didn't ask me what I wanted again."

I chew my mouthful before replying. "I can have it changed," I say, holding up a hand to get the waiters attention.

She immediately grabs it, slamming it down on the table. "No, don't do that."

"Then eat your steak, Bella."

I finish up and drop my napkin on my plate. Bella's eaten half of hers and now she's pushing it around her plate like a sulking teenager. I check my watch again and this time she catches me. "Do you need to be somewhere?"

"A meeting, but eat, I have time."

She shakes her head, "I'm not that hungry."

"Would you like it boxed so you can have it later?" I wave the waiter over before she replies and ask him to box it up.

Ten minutes later, I pull up outside Tremos. "You're quiet," I state.

"I'm just . . ." she sighs. "Taking it all in, I guess."

I get out of the car and head to her side, opening the door. She steps out and I press against her, trapping her. "You're over-thinking," I whisper, pressing my lips to her neck. She tilts her head slightly. "We're enjoying each other's company. Just go with it." I feel her relax, and I pull back to press my lips to hers. "I won't be home until late," I add. "But you'll be in my bed when I get back." Then I take her by the hand again and lead her inside.

CHAPTER TWELVE

Bella

The days blur past. I go to work each day, with Aiden insisting he drive me and pick me up. He takes me to dinner every evening before dropping me back at the apartment, and then he continues working, getting home in the early hours to find me curled up asleep in his bed.

Sometimes he wakes me, snuggling up and pressing his erection against my backside, and other times, he lets me sleep, only waking me in the morning in the exact same way.

He lets me touch him and explore his body. And I enjoy it, but I'm always left frustrated, a sentence I never thought I'd say, especially because Aiden is clearly experienced. He doesn't so much as place a finger below my waist unless it's to grip my backside while he kisses me. And those kisses, *fuck,* they're amazing. But damn I want them to trail down my body to settle the ache I have constantly between my legs.

We're locking up on Friday when Aiden pulls up outside the shop. "What the fuck," I mutter, "I told him not to pick me up because we were going for a drink."

He gets out the car. "Don't tell us, you were passing," says Aria, sarcastically. It's the excuse he always uses.

He grins, "I'm working at Tremos from five," he replies, "It makes sense to drop you both there."

"What if we weren't drinking in Tremos?" asks Aria.

"Free drinks all night and the VIP area, why would you go anywhere else?"

I glance her way, knowing he's already won her over. She claps her hands in delight, "Deal. But we'll need to change."

I'm sure Bella has something for you to wear," he relies, opening the car door for us both to get in.

❧

I apply a coat of lip gloss. "If it wasn't free and a guy rolled u to drive me home like that, you'd totally say I should watch out because he's a walking red flag."

Aria laughs, "Aiden is a walking red flag, but let's face it, you're waiting for his pole so what's the point in arguing."

My cheeks redden. "I am not," I cry.

Her eyes widen, "Bullshit. You're so frustrated, even the cakes are suffering."

"What are you talking about?"

"The way you whip the frosting until it's so stiff, it's practically cement."

I narrow my eyes playfully. "How can I be frustrated when I don't even know what there is to be frustrated about?"

"I don't know why you don't just ask him to get you off."

"Because it's embarrassing."

"He's having all the fun here, Bella. I'm not saying fuck him, not unless you want to. But the guy needs to hand out the odd orgasm or what's the point?"

"He's letting me take things slow."

She fixes me with a glare, "There's slow and then there's you and Aiden." She opens my wardrobe and flicks through the dresses I have hanging up. She finds one she likes and pulls it from the hanger, slipping it on and checking herself out in the mirror. Aria looks good in anything; she can get away with the worst fashion and make it look on trend. "What you need to do is step up your game."

"I'm not you," I remind her, "I don't play games."

She begins looking through the dresses again, "I'm talking short," she says, not bothering to acknowledge my comment. "With little to no underwear." She pulls out a red number I've never worn. I got it in a sale even though I hate anything too revealing. It just called to me. "This," she says, grinning.

"No way."

"Yes. With heels, what's the highest you have?"

"Aria, no."

"Bella, do you want him on his knees or not?"

I shudder at the thought, and she giggles, throwing the dress my way. "It's so clingy," I complain.

I go into the bathroom and slip on a thong and bra, followed by the dress. When I step out, Aria is already shaking her head. Relief floods me, for a second, I thought she was going to make me wear it. She closes the gap between us and reaches under the dress, ignoring my protests as she tugs my thong down. "Aria," I gasp, "I can't wear this with no underwear. She wrestles against me to remove my bra.

"A thong doesn't do anything," she argues, "It's literally string."

"But I feel like it's at least a little protection."

"You don't want protection, Bella, that's the whole point."

She steps back, holding my bra and thong in one hand, whilst looking at me. "Much better."

"It barely covers my backside," I hiss, feeling the hem of the dress and tugging it.

"Trust me on this, Bella. If this doesn't work, he's not into you."

I stare open mouthed, not sure if I'm ready to find that out just yet.

I take a breath as the elevator doors slide open, and as if Aiden's been waiting, he looks in our direction from his position behind the bar. I stare straight ahead, determined not to break the second he touches me, and I stride through, heading for the exit. I catch him from the corner of my eye, jumping the bar. "Holy shit that was hot," Aria whispers.

"Bella," he says firmly, and I glance back like I've only just noticed him.

"Hey," I say, smiling.

His eyes scan down my body, "Where are you going?"

"We thought we'd try a few bars first," Aria cuts in, hooking her arm through mine, "Laters."

"Orrrr," says Aiden, taking my wrist gently to halt me. "You could just stay here."

Aria looks around, screwing her face up, "It's not busy yet, we'll come back."

He runs his hand over his jaw, "Bella, a word?"

"Can it wait?" I ask, "It's past wine o' clock."

"Just five minutes," he mutters, taking me by the hand and leading me away.

We get into the office, and he slams the door, "Why are ... erm, why are you wearing ... that?" he asks, trying not to stare at me, yet failing miserably.

I glance down, running my hands down my sides, "The dress?" I ask, "Do you like it?" I turn slightly, giving him an eyeful of my backside.

"It's short," he comments.

"Aria says it makes my legs look great."

He gives a stiff nod, "It does. But remember, you shouldn't really be drawing attention to yourself."

"You think it'll draw attention to me?" I ask innocently, turning again. "Is it shorter at the back?"

I spot the way his jaw tightens. "You need to change," he grits out.

I frown, "Are you being serious?"

"Deadly."

The door opens and JP storms in, he stops in his tracks, his eyes widening, "That's quite a dress," he mutters.

"Out," Aiden snaps and even though it's clear he's talking to JP, I turn on my heel and begin to walk out. His arms are around my waist before I've made it more than two steps. I smile to myself. "Not you," he whispers.

JP smirks, "Gotcha." And he leaves.

Aiden reaches past me and locks the door. "Please go and change the dress," he says, his voice strained. He releases me, putting distance between us.

"I can't, Aria will kill me. She spent ages choosing our outfits."

I move over to his desk, and he follows me with his eyes. I place my hands on it, and bend slightly, "Have you ever had sex here?" I ask, glancing back over my shoulder. His eyes are dark with need and there's a bulge in his pants.

"Bella," he mutters, his tone is strained. "Stop."

I smile innocently, "I'm asking a question." I turn and lift myself up, sitting on the edge and crossing my legs.

"Fuck," he hisses, "Are you wearing underwear?" I give my head a shake and bite my lower lip. "What are you trying to do?" he demands.

"Get your attention," I admit.

"Consider it got," he snaps, closing the gap and kissing me hard. He parts my legs and steps between them. "You're playing with fire." I nod, pressing myself against his bulge. "I'm trying to be respectful," he adds. The roughness of his jeans sends shock waves right to my core and I groan. He closes his eyes, trying desperately to gain some self-control, but I lie back on the desk, lifting one leg up. "Holy shit," he whispers, running his hand along my inner thigh.

Aiden

It's too soon. It's too soon. It's too soon. I swipe my thumb through her wetness, and she shudders, a gasp leaving her swollen lips. *It's too soon.* I rub it over her clit, and she almost bucks off the desk. She's so responsive, just like I knew she'd be. Her scent fills my nostrils, and I inhale deeply. *It's too soon.* "Just a taste," I murmur, watching the glistening wetness gather at her entrance. I grip her inner thighs, spreading her legs wider. "Stop me," I add, breathless, "If I get carried away." I lean closer, using my thumb to rub circles on her clit again. She pants, her legs quivering. I swipe my tongue through her folds, humming my approval, she tastes good, like sweet cherries and musky vanilla.

I lower to my knees, hooking my arms around her legs and using my fingers to part her folds. When I lick her a second time, she grabs a handful of my hair. "Jesus," she cries. I'm desperate to hear her come. I need it like I need oxygen, and I press my mouth to her opening, eating her cunt like I'm starving, releasing my erection and gripping it tightly in my free hand. She tugs at the roots of my hair, occasionally scraping her nails along my scalp. "Aiden," she whispers.

"Stop me when it gets too much," I remind her, rubbing faster as I slide my tongue into her.

"I'm going to . . . Aiden, I think I'm going to-" She stiffens, clamping her legs around my head and lifting her backside off the desk slightly. She shudders, as wetness leaks from her, and I lap it up then push to my feet and release, groaning as my come hits her stomach.

The only sound is our panting breaths as I tuck my cock away. I hold her legs open, staring at her wet pussy as my come drips down her side and onto my desk. I scoop it up and rub it into her skin. She's too relaxed to care. I grab a tissue from the box on my desk and wipe her sensitive folds, she jerks, and I smirk, tucking the tissue into my pocket. I tug her dress into place and take her by the hand to help her stand. Her cheeks are pink, and her lips still swollen. "Have a good night," I tell her kissing her one last time.

"What about the dress?" she asks.

I grin, slapping her backside. "You smell of me," I tell her. "You're marked."

CHAPTER THIRTEEN

Bella

"It worked," I grin, handing Aria her drink. She looks annoyed and I follow her glare over to JP who has a woman sitting in his lap. "Oh dear, what happened to the game?" I ask, sitting down. She throws her drink back in one gulp.

"He's not playing it right," she says sulkily.

"How can he play when he doesn't know the rules, Ari. You keep avoiding his calls."

"He's a man, they're masters at games, Bella, trust me. He's just playing by his own rules. I'm not worried," she adds, shaking her head, "I'll win him back when I'm ready." She brings her eyes to me, "How did it go?"

I grin, "It worked."

She leans closer, "Oh my god, did you fuck?"

"No," I almost screech. "No, but I got that orgasm."

"And?"

I sigh dreamily, "And it was so worth the wait."

Raff joins us, placing a bottle of vodka on the table. "How are my favourite ladies this evening?"

"Single and ready to mingle," says Aria, pointedly.

"You and JP not on the same page?" he asks, glancing over to where JP is now locking lips with the woman.

"Please, JP is not even on my level."

I pour us all a shot and Aria drinks it straight down again. I arch a brow and top her up. It's going to be an interesting night.

※

I'm dancing with Aria when arms snake around my waist. I lean back, expecting it to be Aiden. It's not until he nuzzles against my neck, and I feel a clean-shaven face, I realise it isn't. I turn slightly, smiling awkwardly and trying to pull away. "Relax," he shouts over the music. "We're just dancing."

"That's not a good idea," says Aria, glancing behind me with worry etched on her face.

"Don't be jealous, I've got loads of love to share," he says, grabbing her hand and pulling her to us so I'm effectively sandwiched between them. He thrusts against me, and I wince, shuddering in repulsion.

I'm suddenly released, almost falling forward. Aria lands on her backside and when I turn to see what happened, the guy is pinned against the wall with Aiden's hand around his neck. I help Aria up and she brushes off. "Stupid prick," she huffs.

"Are you okay?" asks JP, cupping her face in his hands and studying her closely.

I see her features soften. "I'm fine," she almost whispers.

The doormen rush over and take the man. "Don't come back in here," Aiden warns as they carry him off. He stomps away without checking on me, letting me know he's pissed.

I roll my eyes and head off the dancefloor, leaving Aria swooning at JP. I sit at the table and grab the bottle of vodka, but before I can pour one, it's taken out of my hand and placed out of reach. I glare at Aiden as he sits opposite me. "You realise that wouldn't have happened had you been wearing something more appropriate."

My eyes bug out of my head. "Victim shaming at its finest," I snap.

"Don't play that fucking card," he growls, "You wore that dress to get my attention, don't act innocent."

"Exactly, I wore it for you, Aiden. That doesn't give other men permission to touch me. Jesus, do you know how fucking pig headed you sound right now?"

"Next time you wanna wear something for me, let's keep it in the apartment."

"I can wear what the hell I like, where I like," I snap, angrily. "Women should be able to roam around in underwear if they want to, without being attacked by desperate men that think they have a right to touch, just because it's on show." I lean over and snatch the vodka back. "Consent is a real thing."

He takes the bottle back, waving to a passing waitress, "Take this away before I end up carrying her home," he says in a teasing tone. She smirks, fluttering her long eyelashes as she takes it, brushing his fingers with her own.

"Of course, boss," she says, in a sultry tone.

I stare at him, "What now?" he groans.

I shake my head in disbelief. "I don't appreciate you making me out to be some kind of alcoholic whilst flirting with your staff," I snap, getting to my feet.

"You're overreacting," he mutters.

"Of course I am. It's my fault a perv grinded against me, and now I'm seeing things, right?"

"Bella," he says sounding exasperated.

"Goodnight, Aiden." I stomp off towards the elevator. I've drank way too much and with everything that's happened tonight, I'm feeling over-whelmed.

So, what if he went down on me? It doesn't mean we're in a relationship. And I was so close to asking if he'd slept with the waitress, I had to get out of there before I embarrassed myself.

I get up to the apartment and strip out of the stupid dress, dumping it in the bin as I pass. I take a hot shower and slip into my fluffy dressing gown. Then I make myself a coffee and take Aiden's laptop and set it on the kitchen worktop. I need an apartment, especially if I want to take things further with Aiden.

I open it up and stare wide eyed at the picture on his screen saver. The man beside him has his arm around Aiden's shoulders proudly. I stare at the blue eyes, and the way his features match Aiden's. *How the hell didn't I see that before?*

Aiden

I hand JP the keys to lock up. I'm done for the night, and I need to straighten things with Bella. I was mad when I saw that guy with his arms around her . . . and jealous, *fuck was I jealous*. But taking it out on her was out of order, and so here I am again, ready to apologise and make shit right. All for Jakes stupid fucking game.

I enter the kitchen, pausing when I see the laptop open with Bella staring at the picture of me and Jake. It was taken a year ago in Ibiza. Our last holiday together. My heart twists painfully.

"What are you doing?" I snap, and she jumps in fright. I slam the laptop closed and hold it under my arm. "Well?"

"I was . . . erm, I know that guy," she says, frowning in confusion. *Great*. What are the rules if she discovers Jake, even though I didn't tell her. "He used to come in the bakery," she continues. "And he'd always make me laugh, I used to look forward to it . . ." she trails off. "When he stopped coming in, I thought maybe he'd moved away."

"Well, he didn't. He died," I say bluntly, and she flinches at my words. "Why were you on my laptop?"

"I wanted to find a place to live," she explains. I head into the living room, and she rushes after me. "We shared stories about our disastrous dates," she tells me. I turn to see her eyes are full of sadness, "And he wouldn't tell me his name. I would ask him every time he came in, and he refused, telling me to guess, yet even when I did, he'd say I was wrong. I don't remember if I ever said Jake," she almost whispers with a faraway look in her eye. A tear rolls down her cheek and I resist the urge to hold her. "It became a game, and I secretly hoped I never guessed it, so we could carry on."

I place the laptop back on the side. "He liked games," I mutter. "And he was a complete fuck up at dating."

She gives another sad smile, sitting on the couch. "We'd play top trumps on worst dates. And no matter how much I tried, he'd never tell me anything about himself. He said it was more fun that way."

"I'm sorry you found out like this," I mutter, sitting beside her and twisting to face her. "It sounds like you liked him." And the worst part about that statement is the fucking jealousy I feel. She liked Jake and now he's forcing me to play some sick, twisted game with her. *Did he know how she felt? If he hadn't have died, would they be together?* My heart aches.

"I'm sorry you lost him," she sniffles, wrapping her arms around my neck and holding me. "He was a great guy; I can see why you miss him so much."

"Don't waste your tears, Bella," I mutter, "He wouldn't have wanted you to be sad."

She nods against my chest. "I want you to be my first," she whispers. It's so low, I struggle to hear her. She tips her head back, looking me in the eye. "Will you?"

My throat tightens, threatening to choke me. "Bella, you're upset. Don't make rash decisions."

"The reason I'm still a virgin is because I've been waiting to feel this spark. I feel it with you, Aiden."

I shake my head, standing. "You don't know what you're saying, Bella. I don't want to take something so important when I can't be certain you're thinking straight. Plus, you've had a lot to drink."

She wipes her wet, tear-stained cheeks. "You don't want me," she whispers.

I grab her hands and tug her to stand. "Don't be stupid," I say firmly. "Of course I do. You're consuming me right now, and it scares the shit out of me. But I want your first time to be special. So, let's wait until you're truly ready . . . and sober." It was another stipulation in the contract. Bella couldn't be under the influence of alcohol or drugs. But there is some truth in my words. If I'm going to take her virginity, I want her to want it so badly, that she convinces me.

I take her dressing gown cord and unfasten it, letting it fall open. "Luckily for you," I say with a smirk, as I wrap the soft cord around her wrists and secure it. "I'm also good at playing games."

"Oh yeah?" she asks, smiling.

"It runs in the genes," I say, opening her dressing gown wider and admiring her naked body. I take her nipple, watching the flush spread up her cheeks when I tease it. "And I want to spend the entire night playing games with you." I lean down, throwing her over my shoulder. She laughs loud and I swat her backside. "Silence," I hiss, pushing my hand between her legs. She's wet and I smirk as I carry her through to the bedroom. *I don't need to fuck her to enjoy her.*

CHAPTER FOURTEEN

Bella

It's not possible, I can't orgasm anymore. I'm breathless and sweating as I squirm, gripping Aiden's head between my legs as his tongue works its magic. He hasn't given me a break since my last orgasm not five minutes ago. I'm not sure where I start, and he ends. "No more," I groan, "I can't take anymore."

"Remember what happened last time you said that?"

I shudder, and he grips my thighs, holding me still as another orgasm rolls through me. He waits for me to still before dropping beside me and turning on to his side. He throws a leg over me and drags me closer. "Sleep, you'll need your strength for tomorrow."

"Tomorrow?" I whisper, sleepily.

"We're spending the day doing that all again." I groan and he sniggers. "But this time, you're gonna let me fuck your mouth."

Aiden's true to his word. We spend Saturday hardly leaving the bedroom. When we're not wrapped in one another watching movies, we're exploring each other with our mouths. And around mid-afternoon, we order food and sit in bed naked, eating. It's nice to have him to myself and I can't help but picture us having a future.

I drop the last piece of chicken into the box and wipe my mouth with a napkin. "I've enjoyed today," I say, and he eyes me warily.

"Yeah, it's been fun," he says, gathering the leftovers and stuffing it into a bag.

"Fun," I repeat, feeling like a bucket of ice has been thrown at me.

He forces a smile, "Yeah. That's what this is, right? Fun." He must read the disappointment on my face, and he sighs, grabbing my hand. "Bella, I like you, and right now

I'm enjoying this. But if you're asking me to hand out the girlfriend title, I can't."

I nod stiffly, withdrawing my hand. He hasn't made any promises, this is all on me. He turns away, throwing his legs over the edge of the bed. I can feel him slipping away so I say, "For the record, I'm glad I'm not your girlfriend."

He glances over his shoulder with a smirk. "Yeah?" I nod, "I'm free to explore what orgasms feel like with normal human men." I grin, and he spins around fast, diving on top of me and pinning my arms above my head.

"Normal human men?" he queries.

I nod innocently. "Men that aren't robots with a constant hard on." I laugh. I feel him relax.

He kisses me hard. "You can look, but you will be sorely disappointed in what you find, young Isabella." he says in his best Drogo accent.

I giggle as he moves down my body, licking my nipple. "It's unfair to keep my virgin body to yourself." I groan, and he lifts his head slightly to meet my gaze.

"I haven't finished with it yet," he grins.

After a good hour in the shower, washing each other's body, I lay on the bed wrapped in my towel, watching Aiden get dressed. "You work too hard," I tell him.

He grins, "I took the day off," he reminds me.

"Aria is coming over to watch movies," I say, stretching out and yawning.

I watch as he sprays aftershave, patting it into his skin. I love his scent. I run my eyes over his body. He looks good in a suit, and I find myself smiling. He catches it. "What are you smiling about?" he asks, checking his hair in the mirror by the door.

"Just thinking how lucky I am," I say without thinking.

He pauses mid hair sort, and eyes me through the reflection in the mirror. "Just remember what I said earlier, Bella, this isn't a relationship."

I laugh to cover how mortified I feel. "I was kidding."

"I don't want you seeing more into this, Bella," he says firmly. "I've made it clear."

"Jesus," I hiss, "I get the message."

He gives a stiff nod, "Good." And then he leans down to place a kiss on my head. "Enjoy your night with Aria."

I settle down on the couch once he's left and sketch some wedding cake ideas. It's one of my favourite things to do and since the stress of looking after my dad has lessened, I've felt a lot more relaxed and able to create.

Almost an hour later, I hear the bell from the elevator, announcing Aria's arrival. I get up to unlatch the door so she can come straight in and am just about to sit back down when I hear a loud bang followed quickly by a man yelling. I rush to the door and poke my head out, to see Aria and JP. He's glaring angrily and she's missing a shoe.

"What's going on?" I ask, pulling the door open wider.

"Your friend is fucking crazy," states JP, holding up Aria's shoe. "Missed my head by an inch."

"You're lucky, I don't usually miss. And for the record, I hate you," she shouts, "So stop following me around and giving me your bullshit excuses."

The elevator pings again and Aiden storms out looking furious. "What the fuck was that, Aria?" he demands. My breath catches in my throat when Laurie steps out behind him, placing a manicured hand on his arm. She looks amazing and it makes me want to scratch her eyes out. I also want to run back inside and hide, seeing as I am wearing one of Aiden's t-shirts that just about covers my backside, and my hair is piled up on my head in a messy bun.

"Calm down, Aide," she soothes, and I see the way he takes a deep breath as if to calm himself.

"Aria, my VIP area is a mess, what the hell are you playing at?" he asks more calmly, and Laurie rubs his arm as if to praise him. I roll my eyes in annoyance.

"Why don't we ask your friend?" spits Aria, glaring at JP. "Tell them," she snaps, "Tell them how you can't keep your dick in your pants."

Aiden turns to JP. "I warned you this would happen," he growls.

JP shrugs, "The woman's a fucking nut job. I'm sick of her drama, just bar her from the club, and get her out of my sight," he snaps.

Aria grabs a vase of plastic flowers from the table in the foyer, launching it in his direction. It smashes into pieces, the flowers flying across the marble floor. The air is charged with anger and JP closes the gap between the pair. I rush out, squeezing between them, "Calm down," I demand.

"Sort your crazy bitch of a friend out," he yells.

"You're a complete bastard," she screams, breaking down in floods of tears. JP steps back and I turn, grabbing Aria and pulling her into my arms.

"She needs to go, now," snaps Aiden, glaring at me.

"I agree, look at the mess she's made," Laurie agrees, "I've told you before to stop inviting waifs and strays into your home, Aiden."

"It's gonna be okay," I whisper, soothingly as I rub Aria's back. "Aiden, I can't kick her out in this state," I add.

"Well, you know where the door is," snaps Laurie.

"You want me to leave, Aiden?" I ask, arching a brow. It's a risk, he might throw it all in my face and tell me to get out.

"Isabella, this isn't up for discussion. I have to ban Aria; she's trashed my VIP area."

"And she ruined my Saint Laurent bags," Laurie chips in, "The one you got me for Christmas," she says, adding a pout. She brings her eyes to me, "You heard him, it's not up for discussion. Pack your bags." There's a gleeful twinkle in her eye.

"That's not what I meant," says Aiden, but I'm already heading back into the apartment with Aria tucked under my arm.

"Shit, Bells," she whispers, "I can't get you kicked out. I'll go," Aria whispers.

"I'm calling his bluff," I mutter.

"Let's hope he isn't calling yours," she replies, wiping her eyes.

Aiden follows and I smile to myself, "Bella, I didn't mean for you to leave," he repeats more clearly.

"I'll stay with Aria. I have some viewings for apartments next week anyway," I tell him, going into my bedroom and grabbing the bag from under my bed. Aria sits down, biting on her lower lip with worry as she watches me. Aiden places his hands on his hips and then Laurie appears in the doorway.

"It's for the best, Aiden," she tells him soothingly. "Then we won't have to sneak around in hotels because I can come here."

I scoff, stuffing some clothes into my bag whilst Aiden watches helplessly. "You wouldn't have to sneak around if you just left your husband," I point out, my voice laced with sarcasm.

"You wouldn't even be here if he didn't want your virginity so badly." she counters.

I laugh. "And how does that feel, to know I have something you gave away long ago?"

"At least I can please him," she cries, curling her hands into fists with anger.

"So can I and I don't even have to open my legs," I yell.

"Enough," Aiden shouts.

I take a calming breath, "Please go and fetch my things from your room," I tell him, giving Laurie a smug smile.

"You're not fucking leaving," he snaps, "Aria, I'm billing you for the damage to my club. And you're barred for the next month."

"Aiden," Laurie argues, with outrage.

"And you," he hisses, pointing a finger in her face, "Don't own me. You left, Laurie. Not me. So, stop fucking acting like my wife cos thankfully, you saved me from that hassle."

He turns on his heel and marches out. Laurie stamps her foot, rushing after him and I turn to Aria, smiling. "I knew that would work," I whisper, feeling smug that Aiden put Laurie in her place.

Aiden

I get as far as the living room before Laurie grabs my arm and I spin to face her. She's angry, her entire face is red, and her fists are curled into tight balls. "She's sleeping in your bedroom?" she hisses.

"I don't owe you an explanation," I snap.

"You do when you're crawling back into my bed."

"I haven't been in your bed since I started . . ." I pause, not knowing what to say. Bella appears, leaning in the doorway.

"I don't want to cause any trouble," she says, folding her arms.

Laurie stands in front of me and places her hands on my chest. "It makes more sense if she stays with her friend, look at the trouble it's causing just having her here. You keep telling me there's nothing between you, so why do you want her to stay."

I can't look away from Bella. I hate the sadness I see in her eyes. I have two more weeks. Just two. "We all just need to take a breath," I say.

Bella's expression changes to disappointment and my heart aches. "I'm leaving," she whispers, going back into the bedroom.

"Fuck," I mutter, following . . . again.

"Why?" I ask.

"I'm not okay with it," she says, shrugging. "I thought I could be, but I'm not."

Laurie huffs, "Let her go, Aiden. I'm free tonight, I can stay over."

"Don't you see?" asks Bella, "You say you can't commit, and you don't want to settle down, but that's what you're doing with her. You're second best to her husband, yet you hang around waiting for his scraps. You're putting your life on hold for her."

"I'm not," I mutter, and Jakes words come flooding back. *'She uses you. She keeps you dangling so she can call when she's bored.'*

"It's fine," cries Bella, "I don't care. If you want to be with her, then be with her. But stop forcing me to stick around."

"I haven't forced you," I almost whisper.

"I sleep in your bed, not by choice but because you carry me in here if I even try to go into my own room. I can't bathe or shower unless you're in there with me," she argues, counting each point on her fingers. "You insist on taking me to work and picking me up. You won't let another man near me without having him frog marched out of your club. I can't wear anything too revealing because it sends you over the edge. You wrap me in your arms every single night, and you do delicious things to my body." She takes an unsteady breath, "You're doing all the things a boyfriend would, Aiden."

"Except sleep with you," cuts in Laurie, "But he comes to me for that," she adds smugly, and I clench my jaw in anger.

Before I can demand she leaves, Bella rushes at her, grabbing a fistful of hair and yanking her head down. "Fuck you," she screams, and Aria laughs, clapping.

"Jesus," I hiss, pulling them apart. I hold Bella around the waist.

Laurie touches her hair, shock evident on her face. "She attacked me," she screeches. "Like an ally cat."

"Laurie just go," I snap.

She glares at me. "You're kicking me out?"

"You heard him," yells Bella. "Get the fuck out."

"Aria, you too," I snap.

I wait for them both to leave before kicking the door closed and releasing Bella. She grabs some more clothes, stuffing them in her bag. I snatch it, pulling them all out and emptying them on the floor. "Will you stop packing," I shout. "I don't understand what's happening. This was between JP and Aria, and now somehow, you're leaving. When we spoke about this being fun, you said you were fine with it."

"I thought I was. Turns out seeing her with you like that, turns me into a lunatic. It did the same to you when you saw another man touch me," she points out.

I nod. "It did," I admit. "But not because I'm in love with you, Bella. It's because I'm selfish and I don't want another man to touch what I want." *There, I've said it.*

She shakes her head in disgust and picks some clothes up from the floor. "You're a bastard."

I still her hands and pull her towards me. "I haven't pretended I'm not. I was a bastard last night when you let me do all of those things to you. I was still a bastard today when you were sucking my cock, and I will still be a bastard tonight when I go and fuck Laurie or some other desperate bitch."

"Fuck you, Aiden. Stay the hell away from me."

"Until later when you're in my bed," I snap, "Because let's face it, you aren't going anywhere. You have nowhere to go, and you thought that by putting me in that position with Laurie, you'd be able to force my hand," I hiss. She stares down at the ground. "It's backfired, because you don't want to leave any more than I want you to. So do us both a favour and stop the dramatics, Bella, because I didn't change the fucking rules."

I leave the room, slamming the door. Aria looks up from her mobile. "She might need you," I mutter, and she rolls her eyes.

"Fucking men," she snaps, stomping past me.

CHAPTER FIFTEEN

Aria

Aria hands me a tissue and I dab my eyes. "How did this end with you in tears?" she asks, smiling. "If I'd known, I wouldn't have lost my shit."

"What happened?" I ask.

She rolls her eyes, flopping down on the bed beside me. "I walked into the club, and he was practically having sex with some bitch, grinding up her like a horny teenager. He was texting me all last night telling me he really liked me and didn't want to play games. Fuck men and fuck JP. I'm not being the plaything that waits around for him to decide if he wants me or not." I wince, it's exactly what I'm doing with Aiden, and when Aria realises what she's said, I see the panic in her face. "I'm so sorry Bella, I didn't mean you, I just meant..." she trails off.

"It's fine," I reassure her. "I mean, you're right, I am waiting around for him to choose me." I groan, laying back and staring up at the ceiling. "It gets more complicated," I add. "Remember no name guy from the bakery."

She nods, smiling, "Yeah, mystery man that had us both in knots?"

"Turns out he's Aiden's brother."

She glares at me, "What the fuck?"

"Right. I mean, how's that for small world."

"I was starting to think we'd poisoned him when he stopped coming in," she adds thoughtfully. "Did you finally get his name?"

"Jake," I reply. "Aria, he died."

Her mouth falls open and she gasps. "Oh my god, that's awful. He was so young. How?"

"Same age as Aiden," I reply, "They were non-identical twins. And, I haven't asked for details. Aiden doesn't want to talk about it. I think he's still grieving."

"Understandable. So, you think all this weird behaviour is down to grief?"

I shrug, "Maybe. It sounds like Jake hated Laurie and wanted Aiden to stay away from her."

"It's not your job to carry out his dying wish, Bella."

"Yeah, I know that. And I'm not. Aiden will do whatever he wants, but a part of me can't help wondering that maybe, if he just feels what it could be like to be in a real relationship, with actual love, he might like it."

She frowns, "Do you really think he's got the staying power for a full-on relationship? And honestly, do you think you can tame a guy that's been a player for God knows how long? He's already broke your heart and you're not even together."

"He never lied to me, Aria. He was straight with me and said he can't do relationships. I can't be mad when he was upfront."

"And now you're making excuses," she says gently. "I get his appeal, he's hot and brooding, but he's a walking red flag, just like JP. We deserve better."

"I'm not ready to walk away," I admit.

She grabs me into a hug, "I'll be here when he breaks you some more," she reassures me. "And I highly recommend that you stay in your own room, or you'll end up sleeping with him and you really don't want to do that." She kisses me on the cheek. "I'm going home to sleep off my mood."

I spend the next ten minutes taking all my things from his room and effectively moving back into my own. I test the lock on my door, satisfied it works and vow to use it until he gets the message. If nothing else happens between us, I'll at least be around as a friend when Laurie breaks his heart. Knowing he's Jakes brother makes it feel different. Like I have a responsibility. And Aiden did save me, he could have walked away, and I'd never have known what my dad had done. *Dad*. I sigh, sitting on my bed and grabbing my mobile. It's the longest I've ever gone without speaking to him. I send off a text.

> **Me: How are you, dad?**

His reply is instant, giving me hope he's stayed sober.

> **Dad: Bella, I miss you so much. How are you?**

> **Me: I'm good. I miss you too. Are you coping?**

> **Dad: I haven't touched a drop since you left. And I've been going to meetings twice a week. My support worker is pleased with my progress.**

I smile, my heart swelling with hope. It's not the first time he's tried, and a nagging part of my brain is telling me not to get too excited.

> **Me: That's great. I'm proud of you.**

> **Dad: I met someone. She's really nice, I think you'd like her.**

He hasn't shown an interest in any other woman since mum, but surely this is a good thing. He's looking forward and not back. I want him to be happy.

> **Me: If she makes you happy, dad, I'll like her x**

I put my phone on silent and pick up my drawing pad, adding colour to my early designs. It helps to take my mind off everything Aiden related, and I soon feel myself getting tired. I lock my bedroom door and get into bed. After our fight, I'm sure he'll leave me in here, but I'm not risking it.

Aiden

JP, me and Raff are all sitting in silence in my office. The weight of the night is heavy on my shoulders, and I have a feeling I've fucked it all up with Bella. I shouldn't have gone in so hard, and I shouldn't have let my feelings take over.

JP props his feet up on the edge of my desk. "There are other clubs," he says with a shrug.

Raff nods in agreement. "He's right. It's not worth all this stress."

"Me and Jake worked too hard to get this place up and running. It means everything to me and it's the last place I have that reminds me of him. I can still feel him here, I can hear his laughter and see him behind the bar shaking cocktails to impress the ladies." I sigh, fighting the urge to cry. I haven't broken down once since he left me, and I won't start now. The entire game's been one big distraction, maybe that was his plan all along to save me dropping into depression.

"Do you think she's left?" asks JP.

I shrug, "Probably. I don't blame her."

"So where do we go from here?" asks Raff.

"If she's gone, I'll do what she wants. I'll fake the whole relationship deal for the next couple of weeks. I only avoided that to lessen her pain in the end, but if that's the only way to do it, I have no choice."

"There's another way," says Raff, fidgeting.

I roll my eyes, "It's not real," I snap. "And it won't ever be."

"Why?" he asks simply.

"Because I like my life the way it is. Yes, she's great and I love spending time with her. But eventually, I'd miss all this. And none of it is real, the entire thing started on a lie to get her to need me. Imagine if she found that out further down the line. No, it just wouldn't work."

"When we first came up with the plan, it didn't feel this hard," mutters JP. "She wasn't real to us then. And now she's here, it's like she's bewitched us all. She brings us damn cupcakes home every night," he adds.

"Good cupcakes," agrees Raff.

"She doesn't deserve any of this," adds JP.

"Don't you think I know that?" I snap. "But Jake did this, and whatever reasons he had, I can't back out and I can't lose my club. We can't lose it. We love this place." I sigh heavily, "If my brother wasn't dead, I'd kill him." I look them in the eye, "It's almost over and then we can go back to how it was before."

♥

It's almost five in the morning when I decide I can't hide any more. I head up to the apartment and open the bedroom door quietly. *She isn't there*. My heart hammers hard in my chest as I march over to the wardrobe and fling open the door. All her stuff has gone. I check my bathroom and it's the same, empty. *Fuck.*

I go to her room, pushing the door, to find it locked. I frown. She's never locked the door before, but at least she's still here. I tap gently on it, "Bella?" There's no answer so I try again, this time knocking louder. "Bella?"

"Go away, Aiden," she mumbles.

"Let me in," I mutter, resting my forehead against the door. "Please."

"No."

My heart sinks. I should just be pleased she's still here, but I didn't realise how dependent I've become having her beside me all night. "Don't you want me to keep you warm?"

"Go to bed, Aiden. You made yourself perfectly clear. I'm done."

I sigh, heading back to my room.

♥

I hear giggling and it wakes me from my slumber. I groan, stretching out and opening one eye. It's almost ten a.m. and I am not ready to get up. The giggling comes again, and I narrow my eyes, pushing myself to sit. I'm intrigued, so I grab my shorts and pull them on, then follow the sound of the giggles into the living room where Bella is dressed in sporty leggings and a cropped top. Behind her is a man dressed in sports gear, and he's got his hands on her hips as she squats.

"What the fuck is going on?"

She raises her arms over her head slowly and tips to one side, all the while being supported by Mr. Muscle. She smiles wide, "Sorry, did we wake you?"

"Obviously."

"This is Cal, my personal trainer. Cal, this is my landlord."

I arch a brow, *landlord*. "You have a personal trainer? Since when?"

"Believe it or not, Aiden, you don't know everything about me." She turns, bending so I get an eyeful of her backside. I have no doubt this is some kind of game to show me what I'm missing, but believe me, I already know. "I've neglected my sessions since all the stuff with my dad, I've decided to get back on it and Cal here is amazing at working my body hard, aren't you Cal." *My god is she flirting?* Cal grins, his eyes running over her body in much the same way as mine. He wants her. *Almost as badly as I do.*

Bella

Cal works me hard and as I drop down on the grass and stare up at the sky, I wonder why I do this to myself. My lungs burn and my legs ache. Cal grabs my left leg and rests my foot on his thigh while rubbing my muscle. I groan, it feels good. "So, was that guy just a landlord?" he asks casually. I smile to myself. Cal's made no secret he likes me, and I'm not complaining because he's gorgeous. His body is perfect, sculptured by the Greek gods according to Aria. Maybe I should just . . . I give my head a shake, what the fuck am I thinking. I can't sleep with Cal out of the blue. That would be reckless.

"Yes," I finally answer as he rubs my other leg. *His hands do feel good*, I muse.

"And you're still single?" he asks.

"I am."

"Yet you still turn me down," he teases.

I grin, "I don't want to lose a good PT."

"You're killing me here, Bella," he says, holding a hand over his heart.

Maybe I should. Maybe getting rid of my virginity, will put an end to the turmoil I currently feel. *Maybe I would stop craving Aiden if I just moved on.*

"Yah know, my place is just over there," nods Cal as if reading my mind. "We could warm down and then have a coffee? Look at sorting out a proper food plan?"

I put my hand out for him to pull me up. "Lead the way."

Cal's place is a typical bachelor pad. One couch, a television and a coffee table with cup rings staining it. He gets out the laptop and stands at the kitchen worktop. "I have a food plan drawn up," he tells me, and I stand beside him to look it over. His little finger brushes mine and I inhale sharply. There's a definite spark.

"What about you?" I ask, turning so my back is resting against the worktop and I'm facing him. "Are you still single?"

He grins, "Yeah."

My mobile beeps, distracting me. Cal takes his attention back to the laptop and I pull it out.

> **Aria: Aiden said you've started sessions with Cal again. Everything okay?**

I roll my eyes wondering why she's spoken to Aiden.

> **Me: Yeah, I'm good. I'm at his place now.**

> **Aria:** The last time you worked out, was because you were depressed. Should I be worried?

> **Me:** Don't be ridiculous. I need a boost. Besides, he's fit ☒

> **Aria:** Okay, officially worried because you don't even sound like you right now.

> **Me:** You were right last night, Ari. I am too good for Aiden. Fuck him. Cal is flirting and I'm not against it.

> **Aria:** So now you're moving on to Cal?

> **Me:** I'm considering losing my burden to a nice guy that I have no connection with.

> **Aria:** That's crazy. You're upset over last night and not thinking. Meet me, let's talk about this.

I tuck my mobile away. I'm so sick of talking. My virginity has been the topic of so many discussions, always demanding the top conversation slot. It's even been the butt of my friends' jokes. *I'm done holding on to it.*

"Everything okay?" asks Cal.

I shift closer so our arms brush, he eyes the connection. "Where were we?"

He stares at me, and my breathing quickens. He leans closer, until his lips are a breath away. "Am I reading this all wrong?" he whispers. I give my head a slight shake, too scared to speak. His lips brush mine, like he's giving me the chance to back out. Instead, I slip my arms around his neck and slide between him and the worktop. His hands cup my face, tilting it slightly before he seals his lips over mine in a slow kiss. There's no urgency or rush as he tastes me, and he's gentle, just how I like it. And it's nothing like Aiden's.

He runs his hands over the bare skin on my back, sliding them up my arms and resting on my shoulders. His eyes darken and his chest heaves with controlled breaths. He carefully slides the straps of my top down until my breasts are exposed, then he lowers his mouth to my nipple, sucking it into his warm mouth. My head falls back, and I close my eyes, enjoying the way he swirls his tongue over the swollen bud.

My phone vibrates and he reaches into the waist band of my leggings, pulling it out and holding it out for me to look at, all the while still teasing my nipple. Aiden's name flashes on the screen. I cancel the call, taking the phone and laying it face down on the worktop.

Cal's fingers hook into my waistband, and he pushes my leggings down, kneeling before me and peeling them away. He takes my leg and guides it over his shoulder, and then I feel his hot breath at my opening. I grip the worktop, staring down in wonderment as he runs his tongue through my folds, keeping eye contact. It's hot. He keeps an intense pressure on my clit, and I'm so close to coming, that when he pushes a finger into me, I cry out. I've needed the intrusion for so long, it's a relief.

He stands, kissing me so I can taste myself. "Are you sure about this?" he asks, his voice strained. I nod, gripping his hard cock through his shorts. He hisses, leaning past me to grab his wallet where he retrieves a condom. He shoves his shorts down to his hips and I stare at his thick cock as he sheathes it in rubber. It's on the tip of my tongue to explain I'm a virgin, when a loud bang on the door causes the words to die on my lips.

"Ignore it," he whispers, lifting me onto the worktop, then dragging my backside right to the edge.

"Bella?" It's Aiden. I freeze, staring wide eyed at Cal. "Bella, open the fucking door."

"Oh my god," I whisper. My heart slams in my chest.

"Is that your landlord?" asks Cal in a hushed voice.

I nod, gripping his shoulders tightly and holding my breath while I listen for any movement outside. "Just stay quiet, he'll leave," I whisper.

"Why's he here?" he asks.

"The door's locked, right?" I add.

"What's he doing here, Bella?" he asks, his voice angrier now.

I shrug, "I have no idea."

"Bella, I know you're in there," Aiden yells, banging harder. "Open the fucking door or I'll kick it in."

"You should deal with that," mutters Cal, tucking himself away.

"He'll leave in a minute," I reassure him.

"Please, Bells, don't have sex with him, I'm begging you," mutters Aiden and my heart twists at the pain lacing his words. "Not because of me."

Cal pulls my top into place. "Put him out his misery."

I jump down off the counter, pulling my leggings up. I pause at the door, gathering myself before unlocking it and opening it just enough for him to see me. Our eyes connect and I'm mildly satisfied to see he looks stressed and maybe even desperate as his eyes run over me.

"Have you done it? Did you sleep with him?" he asks, urgently.

"What are you doing here, Aiden?" I whisper hiss, angrily.

"Did you fuck him?" he repeats. I give my head a slight shake and he exhales in relief, taking a few steps and running his hands through his hair. "Thank god," he whispers to himself.

"How did you find me?"

He stills, "Aria." I roll my eyes, and he rushes to defend her, "I saw your text over her shoulder. She tried to stop me coming here."

"Well, now you've seen me, you can leave. I mean, this is taking our friendship too far."

"I'll do it," he blurts out, "I'll try it, with you." Words get stuck in my throat as my mind races. "I've been a complete prick, and I'm messing this up. But I can't stand to think about you with anyone but me. I'll give the relationship thing a go."

"Cal's in there waiting for me," I say, "We almost, we're about to . . ." the words trail of and Aiden glares at me. "You can't just turn up here and demand I stop what I was about to do because you've had a change of heart," I cry, "I was ready," I add, "He put a condom on." Aiden curls his fists by his side. "I wanted to see if he was different," I mutter.

"Of course he's fucking different, Bella. He's not me. But what we have . . ." He growls angrily.

"He's not rough, he takes his time like he wants to be with me."

Aiden takes a calming breath, "I want to be with you, Bella. I'm here telling you I want to be with you."

"You're too late," I yell, "I just came on his tongue," I wail feeling mortified. Everything that's just happened suddenly hits me and I feel dirty. Like I've cheated. I slam my hands over my mouth, "Oh my god."

"I know you want to hurt me the way I've hurt you," he mutters, "It's working. But we can start a fresh, okay. No more games. No more lies. Just me and you, like you want."

I suddenly feel exhausted. "I need to say goodbye to Cal."

Aiden looks panicked, "No, don't go back in there," he yells, and I close the door and lock it. He slams his hand against it, yelling a string of profanities. "Bella, open the damn door."

When I go back into the kitchen, Cal is leaning against the counter staring at the ground with his arms crossed over his broad chest. He glances up when I enter. "I'm sorry," I mutter.

"It's fine," he says, stepping closer and tucking my hair behind my ear. He cups my jaw, rubbing his thumb over my cheek. "Do you know how long I've thought about that exact moment?" he adds, smiling.

I laugh, and a sob escapes. "I'm so sorry. It's complicated. I didn't mean to drag you into it."

"Hey, I'm not complaining. And when he messes up again, I'm here waiting to help with the rebound." He grins and I press my forehead against his chest.

"Why can't I fall for you?" I murmur.

"Maybe our time hasn't come just yet?" he suggests, stroking a hand over my hair. "You should go before he explodes," he adds, kissing me on the head.

When I step out, Aiden looks relieved. He stops pacing and holds out his hand. I stare at it for a minute before taking it. "You need to get a new personal trainer," he mutters, kissing me on the head. "And a shower," he adds.

Shame washes over me again. I've never done anything like that before, it was so unlike me. And I realise just how much Aiden is affecting me.

"What happens now?"

"We start a fresh," he says, opening the car door for me to slide in. He leans in and grabs the seatbelt, securing it around me. "Next time I find you with another man, it ain't gonna end well." He kisses me on the head again before closing the door.

CHAPTER SIXTEEN

♡

Aiden

We drive back to Tremos in silence. I can't shake the thought of Bella with someone else. The fact he saw her orgasm makes me want to rip his eyes out. I grip the steering wheel tightly. And I deserve this, I know I do. Each sordid image my mind has created, I deserve to have, because it's exactly what I've done to her every time she's seen me with Laurie.

We walk through the club, and JP and Raff pretend to busy themselves, avoiding any eye contact with Bella as she hangs her head like she's ashamed. Once we're in the apartment, I throw my keys on the side. "Go and shower," I mutter coldly. "Wash every inch of him from your skin."

Her eyes glisten with tears and she wraps her arms around herself before going to the bathroom.

I pull out my mobile and head into the kitchen, closing the door. I dial Raff who answers on the first ring. "She okay?"

"Yep. All intact."

"And the PT? Is he in one piece?"

"Yep."

"Now what?"

"Call the solicitor. Tell him to be here at nine tonight," I say.

"You're going directly to him?"

"If he sees it with his own eyes, he can't argue it."

Bella

I rest my hand against the kitchen door, stilling at Aiden's words. *See's what?*

I hear him disconnect the call, so I rush back towards the bathroom, closing the door and leaning against it.

There's something more going on. None of this makes any sense. Aiden turning up like that, practically kicking the door down. And the way he's suddenly changed his mind about a relationship. And forgiving me for being with Cal. Just like that. No questions, no anger. It's almost like he doesn't care, as long as I haven't had sex.

Aiden taps on the bathroom door, and I jump in fright. "Yeah?"

"Open the door," he says. I glance down at my gym gear, wincing. I pull my top off and grab a towel to cover myself, pulling the door open. Aiden eyes me suspiciously. "You okay?" he asks. I nod. "I'd like to cook dinner tonight," he states. "Are you free?"

"You don't cook," I say, frowning.

"Is that yes?" he asks, sounding irritated.

"Sure."

"Great, I've got some errands to run." He leans closer, kissing me on the lips. I test the waters, cupping his cheek and pulling him closer to take the kiss deeper. He allows it for a second before pulling back.

"Maybe we could shower together," I suggest, seeing as he's always insisted getting in with me.

"I'd love to, but I have shit to do if I want to get back in time to make dinner."

"Our first as a couple," I say, adding a smile.

He forces a tight one in return. "Yep."

"Are you mad with me?" I ask, running a hand over his chest.

"I'm mad with myself for almost blowing it," he admits.

"So, let's put things right," I say, opening the bathroom door wider and dropping my towel. He stares at my breasts, almost lost for a moment before shaking his head and bringing his eyes to mine. "Later, Bella. I promise."

I shower and dress in comfortable clothes. I pull my hair into a messy bun and curl up on the couch, going over everything that just happened in my head, trying to get it straight. But no matter how many times I go over it, it doesn't add up. I call Aria.

"Oh my god, I was so worried," she cries. "I'm so sorry. I was talking to JP trying to sort everything out, and Aiden saw your text. And yah know what else is weird. He put a call in and had Cal's address in seconds."

"Weird," I agree.

"Are you okay? Is Cal?"

"Yeah, we're both fine."

"Did you . . . yah know, do the deed?"

"I didn't get chance, but we were close. Aiden turned up like a crazy ex."

"Yeah, he went off here before he left. He was so mad."

"It doesn't add up, does it?"

She pauses, "It's definitely weird. Tensions were high but why is he so bothered when he's made it clear he doesn't want a relationship."

"Apparently, he's had a change of heart. The threat of me with someone else woke him up and now we're officially a couple."

The silence stretches whilst she processes my words, "Yeah, that does seem odd."

"So, it's got me thinking, is he just after my virginity, or is something else going on?"

"Like what?" she asks.

"I don't know," I mutter. "Jake keeps popping into my head. Is it really a coincidence he came to the bakery every day, and then his brother turned up to rescue me from men I've never heard from?"

"When you say it out loud, I guess it raises suspicions. Where is Aiden now?"

"Out. He wants to cook us dinner this evening, yet I overheard a phone call where he arranged for a solicitor to come over at nine." I stand, heading for Aiden's room. I put the phone on loudspeaker and place it on the bed whilst I pull open Aiden's bedside drawer. "The entire thing feels off," I add, finding nothing in the drawer but condoms. I slam it closed, sighing and looking around. "Do you think you could come over to Tremos?" I take the phone into the walk-in wardrobe.

"Sure, why?"

"I need you to distract JP and Raff, and Aiden if he turns up too early."

"What are you going to do?"

I pull down a box and lift the lid, rummaging through the photographs of Aiden and his brother. "I'm going to search Aiden's office."

"What exactly are you hoping to find?"

"I'm not sure. But if there's a solicitor involved, maybe there's a paper trail?"

"You could just walk away," she suggests. "Leave and never look back."

"I could," I agree, "But if today is anything to go by, he'll come and find me. I need to know why I'm suddenly so important to him."

"Okay, I'm in," she says. "I'll text you when it's safe."

I search the apartment. Every cupboard, every drawer, even behind spaces, and I find nothing unusual. It's another hour before Aria messages me.

"Now."

My heart hammers in my chest as I take the elevator down to the club. I step out, to find the club empty. I push the office door and hold my breath, relieved when Aiden's chair is empty. I go inside, closing the door quietly behind me.

I sit at his desk and have a brief look at the various letters and paperwork strewn across his desk. There's nothing that stands out. I open his drawers and find bills and random paperwork that means nothing to me. I slouch back in his chair, huffing. *Maybe I'm being paranoid.*

Something catches my eye under the desk, a middle drawer, set back so it's almost hidden. I pull it, but of course, it's locked. *Shit.* I search the drawer again, this time finding a keyring with four small keys. I try each one, almost laughing in delight when the last key fits.

In the drawer is a file, I set it on the desk, staring at it. This could be nothing, or it could change everything and as I open it, I feel sick with nerves.

Pinned to the top of the inside cover, are two photographs of me. One of me leaving work and the other of me behind the counter serving a customer. My full name is scrawled in messy handwriting on the bottom of each one.

On the other side is an official looking letter from a law firm. **Dobson Law & Co**.

I scan my eyes over the document. It appears to be some kind of contract and when I lift the page, I see it's been signed by three people. Aiden Tremos. Jake Tremos and Drake Dobson. I frown, *Drake.* The solicitor he introduced me. I go back to the first page, staring at the bullet points that stand out.

- Sexual intercourse must take place whilst Isabella is a virgin. It must take place between Aiden and Isabella.

- Proof must be given by GP examination unless other means of proof can be provided. (To be discussed and agreed between Drake and Aiden).

- Isabella must be fully consensual.

- Aiden must spend a minimum of six to eight weeks with Isabella, getting to know her.

- Sexual Intercourse must not take place whilst either party is under the influence of drink or drugs.

I gasp, sickness bubbling in my stomach. It's like a cruel joke. Everything's been a lie. None of it was real.

The contract outlines that on completion of the 'task' Aiden will get the fifty-percent share that Jake owns in Tremos. *All this for a fucking night club.* I shove the file away, fighting the tears that want to fall. *Is it even legal?*

A sealed envelope slips from the file, taunting me. I trace my finger over Aiden's name on the front, along with the words, *Not to be opened until the club is fully signed over to Aiden.*

Fuck that. The rules no longer apply. I rip it open.

So here we are brother, I'm guessing if you're reading this, I must have croaked it no less than six-months ago. I hope you gave me a proper send off, I know how tight you can be.

You must be wondering why? It's simple, I thought you would need a distraction from your loss, that being me, shithead. And don't even pretend you're not bothered; I know you loved me despite insisting I was delivered by the stalk and dropped on our family.

What I'd give to have seen your face when Drake gave you the contract. As if I would just hand it over. You know me better than that, and let's not pretend you wouldn't have done the same.

So, why her? I spent months finding the perfect woman for you, and she is it, brother. Isabella is like a breath of fresh air on a stuffy day. She brightens the world, which I'm sure you've discovered by now. I made no secret of the fact I hate Laurie, and if I can come back as a ghost, I'll be haunting that bitch. But in case I don't, take this as a sign, Aiden. She broke your heart, and you've wasted too much time trying to forget her, only to have her pick you up anytime she wants. You'll never heal if she has her way. With Bella's help, you'll love again.

So, the terms were set and I'm praying I gave Bella enough time to convince you she's the one for you. She deserves happiness and I know you can give her that too. Make me proud, brother. And make her happy, for me.

I love you, Aiden.

Jake x Your better-looking twin.

I'm crying so hard; I can't catch my breath as I stuff the letter back in the envelope. I hide it at the back of the file and stuff everything back into the drawer. Aria was right, I should never have come looking.

Jake was so kind and sweet, why would he do this to me?

I stagger back up to the apartment, sending Aria a text message telling her I didn't find anything, mainly because I can't face her right now. I can't face anyone.

I go into my bedroom, collapsing on my bed. This must be what heartbreak feels like as I rub the pain my chest. I really thought he liked me. All the drama and the chasing he did, I thought that was because he was battling with himself. Turns out that he didn't like me at all, not as a girlfriend and certainly not as a friend, because no friend would do this.

I dry my eyes and take a breath. I open the music app on my phone and put a plan into action. *Fuck Aiden. And fuck Jake.*

☙

I wake with a start, sitting up to look around my dark bedroom. I grab my phone and see it's half past seven. My eyes are swollen, and my throat is sore from the crying. I freshen up, trying my best to look slightly less broken and when I go into the living room, Aiden is just arriving home. His hands are full of bags, and I watch him struggle, taking a seat on the couch. He places them by the kitchen door, and I feel his eyes assessing me. "Everything okay?" he asks. I nod. "Have you been crying?"

Fuck. "Yeah," I almost whisper. "I watched The Notebook; it always gets me."

He laughs and I picture punching him right in the throat until he chokes on all his lies. "What have I told you about watching that romance crap? It isn't real, life doesn't work like that."

I want to scoff at how true his sentence is. "It's all lies," I say firmly, and he pauses, confusion playing out on his expression. "Love," I clarify, "Everyone is so selfish looking out for themselves, how can real love exist?" I ask.

He looks slightly relieved at my odd rambling, "Exactly. Glad you're finally seeing sense."

Aiden

I head into the kitchen and unpack the shopping. Bella looks exhausted and I wonder if that's mostly my fault. Damn Jake. And now everything is set to go ahead, I almost feel a mix of relief and guilt. It's making me paranoid and I'm examining every expression on Bella's tired face, wondering if this will break her.

I cook duck breasts with vegetables. Not exactly Gordan Ramsey, but its edible and with my lack of skills, it's the best I could do at this short notice. I set the table up with candles and flowers. I've even splashed out on a bottle of Champagne, instead of taking it from the bar. Hopefully by the end of tonight, I'll have something to celebrate.

I go back into the living room and Bella looks lost in thought. "Dinner is served," I say, causing her to jump. She offers a sad smile and follows me through to the kitchen. She stares blankly at the table as I pull out her seat. She lowers and I tuck her in, placing a gentle kiss on her head. "You look shattered," I whisper, squeezing her shoulders. She shudders under my touch, and somehow, I don't feel like it's with need.

"It smells delicious," she mutters, shifting slightly so my hands fall away.

I take my seat; my mind racing to try and work out what's going on. "Is everything okay?"

"Champagne," she says, ignoring me and nodding at the bottle, "What's the special occasion?"

I take the bottle and pour her a glass, "Us," I reply, and she takes the glass before I've even pulled the bottle away. I frown, watching as she downs it, coughing as the bubbles tickle her throat. "Careful. This is expensive shit, you'll be on your back," I joke, as she thrusts her glass under the bottle for a refill.

Her lip curls slightly at the corner, "That's how you want me, isn't it?" The way her eyes burn into mine, makes me shift uncomfortably. Before I can raise my concerns, she claps her hands in delight and jumps out of her chair. "I forgot, I made you a surprise," she announces, "A playlist. It's what couples do," she says, connecting her phone to the built in speaker system. She grins, pressing play and taking her seat as Gnash's, I Hate You, I Love You, fills the room.

We eat in silence, occasionally she sings the lyrics 'I hate you' and I'm wondering if she's singing those words to me. My concern deepens when Eminem's, Love The Way You Lie, comes on.

I fidget uncomfortably, if only she knew how these songs were so close to the truth. But she doesn't seem to be taking any notice apart from humming the odd part with a far-away look in her eyes.

"Not exactly love songs Bells," I tease.

She grins, popping some duck into her mouth and I relax a little. At least she seems to have cheered up. "They all have meaning," she says, "I connect with them."

When Alec Benjamin's, Let Me Down Slowly, comes on, I stand abruptly, taking her by surprise. "I'll clear the dishes," I mutter. I'm being paranoid, I need to relax and get my shit together. I check my watch and Bella notices, "Eight-thirty," she confirms. "Any plans?"

I turn the taps on, keeping my back to her. "No plans," I say.

She causes me to jump in fright when she slides her arms around me. "Maybe we should make up properly?"

I smile to myself; she's playing right into my hands. "It's been a long day," I reply.

"You've waited long enough," she says, as I turn to face her. "Unless you're put off by earlier?"

Her sad eyes cause an ache in my chest, and I cup her face. "Fresh start, remember?" I whisper, kissing her gently.

She nods in confirmation, "Fresh start," she repeats. "No more lies." Her eyes pierce me, like they're waiting for my confession. *Damn this guilt.* I slam my lips to hers and lift her into my arms, wrapping her legs around my waist and carrying her to the bedroom. I'm too close to quit now.

I lower her to the bed, not breaking our kiss as I crawl over her body, forcing her to lie back fully. I try to slow my kisses, her words from earlier about Cal being gentle, haunting me. *Fuck.* Why am I thinking about that now?

I pull back and she frowns, "Are you okay?" she asks. I see hope in her eyes, she wants this, *so why am I being a fucking pussy?* I stare down at her, a thousand things going through my mind. "Aiden?" she says gently, snapping me from my thoughts. "You don't have to do anything you don't want to," she adds, gently cupping my cheek. *Those damn sad eyes.*

I give my head a shake. "I'm fine," I mutter. I slam my mouth to hers, hard and demanding, just how I like it. I move down her body, pushing her top up. *Did he kiss her here? Fuck, Aiden, stop this shit.*

I lick her smooth stomach, nipping her skin between my teeth. When I glance up, she's wiping a stray tear. "Shit, are you okay?" I sit up and she does the same.

"Yeah, I'm just nervous with it being my first time," she says softly.

"Do you want to stop?" I ask.

She shakes her head, "Not if you don't?" I shake my head too, and she gives a stiff nod, pushing to her feet and lifting her top over her head, dropping it to the floor. I take a moment to appreciate her flawless body with her perfect curves. I'll miss her being wrapped in my arms every night. Her warmth. Her breathy moans when I make her come. I groan and she stills, "Keep going," I mutter, not meeting her eye.

She slides her leggings off, standing before me naked. "Now you," she says.

I lift myself off the bed, and she takes the hint, taking hold of my shorts and tugging them down. My cock springs free and I grip it, easing the ache as I rub it. I grab her wrist, tugging her back onto the bed, she yelps in surprise, but I don't give her time to react as I lean over her, kissing down her body hungrily. I drop to my knees and part her legs, licking through her folds. She bucks up, groaning and all my doubts are forgotten. I push my finger inside, something I've not done as yet, and fuck she feels tight. I add another, moving them slowly at first to help her adjust to the intrusion.

I subtly check my watch. It's ten to nine but if I don't fuck her soon, I'm going to combust. "Tell me you're on the pill?" I ask, knowing she is because I've seen them in her bedside drawer.

"Yes," she whispers.

"Thank fuck," I mutter, climbing between her legs and gripping my cock. I rub the head through her folds, "Are you sure?" I ask, one last time.

"If you are," she says, and those fucking eyes send me on another guilt trip.

"Bella, are you okay with this or not? I need you to say the words."

She hesitates and for a second, I think she's going to say no. I stare down at my glistening cock, taking a breath to calm myself. "Just do it," she whispers.

CHAPTER SEVENTEEN

Bella

He's torn, I can see the conflict playing out in his eyes, and right as I think he's about to stop, he lunges forward, groaning. I cry out in surprise. Aiden stills, gently rubbing his nose against mine, "It's okay," he reassures me, "You're fine. Breathe."

I take a shuddering breath as the pain continues burning between my legs. It's done. *I'm finally rid of my virginity.* I don't feel as elated as I thought I would. "You okay?" he whispers, placing kisses along my jaw. I swipe away the tears trickling down my cheeks and he stares at me with concern. "Bella?"

I nod, not trusting myself to speak. He kisses the tear trails, whispering words of encouragement. "I'm going to move again," he warns me, and I immediately stiffen. He laughs a little, "Relax, Bella. It gets better, I promise."

I take another calming breath and give a nod before turning my head to the side to avoid his kisses. This is a transaction, and I don't want his nice words or his tender kisses.

He buries his face into the crook of my neck, and I close my eyes, resisting the urge to hold him. Instead, I stuff my hands under my backside, preventing me from touching any part of him as he moves faster. "You feel amazing," he whispers. I swallow the bile in my throat. "I need to switch," he adds, gripping me tighter and turning us so he's lying on his back and I'm now sitting over him. I notice the blood on the sheets and wonder if he chose white on purpose. He grips my hips hard enough to bruise, and he guides me to move. I wince as more pain rips through me. I feel fuller this way and it's uncomfortable. He takes my hands and places them against his clammy chest. But it gives me leverage to lift, like he's shown me. I move more freely, and he releases his hold on my hips, sliding his hands to my breast instead, pinching my nipples.

There's a warmth in the pit of my stomach. It whirls around until I feel the familiar buzz of an orgasm. I'm on the brink and Aiden notices, moving his thumb between my legs and pressing against my clit. I cry out, shaking uncontrollably. It feels different this way, more intense and out of control. Aiden slams up into me, chasing his own release as I come down from mine. He growls, his face contorting in pleasure, looking more beautiful than I've ever seen before. I hate that.

He stiffens, tugging me to lie against him as he empties into me. His chest rises and falls with exertion and we both still, reeling in our own thoughts.

I hear footsteps and Aiden shifts slightly. I glance back, and Drake has the decency to look uncomfortable. JP appears beside him but immediately covers his eyes, "Jesus, cover her up," he snaps.

Aiden pulls a sheet over us, taking my face gently in his hand and turning me to look at him. "I'm sorry," he whispers. If I didn't already know why he was apologising, I'd be so confused by now. I almost feel sorry for the naïve, unsuspecting me. Relieved I saved her in time. "Sign the paper's Drake," he snaps.

"Why are you sorry?" I whisper, wiping more tears. They escape, dripping from my face and onto his bare chest.

"I didn't lock the door," he whispers, wiping my cheek.

A sob leaves me, and I'm unable to hold back as I climb from him. He gently touches my back, "Are you okay? Did I hurt you?" He sounds worried, which makes everything feel so much worse. I rush to my room, slamming the door and locking it.

I cry until my body aches and my heart is shattered. Aiden doesn't try to come in and console me. Why would he? He's got what he needs. I perch on the edge of the bed, still wrapped in the white sheet from Aiden's bed. I feel humiliated and embarrassed. A part of me thought he'd confess, that he wouldn't take it all the way. And when it became obvious, he wasn't going to, I went along with it. *Why did I do that?* Why did I think it would feel better? Finally, being free? It doesn't. It comes with shame and hurt. I groan, rubbing my hands over my tired face.

I'm not sure how long I sit there staring at the floor, but I'm interrupted when there's a light tap on the door. "Bella, let me in. I'm worried."

It's a little late to start worrying now, I think, bitterly. I ignore him, and head to my shower. I need to wash him from me. I can smell his aftershave; it makes me feel sick.

Half an hour later, I dress slowly in jeans and an oversized jumper, feeling a mixture of nerves and emptiness. I unlock my door, surprised to see Aiden sat on the floor, leaning against the wall opposite my room. His head is in his hands. *Good*, I hope he feels like shit. He looks up, worry marring his perfect features. "Bella, are you okay?" he asks, scrambling to his feet. His eyes land on my bag and he frowns. I pass him, heading straight to his room to collect my clothes from the floor, stuffing them in with the rest of my stuff.

He lingers in the doorway, and I face him, making sure to look him in the eye. "When I first met Jake," I begin, wincing at how raspy my voice sounds from all my tears. "I thought he was a bit of a twat." I give a slight laugh, and he stares down at his feet. "He came in every day. Made crap jokes, ate a chocolate cupcake, just hung around. Aria thought he fancied me," I smirk at the memory of her teasing me whenever he came in. "I warmed to him," I admit. "In the end."

"What's this got to do with Jake?" he mutters.

"I forgot," I say, sadly, "You don't like to talk about your brother. But you should," I tell him, "It keeps his memory alive. Remembering all his quirks, his pranks, and the places you hung out together," I add. "I bet you have plenty of those, especially here." He finally looks up, his eyes meeting mine. "I never thought Jake would turn out to be so scheming," I mutter, with disappointment lacing my tone. I zip up my bag and lift it from the bed. "I should have trusted that first instinct. He was a twat." Aiden briefly closes his eyes, and I imagine he's feeling less smug over his conquest. "I know the truth," I finally admit.

I shove past him and head into the living room. "God," I cry, "All those times I told him about my fucking shitty dates," I snap, angrily. "In exchange for tales of his escapades with his brother. With you!" I yell, stabbing a finger to his chest. "All along he was plotting, weighing me up, seeing if I could be the one to tame his slag of a brother. Every story, every line, it was just to reel me in so he could drag me into this childish game," I scream.

Aiden holds his hands up in a defensive manor. "He was trying to make us both happy."

"Great," I cry, "How's that working out for you because I don't feel fucking happy right now," I yell. He closes the gap between us, reaching for me but I shake my head, "Don't fucking touch me."

He steps back, pressing his lips together in a firm line. I've never seen him so quiet. It's a nice change and if I didn't already know the deceiving, lying prick, I'd think he looked like a nice guy.

I take a breath. "If you'd have just told me, Aiden. If you'd have just said you needed my help, I'd have given it to you. It was never that important to me." He keeps his eyes trained to the floor, but I see the way my words hurt him in how he clenches his jaw. "I wanted to be friends with you, maybe more, but I would have been happy at friends."

I head for the door. "Where will you go?" he asks.

I shrug. "I would rather sleep in a shop doorway than be around you for another second." I place my door key on the small table and pull it open. "I hope it was worth it. This club is amazing, and I get the appeal. But when the lights go up, and the party stops, you're just a sad, lonely man. And eventually, when the novelty wears off, you'll look around and see the reality. No one cares about you, Aiden. Laurie is a married woman that won't ever leave her husband, at least, not for you, because she left you to go to him. And your friends get their kicks by watching you make a shit show of your life. If they were good people, they'd have stopped all of this to tell you that what you could have with me, would be worth it."

Aiden

She closes the door gently. A part of me wished she'd slam it, because anger is way better than disappointment. I rest my forehead against it and release a long breath. Of course she fucking knew. It makes sense now. The songs. The way she behaved at dinner. How didn't I see it?

I growl angrily, slamming my fist into the drywall over and over. It breaks, and I shake my hand, wincing as pain radiates through my knuckles. "Are you happy, Jake?" I yell, looking up like he'll magically appear. "Is this how it was supposed to end?"

I pace the apartment. I should be happy now, the club is mine, along with some of the other smaller businesses. But I feel like crap knowing I've hurt her.

After half an hour, I head downstairs, unable to resist the urge to drown my sorrows any longer. JP is behind the bar. He looks up when the elevator opens and I see his eyes are full of regret, just like mine. "Whiskey bottle," I grate out, taking a seat.

He grabs it, placing it on the bar. "She knew, didn't she?" he asks. "I saw it in her eyes."

"Not now, JP," I mutter, unscrewing the cap and gulping a few mouthfuls from the bottle.

"She couldn't even look me in the eye," he says sadly. "She marched out of here looking full of shame. We did that to her," he snaps. "And by the looks of you, it doesn't feel like you thought it would."

I slam the bottle down. "Fuck you."

"I told Raff this was a bad idea, and we should call it off. How are we gonna carry on as if it didn't happen?"

I snatch the bottle up and head for the office, I can't deal with his shit right now. I just want to get wasted.

※

I lift my head up from the desk, blinking a few times to clear the fog. *Fuck*, how much did I drink? I lift the bottle, bringing it closer for inspection and noticing it's empty. I smirk. That explains why my head is pounding and my mouth's dry.

The office door swings open, and I make out a blurry figure, soon realising its Aria by the enraged screaming coming from her. I wince, holding up my hand while I sit straighter. She becomes clearer and I offer a smile. She doesn't return it, instead glaring at me. "Well, get it over with," I slur.

"You fucking piece of shit," she yells, and her hand stings my face as it connects.

JP pulls her back, holding her arms by her sides. "Enough," he warns.

"Why would you do that? What did she ever do to you?"

"Let her go," I mutter. I deserve her anger.

JP releases her and she spins on him, shoving him back. "Did you know?" she asks. He stares down at the ground, placing his hands on his hips. She gasps, slamming her hands over her open mouth. "Oh my god, you did," she whispers.

"I'm sorry-" he begins but she slaps him too, screaming in anger.

"Fuck you," she yells. "You're all pathetic."

"We had no choice," I mutter, already sick of her screeching. "Shouldn't you be with her?"

She scoffs, "Yeah, I should, Aiden. But you know what, she's so heart broken and ashamed, she won't tell me where she is. She doesn't want to see anyone, not even me." My heart twists painfully. I hate that she's on her own. "I can't believe what you've done," she whispers, "It's so fucked up."

"She'll get over it," I mutter. "No one suffers with a broken heart forever."

Aria screams again, this time tipping over my drink's cabinet. The contents crashes to the floor, smashing and spilling out. I stare at the mess, unable to find the strength to be pissed. "She'll never trust a man again. You did that. I hope it keeps you awake at night. I hope you never find happiness again. You don't deserve it." She spins on her heel, and JP steps in front of her.

"Please, Ari, just hear me out."

"I never want to see either of you again. Ever." And she marches around him and leaves.

"That went well," I mumble, lying my aching head back on the desk.

CHAPTER EIGHTEEN

Bella

I open the front door to my home, the one I grew up in. The last time I was here, I met JP looking all big and scary. If I'd have known then, what I know now, I would have walked straight back out, refusing to even listen to any of it. Sometimes, ignorance is bliss.

"Dad," I call out, and he pops his head around the kitchen door looking surprised.

"Bella." he says with a huge smile. He rushes over, wrapping me into a tight hug and it's enough to send me over the edge. He pulls back, holding me at arm's length. "What's wrong?"

"It was all a lie, Dad. Aiden used me," I whisper.

His hands fall from my shoulders, "He went through with it?"

I gasp. I didn't think it would be possible to feel any more pain, but I was wrong. "No," I murmur, shaking my head. "Please, Dad, tell me you weren't in on this."

"I thought he'd make you happy," he rushes to tell me. "He said he wouldn't let you get hurt."

I crouch down, holding my hands to my aching chest whilst I sob uncontrollably. "How much?" I whisper.

"Bella, please believe me. I thought it would be a good idea because he'd get you away from me."

I stand, "I thought, I thought," I scream. "Well, you thought fucking wrong." He takes a few steps back, tears filling his own eyes. "I have spent years caring for you when it should have been the other way around. You let me down," I yell. It's words I've been holding back for too long, and now I've started, they're just pouring out. "So next time you think you're doing me a favour, don't."

"I haven't drunk since you left," he whispers, like I should be proud.

"I don't care," I hiss. "I am done with you." I pull my purse out of my bag. "In fact," I say, "Have a drink on me."

And I throw a twenty at his feet. "Mum would have hated what you've become," I whisper.

He reels back, my words cutting him like a knife. I don't feel bad, he's hurt me too much. The one person that is supposed to be there for me, and I can't think of one time when he was. I leave him standing in the kitchen, clutching his chest, his silent tears spilling down his cheeks.

❧

I walk around aimlessly for a long time. I'm aware that my mobile is ringing over and over, but I leave it in my bag, ignoring it. I can't face talking to anyone that knows about any of this situation. I'm too humiliated and I feel so ashamed because I went through with it. How would I explain that?

I stop at Cal's door. I don't know how I've ended up here, it wasn't a conscious decision. But I ring the doorbell anyway. He opens the door and his smile falters. I must look a state with swollen eyes and puffy cheeks, but he recovers quickly, forcing the smile again. "Hey, come in," he urges, taking my bag from me.

I sit on the couch while he makes a coffee. When he returns, he sits opposite me and smiles kindly. "Okay, start at the beginning," he says, relaxing back. And I do. It tumbles out from start to finish, and all the while, he stares wide eyed. When I finally finish, he takes a deep breath, releasing it slowly. "Wow." He moves to the couch beside me and wraps me in his arms. "I don't know what to say apart from he's a scum bag."

"I'm so sorry for just turning up like this. I couldn't face anyone, but I also needed a friendly face."

He gently rubs my back. "Anytime, Bella. You know that."

"Personal trainer and therapist," I joke, wiping my eyes.

He gives a sympathetic smile. "Look, relax, get some rest. I'll make us some food. Get your head straight."

I smile gratefully. "Thanks."

He places a blanket over me before heading in the kitchen. I close my eyes. They feel so heavy, and it's not long before I feel myself drifting off.

♡

"Stay the hell away from her or I'll kill you myself." I wake with a start right as Cal is placing my mobile back on the table. He winces, "Sorry, I didn't mean to wake you, but your phone just kept ringing," he explains.

I sit up, wrapping the blanket around me. "It's the reason I didn't go to Ari's, he would have turned up there."

"Look, I've been thinking. How about you stay here?" I'm already shaking my head. "I have a spare room, Bella. It's not a problem."

"I can't impose on you, Cal. It's bad enough I turned up here after everything I did to you."

He smirks, "I believe it was me doing it to you," he teases, and I blush. "Jokes aside, I've always wanted a roommate. What have you got to lose." The last time I agreed to this, I lost a lot, but I remain silent. "At least come and check the room out," he adds.

We head down the hall and he pushes the door open, revealing a bright, freshly decorated room. "No one's ever stayed in here," he says. "It's a blank canvas and you can put your own stamp on it."

"It's beautiful," I whisper.

"Stay tonight and think about it. We can discuss rent tomorrow if you decide to take me up on the offer. No strings attached, Bella." He gently rubs my arm. "I've put some leftovers in the fridge if you want them, help yourself. And try to get some more rest."

꼬

I spend the next few days in hiding. I agreed to a trial run at Cal's and after we settled on rent, I went back to my room, and I've hardly left since. I can't eat, and every time I try, I just feel sick. I haven't been to work and apart from the odd text to confirm I'm still alive, I haven't spoken to Aria. I can't face the questions I know she'll fire at me the second she sees me.

There's a light knock on the bedroom door and Cal pops his head in, just like every morning, he holds up a brown paper bag containing a pastry. "Breakfast?" he asks hopefully. I stop drawing and give a nod. "Thank god," he says dramatically, "I've had to eat both pastries these last few days. It's not good for my waistline."

I follow him into the kitchen. "Are you supposed to eat this stuff in your line of work?" I ask.

He narrows his eyes playfully, "Are you judging me?"

I smile, "It makes me feel better when I see healthy people eat crap."

"Hey, a little treat doesn't hurt." He slides one pastry to me and sits opposite me to tuck into his own. His eyes glance at the drawing pad beside me. "Can I see?" he asks. I nod, pushing it towards him and he flicks through. "These are amazing, Bella."

"I love drawing," I say, shrugging.

"But these designs are perfect, can you make them too?"

I nod. "Yeah, but Aria isn't keen on taking her business in that direction. Orders can flood in, and she doesn't like to over commit."

"Have you thought about selling the designs?" I shake my head. "You could put these online. Have you got a website?" I shake my head again, smiling at how excited looks. "I can sort that. I'm serious, Bella. You have an amazing eye for this stuff, and I reckon brides would buy these to hand to their cake designers."

I take the pad back and stare at my latest creation, "They are beautiful," I mutter thoughtfully.

"And it would be good to have a focus," he says, "Build a future. I got you something whilst I was out," he adds, reaching for a bag. "It's totally up to you, if you don't want to use it, I won't be offended, but I thought you could use a fresh start."

I take the bag and warily look inside. "A mobile?" I ask, taking the new phone out.

"It's a good way to start again. If he doesn't have your number, and doesn't know where you're living, he can't keep hassling you."

"Did anyone ever tell you that you're a great friend?" I almost whisper, feeling emotional.

Aiden

I stare at the empty bottle wondering how I drank it so fast. I wave to the bartender but JP steps in, shaking his head. "No more," he says firmly.

I scoff, "You know what you are, JP?" I slur. "A fun sponge. Always there with your words of advice, telling me to sort my shit out." I laugh at nothing in particular and point a finger in his direction. "Fun sponge."

"I'll take him upstairs," says Laurie, wrapping a gentle hand around my arm. "Come on, baby," she coos, and I shudder in repulsion. It's not the first time she's been waiting in the wings to drag me off upstairs, and I don't exactly fight her off. Why would I? She's all I deserve.

We stumble into the apartment, and I fall back on the couch, attempting to kick my shoes off. Laurie is there in a flash, grabbing my foot and easing it free. I take in the tight dress she's wearing. *Why is she always in red?* "I'm starting to think you're drinking so much to avoid me," she says, removing my other shoe.

"It's not working," I muse, "Cos here you are again."

"I'm worried about you. This is so unlike you."

"You don't know me," I mutter, looking away. I stare at the blanket hanging over the back of the couch. The same blanket Bella used to wrap around herself whenever she fell asleep in this exact same spot, waiting for me to come home. I pull it closer and press it to my nose, inhaling deeply. Her scent is fading, and I hate that.

"I should wash that," says Laurie making a grab for it. I hold it tighter, and she glares angrily. "This is not healthy, Aiden. Fuck, when are you going to pull yourself together?"

"Just go," I mutter.

She sighs. "You'll never move on if you keep drinking and laying with her damn blanket," she snaps. "Let's just get back to normal." She runs her hand up my thigh, giving me a sexy smile. A few months ago, that would have worked. But now, all I can see is Bella and all I feel is guilt. It's consuming, and the only time it eases a fraction, is when I'm wasted.

I tune back in to Laurie, realising that somehow, she's pulled my trousers down to my thighs. "That's it, baby. Focus on me," she whispers seductively, gripping my cock.

I close my eyes and picture Bella. *My beautiful Bella.*

Bella

"It's been a month," Cal reminds me as I sit in the passenger seat of his car, across from the bakery. "Of course you feel anxious. But it's normal."

I give a stiff nod, gripping the door handle so tightly, my fingers hurt. "But what if he turns up?" I ask. I didn't get a wink of sleep, which is making my anxiety about returning to work, ten times worse.

"He found out you were living at mine over a week ago according to Aria, and he hasn't shown up yet."

He's right, I know he is, but I can't help worrying. I'm not ready to face him, I don't even know if I'm quite ready to see Aria face to face, which is shit, because she's my best friend. "Aria isn't going to grill you," Cal adds, giving my arm a reassuring squeeze. "She's fully up to date on everything and she's just excited to have you back at work," he says. I know he's been updating Aria on my behalf, mainly to stop her worrying. But still, I know her too well and she's going to ask questions.

"Okay," I say, taking a deep breath, "I've got this."

"You have," he agrees.

I get out of the car, leaning back in, "Thanks, Cal, I appreciate you."

He grins. "Go be a bad ass boss bitch. I'll pick you up later."

When I enter the shop, Aria squeals in excitement, and runs over, wrapping me in a hug. "I have missed you so much."

I smile, "I've missed you too, Ari."

She holds me at arm's length and assesses me. "You've lost weight," she notes.

"The joys of living with a PT," I say, shrugging out of my coat. "Cal is a great cook, and he force feeds me vegetables."

She takes my things from me and heads into the back room to hang them up. "Well, you look great, not that you needed to lose weight."

I move behind the counter, running my hands over the cool glass. "It feels weird being back after so long off," I say.

She returns, "It's been so quiet without you. I saw the website, it looks great."

I smile, "Yeah, it's really happening isn't it. I thought Cal was talking crap, but I've made some sales and even had a commission."

She grins, "Oh my god, that's amazing. Which brings me to a business proposition," she says, and I eye her suspiciously, "Of sorts," she adds, heading for the door and turning the sign to closed. "Let's get a coffee and talk about it." Aria never closes the shop, which just makes me more suspicious.

We sit out the back with a coffee and she takes a deep breath. "What if we made the wedding cakes?"

I frown, "The shop isn't big enough, and the kitchen certainly isn't. It wouldn't work."

"Next door is for sale," she says, her eyes search my face for a reaction.

I laugh, "Have you won the lottery, and this is your way of telling me?"

"No."

"Next door is a florist, Aria. It would cost a fortune to kit it out."

"We could knock through," she continues, ignoring me, "Extend the kitchen. Then have one side for the bakery and the other for wedding cakes."

"Have you hit your head?" I ask, shaking my head with a smirk.

She reaches into her pocket and pulls out a crumpled piece of paper. "A few weeks ago, your dad came to see me."

I inhale sharply, she's caught me off guard and feel my anxiety dial up a notch. "He gave me this," she adds, holding out the paper.

I shake my head. "Whatever it is, I don't want it," I snap, making no move to take it. She opens it out and I stare at the cheque, it's signed Aiden Tremos, which instantly makes me feel sick. "What the fuck is this, Aria?" I snap.

"Your dad insisted that Aiden make the cheque to you," she says.

I scoff, "That was good of him," I say, my voice dripping with sarcasm.

"I'm on your side, Bella. Trust me, I told your dad exactly what I thought of him. But when I saw the amount of this, I took it, because you deserve it after what those fuckers did."

"No amount of money will make it right," I snap. "I don't want anything from any of them. Accepting that cheque will make them feel better. But it won't erase what they did."

"You're right," she agrees. "It won't. And maybe you taking it will ease their guilt, and we don't want that because they deserve to feel bad. But this money could make such a difference in your life. You could buy the florist and make it yours. It will be your future."

"Paid for by the man who has destroyed me," I cry, feeling tears building.

"Exactly. Nothing will take away what he did. If you cash this, it doesn't change anything except your opportunities. When will you ever get this chance again?"

I sigh heavily, "I feel so ashamed," I whisper. "And it doesn't matter what I do, I can't shake it."

"You did nothing wrong, Bella," she says, wrapping an arm around my shoulder.

I side eye her, "Didn't I? I slept with him. I knew his plan and I still went ahead. I could have stopped him at any time, but I chose to stay quiet." My words come out on a choked sob.

"Sometimes we do things we wouldn't usually do when we're under extreme distress or pressure. You just found out his plan and it shook your world, you weren't thinking."

I shake my head angrily. "I'm as bad as him."

"No you're not," she cries, "Don't you dare blame yourself."

"I wanted rid of my virginity."

"Because it was causing you so much trouble. No wonder."

"But I gave it to him," I yell, "Why did I do that?"

She shrugs sadly, "I don't know, Bella."

"Because..." I sniffle, hating my next words, "Even after everything, I wanted him to get his stupid fucking club. He went to so much trouble, I thought how important it must be for him. So, I went through with it for him."

"Oh Bells," she whispers, hugging me harder. "You fell in love, no one can blame you for that."

"I hate myself for giving a shit," I sob.

"You can't just turn your feelings off, even when they don't deserve them."

"JP?" I guess.

She shrugs, "I want to hate him," she admits.

"Aria, please don't avoid him because of me and Aiden."

"I can't be with a man that supports that sort of behaviour," she says firmly.

"Have you heard from him?" I ask, wiping my own eyes.

"Yeah. He's got a lot on, and he seems to want to vent to me. Even when I make it clear I don't care, or I don't want to know. He said I'm the only one he can talk to about how he feels."

"Pity he didn't feel that way before," I say, and she nods in agreement.

"If it helps, Aiden is totally off the rails. Drinking, not running the business."

"Good," I mutter. "I'm glad he's suffering." And I ignore the twist in my heart.

※

Cal picks me up and I fill him in about my first day back. And later, as we cook dinner together, I tell him about the cheque.

He glances up, his chopping knife held mid-air, "Shit, what did you say?"

"I didn't take it," I mutter, stirring the sauce. "I don't want anything from him."

"It's your choice," he says, frowning, "But I'm kind of on Aria's side with this." I stare open mouthed, and he shrugs, "You deserve that money." I thought out of everyone, he'd be on my side.

"It'll be like I've prostituted myself," I tell him.

"He took it anyway, Bella. The least he owes you is the money he was paying your dad. And let's face it, what will your dad spend it on? Booze most likely. You said you paid the mortgage and bills whilst you lived there, yet it's all in his name. You won't get any of that back, so see this as your return on the property."

I smirk, "It doesn't matter how I dress it up, it's still money that Aiden paid dad for his part in the entire thing. And Aria wants me to buy the florist beside the bakery and open it as a wedding cake shop."

"Then what the hell are you waiting for? It's a sign. Your future depends on it."

CHAPTER NINETEEN

Aiden

I down my black coffee and shake out my stressed shoulders. It's the first day I've woken sober since she left me. And it's the first day I've wanted to be in the office and actually do some work.

I gather the empty whiskey bottles from the desk and place them in a box, then carry them into the bar for recycling. JP glances up from where he's sitting in one of the booths. It's almost lunch, and we don't open until after six, but it's not unusual to see him here early just lately, picking up the slack for me. I dump the box on the floor and join him. "Morning," I say. He eyes me before turning his attention back to his laptop. "Anything I can help with?" I know him and Raff are pissed at me, I don't blame them, but I hate being ignored.

Eventually he sighs, "I'm doing the weekly order."

"I'm sober," I point out. "I thought it was time I got my shit together."

He gives a stiff nod. "Good to have you back."

"Are we supposed to congratulate you?" comes Raff's voice as he enters the bar, dumping his gym bag on the ground and sitting beside JP. "Cos let me tell you, I'm not as easy to get round."

I smirk, "I'm not trying to get around you, Raff. I'm simply saying I'm done with the drink and partying."

"What about sorry?" he snaps. "Where's the fucking massive apology you owe us for keeping your bar afloat whilst you locked yourself away."

"I'd do the exact same for both of you."

"But you never have to do you, Aiden. Because we don't pull that shit."

"Okay, I'm sorry you had to clean up my mess," I say, shrugging. "But in case you didn't realise, I was kind of drowning."

"Fuck you, Aiden," he spits. "All that shit for this place, and then you just turned your back. If it hadn't been for us, you wouldn't even have the club anymore. It would have all been for nothing."

"You're right," I mutter. "I'm really sorry. And I appreciate you sticking around and saving my backside."

He relaxes a little. "Don't do it again."

"In other news, Bella banked the cheque." JP avoids eye contact, "But then you knew that, right?" I guess.

"Aria mentioned it," he mutters.

"And you didn't want to tell me?"

"I'm only just getting Aria to speak to me, I don't think she'll be happy if I feed information back to you."

I give a knowing nod. "I just hope she spends it on a new place, I hate the thought of her sharing with that fitness freak."

"As long as she's happy, it doesn't matter," says Raff, firmly, exchanging a look with JP.

"What?" I ask.

"Nothing," he reassures me.

"Raff, I saw that look, what do you know?"

He sighs, "She's buying the florist beside the bakery. Apparently, she's got big plans to make it into some wedding cake venture."

I let that information settle in. I'm glad she's doing well, and that she's using the money to set up a future. I didn't think she'd accept it, but I'm relieved she has. "You miss her," says JP, breaking my thoughts.

I stare down at the table, "More than I ever thought I would," I admit. "And hearing all about her plans, makes me realise how much. I want to be the one she tells everything to." I sigh, scrubbing my hands over my face. "Yah know what she said to me right before she left? That if I'd have told her everything right from the start, she probably would have helped me."

"Sounds like something she'd do," says Raff, fondly. "She's a good woman."

"If you could start again, would you tell her?" asks JP.

I stand, "I'd have sold the club," I confess, "Then I would have spent time getting to know the woman my brother insisted was my perfect match." I slide the letter Jake left me, onto the table. "I finally read it," I say, "It explains why he did it."

"That's the thing with hindsight," says Raff, taking the letter. "But it can't be changed now, Aiden. Leave Bella alone."

Bella

I'm a shop owner. I stare at the empty florist, taking it all in. Cal joins me, smiling wide. "Congratulations."

"Are you going to let us in, or should we just stand here looking?" asks Aria, stepping from the bakery to join us on the pavement.

I hold up the keys, smiling as I push it into the lock. "I can't believe it," I say, "I own a bloody shop!"

"You did good," says Cal, stepping in behind me and looking around in awe.

"And the builders are starting tomorrow?" Aria clarifies. I nod. We've spent weeks picking out ovens, mixers and cabinets, but back then, it didn't seem real. Now, as I stand in the empty shop, it feels very real and a little scary.

"Things are finally looking up," says Cal, giving my hand a reassuring squeeze.

I turn to him, "Thank you for helping me," I say sincerely.

He grins, pulling me into his arms. "You don't need to thank me."

"You've all been amazing. If it weren't for you, Aria and Jake, I don't know if I'd have done any of this."

"We're so proud of you, Bella," says Aria. "Most people wouldn't have made it through this, but you did. And look at this place, it's perfect."

Cal grabs me around the waist and spins me around, I laugh, wrapping myself around him. "Now, enough of the soppy bullshit, let's get this place cleaned."

As he slides me down his body, I glance out of the window and notice a car slowly driving past, with Aiden at the wheel. Our eyes connect and for a minute, everything seems to fade away, and all that's left in the moment is me and him.

"Bella," Aria calls from the back room, "When is the sign coming?"

I look away from the window. Neither have noticed my sheer panic at seeing him and I pull myself together quickly. "Erm, tomorrow," I reply. When I glance back, the car is gone.

※

The days blend into one. I'm so busy with the shop, I haven't had time to think about anything else. Including Aiden. Maybe his drive by was a complete accident. And if it was, he hasn't been back to try and talk to me. Which I'm grateful for. And I didn't bother to tell Aria or Cal, I couldn't have the mention of Aiden ruin my big day.

I'm sure eventually, I'll come across him, maybe in the street or a restaurant, and I'll have to face my demons. But right now, I want to enjoy this time with my best friends without the stress and drama that Aiden brings.

"The builders are all done," says Aria, popping her head into the bakery where I'm currently baking cupcakes for tomorrows opening.

I wipe my hands down my apron and follow her out, and back into my shop where I thank the foreman for everything. I've been super fussy with minor details, and I know he's secretly wanted to throttle me more than once. I made sure to pay extra with daily cupcakes as an apology though.

Once he's left, I turn to Aria and we both give a little excited squeal. "I can't believe I'm opening tomorrow."

"You've worked so hard," she says.

I grip onto the worktop and squeeze my eyes closed as a dizzy spell passes through. I've been feeling off all week, which is more than likely due to the late nights and early mornings I've been putting in.

Aria watches me carefully, "You still not well?"

"No. Once the opening is out of the way, I'm sure I'll feel better. But if I don't, I'll go and see the doctor."

❥

The following day, me, Aria and Cal spend the morning making sure everything is in place.

Beautifully decorated cakes fill the display cabinets and taste samples are carefully placed on tabletops. Balloons with my logo across them, bob up and down in the window and there are iPads on the counter so that people can access the website to see more designs.

I check my watch, there're five more minutes until the doors open and Cal is stationed outside the shop to hand out cake samples. Aria glances out the window, "There's a line of people," she says excitedly.

I take a deep breath. I feel so sick with nerves, that I have to take a seat. Aria pulls a paper bag from behind the counter. "I got you this," she says.

I smile, taking it, "You didn't have to get me anything."

"It's not a present," she mutters, and I peer into the bag and gasp, slamming it closed. "It's just to make sure," she rushes to tell me.

"I'm not bloody pregnant."

"So do the test and prove me wrong," she says simply. "You have a few minutes."

"You want me to do it now?" I hiss.

"You just have to pee on it, once I see it's negative, I'll feel better."

I groan, heading out back for the bathroom. "I'm on the pill," I call out to her.

"It's not fool proof," she calls back.

I pee on the stick, then put it back in the box and place it on the counter. Then I go outside to open my shop for the very first time. Cal starts clapping as I hold up the scissors, and the line of potential new customers join him. "I now pronounce Bella's, open," I say with a huge smile as I cut the red ribbon.

I spend the next twenty-minutes chatting with the customers and pointing them in the direction of my website. Cal is huge on me having people sign up to my newsletter updates. Apparently, it's a good way to keep customers returning.

I step behind the counter, smiling at the amount of people I have in the shop. "This is great, isn't it," I whisper.

"I just had a bride sign up for a cake," Cal tells me. "She's going to browse the site for ideas," he adds excitedly.

"Did you check the test?" Aria asks and Cal arches a brow, waiting for me to explain.

I roll my eyes, "Aria got me a pregnancy test. Not the present I was expecting on my opening day."

"You're pregnant?" he gasps.

"God no. She's over-reacting. I did the test to shut her up."

"So it's negative?" asks Aria.

I groan, grabbing the box off the counter out back. "I'm run down," I explain, pulling the test out a little. I stare wide eyed, before shoving it back in the box. My heart slams wildly in my chest.

"So?" Aria pushes.

The shop door opens, and I glance up to see Aiden staring back at me. My world feels like it's imploding and him turning up is like a bad omen. This can't be happening.

"What does it say?" Aria asks, this time sounding less patient.

I swallow the lump in my throat, my eyes still fixed on Aiden. "Positive," I mutter.

Aria gasps and Cal utters a string of curse words. And then, as if they both sense at the same time that I'm not reacting, they follow my line of sight to where Aiden is.

It all happens so fast. There's movement and bustling. I hear Cal yelling and Aria is standing between them, but Aiden doesn't take his eyes from me. Cal is shoving and pushing, Aria is getting caught in the middle. Aiden doesn't react, his face stays calm, and his eyes are burning into me and in that moment, I feel like it's just me and him.

Me, Aiden and our baby!

CHAPTER TWENTY

Bella

Seeing him standing there, in my shop, on my special day, is all too much. What is he thinking? He hasn't contacted me at all, and he decides that this is the best day to do it. *My grand opening.* He looks well. The dark suit he wears fits snug, and his white shirt showcases his muscles perfectly, with his tattoos peeking out over the collar. His pure bulk makes him look intimidating; I don't feel intimidated though. Just annoyed.

As usual, my friends are there to put a barrier between us. And despite Cal trying to shove him from the shop,

Aiden isn't budging. "This is her day; how dare you turn up and ruin it," he yells.

My attention moves to a few of my customers who are huddled together, looking like they need an escape. I take a deep breath and march towards the scuffle. Cal notices and steps back. I give him a grateful smile then turn to Aiden. "This isn't fair," I mutter, avoiding eye contact. "Please leave."

He stuffs his hands in his pockets, hanging his head in what I want to believe is shame, but I know Aiden doesn't feel like the rest of us. "I just came to say congratulations and good luck."

Aria scoffs, coming up behind me. "That's what you came to say?" she shouts angrily. "Not, sorry for using her, or for being a complete, selfish twat?"

"Aria," I hiss, glancing around, aware that everyone is listening.

"I tried to call, but the number didn't connect," he says, his bright blue eyes finally reaching mine. "I've been wanting to come and say it face to face," he adds.

I hold up a hand and he stops speaking. "Just leave, Aiden. This day is too important for me."

I turn away from him and offer my customers a reassuring smile. "Sorry about that, please stay and help yourself to more cake. I'll be right back with champagne." And I rush into the back room, closing the door.

I take a few deep breaths, squeezing my eyes closed to stop myself from crying. I refuse to shed anymore tears over him. I'm moving forward and this is my new start. I groan, grabbing the pregnancy test from my pocket where I'd shoved it when I spotted Aiden. New start? *Fat chance.*

Aria knocks lightly on the door, and I let her in. "He's gone," she says with a sympathetic smile. "Are you okay?"

"No."

"Shit, Bella. I really wanted it to be negative," she whispers, taking it from me to stare at the little window. "Ten weeks," she mutters, "That's still early on."

"A reminder of what he did to me," I spit angrily, "Like a little ten-week anniversary gift."

"Perhaps do a second test to make sure. You can get false positives," she suggests hopefully.

"What are the chances when I'm having sickness and dizzy spells," I mutter. "I was on the pill, how the hell does this happen on the first time when I'm on the pill?"

"Were you regular with it?"

I shrug miserably, "What with everything going on, I probably missed one or two. I was taking it for my periods, I didn't even think about it as a precaution because I wasn't having sex."

"The fucker should have worn a condom," says Aria, "He knew he was gonna have sex with you."

I shrug, "It's too late to play the blame game now. Anyway, I have a shop to run."

I pop the cork on a bottle of champagne and begin to fill the plastic glasses I'd purchased for today. "I'll figure this out later."

Aiden

I knew she wouldn't be pleased to see me, but I wasn't prepared for the hurt in her eyes. It cut right through me. She's never looked at me like that before, not even after she found out about the deal.

When I get home, Laurie is in the kitchen chopping vegetables. I frown, "What are you doing here, and how did you get in?"

She smiles, "Surprise."

"I don't like surprises," I say firmly. "Seriously, how did you get in?"

"I had a key cut," she admits, "I was worried when you were drinking so much. I did it so I could come and look after you."

I narrow my eyes, "What the fuck?" My mobile rings before I can lose my shit, and I answer. "JP?"

"Hey Boss, fancy a few drinks at the Cabana club? I need to get away from this bar that you keep me imprisoned behind."

"Yeah, I'll meet you there in about half hour?" I say before disconnecting.

I head for the shower with Laurie hot on my heels. "Dinner will be ready in ten minutes," she says.

"Laurie, if I wanted to have a wife to answer to; I'd have married you. Go home and nag your husband."

"You need to build your strength; you weren't eating right for weeks."

"I can order in, like I have done for years."

I begin to strip off and she lingers in the doorway watching me. "Homecooked is better."

"I don't have time," I say, kicking off my trousers and shorts.

Her eyes run down my body, and she bites on her lower lip. "How about I help you shower?"

"How about you go home."

"Aiden, come on. I've stuck around to help you when no one else would," she argues, and I feel a twinge of guilt. She has been here to check on me every day.

"Laurie, I appreciate you being there for me, but you have a husband. You should go home and spend time with him."

She scoffs, "He doesn't notice I'm not there. And since when did you care about my marriage?"

"I've already fucked my own life up. Don't let me ruin yours too."

She stands in front of me, running a manicured finger over the tatts on my chest. "You still have the club, and you have me. I know you feel bad for everything with that girl, but she's gone now."

"Bella," I grit out, because she damn well knows her name yet always refers to her as 'that girl'. "Her name is Bella."

"Whatever. Either way she's left. But I'm here. Nothing's changed."

I remove her hand from my chest. "Exactly," I mutter bitterly. "I've re-evaluated my life and this," I say, indicating between us, "Isn't what I want. Leave your key on the way out.

Bella

Cal sits on my bed, watching me apply my make-up. "I won't be able to drink, what's the point," I say with a sigh, as I apply mascara.

"Aria wants to celebrate your shop opening, don't be a killjoy," he says. "I'll be there around ten."

"After your date," I say, wiggling my brows.

He grins, "I want to see you having fun when I arrive. No sulking in the corner."

"What if I see them?" I mutter, turning to face him.

"What if you do?" he asks with a shrug. "You live close by, it's gonna happen one day. All you can do is ignore them and make sure they see they don't affect you."

"But they do," I admit.

He stands, kissing me on the head. "You don't have to show them that." He heads for the door. "Have fun, you can't spend the rest of your life avoiding them. And you can't hide away."

"I'll have fun if you promise not to bin this date off for a stupid reason."

He smirks, "My reasons are valid."

I roll my eyes, and he laughs harder, leaving. It's the eighth date he's been on this month alone, and they never get past the second date because Cal is too fussy.

Aria arrives ten minutes after Cal leaves. She's looking hot in a black jumpsuit that clings to her ample chest. When I eye her suspiciously, she shrugs, "I might meet Mr. Right tonight."

"Is JP coming then?" I tease, because we both know he's her Mr. Right.

She narrows her eyes. "Haha, very funny."

We choose a quiet wine bar. The sort with low lighting and a solo singer setting a somber mood. Aria gets us both a glass of wine, only mine is non-alcohol, and I stare at hers longingly.

"Let's talk about the elephant in the room," she begins.

I groan dramatically. "Let's not. I have no idea what I'm going to do, and you badgering me about it, isn't helping."

"I'm not badgering," she replies innocently. "I'm simply helping you come to a decision."

I roll my eyes, "Next you'll be telling me to tell Aiden." She gives me a look that tells me that's exactly what she was thinking. "Oh, fuckoff, Aria," I cry. "He shit himself when I mentioned a relationship. I guarantee the last thing Aiden Tremos wants, is a baby."

"But if you decide to keep it, you'll tell him, right?"

"Why do you suddenly care about Aiden?" I demand.

"I don't. But he does have rights and if you don't tell him, and he finds out . . ." She trails off.

"I don't owe him anything. I certainly don't plan on tying myself to him forever."

"So you're not keeping the baby?"

I sigh heavily, "No . . . yes, no. I don't bloody know, Aria. But if I keep it, Aiden can't know."

"You're right," she says, holding her hands up in submission. "He doesn't deserve to know. I'm sorry."

I smile, "Let's not talk about Aiden Tremos tonight. I don't want to think about it. We're celebrating right?"

She taps her glass against mine. "Yes we are."

After an hour of shop talk, we meet up with some of our friends at the Cabana Club. Aria immediately wanders off to scope the talent, and I head for the bar. It's busy and no fun when you're the only sober one, but I promised Cal I'd try and relax, so I order shots for everyone else, and grab a lemonade for myself.

Jack takes his gratefully as I place the tray on the table. Aria rushes up behind me, gripping my arm. "Bella, JP is here," she hisses.

My stomach tightens and my heart beats wildly. I find myself scanning the area for Aiden. "Who's he with?"

She shrugs, "I have no idea, I ran the second I saw him. Do you want to leave?"

Cal's words play through my mind and I give my head a shake. "No. I'm done running."

"Who we running from?" I turn at the sound of Cal's voice and smile with relief. He pulls me to him, wrapping his arms around me. "Why do you look so sad?"

"Aria saw JP," I mutter.

He tips my head back to look me in the eye. "It doesn't mean Aiden's here, and if he is, it will all be okay."

I want to believe him, but a part of me is terrified. "This is because I banked the cheque," I say, "Now he thinks he can just keep showing up in my life."

"Maybe," Cal agrees. "But it's done now. You just have to ignore him until he gets the message."

"It'll get even more awkward when she starts showing," hisses Aria and I elbow her in the side.

"We're not talking about that, remember."

Cal hugs me tighter, "She's got a point," he whispers in my ear.

Aiden

"Stop looking for her," says Raff from beside me. I give the crowd one last scan before turning my back on it and smiling at Raff. "She hates you, don't ruin her night."

"Thanks for the reminder," I reply, dryly.

JP joins us looking pissed. "I wanted one night where Aria wasn't in my head, and then I fucking bump into her," he complains.

"She's got to forgive you eventually, brother," says Raff, slapping him on the shoulder.

"How come he gets sympathy?" I ask.

Raff grins, "He isn't as big a prick as you."

I roll my eyes and turn back to looking down on the dancefloor. And that's when I see her. I inhale sharply, my heart swelling with hope even though she's in the arms of the fitness freak.

I go to the bar and pay for a bottle of expensive champagne and ask the bartender to take it over to Bella, who's now sitting with her friends at a table.

I watch as he taps her on the shoulder. She listens to whatever he's saying, her eyes glancing around the bar, searching for me. And then she turns to the fitness freak and says something in his ear. Cal looks up and his eyes meet with mine. He looks instantly pissed and says something to the bartender. He nods once then heads back in my direction, the champagne still in his hand.

"She declined the champagne," he reports back, and he puts it down in front of me.

I smirk, *of course she did.*

JP joins me, eyeing the bottle. "You celebrating?"

"Nope, but they are," I reply, nodding towards the table. "She declined it though."

He laughs, "Only Bella would turn down a bottle of champagne."

"I don't blame her. It's gonna take more than this to get in her good books again."

"Is that what you want?" he asks.

I think over his question. "Yes," I say, firmly. "More than anything."

"To ease your guilt or because you like her?"

"Both."

"Then get her alone. You don't stand a chance of getting her to hear you out with muscles one side of her, and her psycho bff, the other."

He takes the champagne and heads back up to the lounge area, leaving me to watch Bella and her bodyguards and wait for my perfect opportunity to pin her down and listen to what I've got to say.

Bella

I'm in the bathroom, waiting in line for the toilet with aching feet and a real craving for my bed. Being pregnant is no fun. I'm exhausted and the thing isn't even the size of a bean. I groan out loud, getting me a few curious glances from the other women in line. I can't believe Aiden thought he could buy me off with champagne. Like him flashing the cash would make me forgive him. *Prick.*

"Ladies, would you give us a minute?" My head whips up at the sound of Aiden's voice and I stare open mouthed as he fills the doorway.

The women smile wistfully, all heading for the exit. "No," I snap, "Don't go." They don't listen, filing out one by one. *Great.* "What happened to safety in numbers?" I cry after them.

"We need to talk," he says, fixing his blue eyes on me.

I shrink back slightly, without Cal and Aria as my armor, I feel weak. The toilet flushes and a woman steps out. She keeps her head lowered as she washes her hands while we wait patiently in silence.

Once she's gone, Aiden closes the gap between us, so I'm trapped between the sink unit and his hard body. "You won't even look at me," he mutters.

"What the hell do you think you're playing at?" I hiss.

"I just need a minute of your time, Bells."

"Isabella," I correct him. "Only my friends call me Bells."

He clenches his jaw, and I know he wants to yell at me for being so stubborn. "Just hear me out," he pleads.

"So, talk, Aiden. You've gone to all this trouble to force me to listen," I yell.

"I messed up," he begins, and I scoff, folding my arms. "And you have every right to hate me."

"I do," I cut in.

"But, please, try and understand why I did it. I know you saw Jake's letter, it was open." I stay quiet, not confirming nor denying my snooping. "He thought we'd fall madly in love and live happily ever after."

"It wasn't up to him to try and make that happen," I snap.

"But he saw you needed someone and wanted me to settle down. He grabbed the opportunity."

"I didn't need anyone," I yell. "Least of all, a lying, cheating playboy like you." I take a deep breath to calm myself. "Look, you've said your piece, and honestly, it doesn't make me feel any better. Your brother played a game with my heart. I can't forgive either of you."

"Bella, please!"

"What do you want me to say, that I forgive you?" I ask, "Would that make you sleep better and ease your conscience?"

He stares down at the ground. "No, probably not. But I want us to be able to be in the same room and be civil. Aria won't see JP, even though we both know she wants to. Everything is a mess, and I just want it to be okay," he says, desperately.

"Are you trying to make me feel bad?" I snap. "JP wasn't innocent in any of this and that's why Aria won't speak to him. I can't control what she chooses to do."

He rubs his hand over his brow, stress evident in his expression. "Why did you go through with it?" he asks, looking me in the eye. "Once you knew, why did you let it go ahead?"

This time it's me that looks away. "I keep asking myself the same thing," I mutter bitterly. "I thought my virginity meant nothing to me, so I let you have it to save yourself. A part of me was hoping you'd confess, but the more time that passed, the quicker I realized that wasn't going to happen. You'd gone to all that trouble to strip me of my virginity, and if I stopped you, you'd have lost everything. Then it would have all been for nothing," I mutter. Sadness fills my heart. "That's how pathetic I am," I add, raising my eyes to meet his. "Still thinking of you, even at a cost to myself."

"You're not pathetic," he rushes to tell me. "You're kind and thoughtful and I didn't see that until it was too late. Tell me how to make it right."

"If you think you can make it right, you really don't understand how much you hurt me, Aiden."

"Then show me. Scream, lash out, do whatever you want to make it feel better."

I scoff, "I'm not like you, Aiden. I won't willingly hurt someone I care about." I shake my head, "Cared about," I correct.

"So this is it? This is how it ends?"

I head for the door. "It ended the night you broke my heart, Aiden. Goodbye."

Aiden

"You look happier," JP notes as I take a seat at our table.

"I saw Bella," I tell them.

Raff groans. "But you didn't go over to her, right?" I shake my head, and he relaxes.

"I followed her into the bathroom and forced her to speak to me."

He glares at me, "Tell me you're joking. Jesus, leave the woman alone, you've already done too much."

"Did she talk to you?" asks JP.

Raff nudges him. "Don't encourage this stalking bullshit."

"Jakes right, they're good together," he argues.

"Jakes dead. If he saw the shit show that he caused, he'd feel bad."

"I've got to try," I mutter, "I need her in my life."

When we arrive back at Tremos, an hour later, I'm feeling the alcohol buzzing through me. It's the first time I've been drunk since I hit rock bottom, and as I scan the room, my eyes landing on a Bella look-a-like, I feel that familiar pull.

We take a seat at our usual table, and she makes a beeline for me, smiling wide as she leans in to speak. "You look like a guy that knows his way around."

I smirk, "This bar?"

She sniggers. "At the risk of sounding cheesy, do you come here often?"

"You wouldn't believe how many times I've come here."

She arches a flirty brow. "I like you," she states with confidence, "and I'm drunk, trying to get over a broken heart."

"He can't help you there," says Raff, grinning, "He breaks hearts, not mends them."

It doesn't deter her. Instead, she slides in beside me. "I'm going to be upfront. I want no strings, wild sex. And I want it with you."

I can feel my resolve melting. She looks too much like Bella. *Bella*. I shake my head. "As fun as that sounds, I'm out with the guys tonight. If I leave them, to fuck you, they'll just give me shit."

She arches a perfectly plucked brow. "Are you being serious?"

I nod. "I'm afraid so." She huffs and gets up, leaving and moving on to another guy.

"Wow, you're serious about getting Bella to forgive you," says JP and I think I see a hint of pride in his eyes.

"Bullshit. There's no way he can go without sex for the amount of time it will take Bella to forgive him," says Raff. "We're talking months, if not years."

I grin, "You think she'll forgive me?"

"I didn't say that," he replies.

"You do," I say, nudging him playfully. "You think I'll win her round."

He narrows his eyes. "Only because I know you won't give up. You'll wear her down and she's too nice to keep up the hatred."

CHAPTER TWENTY-ONE

Bella

I'm relieved when Cal suggests we spend Sunday at home chilling and watching movies. It's hard to get him to sit still and relax most of the time, but it's exactly what we need.

"How was your date?"

He groans dramatically, "God awful." I laugh because I expected that exact reaction. He never has any luck. "She practically licked her soup bowl like she hadn't eaten in forever, you don't eat like that in posh restaurants. I could feel everyone judging me," he complains, "and she snorts when she laughs. I was trying my hardest not to say anything funny in case I set her off. I can't ever show my face in that place again."

"You're too picky," I say.

Cal rolls his eyes but chooses not to argue because we have had this discussion too many times before. "Shall I come to the doctors with you tomorrow?" he asks, changing the subject and I smile gratefully.

"I would really love that, Cal."

"Any closer to a decision? I noticed you didn't drink last night."

I shake my head. "I've never really thought about kids, it all seems a bit unreal, like a dream. I don't want to be tied to that bastard forever, and keeping this baby would mean just that, but the thought of terminating kills me," I admit.

"There are other options, Bella. Adoption maybe?"

It's not like I haven't used the internet to research. I stay awake well into the night looking it up, but giving a child up destroys my heart even more. I don't want it to feel like I didn't love it, because I do. But the thought of subjecting it to Aiden's rejection lies heavy on my mind. "The pregnancy has come at such a bad time for me. The business is just getting off the ground, and I'm going to be crazy busy if even half of the brides that came to my opening, place an order."

"Is there any right time to have a baby?"

"Yes Cal, when both parents want it," I answer, and he laughs.

"Look, things don't have to change that much. Parents work around their children all the time. You have your own business, so you can take it to work. I can just imagine a mini Bella helping to bake cakes." I picture that scenario and tears spring to my eyes. "Oh, sorry Bells, have I put my foot in it?" he asks, pulling me into a hug.

"No, I just never thought of it like that," I snivel, "Plus my hormones are crazy right now, I literally cry at anything."

We settle down to watch reruns of our favorite biker drama, and I think of different ways in which I can hide this pregnancy from Aiden. *None of which, will end well.*

♡

When I arrive at work on Monday, a florist meets me at the door holding a huge bouquet. "Bella?" she queries, handing me the flowers without waiting for my response. She rushes off and I unlock the shop, going in and placing them on the counter. Once I've dumped my bag and coat, I take the note from them and open it.

I'm never going to give up. Please, forgive me xxx

I throw it straight in the bin. Champagne. Flowers. *So cliché.* But I place the bouquet on the counter. They're too pretty to waste.

‌‌

After a busy few hours, I go to my appointment. Cal's already waiting outside and I'm relieved when I spot him. He grabs my hand, giving it a reassuring squeeze and we head inside.

The doctor takes the pee sample I handed to her and does her own test to confirm the pregnancy. And after sharing my doubts, she talks over various options available to me. She explains everything much better than the internet, and my head feels clearer.

"Until you make a decision," she says, ripping off a prescription, "I want you to take these vitamins. They're vital in the early stages of pregnancy." I take it, and then she adds, "Your first scan will be due around twelve weeks. So I'll refer you to the midwife for around that time. If at any point you make a different decision, just call this office and explain. They'll cancel the appointments for you, and we'll arrange whatever you need. There's no pressure at all, Bella. It's down to you. But because you think you're round ten weeks, I want to put things in place, should you decide to go ahead."

We take a slow walk back to the shop. "What are you thinking?" he asks me.

"That I should keep it."

I feel his eyes on me. "You're serious?"

I turn to him and we come to a stop. "Am I crazy?" I whisper.

"No, not at all." He grins, "Congratulations."

We begin to walk again. "It's not the babies fault it's got a terrible father. And I have enough love to give it for the both of us."

"You're not alone, Bella. You have me and Aria." I notice his smile is still huge. "We can find a bigger place," he adds.

"You still want to share a place?" I ask, wide eyed. I was certain he'd want me to go.

"Of course," he says, grabbing my hand. "I've told you, we're all in this together."

He leaves me at the end of the road to go and meet a client. I walk the rest of the way with a happy heart. It's the first time I've felt like there was light at the end of the tunnel in weeks. It's short lived when I step into the shop to find Aria and Aiden toe-to-toe. I freeze, taking it all in as

Aria shoves him hard in his chest. He doesn't budge but it doesn't deter her from doing it again. "Just leave. She hates you." She spots me and rushes over, "I'm so sorry, I tried to get rid of him."

Aiden turns, his eyes are still full of sadness. I give Aria a reassuring smile. "It's fine. I'll speak to him." I didn't tell anyone about how he cornered me in the bathroom at the weekend. But since then, I've felt more able to handle him, like he'd ripped off the band aid by forcing me to face him.

She gives a stiff nod, propping open the door that joins our shops. She gives Aiden a warning glare as she leaves. "She thinks I'm scared of her," he says, looking slightly amused.

I go behind the counter and shrug from my jacket. "What are you doing here?"

"You got my flowers," he notes, nodding at them sitting proudly on the counter. *Damn.* I should have thrown them in the bin.

"Don't send me anymore," I tell him clearly. "I don't want anything from you."

"Aria mentioned you were at a doctor's appointment," he says casually, picking up a catalogue and flicking through.

"So?"

"Are you sick?"

I sigh. "What do you want, Aiden?"

"You weren't drinking on Saturday. You sent the champagne back too." He places the catalogue down and stares at me like he's expecting me to explain myself.

I place my hands on the counter to show I'm not threatened by him being here in my space, and I fix him with a look of contempt, hoping I'm conveying everything I feel about him in my stare. "I don't like you, Aiden. I don't want gifts. I don't want apologies."

"How about dinner?" he suggests, and I want to scream. "No thank you."

"You can choose. No expense spared."

I scoff. "You really think this can be fixed with money."

"Everything has a price," he points out.

I shake my head sadly, heading for the conjoining door. "I paid the price. Now please leave me alone."

I hear the shop door open and close and release a breath. "You okay?" asks Aria, gently rubbing my arm. I watch Aiden get into his car and nod. "How did it go at the Doctors?" she asks, and I give her a big smile.

"I've decided to keep the little bean."

Aria squeals in delight, throwing her arms around me. "I'm so happy for you. And I'll be there every step of the way. I'll be the best aunt."

"Good, because I'll need all the help I can get."

"And Aiden?" she asks, wincing.

I shrug. I haven't decided what to do about him. I hope he'll get bored before I have to tell him. But who knows with him, maybe I'm worrying about nothing, and I'll tell him, and he'll run a mile. We all know he can't commit."

Aiden

I head back to the apartment with a heavy heart. Bella's not falling for all my usual shit, which I expected, but it doesn't give me much hope for winning her over.

My mood doesn't improve when I spot Laurie sitting on my doorstep with a bag at her feet. She looks up as I approach and it's obvious she's been crying. She pushes to her feet, tipping her head for me to kiss her on the cheek. I hesitate, but do it anyway, like an old habit that's hard to kick. "Are you okay?" I ask, unlocking the door.

"No, he's kicked me out," she sniffles, following me into the club.

I stiffen at her words but show no reaction as we head through to the elevator. "Does he know about us?" I ask, punching in the code.

She pulls out a tissue and dabs her eyes. "No. He's in love with someone else." A few more sobs leave her. "She's eighteen," she suddenly wails angrily. "How can I fucking compete with a someone barely legal?"

I sigh as we go into the apartment. "Do you care?"

"Of course I care," she spits.

"Laurie, you've been seeing me for years behind his back. We fucked on your wedding day."

"That doesn't mean he can leave me," she snaps.

I pour her a whiskey, placing it on the kitchen table and she sits down, placing the bag down. "I need a place to stay."

I'm already shaking my head before the sentence is finished. "No."

"You're going to see me out on the streets?" she wails.

"Laurie, he's loaded, ask him for money to get your own place."

"He's blocked all my cards," she cries. "Said he knows I've not been faithful through the marriage so until we've seen lawyers, I can't have a penny."

"He can't do that," I mutter, "I'll put you in touch with a great lawyer."

"You have to let me stay, Aiden," she says quietly.

"No, Laurie, it won't help in your divorce if you're shacked up with your ex. Plus, I don't want to blur the lines between us, not anymore."

"It's too late for that," she spits. "I'm pregnant."

She throws a box on the table, and I grab it. My heart hammers wildly and there's a loud ringing in my ears as I pull out a pregnancy test. "What the fuck is this?" I snap.

"It's yours," she adds. "Before you accuse me of sleeping around."

"Bullshit," I snap, throwing the stick on the table. "You're married."

"And he was too busy fucking his teenage knockoff," she spits bitterly.

I feel around blindly for the chair before lowering into it. "But . . . you don't want it, right?" I almost whisper, terrified of her answer.

"Of course I want it," she snaps.

I stare wide eyed while my heart pumps so fast, I'm dizzy. "You've never wanted kids," I hiss. "In fact, you've always stated that you'd hate to have a kid hanging from you."

"I've changed my mind. Doesn't this mean something to you, Aiden?" she asks, her tone pleading as she stands and makes her way towards me. "We created this child together." She takes my hand and places it on her stomach. There's a definite bump and I panic, pulling my hand free and standing, putting distance between us. *How the fuck didn't I notice her bump?*

"You need to leave," I snap.

"I'm not going anywhere," she hisses, her tone full of venom. "Grow the fuck up, Aiden. It takes two to tango and you were very keen to do the dance. So, we're having this baby and the sooner you accept that the better."

I go into the lounge, perching on the edge of the couch with my head in my hands. *Fuck. Fuck. Fuck.* How have I let this happen? I've been so damn distracted with Bella. The couch dips as Laurie joins me, gently rubbing my back in a soothing manner. I resist the urge to shudder. "You loved me before, Aiden. We can get back to that. I made a huge mistake leaving you before and I know I broke your heart. But this is a sign. We were meant to be together."

A few months ago, before Bella came along, I might have accepted it. After all, I've got to settle down one day and Laurie would be the perfect woman, too distracted getting her lips filled and her hair toned to notice what I was out getting up to. But now, the only person I can imagine spending my life with is Bella. And once she finds out about this, she'll hate me even more. There's no way she'll forgive me now. I stand and her hand falls away. "I need to think," I mutter, heading for the door.

"Aiden, don't run," she calls out with a heavy sigh.

JP and Raff are in my office. Raff drags his feet from my desk and he gets out of my chair. "Sorry, Boss, didn't expect you."

"Clearly," I mutter dryly, grabbing the whiskey decanter and a glass. I half fill it before dropping down in my chair and turning so my back is to them.

JP clears his throat, "Did you go and see Bella?"

"She would have forgiven me," I grit out, taking a large mouthful. "If Laurie hadn't just dropped a bombshell."

"What's happened now?" asks Raff.

"He went to see Bella," JP whispers.

"I came back here, and Laurie was waiting to tell me her husband has kicked her out."

"Probably sick of her whore arse," says Raff. "I don't blame him."

I turn my chair. "She's pregnant."

Raff shrugs, "Doesn't he want kids?"

"Not by him," I say arching a brow.

JP's mouth falls open, "Holy shit."

"No fucking way," snaps Raff. "That baby is not yours."

"She said it is."

"And you're just taking her word for it?" he yells. "Jake would lose his fucking mind if he heard this bullshit."

"Why would she lie?" I ask, "If it wasn't mine, she'd keep quiet and raise it with that prick. He's loaded."

"So are you," JP points out.

"Not like him," I say, finishing my drink and pouring a second. "And now, Bella will never forgive me."

"What are you gonna do?" asks JP.

"What can I do? She's keeping it." I put the drink down and scrub my hands over my face. "I've gotta grow up and take responsibility."

"Just cos she said she's having your kid, doesn't mean you have to marry her and settle down," says Raff.

"I've already lost Bella, I may as well accept my fate. Maybe this is karma for what I did to her," I mutter.

"Are you going to tell her?" JP asks.

I shake my head. "I can't watch the disappointment in her eyes," I admit. "I've already hurt her so much, and I can't make this one better, can I? Laurie will always be in my life now. The kindest thing I can do for Bella, is stay away from her."

Bella

The last couple of weeks have flown by. And as I sit waiting to be called in for my scan, I'm a bundle of nerves. So many things are going through my mind. "What if there is no baby?" I whisper and Cal laughs.

"Why would you think that?" asks Aria, rolling her eyes.

"Tests can be wrong."

"What if there's more than one?" asks Aria, gasping.

I stare wide eyed, terror filling me. "Ignore her," says Cal. "The chances of twins is highly unlikely."

I sit straighter. "Aiden was a twin," I hiss.

Cal shrugs, "Still unlikely. Just relax. And Aria, stop winding her up."

"I need to pee."

"Hold it. It makes the scan clearer," Cal instructs.

"How do you know?" asks Aria. "Been to many scans, have you?"

"He's been reading books about it," I tell her, rolling my eyes. "He's taking uncle duties very seriously."

Aria folds her arms, "You're such a suck up."

"I'm prepared so I can answer Bella's million questions when she wakes me every night with another anxiety attack," he teases, and I narrow my eyes playfully. The truth is, I am terrified. I've been having dreams about Aiden finding out and stealing my baby. Or worse, finding out and demanding he move in with us.

I stand, "I really have to pee," I say, rushing towards the toilet. The door to the scan room opens and I freeze at the sight of Aiden and Laurie. They don't immediately see me, but it's too late for me to back track, I'm within touching distance. They're staring at the scan pictures she's clutching, and they're both smiling.

Laurie sees me first and it must feel like all her Christmases' have come at once as her grin gets bigger. "Bella, what are you doing here?"

Aiden's head shoots up and he immediately pulls an arm from Laurie's shoulders. It's like time is stood still, and for a few seconds, we're just locked in each other's pain. His eyes then travel down to my stomach with his brows pulled together in confusion.

Laurie clears her throat around the same time I feel an arm slip around my shoulders and Cal appears. I glance at him, unable to find the words, and he gives me a reassuring smile, before looking at the pair. "Are congratulations in order?" he asks, his voice friendly.

Laurie places her hand on her small bump and I'm instantly jealous. I'm not showing at all, even though I've stood in front of the mirror each night to check. "Sixteen weeks." She slips her hand in Aiden's, bringing him out of his shock. "We were really hoping to find out the sex today, but this little one is as stubborn as his father." She laughs and the sound irritates me. "I say *he* because I know that's what Aiden is hoping for, but secretly I want a girl."

"Congratulations," says Cal. "This is our first scan but we're super excited." He gives my shoulder a squeeze and I force a weak smile. This isn't how I wanted my first scan to go. And out of all the questions I currently want to ask him, my top one is why he hasn't been to see me at all these last two weeks. He said he wasn't giving up, and yet here he is, with Laurie. And they've created a life together.

"Bella?" Aiden mutters, and I'm not sure if he's questioning Cal's statement or if deep down he knows I'm carrying his baby. Either way, we're interrupted when my name is called, and we all turn to the nurse.

"Me," I whisper, "That's me." And I rush into the room.

The sonographer is already waiting, and he instructs me to get on the bed. Aria and Cal look as shocked as me, but we can't discuss any of it now as they each take a seat beside the bed.

Cold gel is squirted onto my stomach and the wand is pressed there, causing me to wince because I'm desperate for that pee. "Do you know roughly how far along you are?" he asks.

"Twelve weeks and two days," I say firmly.

"Yes, I'd say thirteen weeks," he corrects.

I narrow my eyes, "I am twelve weeks and two days," I repeat.

He eyes me warily and Cal gently pats my hand. "She's just had a shock," he explains.

The sonographer gives a stiff nod before peering closer at the screen. "I think you're right," he adds. *Twelve weeks and two days since Aiden Tremos broke my heart.*

We leave the hospital, and Aria is the first to address the elephant in the room. "I can't believe it," she says, "He's having a baby . . . with that witch."

I shrug, "She always did hold something over him. I guess it was only a matter of time." I turn to Cal, "Thanks for rescuing me back there. I felt like all my words were getting stuck in my throat."

Cal grabs my hand, giving it a little squeeze. "You're better off without him Bells, let him shack up with that bitch. Your baby will be surrounded by love."

"How come he hasn't ran from her?" I whisper, tears stinging my eyes.

Aria throws her arms around me. "You did right by not telling him, Bella. If you had of done, you'd have her as part of your life too."

Aiden

The second I get back after dropping Laurie at her mother's, I grab JP and shove him up against the wall. "Did you know?" I yell.

Raff pulls me off, "What the fuck is going on?"

"Bella is pregnant by the fucking gym guru," I snap.

"I didn't know, Aiden, I swear," says JP.

"Shit man, that's tough," adds Raff.

I hate the thought of her being with him. I groan out loud. "Fuck."

"It was gonna happen eventually," Raff says gently. "She wasn't going to stay single forever."

"I just wasn't . . . prepared," I mutter.

"As long as she's happy," says JP.

I nod, even though my heart is aching and all I want to do is see her. "You're having your own kid," says Raff. "It's done. You've both moved on."

Before I can talk myself out of it, I grab the keys to the Audi and head to Bella's shop. I park across the street, and watch her inside, chatting on the phone. There are no customers, so once she hangs up the call, I head inside.

She doesn't look up when I enter, she's busy looking at something on her iPad.

"I'll be with you in just a sec," she says slowly, trying to concentrate on whatever she's looking at.

When I approach the counter, she finally looks up, the smile on her face fading when she sees it's me. I remember a time when she would smile as soon as I entered the room.

"Aiden, what are you doing here?"

"Seems we're both full of surprises," I mutter, fighting the urge to touch her.

"I don't think this is a good idea," she mutters.

"Why didn't you tell me you were with Cal?" I have no right to sound upset, but I can't hide it.

She narrows her eyes, "You failed to mention you and Laurie were expecting," she snaps. "I thought she was married?"

I shrug, sighing heavily. "He left her. Long story."

"Sixteen weeks," she mutters, "Around the same time you were trying to con me."

"I wish I could go back in time, Bella. I would change it all in a heartbeat. I was so wrapped up in Jake's death and getting the club signed over . . ." I trail off. "Sorry, you don't wanna hear all this shit again."

"Are you happy?" she whispers.

I could tell her I am and make this easier. I could walk out of here and never look back, but I owe her some honesty, so I shake my head. "No. I don't want a baby, especially not with Laurie," I add an unamused laugh. "But here we are."

"You loved her once, maybe in time . . ."

"Funny, she said the exact same thing. But honestly, I don't think I ever loved her really. I didn't know what true love was, not until . . ." I trail off.

Bella shifts uncomfortably. "Jake went to an awful lot of trouble to get you away from her. But now a baby is involved, I think he'd tell you to do the right thing by Laurie."

I nod, "I am. But you didn't ask me that, Bella, you asked if I was happy."

The shop phone rings and she looks back, "I need to-"

"Sure," I say and she disappears into the back. I wait a second until I hear her speak, before taking her mobile phone off the side. I unlock it using the code she had on her old mobile, smirking when it works. I enter my phone number, then call my phone so I have her number again.

Bella returns a minute later. I'm browsing through her designs on one of the iPads. "These are great," I tell her.

"Well, you know where to come when you pop the question." She winces.

I laugh, "Can you honestly see me getting married?"

"I didn't see you having kids," she mutters.

"Good point. I never asked you," I say, moving closer to her. She steps back. "Are you happy?" Without hesitation, she nods. My heart crushes. "I'm glad," I tell her, feeling like the words are choking me. "Take care, Bella." And I force myself to leave.

Bella

The second the shop door closes, I burst into tears. Hot, fat tears that drip onto the counter. I miss him. *And I hate that*. I watch as Aiden gets into his car. He grips the steering wheel, staring straight ahead, and then suddenly he slams his hands against it over and over. It only makes my tears fall harder. He starts the engine and pulls away at speed, his tyres screeching in protest.

Aiden said himself that he doesn't want a baby. I was right, he wouldn't have been happy if I had of told him and that would have hurt me all over again. I don't want him to be with me because he feels forced to do the right thing, what kind of relationship would that be? I'm glad he doesn't know, and I intend to keep it to myself because he doesn't deserve to be a part of our lives.

I grab my coat and bag. There's no way I can concentrate on work now, even though I'd planned to work late into the evening. It was clear that was our last goodbye. We've both moved on. And even though I hate him with all my heart, it still hurts.

I grab some Chinese food on my way home, it's all I want to eat lately but after my little crying episode, I'm not sure I can even manage this. I get home and head for the kitchen. I plate up the food and pull out my mobile, surprised when I see a text from Aiden. I frown as I open it. He doesn't have this number, or at least, that's what I thought.

> **Aiden:** I'm sorry. I know I keep saying it, and it's just words. But I really am so sorry. I keep messing my life up, Bella, but my one and only regret, is losing you. If you ever need me, I'll always be here for you. Love Aiden xx

I take a deep breath and delete the message. "That's it now," I whisper to myself. "Let him go."

CHAPTER TWENTY-TWO

Aiden

It's been a couple of weeks since I said goodbye to Bella. And me and Laurie have fallen into a comfortable routine. She does all the things I hate, like cooking, cleaning and shopping, and I go to the club and lose myself in promotions and other stuff that keeps me away from the house as much as possible. But today, I can't avoid the twenty-week scan.

Laurie places her hand on my knee, as I drive us towards the hospital. "Are you a little excited?" she asks.

I can't deny I want to know the baby's sex. At this point, I don't even mind if we're having a boy or a girl. It's taken me a while to get used to the idea, but saying goodbye to Bella gave me some sort of closure. I can finally look to my future. "Actually," I tell her, as we pull into the hospital car park, "I am."

She smiles wide. I know she's been waiting for me to show some interest in this pregnancy. It hasn't been easy for her to watch me try and get over Bella. "I know you want a boy, but will you be totally disappointed if it's a girl?"

I smile, shaking my head. "Not at all, she'll be my princess."

I get out, rounding the car and helping her out too. Since her bumps gotten bigger, she's

making sure not to overdo anything, including opening doors for herself. I smirk as she huffs like she's the size of a whale, when in fact, she's got a neat little bump and hasn't put weight on anywhere else. Laurie kisses me on the lips. "I love you," she whispers.

I take her hand and lead her towards the entrance. She's been trying to get me to say it back to her for weeks now, but I won't, I made that mistake with her years ago and she almost broke me.

As we approach the entrance, Laurie pulls back slightly. "Shit," she mutters.

I stop and turn to look at her, amusement in my eyes. "What are you doing?"

"Marcus is here," she explains, and I scan the carpark until my eyes land on Marcus Collins, Laurie's husband. He's standing casually by the entrance with his hands in his pockets and his grey hair shining in the sun, waiting for us to approach.

"He's clearly wanting to speak to you," I say, pulling her towards him, "How did he know we'd be here?"

"I take it you didn't think I'd show?" he asks, keeping his eyes fixed to Laurie who's staring at the ground. "Only, you didn't tell the hospital you weren't staying with me anymore and so they sent your confirmation letter."

"Marcus, now is not the time," she mutters.

"I wasn't going to miss the babies scan just because we're not together," he says firmly.

"What's going on?" I ask.

Laurie glances my way, her face is full of guilt, I know because I've seen that look on her, right before she told me she was leaving me for him.

Marcus sniggers, "Don't tell me she's taken you for a mug again, Aiden."

"Laurie?" I demand. "What's he talking about?" Even though I've already guessed.

"I should have known she'd turn to you once I kicked her cheating backside out," he sneers. "Did she tell you the baby is yours too?"

Laurie begins to cry, and I snatch my hand away in anger. "I had nowhere to go, if you knew the truth you wouldn't have let me stay."

Marcus is laughing hard, and I resist the urge to punch him. "You really are a piece of work, Laurie."

I grab her upper arm, shaking her, "Is he telling the truth?" I yell angrily.

"I don't know who's it is," she cries.

"Bullshit," says Marcus, "We've been trying for a kid for years," he adds. "Did you have unprotected sex with her?"

My world is spinning... again. She's lied to me... again. I release her and take a few steps back. "You fucking bitch," I mutter.

"Please, Aiden. Don't do this, we can be happy."

"Stay the hell away from me."

"But what if it is yours?" she cries.

If there's a small chance, I'm not gonna risk not knowing. "Let me know when the kid is born, I'll have a DNA test." I march back to the car, leaving Laurie screaming at Marcus.

I can't breathe. My chest feels tight and as I grip the steering wheel, I try and slow it down. I didn't even want the kid so why am I letting it affect me? *Because,* I think bitterly, *I've spent the last few months trying my best to be the person my child deserves.* Fuck. Weeks of listening to Laurie go on about baby names and which equipment was best. I even had to look at her birthing plan. Who knew that was a thing. I groan, resting my head on my arms. Maybe this is all part of my punishment for hurting Bella the way I did.

I make my way to a bar that's not too far from Tremos. It's the type that older men use for a quiet pint, and that's exactly what I need right now so I can gather my thoughts and clear my head.

I open a tab and ask the barman to keep them coming. Then I find a quiet spot in the corner and relax.

It's almost six in the evening when I settle my bar tab. My vision is blurred, and fuck knows how I'm managing to stay on my feet as I push through the office workers all making their way home after a busy day. It's not until I'm standing outside Bella's shop, that I realise this wasn't a conscious decision and I've drank way too much. I rest my head against the cool glass, watching as Bella and Aria dance around. They're laughing and the sound warms my heart. I squint, noticing the tiny bump as Bella runs her hand over it. She looks good. Glowing even.

Bella

I spin away from Aria and come face to face with Aiden. His forehead is pressed up against the window and his eyes are fixed on me. I gasp and Aria also turns to see what's made me stop. "What the fuck," she hisses, ripping the door open and marching out to where he is. "What are you doing here?" she demands. His eyes don't leave me and I find myself moving towards him. The second I'm close enough, I can smell the alcohol. "Aiden," I say gently, touching his arm, "Are you okay?" He shakes his head sadly.

"I'll call JP," mutters Aria, going back inside.

His hand his hanging limply by his side and I carefully take it, noticing there's dry blood on his knuckles. "What happened?" I ask.

"A wall," he slurs, shrugging.

He looks so defeated and distant, I'm worried. So I lead him inside and sit him on one of the couches. I grab a bottle of water from out back and an ice pack, which I lay on his knuckles. "Did the wall come off worse?" I tease. He doesn't respond so I sit beside him. "Do you want to talk about it?"

His eyes train on my bump and before I can stop him, he places his free hand over it. I gasp, surprised by the emotion his touch brings out in me. "I ruined it all," he whispers. "Why am I such a fuck up?"

I carefully remove his hand and put the bottle of water in it instead. "Where's Laurie?"

He smirks, shaking his head angrily. "Fuck Laurie."

"Aiden, you can't just show up here when you fall out with her," I say, sadly. I can't be his go to.

"She lied to me," he mutters. "Again."

"She didn't go back to her husband?" I ask, because surely she wouldn't do that to him now she's carrying his child.

"The baby isn't mine," he spits. "She used me for a place to stay."

I take a moment to process his words. The fact she lied, just like I'm lying, doesn't sit well with me. Aria appears in the doorway, "JP should be here any second."

Aiden puts the water down and grips my hands in his. "I miss you so much, Bella, it's tearing me apart. Jake was right all along. I needed you and I didn't see it in time," he slurs, "Let me show you. Give me another chance to prove I can change."

I pull my hands free and stand up. "Aiden, you're drunk, sleep it off."

Aiden stands too, grabbing my wrist and pulling me to him. I don't have time to protest before his hands are in my hair and he's got his nose pressed gently to mine. "Bella please, I just need one chance," he begs, and then he kisses me. It's not his usual demanding kiss, but soft and unsure. I don't stop him. It's like the rest of the world melts away and it's just me and him.

Aria clears her throat, bringing me to my senses and I pull away, turning my back on him. "Sorry, but JP is here," she announces.

I head out back, leaving JP to struggle with Aiden. I can't stop thinking about him and how good it felt to be in his arms again. Aria comes in, "Well, that was . . . unexpected."

"Unwanted," I correct.

She arches her brows, "Really? Because you looked pretty lost back there in that kiss."

I groan, burying my face in my hands. "Am I doing the right thing, Aria?" I ask. "Laurie lied to him and look at the state he's in. If he finds out I'm doing the same," I choke on a sob.

Aria grabs a tissue and hands it to me. "No one can tell you what's right or wrong, Bella. Do what you feel is the right thing for you and your baby."

"That's all I'm trying to do," I whisper.

She gently rubs a stray tear from my cheek. "Then what are you so upset about?"

Aiden

My head is on a cool surface, my mouth is dry. I force my eyes open and look around. I'm on a bathroom floor. I recognise the black tiles and quickly sit up, realizing that I'm on the floor in the men's bathroom of my club. My head spins from the sudden movement and I dive to the toilet, hauling myself over it and emptying the contents of my stomach.

When I eventually find the strength to stand, I cling to the wash basin and look in the mirror. It's not a pretty sight. My hair sticks up in all directions and I'm pale with dark circles under my eyes. I splash my face with cold water. I feel so disgusted with myself. Why did I get that drunk? I didn't even want a baby with Laurie, I should have felt relief. But a small part of me was warming to the idea of becoming a dad. A baby was a reason to stop all of this and be someone that Jake would have been proud of.

I head out of the bathroom and into the main bar area where I find JP looking just as rough, with his head in his hands. There's a steaming cup of coffee in front of him and in the booth behind him, lay three sleeping girls. My brain is assaulted with last night's memories, they're sketchy at best, but there were definitely three girls. *Shit*. "Tell me I dreamt last night."

"Nightmare more like," he mutters. "Aria will never fucking speak to me again when she finds out."

"Just don't tell her," I suggest, stealing his coffee and taking a slurp. I close my eyes, letting the caffeine cure me.

"Lying just gets you into bigger trouble," he says, raising a judgmental eyebrow in my direction. "Besides, the one just there," he says, pointing to a leggy blond, "sometimes hangs out with Aria and Bella."

"Shit, did we know that information last night?"

"Yep, you said, and I quote, *'No bitch owns this cock so get sucking,'* You were pretty pissed off with the world last night."

I groan and drop my head to the table. "We haven't pulled this sort of shit since Jake was around," I mutter.

"Yeah, he was the ringleader when it came to orgies."

We share a laugh. "Seriously," I say, sitting up again, "You and Aria aren't together. You haven't done anything wrong."

"She won't see it like that. I'm meant to be proving I can act my age," he says, "That I'm ready for a relationship."

"Well last night proves you aren't," I joke.

"You don't get it, Aiden. She's it for me. And I don't expect you to understand, but I can't imagine my life with anyone else but her."

I want to tell him I fully get it, because I feel the exact same about Bella. But he'd tell me it isn't the same, that it's my guilt talking. So I force my best playboy smile as the women begin to stir. "Ladies, follow me up to my apartment and I'll get you some breakfast." And I lead them away like lambs to the slaughter. If I can save JP's skin by shutting this bitch up, at least one of us will get a shot at happiness. "Leave it to me, JP. I'll sort it."

CHAPTER TWENTY-THREE

Bella

Cal is very strict on my diet since getting pregnant He ensures I eat three healthy meals per day, and he's worked out a fitness plan for me. So, as we take a brisk walk around the park during my lunch hour, I decide to tell him about last night. He isn't Aiden's biggest fan, but he'll always tell me what he thinks honestly.

"So, Aiden stopped by the shop last night. He was really drunk, and Aria had to get JP to pick him up." Cal stops, I keep going before I realise that he isn't at side of me. I turn to face him. "What?" I ask.

"Just odd that you didn't mention it before now," he says.

"You had your breakfast date with Ellie this morning, I didn't want to ruin your mood by talking about Aiden, again." It was his third date to be precise and I didn't want to give him any reason to cancel. I grab his hand and tug him to begin walking again. "It's not a big deal."

"What did he want?"

"He was upset. Laurie lied about the baby being his and he found out."

"Ouch, why would she do that?"

"She needed a place to stay apparently."

"Let me guess, now you feel bad for him because you're lying too?" he guesses.

"You didn't see the state he was in, Cal. He was gutted."

"Don't tell him to make him feel better. Tell him because you think he will be a good dad to your baby."

"I'm not talking abut getting back together," I say.

"Bella, I wouldn't judge you even if you did. I just want what's best for you and the baby."

"He wanted that baby," I tell him. "Aria said he'd really settled down and stopped partying and sleeping around. Maybe he'll want this baby too. I should at least give him one chance, right?"

Cal gives me a tight smile. "He'd be stupid not to want it. Just know I'll always be here for you, no matter what happens."

Aiden

I feed the women once they've showered, and I'm relieved to find Gemma, Aria's friend, has a boyfriend. Who she has rushed off to see in the hope he doesn't discover she was in a three way with me and JP. *Which means she won't be announcing it to Aria anytime soon.* Kaylee and Becky remain. "Any plans today?" I ask.

They exchange a smirk, "Nope, we're both free all day. You?"

I grin, suggestively. "Free as a bird," I tell them. Now I've successfully upset both the women in my life, I have no reason not to go back to how I used to be.

Becky pulls me closer until her lips crash against mine and we tangle our tongues in a deep, hungry kiss. I feel Kaylee approach, watching us for a minute before tugging my head in her direction. She kisses me with the same desperation her friend did.

Becky reaches for the button on my jeans, popping it and pulling out my cock. I sit Kaylee on the counter, pulling the front of her dress down and groping her breasts. She lies back, spreading her legs and guiding my hand there.

Becky lowers to her knees, taking my cock in her mouth. Her hand grips me tightly at the base and I close my eyes in pleasure as she gags.

I focus on the way Kaylee is writhing around on the worktop with my fingers pushed into her wet cunt. I remove them, stuffing them in her mouth while her friend sheathes my cock in a condom. I waste no time burying myself in Kaylee. The women kiss, caressing one another and I marvel at how stupid I've been, wanting to give all this up. This is where I belong. This is my life.

Bella

I take a calming breath before pushing the doors open to Tremos and heading into the bar. JP looks up and smiles wide the second he sees me. "Bella, you're looking great," he says, rounding the bar and kissing me on the cheek.

I force a smile, because I'm still not quite over his part in the entire thing. "I need to speak to Aiden," I say.

"Erm, he was in his apartment but let me just call him."

I roll my eyes, and he pulls out his mobile. After a few seconds he shakes his head, "No answer."

"I could just pop up; it'll only take a second."

The phone in the office rings, "Let me go up first. I just have to grab that call," and he rushes into the office.

I head for the elevator. I'm sure Aiden won't mind me going straight up after what I've got to tell him. I lightly tap on the door, and it opens, like he forgot to close it properly. I wait a few seconds, but he doesn't answer so I push it some more and step inside. "Hello?" I whisper, wondering if he's in bed after his drinking session. I'm certain he'll be hungover.

I freeze at the sound of moaning, unsure if I should turn back and pretend I was never here. I wince, JP's already seen me so that won't work. The moaning comes again. Maybe he's sick. As I go into the kitchen, I'm unprepared for the scene that greets me. Aiden's back is to me as he thrusts into a woman that's bent over the table. Her face is buried between the legs of another woman who suddenly arches off the counter as she orgasms. As her eyes open, she sees my shocked face and freezes. Aiden glances back to see why she looks concerned, and his smile falters. He stops mid thrust but the woman he's fucking doesn't know what the hell's going on, and she starts wriggling to encourage him.

I inhale sharply, "Jesus, Aiden, don't just stop, you'll ruin her entire day." And I turn on my heel and march out.

I hear him call my name, but I don't wait, relieved when the elevator closes before he can get to me. My heart slams hard in my chest and my breathing is heavy as I slump against the wall. It's not the first time I've seen Aiden with another woman, and the second I heard those breathy moans, I knew deep down that's what it was. But I had to see it for myself, to prove that I'm right and Aiden Tremos is not ready to have a baby. I imagine him introducing our child to a different woman every weekend and shudder with repulsion. It's not going to happen.

JP is talking into his mobile when the elevator opens, and he quickly disconnects when he sees me. "Was he there?" he asks, pretending he has no idea what I've just seen. "Don't rush off, lets catch up," he adds.

"Relax JP, it's not a big deal. I was just checking he was okay after last night, and he is. Tell him there's no need to run after me, he can continue his . . . afternoon."

I step outside and breathe in the fresh air. The sun is beaming, and it instantly cheers me up, who was I kidding thinking this would ever be a good idea. I scoff to myself and head in the direction of my shop.

Minutes later I hear footsteps running up behind me, and then Aiden grabs my arm and halts me. I turn to him, forcing a smile, "Didn't JP pass on the message?" I ask innocently.

"Let's not pretend you're fine about what you just witnessed," he mutters, not quite meeting my eye. "I'm sorry."

"It's fine, Aiden, really. What you do in your private time has nothing to do with me. I was simply checking you were okay after last night."

"I'm sorry about that too," he says, adding a cold, empty laugh, "I'm always apologising just lately."

"It's fine-"

"Stop saying it's fine," he snaps and a passing couple glance our way. Aiden winces, "It's not okay," he adds. "I shouldn't have showed up like that, especially not in that state. I didn't even plan to come to you . . . it's just sometimes, you calm the noise in my head." I remain silent and he shifts uncomfortably. "What you just saw," he says, "I haven't done that for so long."

I shrug, "Whatever, Aiden. It's your business."

"I didn't want you to think I'd gone back to my old ways."

I almost smile, "The evidence was pretty damming," I whisper.

"It was a blow out," he says, "After hearing all that shit yesterday, I needed to take my mind off it." He groans, running his fingers through his already messy hair. "Fuck, I don't even know why I'm so cut up. I didn't even want the fucking kid," he grits out. "Imagine me with a baby?" And he laughs again. "I hate kids."

I swallow the lump in my throat. "I'm glad you're feeling better," I mutter. "Take care."

Aiden

JP looks up when I enter the bar. "Did you catch her?"

"Why the fuck did you let her up, JP?" I snap.

"I didn't, she slipped past when I was on a call. I tried to warn you, but you didn't pick up."

"I sorted your problem by the way," I tell him, my voice full of sarcasm. "You're welcome."

"Don't be mad at me cos Bella caught you. It makes no difference anyway, she's with Cal."

"I'm just so tired of letting her down," I admit, sitting on a stool. JP pours me a whiskey, but I push it away, that's the last thing I need. "I can't seem to stop fucking it up. She always catches me at my worst. Her eyes are always full of sadness or disappointment. I hate it."

"Maybe you should sit her down and talk properly," JP suggests.

"I've tried that."

"No, you haven't. You keep turning up unexpected and uninvited. You pin her in the bathroom, go to her shop. Just ask her to meet so you can talk."

I think over his words. He's right. I haven't sat her down and explained everything. "You and Jake were tight. Tell her about him. Explain why you thought it was important to go through with the stupid game."

"What will it achieve?" I ask, shrugging.

"Maybe you can forgive yourself, and maybe she'll forgive you. Then you can both move forward."

I send her a text.

> **Me: I'm aware I'm a massive twat. But please can we meet for dinner so we can talk? Five in our Italian?**

Bella

"Are you going to meet him?" asks Aria as I wipe down the countertop.

"No way. Why would I?"

"So you can clear the air and tell him everything."

I check my watch, it's almost six already but I have no intention of turning up to meet Aiden. What could he possibly say that I haven't already heard? "I told you, I'm not telling him about the baby. This is for the best, Aria."

"What if you telling him makes the difference in his life and he does change."

I stare wide eyed, "Why are you suddenly his biggest fan?"

"I'm not," she says, "I just don't think he'll give up until you've heard him out."

At exactly Six, Aiden walks into the shop. "I knew you wouldn't come," he states.

"Take a hint," I mutter.

"I wanted a chance to talk properly. Not like this where I have to force it on you," he says sadly and for a second, I feel bad.

"There's nothing left to say."

"I want to explain about Jake and how what he did was like normal practise for us," he says.

I sigh and lower onto the couch. He sits beside me. "We were always playing games. Dares, challenges, right from when we were little kids. It drove my mum mad. JP and Raff were just as bad and it became a thing we did. Stupid shit like kissing girls in the middle of class or seeing how far we could push the teacher to breaking point. Childish really," he says trailing off. "I think that's how we all became so confident, getting up in the middle of an English lesson and kissing a girl takes some balls," he smiles at the memory. "Anyway, as we got older it became bigger. Challenges that we set daily like having a threesome with complete strangers or stealing the most expensive car we could find. They'd be either crazy or dangerous, but none of us ever backed down. When I saw Jakes final challenge, I didn't give it much thought. If anything, it just felt like a mild inconvenience for me. You never entered my mind," he admits. "You weren't a real person to me, Bella, just someone Jake named on a piece of paper. And I thought it would be easy. But you turned out to be so much more than a name on a piece of paper." He releases a shaky breath, "You made me feel alive. And I didn't see it back then, but since you left, I've been struggling. Last night was the first time I felt like the old me in such a long time, that I just went with it. But actually, I've realised I don't much like that version of myself. In fact, I despise him. And now in the evenings, instead of craving random women and drunken sex, I miss watching your shit films and snuggling under the blanket." I swipe the tears that are rolling down my cheeks. "I never meant to hurt you, Bella. And I don't mean to keep hurting you. And Jake never meant to hurt you either, he liked you and he just thought he could take the two people he liked the most and put them together so they could live happily ever after. He just forgot what a fuck up I am."

"I appreciate you talking to me," I whisper.

"I'm going to try and be better, Bella. I'm going to prove I can be a nice guy that doesn't mess everything up. And I know you're with Cal, and I know you're happy. But I hope in time, you'll forgive me enough to keep me in your life as a friend." I give a slight nod, and he smiles wide, "Thank you, that means so much."

I feel lighter inside, like a huge weight has been lifted. This feels right, forgiving Aiden and starting over again as friends. For the first time in a while I smile a genuine smile.

CHAPTER TWENTY-FOUR

Bella

Cal squeezes my hand as the doctor puts the cold gel on my stomach. "Twenty weeks already," he whispers excitedly.

"It's gone so fast," I agree.

"Everything feeling normal?" the doctor asks. I nod. "No pains, cramping? And you've felt movements."

I shrug, "I've had some back pain. I think I've had some movement, but I don't really know, it's my first pregnancy."

He smiles, pressing the wand to my stomach. "Okay, let's see what's going on in there."

"Can we find out the sex today?" asks Cal.

"If I can see it, I'll tell you," the doctor replies, "Although sometimes we can't always guarantee."

He spends some time moving the wand, pushing it hard into my stomach and then glancing at my notes. "Describe the movements you felt," he says.

"Erm, just light fluttering's. I told the midwife, and she said it was fine as long as I wasn't bleeding or anything."

"I'm going to ask my colleague to come and take a look," he says, standing.

I immediately panic, squeezing Cal's hand, "Is everything okay?"

"I'll be right back," he says, leaving the room.

"Maybe you aren't as far gone as they first thought?" Cal suggests, "Don't panic, it's probably something and nothing."

He returns minutes later with another doctor. He turns the monitor towards him and away from me, studying the screen hard. I hold my breath, waiting for him to confirm my fears.

"Is it okay if I have a go on the scan, Miss May? We're just having a little trouble locating your baby's heartbeat, sometimes this does happen, it may be nothing to worry about," he says with a smile.

He presses hard, but I don't mind this time, I want to hear the heartbeat desperately. My eyes don't move from the doctors face, but he gives nothing away with his stony expression.

After a few agonising minutes, he puts the scanner down and gives me some tissue to wipe my stomach. We all remain silent whilst I clean myself up.

I push to sit, "You didn't find it, did you?" I ask quietly, and he shakes his head. My heart shatters.

"I am so sorry, Miss May. We can't locate your baby's heartbeat. Your measurements show that the fetus is fifteen weeks, but I'm afraid you have miscarried," he says, "We need to discuss the next steps so can I ask you to stay here whilst I speak to my colleague, and we'll be back shortly."

They leave and Cal pulls me into his arms, but I feel numb, the words from the doctor running through my mind. Maybe they've got it wrong. He didn't even look old enough to know anything about medicine.

A nurse returns to get us, leading us to an office where the doctor is waiting. We sit down and he gives me his condolences again before adding, "So, moving forward." At my scowl, he shifts uncomfortably. "Because your body is showing no signs of expelling the fetus, we will need to perform a procedure called a dilation and curettage. It's a surgical procedure and basically it just means that we will remove the contents of your uterus." He says it so matter of fact that I don't quite take in what he's talking about. A nurse who's been standing at the back of the room moves forward and crouches down in front of me.

"I know this is really hard for you, taking all of this in now when you have just had the worst news ever. But what Doctor Veale is trying to say is that if we don't do this procedure now, then you're prone to serious infection. Your baby has already been in there for some time, and we can't risk waiting." I smile sadly, liking that she at least referred to it as my baby.

"When?" Cal asks.

"We can rush her down today, within the hours," she confirms, and I inhale sharply. I came in here with a baby, and I'll be leaving without one. I give a slight nod and she smiles, gently rubbing my hand.

The doctor continues, going over the procedure and informs me of all the risks. I sign the papers without really taking in anything he has said. I'm on auto pilot.

The nurse then takes me to the surgical ward, where I'm given a sedative to relax my cervix. Cal sits by my bed, his head in his hands. "You can go, Cal. You don't want to be here for all this," I say with a sigh.

He glances up, "How could you ever think I'd leave you to face this alone?" he asks, "You're my best friend, I'm not going anywhere."

I smile gratefully. "Thank you."

"Do you want me to ring anyone, Aria or maybe Aiden?" he asks.

"No, I'll tell them once this is done and I'm back home." I let my head fall back, "I hate that I didn't tell Aiden," I admit. "I feel bad."

"At least he doesn't have to go through this heartache," he says sadly, "You've saved him a lot of pain."

Aiden

"JP, have you spoken to Aria? I'm just outside the shop now and both shops are closed. I can't get hold of Bella," I say into my mobile.

"No boss, not spoke to her all week. Do you want me to call her?"

"No don't worry, I'll go to Bella's."

Since Bella heard me out over a week ago, I've been sending her the odd text to see how she is. But yesterday she had her scan, and when I asked how it went, she didn't reply. I haven't been able to shift the bad feeling in the pit of my stomach all day. Which is why I'm here, to see for myself. But seeing both bakeries closed, has only worried me more, so I head to Cal's.

When he opens the door, he doesn't look pleased to see me. I don't blame him. He's got every right to hate me. "Come in," he says, before I even explain why I'm here.

He leads me through the apartment and lightly taps on a door before entering. Bella is sat up in bed watching television. She looks terrible. Her skin is pale, and her eyes are red and puffy.

"Bella, you have a visitor," says Cal gently and she startles like she didn't know we were even here.

Her eyes fall on me, and they fill with tears. "What's happened?" I ask, moving past Cal and entering the room.

She doesn't speak, and I look back at Cal whose eyes are tearful too. "I need to go to the pharmacy to collect her prescription. Can you stay with her until I get back?" he asks, and I nod.

Once he's left, I turn back to Bella. She's quietly sobbing into her hands. I sit on the bed opposite her and gently pull her hands away from her face. "Bells, what's going on?"

"The baby's gone." Her voice is barely a whisper.

I pull her to me, holding her against my chest and feeling every ounce of pain as she sobs. "Oh, Bells, I'm so fucking sorry."

After a few minutes I shift us back around so that my back is to her headboard and I wrap an arm around her, holding her into my side.

"You're still watching these shit films," I tease, noting that she's watching her favourite romance again.

She wipes her nose on a crumpled tissue. "It's my favourite," she whispers.

"Are you in any pain?" I ask, hating that thought.

I hear the front door and move away from her. She looks confused but I don't want to disrespect the guy in his own place. "I don't think Cal will be too happy," I say as a way of explanation.

Cal comes in with a glass of water and some tablets. He kisses her lightly on the head and hands her the pills. "Take these, baby girl. They'll help you sleep," he whispers gently, and I watch as he strokes her hair.

"If you need anything, just let me know," I say, backing out the door.

Cal follows me out, "Thanks for coming to see her," he says tightly, and I know that this must be awkward for him.

"Like I said, if she needs anything just let me know."

Bella

The days are a blur. Cal gives me all manner of pills and I've lost track of what I'm taking and why. It's a good job he's here to look after me. Him and Aria take it in turns to be with me, even though I've told them to stop fussing. I'm fine. Aria is running both shops, she mentioned that JP and Raff have been around helping, which made me laugh because they're far to big and clumsy to work with delicate cupcakes.

I throw the television remote to the end of my bed and lay my head back onto the soft pillows. I can't stand all this resting. It's driving me crazy. Plus, I'm feeling much better and more like myself.

I decide to shoot a text to Aria and try my luck.

> **Me: I need a night out, what do you think?**
>
> *Aiden: Not a chance.*
>
> *Aria: Sorry, he was looking over my shoulder. I have all three of them under my feet today. But yes, if you're feeling up to it. Friday? x*

Aiden

Friday night soon comes around and the club is heaving. All the promotion works I've been doing seem to be paying off. I've swore off the drink since Bella caught me that day in the kitchen, and it's helping me keep a clear head.

Especially on night like this when I need to network and meet new potential clients. The VIP area is full of Rugby players from a local team. Sports men bring me a lot of business.

I help behind the bar; I smile and chat to lots of people including a few team managers. Jake would have loved this. He was good at talking the talk and could have the VIP area full to the maximum every weekend.

I look over the balcony to the lower club area. It's mainly public that walk in from the street, but we always have people queuing around the corner to get in. I spot Cal entering and I watch, making sure he hasn't been stupid enough to let Bella out partying. I'm horrified when he grabs the hand of another woman who's not Bella. She throws her arms around his neck, and they kiss. Anger rushes through my body and before I can think, I race down the stairs, taking two at a time. I push through the crowd, upsetting people as I shove them out of the way.

Cal sees me approaching him but before he can lie, I bring back my fist and shove it full force into his face. He flies backwards into a group of people standing behind him, and I hear screams and shouting.

"You piece of shit," I yell, leaning over him and grabbing him by the shirt, "Why would you do that to her when she's just lost your baby." I haul him to his feet. "You fucking scumbag."

"Baby?" asks the woman, "Cal, what's he talking about?"

"This piece of shit has a girlfriend; she just lost his kid," I tell her, hitting him again in the face. His nose bursts and blood sprays down his white shirt.

"I can explain," he splutters.

I get into his personal space, "Then get talking."

The doormen appear. "Want us to remove him boss?" one asks, taking Cal by the arm.

"Aiden! What the hell are you doing?" I turn to see Bella glaring angrily at me. Her hands are on her hips and for a second, I'm distracted by how beautiful she looks. *How the hell am I going to tell her?*

"Oh my god, Cal, are you okay?" she cries, shoving past me and rummaging in her bag for tissue. She pulls out a handful and holds it to his nose.

"Tell her," I yell at him.

Bella ignores me, turning to the woman who's crying. "Ellie, are you okay?" The fact she knows her, makes this so much worse and I resist the urge to punch him again.

"Your ex has the wrong idea," Cal hisses.

"I don't see how I got the wrong idea, gym boy," I snap, "I was watching you from up there. I saw you stick your tongue down her throat."

Bella bites her lower lip and winces. "Oh." she says looking guilty.

"Yeah, Oh," says Cal giving Bella a pointed look.

"I am so sorry, Cal," she says, "Go and take Ellie home, I'll sort this." Bella kisses them both on the cheek and then turns to me, looking sheepish. "Can we talk?" she asks.

"I think we need to," I growl, and I storm off towards my office.

I sit at the desk and Bella stands awkwardly in front of it. "So?" I prompt.

"Me and Cal, we aren't together." I'm confused. She's just lost his baby, this makes no sense. When she sees my confusion, she continues. "We never were. You saw us and assumed, and we just never corrected you."

"I didn't assume anything, Bella. He was all over you at the hospital that time, he made it perfectly clear," I snap, "So what, you just slept together and got pregnant?"

Bella doesn't speak for a minute as if she is thinking about her answer. "Something like that. Anyway, all you really need to know is we aren't a thing."

"To be honest, Bella, I'm a little annoyed that you lied to me. I look like a dick."

She has the decency to look guilty. "It wasn't intentional, it just snow balled. I'm sorry."

"You need to apologise to Cal and Ellie," she says.

I raise my eyebrows, "No fucking chance. It's been a long time coming. I thought he was cheating on you," I argue.

"Cal's been great to me, Aiden. If we're going to be friends, you need to make peace with him. For me."

I smile a little. "Maybe I can stretch to a free VIP pass for a weekend."

She rolls her eyes. "One weekend?"

"Fine, six months," I say with a huff.

She smiles, "Thank you."

"I'm not doing it for him. I'm doing it for you and only because I love you," I blurt out. I freeze, and she stares wide eyed.

"I didn't mean...erm I meant..." and then I give up because the words won't come. "Shall we go and get a drink?" I ask, standing abruptly and feeling flustered.

I sit her in my booth and take her a glass of non-alcoholic wine. Aria is dancing with a rugby player and JP doesn't look very happy.

"So," I say, sitting opposite her, "No more lies."

She tenses up, but I don't get chance to pull her up on it because Aria joins us. JP is hot on her heels, but he doesn't say anything as he sits down, looking moody. The tension between them is obvious.

Bella sighs, "What's wrong with you two now, I thought you were getting along?"

"Tell me, how many people do you need for an orgy?" asks Aria, glancing between me and JP. JP shifts uncomfortably.

"Be quiet Aria," he warns.

"I'm really interested," she carries on, not heeding his warning, "I mean, I know three is clearly a threesome but what if there's four or maybe five, let's say..." and she taps her chin like she's thinking "Two men and three women?"

A silence falls over the table and JP looks at me with guilt written all over his face. It's clear she knows everything.

I grin, "I'd say that's a bloody good time, Ari. Are you and Bella wanting to ask us something?"

Before she can come back with a smart answer, which I know is on the tip of her tongue, JP stands. "Let's go," he orders, and she looks at him in shock. "Now."

When she still doesn't move, I watch in amusement as he swoops down and lifts her over his shoulder like she's nothing more than a doll. "Gonna use your office, Boss," he says, and heads off with Aria screaming and making threats to murder.

Bella gives a laugh. "About time."

CHAPTER TWENTY-FIVE

Bella

We sit in silence for some time. I notice women looking over longingly at Aiden, but he doesn't return their smiles. Something in him has changed, because a few months back he would have invited them over to the booth.

"No relationship on the horizon?" I ask, and he frowns. I just want to break the silence, but that question must seem weird coming from your ex.

"No, I've swore off women," he says proudly.

I laugh, "Sorry, What?"

"It's not so hard to believe. It's easier than I thought."

"You've sworn off women?" I repeat, "Like, as in girlfriends or sex?"

"I don't do girlfriends, as you well know. But for the record, both," he says with a cocky grin.

"Are the guy's betting on this?" I ask, laughing.

He looks offended, "Not to my knowledge, but now you've said that I realise that they probably are."

"What's the longest you've been without sex?" I ask suspiciously. If it's not very long, which I suspect is the case, then I want in on this bet.

He thinks for a minute and wiggles his fingers a few times like he's counting, and then grins. "Thirteen years," he says proudly, and my mouth opens in shock.

"Thirteen years, no way."

He nods, still looking proud of himself. "Yep, from when I was born until I turned thirteen," he laughs.

I swipe his arm playfully. "That doesn't count."

"Then, never. There has never been a time when I've been without sex," he admits.

I feel sad for him, all those women and no connection. "Since you were thirteen, you've been having sex? Was that every day, week, month?"

"Maybe a couple of times a month at first, but as I got older it was more regular. And when I got the club, it was more like weekly . . . daily," he says with a shrug, and I see a hint of shame in his eyes. "Let's have a sleepover," he suggests, taking my hand dragging me towards his office.

"I don't think that's a good idea," I mutter without much conviction.

Less than five minutes later, I'm wearing a long t-shirt of Aiden's, and we're curled up on the sofa with coffee. There's a nagging voice in the back of my head telling me this is a bad idea. He's worming his way back in, and now I can't even use Cal as my buffer. But another part of me wants to spend time with him, especially when I feel this sad inside.

"Who was your first time with?" I ask, keen to continue the conversation from the club.

He lets his head fall back with a groan, "My babysitter."

"You had a babysitter at thirteen?"

"She was my former babysitter and we bumped into each other at a party. She was eighteen."

He laughs when I make a face. "So gross."

"And when I was fifteen, I slept with my friend's mum," he admits.

My eyes go wide. "Not JP or Raff's mum?" I gasp.

He shudders dramatically, "God no, Bells, I'm not that bad."

"Oh, suddenly you have morals and standards," I tease. "When did Laurie appear on the scene?" I ask cautiously.

"I was nineteen. Jake and the boys hated her, to me that was a good thing because I knew none of them would use her against me in a challenge. We were fire in the bedroom and so she became like a drug. I needed to have a regular fix."

I suddenly regret asking and he places a finger under my chin, tipping my head back to look me in the eye. "I realise now, all we had was sex. It took meeting you, to see that."

"Are you sad she left again?" I ask.

He shakes his head, "Relieved, not sad. Now, are we watching a film or not?"

♡

I wake feeling stiff and as I stretch out, I open an eye. I'm in a bedroom but it isn't mine. I lift my head slightly and recognise its Aiden's room. I don't even remember falling to sleep let alone getting in here.

I roll to the side and hit something solid. *Aiden*. His arm snakes over me and I freeze. He mumbles something incoherent, and then pulls me to him and tucks me into his side.

He's still asleep, I can hear his deep, relaxed breaths. I feel like I should move but he's so warm and for the first time in months I feel calm, so I snuggle into him and drift back off to sleep.

Aiden

I wake and I'm far too hot. I feel a weight across me, and it confuses me for a second, until I remember yesterday, and Bella. It brings a smile to my face, and I feel content knowing she's here with me. Where she belongs.

I carried her to my bed last night after she fell asleep on the couch. She looked so peaceful that I didn't have the heart to wake her.

We took a step forward last night and talked, something we hadn't done the first time around. But we also agreed to no more secrets, which means I have to tell her about the orgy before Aria or Gemma does.

I sneak out of bed and head to the kitchen. I want to impress her with breakfast, or at least impress her with the effort, because my breakfast skills aren't up to much.

Ten minutes later, I have everything on a tray and I head to the bedroom to find Bella sitting up staring at her mobile. "Cal's been texting. I think he's annoyed with me," she sighs and spots the tray as I place it next to her on the side table. "You cooked me breakfast?" she notes, smiling.

I nod. "Something I've never done for anyone. Well maybe once, but that's another story," I say awkwardly.

Bella eyes me suspiciously and takes the tray, placing it carefully on her lap. "I feel like there's more you want to say."

I perch on the edge of the bed. "I think I slept with one of your friends." I groan, "Actually, I know she was one of your friends. Gemma."

She holds bacon halfway to her mouth. "Wow, Gemma. She likes to put it about, maybe you should get all of that checked," she says, screwing up her face and waving her hand in the general direction of my crotch.

"I just thought that since we weren't keeping secrets anymore..."

Her expression changes, and she puts the tray back onto the side table. "I'm not very hungry. Besides, I should be getting back. Cal didn't want me to go out last night. I'm still supposed to be resting, and he doesn't sound happy in the messages he left." She throws the covers back and I take in the sight of her in my T-Shirt.

"I thought you'd text him last night to say you were with me?"

"I did, he wasn't happy," she mutters.

"You aren't even together?" I say gently, not wanting to upset her.

"He's my friend, he cares about me."

I take a calming breath. I hate that he's dictating who she can see. "I care about you, Bella. But I wouldn't stop you seeing someone if I could see you were happy."

"I'm not arguing about this," she says firmly, and she suddenly bends, gasping and gripping her stomach.

I rush to her, "Are you okay?" I ask, easing her back into bed. She lets me. "Sorry," she winces, "I keep getting these twinges."

"Look, stay. Let me look after you. I can take some time off from the club."

"I can't ask you to do that."

"You're not asking, I'm offering. It's got to be better than bedrest at Cal's. Is he even around during the day?"

"He has to work," she says. "But he's been amazing."

"Let me help him out by sharing the load. I'll even let you watch Notebook."

She smiles. "Wow, true sacrifice."

"Just once though," I add, and she laughs.

Her phone vibrates, and I snatch it off the side before she can grab it.

"Aiden," she screeches, and I grin at her as I leave the room, pressing accept call.

"Cal," I say cheerfully. "Good morning, how's the nose?"

"Why are you answering her phone?" he demands.

"She's resting."

"Bullshit, she just text me back."

"I've had a chat with her, and she wants to stay here for a few days."

"Put her on so I can talk some sense into her," he snaps.

"I think you're still feeling bitter over last night, which reminds me, Bella insisted I apologise. Although, you brought it on yourself, but for her, I'm sorry. Please accept six months VIP membership at the club."

"Fuck you, Aiden," he spits angrily. "What's your game?"

"Why are you so pissed at me, Cal? You knocked her up and got a new girlfriend. Concentrate on your new relationship and let me take care of Bella."

"She'll never let you back in, you're wasting your time."

I grin, "We'll see. I mean, there's nothing standing in my way anymore is there." And I disconnect.

I take the phone back to find Bella sleeping. I turn it off and place it on the side next to her. I take a minute to watch her in her peaceful slumber, gently moving a stray piece of hair from her face before placing a kiss on her forehead.

Bella

I've spent the entire week with Aiden. And I'm not in any rush to leave, because he's been amazing. He's been true to his word and waited on me hand and foot. He's stuck around for every romantic film, including two rounds of The Notebook. And even when he's had to nip out to the club, he's been less than an hour each time, and even text me to check I'm okay. The fact I'm always on his mind, makes me feel special, and I can almost forget the way he's treated me.

But today, after getting the all-clear from the doctor, I've decided to go back to work. So, when he enters the bedroom and sees me fully dressed, he looks confused. I wince, regretting not speaking to him about it properly. I knew he'd fuss, just like Cal did when I mentioned it to him.

"It's just a few hours," I say but he's already shaking his head. I laugh, "I'm not going to break, Aiden. The doctor called and said it's fine, I just can't over do it."

"It's not a good idea."

"Didn't you say you had some meetings today?" He nods. "So, we've both got things to do."

"Will you come back here after work?" he asks.

I sigh, "Aiden, I don't live here. I really should go back home."

"I like having you around," he admits, and I smile.

"I like being here too, but it's not like we'll never see each other again. I appreciate everything you've done for me. You've been the bestest friend." I reach up on my tiptoes to kiss him on the cheek and he swiftly turns his head, so I catch his lips. I pause, a breath away and he uses the hesitation as his chance to kiss me properly.

We break apart and I'm breathless. I forgot what it was like to kiss Aiden Tremos, and as my heart beats wildly, I almost smile. "I should go," I whisper.

"I'll text you soon," he says, pressing a gentle kiss to my head. "Take it easy."

I step into the elevator and my mobile pings.

> **Aiden: I miss you already.**

❧

I don't get time to have a proper chat with Aria because I have bride after bride booked in to discuss designs. It's not like we haven't spoken every day anyway, but I was looking forward to seeing her for a proper catch up.

I'm about to slip out to grab us both lunch, when the door opens and Laurie saunters in. I inwardly groan as a sneer spreads over her perfectly made up face. "Isabella," she greets coldly.

"How are you?" I ask, remaining professional.

She rubs a hand over her swollen stomach and a pang of heartache hits my chest. "We're doing great. You? How far along are you now?" Her eyes fall to my stomach. It's clear I'm no longer pregnant just by my skinny jeans hanging low on my hips. She covers her mouth, "Shit, sorry, Aiden did tell me, but I've got baby brain." She forces a sympathetic smile that doesn't look very sincere. "How are you? Aiden said you're coping well, considering."

The lump in my throat swells and I fight the tears threatening to fall. I won't give this bitch the satisfaction. "I wasn't aware Aiden was still speaking to you after you lied to him."

"Oh sweetie," she says in a condescending tone that instantly irks me. "Aiden and I . . ." she taps her chin thoughtfully. "We're meant to be. And it doesn't matter what happens between us, he always comes running back because no one," she narrows her eyes, "And I mean *no one*, can handle him the way I can."

"You think he's going to take you back when you're having your husband's baby?" I laugh, shaking my head. The woman is delusional.

"You poor thing," she says, smirking, "He already has." And then she turns on her heel and leaves.

I brace myself against the counter. She's lying, of course she is. Aiden's been with me the entire week. Unless . . . well he did pop out here and there, maybe he met her, and they sorted things out. The thought makes me sad. My phone alerts me to a text message.

> *Aiden: Still missing you. It's been a long day. Stay with me tonight. I'll make dinner.*

I stare at the words and realise I don't trust him. I have no idea if Laurie is telling the truth and that terrifies me. What if we get a year down the line and she's still in his life, causing us shit? What if she gives birth and the baby turns out to be his? I ignore the text, turning my phone off and putting it away.

I head home and am disappointed to see Cal isn't here. I take a long bath and get into my pyjamas. It's nice to be home, but I'm missing Aiden's company. I climb into bed and read a book until my eyes grow heavy.

I wake sometime later. It's dark and I feel around for my mobile and turn it on. It's almost midnight. My phone immediately begins beeping with text message alerts. The first is from Aiden.

> *Aiden: Dinner is getting cold, are you okay?*

Followed by . . .

> *Aria: Aiden called and said you've missed dinner? Are you okay?*

> *Aria: Bella, call me. Aiden is seriously blowing up my phone.*

> *Aiden: Bella, why is your phone off? I called by the shop and you're not there. I'm heading over to the apartment.*

That was sent over an hour ago and I wonder if he knocked on and gave up or if he decided to camp out on the doorstep.

> *Me: Aria, I'm fine. Aiden is being dramatic. See you tomorrow x*

I place my mobile back on the nightstand and snuggle back into bed.

"You're not going to reply to me?" I scramble to sit up at the sound of Aiden's voice. I make out a figure in the chair by the window.

"Jesus, Aiden, you scared me."

He moves quickly, crawling over me until I'm flat on my back. "And you scared me, Bella," he hisses. "I was going out of my mind with worry."

A pang of guilt hits my chest. "Well as you can see, I'm fine."

"Unlike the steak I cooked for you, which is now cold and dried up."

"I never said I'd be there."

"You never said you wouldn't," he counters. "Don't scare me like that again, Bella," he adds in a whisper, before pressing his lips to mine. I groan into his mouth, enjoying the closeness. He pulls back, "Where were you?"

"At work, and then I came home. I turned my phone off," I admit. "I needed some space."

He drops down beside me, placing his hands behind his head and staring up at the ceiling. "From me?" I shrug. "Come on Bella, talk to me. No more secrets, remember." The guilty feeling intensifies.

"I saw Laurie," I mutter, and he turns his head to stare at me. "She came into the shop." He pushes up on his elbows. "To rub my face in it mainly," I add.

His brows pinch together, "Hold on, Laurie came into your shop?"

"Did you tell her I'd lost the baby?"

"Christ, No. Bella, why would I tell her that. I haven't seen her since I left her at the hospital the morning of her scan." He looks so sincere, that I find myself believing him.

"I mean, it's obvious looking at you," he adds, adding a sympathetic smile.

"I guess so," I mutter.

"What else did she say?"

"That you were talking again. She gave the impression you were a thing."

He groans, "And you believed her?"

"I didn't know either way," I say defensively.

"I spent last week with you," he reminds me. "You think I had time to go and see her?" I shrug and he rolls over me, propping himself up on his elbows that lay either side of my head. "If you think I can fuck and walk away satisfied, within around half an hour, you're wrong." And he kisses me, not pulling away until I'm breathless. "I'm not interested in anyone else, Bella. Just you."

"For now," I mumble, hating how needy I sound.

"Laurie calls and texts constantly. She turned up three times to the club last week and I had her removed the second she tried to speak to me. We're done. For good."

"Not if the baby is yours," I say.

"That baby is not mine. I always used protection, and her husband told me straight they'd been trying for a baby."

"But you still want a paternity test."

"Cos I can't have her keep popping up in my life trying to convince me the kid is mine. And she'll do that, just to come between us. The test will put an end to it all, and it'll put your mind at rest."

"I don't want her turning up at my shop, Aiden," I whisper, stroking my hand down his cheek.

He leans closer, kissing me again. "I'll sort it." This time, when he drops beside me, I notice the bulge in his jeans. He adjusts himself, smirking. "Sorry."

"If you're staying over, you need to undress," I say, biting my lower lip.

He laughs, unbuttoning his jeans and lifting his backside to slide them off. "Don't get any idea's, I'm here to make sure you rest."

I get out of bed, heading for my drawers where I grab a silk nightie, before heading for the bathroom, "I need to pee," I say. When I return in just the nightie, Aiden stares wide eyed. "What?" I ask, innocently.

"It won't work," he says, narrowing his eyes, "I can see what you're trying to do."

I run my eyes over his bare chest. My first time wasn't exactly perfect, and I want to try again. I slip into bed and turn out the bedside light, keeping my back to him. Aiden snuggles up behind me, wrapping me in his arms. His erection pokes my backside, and I shift closer. He hisses and I smile to myself. "Bella," he grits out, placing a hand to my hip to still me.

"We spent weeks not having sex and just pleasing each other," I remind him. "If you don't want me, we can just-"

He leans over to kiss me hard, "I do want you, Bella. That's not why I'm holding back. I don't wanna hurt you," he says, placing kisses over my face. "Now go to sleep."

I smile. It's nice he's thinking about me like that, with concern and love. "I really feel fine," I say. "Maybe if we take it slow?"

He groans. "You're making this impossible."

I grin, turning over and sliding my leg over him, before lifting myself to sit over him. I feel his stiff cock brush against me, and I shudder. "Can we just try?" I lean down to kiss him, making sure to rub against him. I slip my hand between us, easing him into me.

His fingers dig into my thighs, and he groans, "You're so tight," he murmurs.

"Is that a good thing?" I ask, wincing as I stretch to adjust to his size.

"Fuck, yeah, Bella. It's a really good thing."

I take him as far as I can, then still. "Does that feel okay?" he whispers, reaching up to tuck some of my hair behind my ear. I nod and he smiles, "It feels really good for me."

I brace my hands against his chest and lift slightly. It sends tingling sparks through my body, and I release a breathy sigh. Aiden's hands travel up to my breasts and he massages them, teasing my nipples. "I missed this," he whispers, "I'll never mess up again."

I lean down to kiss him, gasping at the pressure against my clit. I shift slightly, realising how good it feels to have my breasts brush his chest whilst my lips find his. I keep in this position and ride him. Every nerve ending in my body feels alive, and the way he's cupping my face while I fuck him, makes everything feel so much more sensual. We're not just fucking anymore, we're making love.

CHAPTER TWENTY-SIX

Aiden

I wrap Bella in my arms, stroking her hair whilst she falls to sleep. Things have shifted between us, and there's no denying that what we just did, was far from fucking. We made love. And it doesn't scare the shit out of me like I thought it would. If she wasn't so exhausted, I'd do it all over again right now, because I can't get enough of her.

We wake the following morning wrapped around each other. I'm easing my erection into her before she's opened her eyes. She doesn't protest, only groaning with pleasure as I take what I need.

There's a knock on the bedroom door, and Cal pops his head round. I still and Bella half sits, looking flustered. Cal falters, "Sorry, I didn't know he was here," he mutters, his disapproval obvious in his expression.

I keep my cock buried inside of her, wishing the prick could see. "I'll be out in a sec," she says.

"I'll put the kettle on," he mutters, leaving.

I grip a handful of Bella's hair, tugging her head back so my mouth is at her ear, "Does he often barge in here?" I ask, withdrawing slow and slamming back in. She gasps. "How many times has he come in here when you're naked?"

"Aiden," she pants, as I fuck her harder. Jealousy is driving me and I'm losing control, feeling the urge to mark her before she goes out there to speak to him. I push her onto her front, placing my legs either side of her thighs, watching my cock disappear into her. She shudders, groaning into her pillow. I follow, growling loud enough for him to hear.

I climb from her and she roles onto her back. Her cheeks are flushed pink, and she's got a just fucked look about her that satisfies me. Cal will know that look, and he'll know I'm the one that put it there.

"That was primal," she remarks, sitting up.

I grab her round the waist and pull her back. "Who said we were finished?"

She bats my wandering hands away, laughing as I take her nipple in my mouth. "What's gotten into you?"

I drop back, staring up at the ceiling. "What's happening here?" I ask and she snuggles into my side.

"You're asking me?" she asks with a laugh.

"I know what I want, Bella. I need to know if you want the same?"

"I like spending time with you," she admits. "And I like how you are. I feel like this is the real you."

"It is," I reassure her. "Everything is out in the open now, no more lies."

"I want to take it slow," she whispers.

"A bit late for slow," I tease.

"I mean, let's not stick labels on this just yet. And I need you and Cal to be okay around one another."

I groan. "I don't like the guy, and can you blame me?"

She sighs, placing a kiss on my lips before sitting again. "Let me go talk to him. Take a shower and I'll bring you coffee."

It's twenty long minutes before she returns and she gives me a sheepish smile, placing a coffee on the bedside table. I sit up and she slides into bed beside me. "There's something I need to tell you." I stiffen at her words. "But please let me just explain before you get angry."

"Here we go," I mutter. "Has lover boy kicked off cos we're back together?"

She sighs, "We haven't said we're back together, Aiden. I said we'll take it slow. Cal wasn't the father of my baby."

I take a second to process her words, "What?"

"He only said it because he could see I was upset when you and Laurie turned up. He was trying to rescue me, and it got out of hand."

I get out of bed, staring in disbelief. "We said no more lies," I snap.

"We did, and that's why I went to check with Cal that he was okay for me to tell the truth."

My brows pinch together. "Hold on, you wanted to check with Cal to see if you could expose the fucking lie?"

"I knew you'd get angry," she mutters, shaking her head.

"So, who's the father?" I demand.

"No one you know," she says, her eyes pleading with me to calm down.

"I want his name, Bella. How many have there been since me?"

"We don't need to do this. It doesn't have to be a big deal."

I glare, anger pulsing through me. "How many?" I yell.

"One," she cries.

"So you and Cal?" She shakes her head. "I fucking punched him," I shout. "I thought he'd cheated on you."

"If you'd have just told me about Laurie, I wouldn't have been so shocked."

"Don't put this on me. I didn't have to tell you shit," I snap, "We weren't together. I didn't owe you an explanation."

Her eyes widen, "Likewise."

"This is different, Bella. You could have told me the second we started talking again. You've had loads of opportunities."

She buries her face in her hands. "I know I should have."

I scoff, "but you needed Cal's permission, right?"

"I didn't want this war to continue between you both," she explains. "It was getting too much."

I grab my jeans and pull them on. She watches in silence whilst I dress. "I need some time," I mutter. The last twenty-four hours have been amazing, and I'm hurt she didn't tell me everything.

"What about us?" she whispers.

"Like you've already pointed out, you want to take it slow." And I storm out.

♡

I find Raff in my office. He looks up in surprise. "Thought you weren't coming in until late?"

"Yeah well, change of plan."

He gets out of my chair, and I sit in his place. "Bella drama?" he guesses.

"That obvious?"

"Well, lately, it's always Bella or Laurie."

"Cal wasn't the father of her baby."

Raff laughs, "Shit, you punched him."

"Right!"

"Why did they lie?"

I shrug. "She said it was a spur of the moment thing when she saw me with Laurie."

"Who's the father then?"

"She didn't tell me."

Raff sits opposite me. "Do you think you know him?"

I frown, "I do now."

He grins, "Just weird she won't say."

I shrug, "I didn't really push her to be honest. I just wanted to get out of there. She said I didn't know him."

"Unless you do and that's why she won't say."

"She only knows you and JP," I point out.

"And you," he adds. I stare, waiting for him to continue. "What if it was yours?"

I scoff, "Don't be ridiculous. She'd have just told me."

"Would she?" he asks. "She saw you with Laurie, why would she announce it after that?"

"I mean before that, she'd have called me when she found out."

"She was really angry and upset, Aiden. I'm not convinced she'd tell you. How far along was she?" I shrug, realising I've never actually asked her. "Don't you think you should find out?"

I groan, scrubbing my hands over my face. "She'll never tell me now, I've just walked out because she lied about Cal."

"So go to the source of the lie. Ask Cal, it's the least he owes you."

♥

Cal is in the park. He wasn't hard to find seeing as he conducts most of his sessions here. I wait for him to finish up with his client before heading over. He eyes me warily, maybe expecting another punch, instead, I hold out my hand for him to shake. After a few seconds, he grips it firmly. "I'm sorry," I say. "I shouldn't have hit you. My feelings towards you came from a jealous place," I admit. "And now Bella's finally explained everything, I realise I was out of order."

He nods, "I appreciate your apology."

I hand him the bottle of water I purchased from the hut on the park, and he takes it gratefully. I take a seat on a nearby bench, cupping my coffee. "I just can't get my head around it all."

He sits beside me, "Yeah, it's a lot."

"And I realised I never even asked her how far along she was," I admit, I give my head a sad shake. "I was so pissed she lied, I just walked out."

"Bella hates lies," he tells me. "And I shouldn't have forced that on her. I just saw her struggling when she was faced with you and Laurie together," he sighs heavily, "She'd already been through so much."

"Thanks to me," I mutter.

"Which is why she didn't want to tell you when she found out." He takes a mouthful of water. "Me and Aria said she should tell you the truth. But you really hurt her, Aiden."

"I know," I mutter.

"And she said you didn't want to be a father, that you weren't ready." I stiffen at his words, but he continues, not noticing. "But I'm glad she finally told you. Now you can start a fresh with no lies standing in the way."

I get to my feet, rage pulsing through me. "Thanks for the chat. I should go and see Bella now." And I stride off in the direction of the shop.

Bella

My heart feels heavy. I thought telling Aiden part of the truth, might ease the guilt that's eating into me. It didn't. And now he's ignoring my calls, angry because I lied about Cal. Imagine how he would have reacted knowing the truth.

The shop door opens, and I glance up to find Aiden standing there. He still looks pissed, so I move around the counter, towards him. "I can't do this now, Aiden," I snap. "We'll talk later."

He scoffs, "How far along were you?"

His words stop me in my tracks, and I frown in confusion. "Huh?"

"I never asked you how far along you were."

My heart thuds hard in my chest. "What does it matter now?"

He sniggers and I'm instantly on high alert. "Oh, it matters, Bella."

"Where's this going?" I almost whisper, anxiety gripping me tightly.

He steps further into the shop, turning the sign in the window to closed. "Is there anything else you'd like to tell me, Bella?" he asks, moving to the conjoining door that leads to Aria's shop, and locking it.

I back away, going behind the counter to put distance between us. "No." His eyes finally land on me, and anger is raging in them. It makes me want to run and hide, but I stand my ground. "What's going on?" I ask.

"I've been so fucking stupid," he mutters, and I swallow the lump in my throat. "I didn't even think for one second it could be mine." *Fuck.* "Out of everyone, I never thought you'd lie about something so important."

"Aiden . . . I-"

"So, I went to see Cal. My world tilts, "And he told me the truth."

"I can explain," I mutter feebly.

He slams his hand on the countertop, and I jump in fright. "I can't wait to hear it," he grits out.

"I was upset . . . I was really depressed and . . ." Tears slip down my cheeks. "I didn't mean to lie."

"But you did, didn't you, Bella," he spits the words. "Over and over. You let me run around after you, all the while hiding the fact that it was my baby you lost." He shakes his head in disbelief. "I lay with you while you cried. My heart broke for your loss," he yells. "Not knowing it was my loss too."

I sob, my shoulders shaking. "I'm sorry."

"Sorry you got caught."

"You didn't want kids," I remind him. "You told me that."

"I wouldn't have said that if I knew the truth."

"I was hurting," I cry desperately. "I wasn't thinking straight and then it just became easier to let you think it was Cal's baby."

"You've had the moral high ground all this time," he says with disgust, "And it turns out you're a deceiving, lying little bitch, too."

I shake my head in denial, unable to speak through my tears. "You wouldn't even look at me when I hurt you. You made me feel like I was the evilest man on the planet. And then you do this. Was it punishment?"

"No."

"Did you want to pay me back for what I did?"

"No."

"Does Aria know?" he demands. When I don't reply, he laughs. It's cold and empty. "Of course she fucking does. She made JP grovel for his forgiveness, and she kept this from him."

"It's not her fault," I mutter. "This is all on me."

"Do you know the worst part?" he asks. "Not the fact you lapped up all the attention while I ran around after you. Not the way you had me grovelling for your forgiveness. Not even the way I let you call all the shots just so you'll give me a chance. It's that I didn't even see this coming. It's the fact you knew what Laurie did, and how that hurt me, and you were doing the exact same thing. Lying to get what you wanted."

"It wasn't the same," I cry.

"She lied to keep me, you lied to keep me away. And once the problem was gone, you reeled me back in."

"That's not how it was."

"Then tell me," he yells, "Tell me how it was, Bella. Because it feels like you got everything you wanted. The shop. The baby. And now that hasn't worked out, you've come for a second try?"

I shake my head, confused by his words. "What are you talking about."

He slams a packet on the table. "Take it," he hisses.

"What is it?"

"The morning after pill."

My frown deepens. "I'm on the contraceptive pill."

"You said that before and you got pregnant."

"I'd fucked up a few times, missing them or getting sick. I didn't get pregnant on purpose, Aiden."

"Maybe not last time."

"You think that's what I want now?"

"I couldn't work out how you went from hating me, to climbing back into bed with me," he sneers. I slap him hard, immediately crying out as the pain burns my hand. I hold it to my chest, my tears falling faster. His jaw tightens and his eyes blade with anger. "Take the fucking pill and prove me wrong."

"Where did you get it?" I sniffle, picking the packet up.

"I have a doctor friend, he's good in emergencies like this."

I arch a brow, "You use him often do you?"

"All the damn time. I just never thought I'd need him with you." I pop the pill from the packet and swallow it, taking my bottle of water and washing it down. Aiden grabs my chin, "Open," he orders. I do, sticking my tongue out. He shoves me away in disgust. He reminds me of how he was before, and I'm struggling to see who the real Aiden is anymore. "We are over, Bella," he says firmly and my heart stutters. "Don't contact me, don't turn up where I am, and don't come in any of my bars or clubs. If you do, I'll have you removed immediately."

I stare open mouthed. "You're not even gonna talk about it?"

"There's nothing to say. You lied over and over, even when we agreed to no more lies. I can't even stand to look at you, Bella. We're done." And he turns around, and leaves.

I send Aria a text explaining I'm sick and heading home. She's busy and doesn't rush round to see me. Which is a good thing, because I'm a mess.

I get home, drop my things by the door and go straight to my room where I crawl into bed, and close my eyes.

This morning, I felt happy. For the first time in months, things were looking up. And even after Aiden stormed out, I didn't think it would end like this. I thought he needed time to cool off. The venom in his words and the hatred in his eyes, haunt me. My throat tightens and I make a grab for the waste bin, emptying the contents of my stomach. *How many times am I going to let Aiden Tremos affect me like this?*

A few hours pass before I hear Cal call my name. "In here," I mutter.

He pushes the bedroom door open and winces, "It stinks in here," he states. I point to the wastebin, not bothering to give an explanation. He screws his nose up. "You have a visitor."

My heart leaps and I jump out of bed, rushing into the living room, my heart sinking when I see JP holding a box. He gives me a sad smile, letting me know that he knows. He places the box on the couch. "He asked me to drop this round."

I lift the lid and see my things from his apartment. Cal lingers in the doorway, "What's going on?"

"He said to keep anything he's left here, or throw it, whatever," JP adds.

I nod stiffly. I only have a t-shirt and now I'm wondering if he did that on purpose, never leaving anything so he wouldn't have to face me when it all came to an end.

"Bella, what's going on?" Cal repeats.

"He also asked me to give you this," he says, holding out a brown envelope. His face is full of guilt as I take it. "I think once he cools off, he'll rethink this, but right now, he's angry and there's no talking sense into him."

I open the envelope. It's a solicitors business card with a name scrawled on the back. "What's this?"

JP shifts uncomfortably. "He wants half the shop."

I inhale sharply, gripping the back of the couch to stop myself collapsing. "No," I whisper.

"Why would he do that?" Cal demands, wrapping his arm under my arm and supporting me to sit down.

"The guy on the card is your point of contact if you have any questions."

"I have plenty of questions," I manage to say.

"Aiden won't see you," JP confirms.

"He's a coward," I whisper.

"He's upset and angry. It's best you go through the contact than approach him yourself" JP warns. "And if you need anything, call me," he adds, turning to leave. "For what it's worth. I'm sorry it ended like this; I thought you were it for him." And he leaves.

I choke on a sob and Cal crouches before me. "Bella, talk to me."

"You told him about the baby," I say through tears.

He frowns, "He said you told him?"

I shake my head and his eyes widen. "Oh shit. Bella I'm so sorry. He made me think you'd told him."

I force a sad smile, "It's not your fault. It's mine. I should have."

CHAPTER TWENTY-SEVEN

Aiden

The thing about anger is it drives me to work harder in my businesses. And after the last few months of distractions, I'm relieved to be back doing what I do best. It's been over two weeks since I last saw Bella. And this time has been much easier to stomach, mainly because I have no guilt weighing me down. Having my solicitor, Drake, as the go between, as also helped because I haven't had to see her.

Drake sighs, and I already know I'm not going to like what he's about to tell me. "Bella would like to *sell* the entire business to you."

I frown, "She only started the business because of the money I gave her."

"She doesn't want to be partners in business."

"I don't give a shit what she wants. I have no idea how to run a cake business," I snap. "I want half because I put money into it."

He sighs again, irritating me further. "Technically you weren't investing, Aiden. We both know the reason you gave Bella that money and it wasn't to invest."

"As I understand it, she hasn't got herself a solicitor, Drake, so this should be easy. Get her to sign the damn papers." I slam the phone down just as JP enters.

"Problem?"

"Bella won't sign the papers."

He shrugs, "I don't blame her."

"If it wasn't for my money, she wouldn't have the shop."

"If you hadn't of tricked her, you wouldn't have paid her," he counters.

"You should reason with her," I say thoughtfully.

"No."

"It's not a polite request, JP. I'm your boss and I'm telling you to make her sign the fucking papers."

"You want me to go heavy on Bella?" I nod. "You've lost your mind. Why not just take it all, Aiden? She's offering for you to buy her out and you can own it all." The fact he knows this, pisses me off and he realises his words too late. "Fine," he snaps. "I'll go and see her."

I pull my copy from the jar and slide them across the desk. "Make it clear. Half."

Bella

I'm putting the finishing touches to an amazing five tier wedding cake. If I ever got married, then this is the cake I'd have. Decorated with hundreds of handcrafted, tiny daisies, cascading like a waterfall down one side of the cake. Trying to imagine my wedding when I feel so broken, is hard. But it's not the first heartbreak I've felt. So, each day, I've pushed myself to get out of bed and paste on a smile. I've cheered brides on and made their dreams reality. All whilst silently suffering.

JP enters and I smile. He's been checking up on me regular, although I'm certain he gets updates from Aria. "Wow, Bella, that's amazing," he says, eyeing the cake.

I take a step back to admire my work. "I know, right, I love it."

"How are you?"

I shrug, "Pushing on. How's Aiden?"

He looks away, just like he always does when I ask. And I ask every time, because I can't believe he's getting on with his life like we never happened. "You know Aiden," he mutters. "Actually, he's the reason I'm here."

"Oh?"

"He's unhappy about your request for him to buy you out."

"I know, Drake called me."

"So, have you thought anymore about it?" he asks hopefully.

"I will not work with him, JP."

"Technically, he'll be a silent partner."

I scoff, "When has Aiden ever been silent about anything? We both know that won't happen."

"So, make him sign something. Yah know, if you got a solicitor like I suggested, this wouldn't be an issue."

"I don't have money to throw at a solicitor, and even if I found someone in my price range, Aiden would make sure his solicitor tore them to pieces. I don't want to fight about this. I'm just asking he be reasonable."

"I don't think you have much chance of that right now."

I groan. "I'll talk to him myself."

His eyes widen. "That's not a good idea."

"He's not bullying me anymore. And does he think we can go into business and never speak? He's acting ridiculous." I pause, "Hold on, did he send you to put the frighteners on me?" After all, JP is the henchman. He glances down and I give a cold, empty laugh. "Leave the papers with me, I'll take them to him myself."

"Bella," he mutters, shaking his head.

"Leave now or I'll call for Aria."

He narrows his eyes, "Unfair," he whisper hisses before leaving.

It's almost seven in the evening by the time I lock up and head for Tremos. It seems strange coming here when I know I'm not welcome, but luckily, the door is propped open for a delivery, and I scuttle pass the delivery guy and head inside.

Aiden is talking with a small group of men, but the second he sees me, he excuses himself and heads my way. He grabs the top of my arm, marching me towards the office, where he shoves me inside before slamming the door. "What the hell are you doing here?"

"Didn't your henchman warn you I was coming?" I ask, holding up the papers.

He places his hands on his hips and stares at the ground, "You didn't need to hand deliver them." I hate that he looks so good, and yet I feel so . . . lost.

"I like to face my problems rather than get staff to deal with them."

"You've seen sense and signed them?" he asks, finally meeting my eye.

"Why do you want to share my business?"

"I paid for it," he snaps.

"You paid for my virginity," I counter, "To ease your guilt."

"And now you've got your own back, you can sign half over, and we can move on."

I narrow my eyes, "This isn't a game to me, Aiden. I've built this business up and now you just want to take half to hurt me."

"It's good business sense," he snaps.

"It's a game. It's all you know." I cry out in anger, "Why do you want to share this when you hate me." I think I see him soften slightly but he recovers quickly.

"Sign the papers, Bella."

"I'll sign," I eventually say, "If you agree to be a silent partner."

He scoffs, "You don't have the right to come here and make demands."

"This is my life," I cry, "You've already taken so much from me, and it's clear you're only doing this to punish me, so agree to be silent and I'll sign the fucking papers, and you won't have to deal with me again."

He eventually gives a slight nod. "I'll have Drake add the clause in."

I hand the papers back to him. "Thank you."

❦

"Did he agree?" asks Aria the following day.

I nod and she claps her hands together, smiling. "That's great news."

I hate that I'm about to crush her dreams. "It doesn't change anything."

Her smile fades. "But if he stays out of the business, you can run it how you like. Plus, he can put in a cash injection. You can get some more equipment, expand to meet the demand." I take her hands and tears fill her eyes. "Don't," she whispers sadly, "Don't give me that sympathetic look."

"I'm not leaving you, Aria."

"You are," she cries dramatically, and I can't help but laugh. "If I can't see you in the flesh, or touch you, then you're leaving me."

I nod in agreement, "You're right. But we discussed this already, and you know why I have to do this."

The shop doorbell rings, and I kiss her on the cheek before heading back into my shop where I find Aiden. I inhale sharply before composing myself. "That was quick," I say, forcing a smile.

He hands me the papers and I take them over to the desk. "You should have someone read over that," he mutters.

I pull a pen from my drawer and skip through the pages. "I'd rather just get it over and done with." I spot the extra clause and turn to the final page. "How will this all work?"

"You'll run things, and I'll take half the profits," he says, with a slight smirk. Just the thought of breaking my back for him to take half, makes me sick.

"And what happens if you decide you want more?" I ask, "How do I know this will be my final battle with you?"

"You'll just have to trust me."

I roll my eyes, "That's the problem, I don't." But I scribble my name on the dotted line and slide the papers back to him. Our hands touch and I snatch mine away like he's burned me. "Is that it, is the agreement done?"

He nods. "We're officially partners."

"Good, because I'm hiring a manager to run the shop."

Aiden

I stare wide eyed. "What?"

She nods, as if to confirm her words. "I'm holding interviews at the end of the week."

"Why would you do that? It makes sense for you to run things, you know the business."

"You're a silent partner, remember?" I almost whisper.

"That doesn't mean you can pull shit like this," I snap, angry she's tricked me.

"You might be able to swan around here like you never felt a thing, but I can't. I tried to ask nicely for you to set me free, and you refused, so I have no choice."

"But you love this shop."

She smiles sadly and tears balance on her lower lash as she looks around, "Yeah, I do, but lately it just reminds me of everything bad in my life."

Her words hurt but I keep my expression stone. "What do you plan to do if a manager is running this place? Will you still bake the wedding cakes?"

She shakes her head. "No. I'm giving up on that dream too."

"Bella," I whisper. This isn't what I wanted. Without baking, what does she have?

"Anyway," she says, wiping her cheeks and forcing a laugh. "I'll let you know who I choose. And I'll be keeping a close eye on everything. Plus, Aria will be around to keep things running smoothly. It won't affect your half of the profits."

"It's not that..."

"The decision is made, Aiden. Do you want me to call you, or should I call Drake with the details?" She laughs again, "I don't know how all this stuff works."

"Call me," I say, turning to leave. I pause at the door. "I hope you know what you're doing."

"For once, I think I do."

I glance up at the sight of JP in a smart shirt. "Are you meeting Aria's parents?" I joke.

He scoffs, "No. We have dinner with Cal, his new girlfriend and... Bella."

I frown. "A couple's dinner, but with Bella?"

"I'm running late, I should make a move." I stand and he hesitates. "Is she seeing someone?" He shakes his head. "So why do you look like you're hiding something?"

It's been a month since Aria hired some guy to work the shop. She landed on her feet with him being a baker as well as having managerial experience. And JP assures me he's gay, but now as he edges towards the door, I'm wondering if that was a lie too.

"I can always turn up and see for myself," I warn.

"You don't know where we'll be," he says, smirking like a child.

"Bella Italia?" I guess and his smirk fades. She always goes there because she loves it.

"Fuck sake," he mutters. "Aria will have my balls if she finds out."

"Since when do your loyalties lie with Aria over me?" I demand.

"Since she took me back on the condition, I stopped telling you about Bella?"

I narrow my eyes, "Was that an actual condition?"

"You're missing the point, Aiden. There are things Bella doesn't want you to know."

"Like when she was pregnant with my kid?" I snap. "Did you know about that too?"

"No of course not."

"What is so important, Bella thinks I'd actually give a shit?"

"She's leaving. Moving away," he mutters. "But you didn't hear it from me."

It's not the words I was expecting, and I stare for a few silent seconds. Then I take a breath and shrug. "Is that it, I thought it was something bigger."

He eyes me, knowing full well I'm talking shit. The news is the worst I've heard in a long time. "Now you know," he mutters, leaving.

I wait for him to leave before swiping my hand over the desk and sending paperwork flying. *Where the fuck is she going to go?* All her money is tied up in the business. *Is that why she wanted me to buy her out?* Then I spend the next few hours, refreshing Bella's social media, waiting to see if she puts pictures on so I can see who she's with. Like that will somehow explain her sudden urge to pack up and go.

♡

It's almost midnight when I spot Bella marching towards me. A small part of me is thrilled at seeing her. But I don't budge from between the two women that are trying their best to get my attention. Bella stops at the table. "Can we talk?"

I place my arm around one of the women casually. "If it's to tell me you're leaving, I already know," I reply in a bored tone.

"It's not, well it is, but I just wanted to explain some stuff."

"I'm busy," I state and the women smirk.

"This is the last time you're ever going to see me, Aiden. If you ever felt half of what you said, you'll talk to me." She marches towards my office.

I go after her, secretly desperate to hear what she's got to say. We go into the office, and I sit in my chair, crossing one leg over the other at the ankle and waiting for her words.

"The morning I caught you with those two women," she begins, looking uncomfortable. "That was the day I wanted to tell you the truth about the baby. I felt awful knowing what Laurie had done to you, and so I came to tell you then."

"Only you didn't," I say, shrugging.

"No, because I saw the women and it threw me, I was embarrassed, so I left. You came after me and said you didn't care about Laurie, that you felt relieved because you didn't want kids."

"I didn't want them with Laurie," I snap.

"How was I to know that?" she asks. "You seemed so certain."

"What do you want me to say, Bella? That I forgive you? Because I don't. There were so many times after that, when you could have told me. We were working things out."

"I thought it would be kinder if I didn't tell you," she whispers, "So you wouldn't have to feel the same pain I did."

My heart twists but I ignore it. "I felt it for you anyway," I snap. "Don't try and convince me you were sparing me. You lied because it suited you. I'm sick of women thinking they can lie their way in and out of anything."

"Maybe you should look at why women lie to you, Aiden," she snaps. "Maybe you should treat them better and they wouldn't get hurt and do things that hurt you too."

I roll my eyes, "Maybe you should be on your way."

"I don't know why I thought this would be a good idea," she mutters.

"You wanted me to forgive you, Bella. And it hasn't worked."

"I thought I deserved the same forgiveness I showed you after you hurt me," she says, nodding. "I was stupid to think you were that reasonable." She pulls the door open, and I feel panicked, I'm not ready for her to leave.

"Where are you moving to?" I ask, hating that I care.

"Far away from here," she says, almost looking relieved. "A fresh start." She takes a few more steps then turns back, "Was it just kids with Laurie you didn't want, Aiden?"

I smirk, "Are you asking if I wanted kids with you?" She gives an unsure nod. "No, Bella. I didn't want kids with you either, especially not after everything."

She gives another stiff nod. "That's what I thought." And she leaves.

I sit staring at the closed door for a further few minutes before jumping up and running after her. I can't let her leave, I love her. *What the fuck was I thinking?*

CHAPTER TWENTY-EIGHT

Bella

I pull up in my little hatchback outside my dad's house. I stare at the run down little terraced and wonder for the hundredth time whether I should just leave without seeing him. The rain is pouring down fast and I'm wearing summer clothes and sandals, it's typical of the British weather.

I make a run for the house, holding my jacket above my head. I knock on the door, reasoning I can't just walk in. It no longer feels like my home. A small lady with greying hair opens the door. "Oh, my goodness, come in quick it's pouring down," she insists, stepping to the side. I go in and she shuts the door and turns to me. "Finally, I've been wanting to meet you for some time. He's told me so much about you, Bella." I'm confused and she realises by my baffled expression, "I'm Claire. Come on through, he'll be so pleased to see you."

I follow her, noticing the house is clean, not what I expected seeing as I did all of that. The sitting room has had a lick of paint, and it looks bright and fresh. Dad is on a new sofa, watching television and even he looks clean and well groomed.

"Look who I found standing in the pouring rain," announces Claire excitedly, and dad looks up.

When he sees me, his eyes brighten, and he stands. "Bella, wow you look amazing," he says, looking surprised to see me. He pulls me into a hug.

"Hey Dad," I whisper, hugging him back. I'm shocked by his physical appearance. He's thin, and he looks so tired and gaunt.

We sit down, and Claire goes off to make a drink. "So, Claire is…?" I ask, and he blushes slightly.

"She was my nurse; things have progressed, and she moved in last month."

"Nurse?" I repeat. "You've been sick?"

He laughs, "Don't tell me you thought I looked well?" he teases.

My smile fades, "Is it serious?"

"I haven't seen you in such a long time, Bells. I don't want to waste it talking about me getting old. How have you been?"

I shrug, "Up and down. I brought a shop," I add, "Just a small bakery, but it's busy. I specialise in wedding cakes."

"That's fantastic. Well done you."

Claire returns, placing a tray on the table with tea and biscuits. She sets about pouring each of us a small cup. "Did you hear that, Claire, my little girl is a businesswoman."

She smiles too, "Amazing. You always said she'd do good things. Maybe we can come and see it?"

"Actually, that's why I'm here," I explain. "I'm moving away."

Dad instantly looks upset, but he covers it well with a grin, "Anywhere we know?"

I shake my head, "No. It's quite a way."

"That's not a good-" Claire begins but dad shushes her.

"It's a great idea. A fresh start is exactly what you need."

I nod in agreement. "What about your shop?" Claire asks.

"I've hired a manager. And I'll call regular to check he's doing okay. Who knows, maybe I can branch out."

I take out a piece of paper with my phone number, placing it on the table. "This is my number if you need me. Eventually, I'll forward my address and maybe you can both come and stay?"

Claire exchanges a worried look with dad, but right now, I don't want to know the reasons behind it. Because no matter what, I can't stay here. Nothing can change that.

Aiden

"Relax," says Raff, holding me against the nearest wall.

I growl out in frustration. "Just tell me," I yell.

Cal gives Raff a look that says, *'take him away'*. "I have no idea where she's going, Aiden. But if I did know, I wouldn't tell you."

"Not helping," snaps Raff.

"She's freed herself," Cal continues. "And I'm glad. I hope she meets the perfect man who will treat her like the queen she is."

"Fuck you," I spit, pushing Raff away and rushing down the steps.

We go to the nearest bar, and I order two beers and two shots. "Not a good idea," says Raff.

"How the fuck can she just disappear?" I demand, knocking the shot back.

"Maybe it's for the best," he mutters.

"Why do I keep fucking up?" I yell and a few of the other customers glance my way. "Why the hell did I tell her I didn't want kids with her?"

He frowns, "She asked that?"

I nod. "And I told her there was no chance after everything." His frown deepens, "What?" I ask.

"It's just a weird thing to ask, isn't it?" I shrug, thinking back to her earlier words. "Like she's checking she's made a right decision?" he pushes.

"You're saying she's pregnant?" I ask.

"I'm saying it's a weird thing to ask, Aiden."

I shake my head. "She's not. I saw her take the morning after pill myself."

"I think you should see this as a sign, man. She's gone. It's for the best."

Maybe he's right. And after everything we've done to one another, this feels final. She's gone and now we both get to see what life is like now we're fully apart.

I take another drink and sigh heavily. "I joined a dating app."

He stares for a long moment before a smirk spreads over his face. He laughs, "You had me there." When he sees I'm not laughing, the smirk fades. "You're serious?"

"And, someone messaged me. We matched."

"You matched," he repeats, "Just hearing you say those words gives me nightmares. What the hell made you join a dating app?"

"I always find women in bars, right? My thought is, if I meet someone outside of a bar, maybe re-invent myself somewhat, I can change my behaviour."

He pinches the bridge of his nose. "Aiden, just stop shagging around."

"Exactly. That's the plan. I'm going to meet Emmie in a coffee shop."

He eyes me, "You're serious?"

"Yes."

"Holy shit. Aiden Tremos dating."

I grin. "Jake would love it."

"Jake would have you sectioned. You don't date, in fact you do everything you can to avoid it."

"Well, being with Bella made me realise there's more to it than I thought."

"You weren't even dating Bella," he cries.

"We spent a good few weeks there where things were really good. It's not my fault she messed it all up."

He rolls his eyes. "And you were so innocent."

"We both fucked up, so maybe you're right and we're just not good for each other. I'm going to meet Emmie and try to do things properly."

Bella

I arrive in St Monanas in the early hours. The small cottage I've rented on a short lease, takes my breath away, much like the tiny Scottish village did on my drive through. I push the green wooden gate, smiling when it creaks in protest, and head up the path. There are flowers either side of me, and I can't wait for daylight so I can take in their beauty.

I find the key under the matt, just like Mr. Limes instructed. Inside, the smell of lavender immediately hits me, reminding me of my mum. It feels like a sign, maybe she's right here with me.

I place my bag on the floor and close the door before turning on the lights. I gasp in delight, it's exactly how I pictured it. Cosy, cute and with all the original features a cottage boasts, including wooden beams. Aria would hate this. But to me, it's homely. I feel like I've made the right decision and when I pull out my mobile to send Aria a picture of the ornamental horse on the fireplace, and realise I have no signal, it's almost like this cottage knows exactly what I need. Peace and quiet.

I briefly check the kitchen and notice Mr. Limes has left me a fresh pint of milk in the fridge. It's just another reason to make me smile. But I'm far too tired to make a drink, so I head upstairs to find my bedroom.

I'm relieved to see the bed is made up, and almost cry happy tears when I realise it's freshly washed. I'd ordered home comforts like this and the towels, to come directly here. Everything was so last minute, and I didn't want to drag everything over in my car. Besides, I wanted new things for my new start. I must remember to buy my new landlord a gift to show my appreciation.

※

I manage a few hours' sleep but excitement to explore wakes me the second the sun rises. Once I'm showered and dressed, I head out. The village is literally a two-minute walk, and I was told everything I'd need was there. But right now, all I'm craving is a hot breakfast and a coffee.

I find a small coffee shop and head inside. The smell of fresh bread hits me and my stomach growls in anticipation. There's a woman behind the counter around my age and she smiles wide. "Hi, I'm Blair," she introduces, holding out her hand.

I shake it, returning her smile, "Bella."

"Are you just passing through?" she asks.

"No, I'm renting the cottage over the road, April Cottage."

"Aww, Mr. Limes' place. Welcome, I own this place. And you're first order is on me, so what can I get you?"

"Thank you so much, I'll take a coffee."

"And you have to try my home baked bread with jam."

I nod and take a seat. Minutes later she brings over a coffee and two thick slices of toasted bread, smothered in butter and Jam.

She takes a seat opposite me, "Let me fill you in."

We spend some time chatting. She tells me about some of the places to see and where to go for things like groceries. She tells me about the two village pubs and how everyone knows everyone, so I should get used to people dropping in and chatting. It sounds like the perfect place. She offers to meet me later and introduce me to some of the locals.

Blair points me in the direction of the local bakery, I want to see if they have any vacancies, but she seems to think that there won't be any. She told me to try the local farm though as they need help in their farm shop.

I pass the doctors surgery on route to the bakery and decide to pop in and fill out any forms. The receptionist hands me a clip board. "Would you like to meet the doctor today and perhaps get a health check?" she asks with a friendly smile, "he's free now."

I'm not used to such an efficient service, it's refreshing. "That would be great."

After the forms are completed, I hand them and she leads me along a passage, knocking lightly on the door. "Come in," shouts a male from the other side. She glances back at me with a glint in her eye, before opening the door to announce my arrival. "A new patient, Doctor."

The Doctor stands, and I momentarily forget to breathe. He's gorgeous and not in a big, muscle Aiden kind of way, but a Chris Hemsworth kind of way. The receptionist smiles at me like this was what she was waiting for, to see my reaction.

He shakes my hand. "How lovely to meet you, Mrs...?" and he waits.

I continue to stare open mouthed, unable to find any words. *What's my name?* He smiles, shifting uncomfortably under my gawping eyes, then he glances to the receptionist, probably wondering if I'm some kind of mute.

"Bella," I huff out, grinning like an idiot.

"Come in, take a seat. I'm doctor Lain. Grant Lain." I sit opposite him. He glances through my paperwork then stands. "Can I?" and he holds up his stethoscope.

I give a nod, and he proceeds to round the desk, rubbing the metal against his palm, "I'll warm it up," he adds with a small laugh. He stands behind me and places it down the back of my shirt and against my back. He listens before moving to my front where I open my top slightly, so he has access to my chest. After a few more seconds, he gives a satisfied nod, then takes my blood pressure.

"Slightly higher than I'd expect," he says, "Are you feeling well in yourself?" I nod again, and he laughs. "You can talk, can't you?"

I blush, *I'm such an idiot*. "Sorry, I'm a little tired. It was a long journey through the night."

"London to Scotland really is a long journey," he agrees.

"There is a reason for me popping in to register today," I add, "I'm pregnant. Only a few weeks but I recently miscarried and so I'm a little stressed and anxious."

He sits back down and makes a note. "Okay, well congratulations. You and Mr. Bella May must be very pleased."

"There is no Mr, just me," I confirm.

I have to get used to that line in a small village like this. People will probably talk about the single pregnant woman that's run away to Scotland.

"Sorry, I shouldn't have presumed like that. How far along do you think you are?"

"Only four weeks, very early stages. I'd taken the morning after pill but was sick within an hour of taking it, I stupidly didn't really think much of it at the time."

"Would you like to discuss options?" he asks, frowning.

I shake my head, "No, I want to keep the baby. It was a mistake to take the morning after pill."

He smiles, "It worked out well then," and he gives a laugh to ease the tension. "Let's get you started on vitamins. I'll send for your notes today and then I'll be in touch. But you've come to the best place, Bella, we'll keep a close eye on you. So for now, rest and take it easy."

I release a long breath, "Thanks. I appreciate you seeing me."

"This isn't London," he says, "We'll always see you no matter what time or day." I stand, and he follows. "It was lovely to meet you, Bella. I look forward to seeing a lot more of you." Images of my smear test flash through my mind and I cringe. I can never have a smear again.

The bakery is a few doors up. The lovely elderly woman tells me she doesn't have a vacancy, but she'll hire me anyway because she could do with the help now she's getting older. I'm so happy I could cry. It's only a few hours a day, which is perfect for me, and with the monthly money from the shop back in London, I'll be fine.

Life here is going to be amazing. I can feel it.

Aiden

It's been weeks since Bella left and even though she's still on my mind most days, I'm starting to relax in the knowledge, we've both made the right decision. When I popped into the bakery last week to collect the books, Aria wasted no time filling me in on how amazing Bella's new life is. She even made sure to tell me all about the hot doctor she'd met. And although I left there feeling jealous, which was clearly Aria's intention, I know it's the right thing for Bella. She deserves to be happy.

I take a deep breath to clear my mind, and turn back to the stacks of paperwork in front of me. JP pops his head around the door, "Any news?" he asks.

Laurie is having a c-section today and the DNA test will be done right after if all is well. I shake my head. "Aria asked me to go to Scotland," he adds, stepping further in.

"A mini break," I say, my tone teasing, "Whatever next, marriage?"

"You sound bitter," he says, also grinning.

"Just be careful, that scary little she devil will get her claws into you, and you'll become her little bitch."

"I welcome the pain," he says, smirking.

"Why Scotland?" I ask, tapping some figures into the calculator. When he doesn't reply I glance up and he shifts uncomfortably. I sigh, "She's in Scotland." Everyone is treating it like some big secret, scared I'm going to chase her down and drag her back here. I roll my eyes in irritation, "Just go to Scotland, JP. Say hi to the Doctor from me."

"Aria told you?" he guesses.

I scoff, "Of course she did. She couldn't wait to tell me. But I'm good with it. I don't know how many times you want me to say I'm over Bella. So I don't care where she is or who she's fucking. I'm done."

He gives a nod, a smirk playing on his lips. "If you say so."

I ignore him, letting him leave. I'll need to cover his shifts whilst he plays happy families. I groan out loud, grabbing my mobile and opening up Bella's social media. I haven't been on since she left, and part of me is praying she's locked her account so I can't see it. Her beautiful smile fills my screen and my heart twists. I swipe through her recent pictures where she's at the beach with a group of people, looking amazing in a bikini. She's started to put weight back on and she looks healthier for it. The next picture catches my eye, and I stop scrolling. She's with a tall guy. He's clean cut and preppy looking, most likely the doctor. They're staring at one another and laughing, and I hate that I'm not in on the joke.

I sigh heavily and put the phone down. I'm torturing myself with my past, and if I don't stop, I'll be driving to

Scotland just so I can hear her laughter or smell her vanilla perfume.

I lose myself in office work until my phone alerts me to a text message. It's a picture. I wait for it to load on to my phone. A close up shot of a tiny baby's face fills my screen, it's captioned. 'A baby boy. Send your doctor.' I'm holding my breath but I'm not sure why. I knew this day would come and it's time to find out what my future holds.

I fire off a text to my doctor, asking him to complete the test. I look at the picture again. It's hard to see who he looks like; he's just a baby and he doesn't look like anything but a sleeping baby. I expected my heart to react in some way but maybe it's protecting itself until I know the truth. I go to the safe and pull out an envelope ready for the doctor, I pay handsomely for the extra services I keep using.

Bella

The weeks are blurring into one, each passing as quickly as the last. I find myself missing home, yet not wanting to leave here because it's perfect. The people are friendly, and there's a sleepy feel to the village, a stark contrast from London. I can even leave my front door unlocked, which is perfect for when the doc pops around to check on me, which he often does seeing he lives right opposite me.

"How's the sickness?" asks Grant, sitting in the flowery armchair by my window.

I've spent the entire morning laying on the couch battling the 'morning' sickness which seems to last most of the day at the minute.

I open one eye to see him watching me. "I can't even go into the garden to enjoy this beautiful weather," I complain. "I hate spending my Saturday like this."

"Ginger tea?" he suggests, standing and heading for the kitchen. "The farmers boys are celebrating Georges thirtieth birthday in the village; I've just passed them and it's messy. I feel like there will be many complaints in the Dog & Sheep," he shouts through to me.

I slowly sit up, hoping that the movement doesn't make me vomit. "I wish I was out getting messy instead of being in here feeling miserable."

Grant returns, placing my tea down, and sits next to me. "When do your friends arrive?"

I check my watch. "Any time now," I say, "They set off early."

I'm nervous about seeing Aria, mainly because I've yet to reveal the pregnancy. I didn't hide it on purpose, I just didn't want to put her in an awkward situation with JP, especially if the worst happened again. But now I'm twelve weeks, and Grant seems fairly certain the pregnancy is healthy, there's no reason not to tell her.

As if his question conjures her up, there's a knock at the door. I don't even have to shout come in before Aria is bounding into the tiny cottage like a puppy dog. "Oh my god I love this," she squeals looking around through wide eyes.

I smile and stand, Grant follows my lead. She throws herself at me and we hug for a long time. It feels good to finally see her but weird that she's here in my new life.

A shadow appears in the doorway and JP enters carrying a couple of bags. He bends to get his huge body through the cottage door. Once inside he places the bags down and eyes Grant suspiciously. Grant puts his hand out to him. "Grant Lain, you must be JP."

JP shakes his hand, and I breathe a sigh of relief, for a minute there I thought he was going to ignore him. "Bells," he rumbles, with a nod of his head.

"Good to see you JP."

Aria suddenly reaches for my wrist and turns me towards her, eyeing my small bump with shock. I give my head a slight shake, I'm not ready for JP to know who will undoubtedly tell Aiden. She pulls me into another hug to disguise her discovery. "You look amazing," she whispers.

"I don't know about you, JP, but I could do with a pint, do you fancy it?" asks Grant.

JP nods, "I'm not gonna turn down a drink." He gives Aria a quick kiss on the head. "Catch up with Bella and meet us later?" She nods and he leaves with Grant.

I lead Aria out to the back garden where we are surrounded by bright flowers. I purchased a garden table just so I could sit here and watch the bee's enjoying the fruits of my hard work. Since coming here I've become a bit of a green fingers.

"What the actual fuck, Bella?" she hisses, "You didn't think to mention that you're pregnant again?"

"I'm sorry, I know I really should have but I wanted to wait until I'd had my twelve-week scan, after last time I didn't want to get anyone's hopes up."

"When did you find out? How the hell did it happen. Is it the doctor?"

I laugh. "Grant's my friend. *A really hot friend*," and I wiggle my eyebrows. "It's Aiden's. I haven't slept with anyone else and honestly; I don't want to."

"The whole reason you and Aiden split was because of lies," she reminds me.

I nod, "I know. He lied, I lied. And now I'm keeping more secrets." I sigh. "You saw how he was before I left, Aria. I can't risk being hurt all over again. He took half my business just to spite me," I say with an empty laugh. "He hates me and that's no way to raise a child."

"He was angry, Bella. We all say things when we're upset."

"I'm not taking the risk. He's entitled to walk away, and I respect that. But I already lost one baby, and I won't lose another. I'm not asking him for anything, so he doesn't need to know."

Aria takes my hand in a reassuring squeeze. "You're right. He won't find out from me."

"Is he okay?" I didn't plan on asking but it slips out.

Aria gives a shrug. "I don't ask JP about anything Aiden related, and he doesn't tell me. I've seen him a couple of times when he's popped into the shop to get the books. He's the same arrogant arse he's always been."

"And the business, how's things working out?" I miss working with Aria, but I still send my designs to Guy to create, making sure to keep my stamp on the place. And he's amazing at bringing my creations to light. I also run the website and do the books.

"I love Guy," she says with a smile. "We have fun and if I can't have you, he's the next best thing."

"That makes me feel better about deserting you," I admit.

An hour later we join the guys in the pub. It's still rammed with the farmers plus some other locals. The sunshine seems to have everyone out. JP is fitting in well and chatting with random locals, but it's how this place is. It's how I got sucked in.

CHAPTER TWENTY-NINE

Aiden

"Honestly, it's amazing, Raff. The views, the country girls."

JP is going on about his recent visit to Scotland. It was so amazing they extended their stay and had five days instead of the two they were originally going for.

"Any chance you could get on with restocking the coolers instead of gossiping like a girl?" I snap. "Who the hell are you, talking about views? You sound like a pussy." I scowl.

"Why are you at the bar anyway?" he mutters, grabbing a box of Bud off the bar and opening the fridge.

"I can work where I want," I snap, scanning my eyes over the accounts book for the bakery. I don't tell him it's because I'm itching to know all about Bella and what she's doing these days.

"Ignore him," says Raff, "he's been moody over anything Bella related."

I scoff, "Whatever," I mutter. "I'm not moody over these accounts, the place is running a tidy profit." I smirk, "In fact, I'm regretting not taking it all."

"She's worked hard for that place, man," JP mutters.

"Where is she now, JP? Not working her backside off in the shop. She's ran off and left someone else in charge."

I gather my paperwork and head for the office, JP is ruining my vibe, and I've come up with an idea . . . one that means I have an excuse to speak to Bella.

I sit at my desk and dial her number. After four rings the line connects. I hear a scuffling and a giggle, *her giggle*. My heart beats a little faster. Eventually she speaks. "Don't hang up, one second." She's laughing. I wait patiently listening to any sounds that give me a clue to her new life. "Hello," she finally says, sounding out of breath.

"Hey Bella, it's Aiden." It satisfies me to hear her sharp intake of breath. *I still affect her.*

"Oh, Hi."

"I've just been looking over the books for the shop, it's doing really well."

"Erm, yeah it is, Guy's doing a fantastic job at running it."

"So, I was thinking. You were right before; I should take it all on." There's a pause and I wait to see how she'll react. I miss our heated fights.

"Aiden, you can't do that. I need that income. I didn't fight you before because I felt guilty, but I will fight you on this," she says clearly and calmly.

I can imagine that she's pacing, panicking and trying to find all the reasons to convince me not to do this. "It was my money that paid for it," I remind her with a smirk on my face.

"You gave the money to me. I've come to rely on that extra income, Aiden. You can't just take my business," she snaps.

"The business you paid for with my money. I could tell a judge I loaned you that in good faith. There's a clear paper trail from my account to yours. A small claims court would cost you a fortune in fees, which you'd have to pay should I win."

She falls silent for a few seconds. "Aiden, please don't do this to me. You have the clubs and a bar and half of my shop. I have nothing if you take the rest. You don't need to do this. At least offer me a fair price."

I scoff. "I already paid. It's just business, Bella. Nothing personal. Besides, Laurie had the baby. I'm waiting on the results, but if he's mine, I'll need the extra money to pay towards my sons' upkeep." I don't know why I say it. It must hurt her since she lost our baby, but it flows out of my mouth before I can talk sense into my brain.

"Congratulations," she mutters, "Considering you didn't want a kid you're pretty keen on stepping up."

"I didn't say I didn't want a kid, Isabella, I said I didn't want one with you."

"Jesus Aiden, do you sit and practice nasty lines to throw at me? Were you bored so you thought to yourself, I'll give my ex a call seeing as I hate her so damn much, and I'll throw some shit at her to ruin her fucking day. Well, mission accomplished, you've ruined my day so well done you. You aren't having the business, I need it. So, take me to every court in the world, the answer won't change. I moved away, I gave you half, I left my friends and still you want to destroy me."

"Bella, calm down, think about your blood pressure." I hear a male's voice and my skin prickles. *Is she ill?* She covers the mouthpiece, so I can't hear what's being said, and then she comes back on the line, "Aiden, I have to go."

"Have you moved on, Bella?" I find myself asking. I close my eyes, waiting for the answer.

"I'm happy here, Aiden, and I won't be coming back, so you can relax. Good luck with Laurie and the baby, I hope it's the outcome you want. See you in court." She disconnects the call.

I stare at my mobile with my heart twisting painfully. I'd never really thought about Bella never coming back.

※

My mobile vibrates across the polished desk, making a loud humming sound. It's the doctor. I snatch the phone up and connect the call. "Aiden, I have your results in. Congratulations, you've had a lucky escape, he isn't yours."

Relief floods my body and a weight lifts from my shoulders. I release a long breath, Thanks, Doc. Can you email me the results so I can forward them to Laurie."

I pull the results up and call Laurie. "Hey gorgeous," she purrs, and I roll my eyes, motherhood hasn't changed her.

"Laurie, he's not mine."

She lets out a frustrated cry and I move the receiver from my ear on a wince. It's clearly not the news she was hoping for. "He has to be, he looks just like you."

"I've sent the results to your email, Laurie. He isn't mine. I suggest you concentrate on being a good mum and sorting your marriage out."

She begins to sob, "Can I still see you?"

"No Laurie, I've moved on. We need to accept that we were over years ago. It was sex and nothing more." She hangs up on me. That's two women I've upset in one day, I'm on a roll.

I send a text to Bella.

> **Me: Good news, the baby isn't mine. Keep your share of the business. It was good to hear your voice, Bella. I've missed you yelling at me. Aiden x**

I wait for her reply, it comes a few minutes later.

> **Bella: I'm sad you are so full of hate. You could be happy, but you choose not to be. Take care.**

Bella's right. It's time to let go of the hate and move forward. Her and Laurie are out of my life. Maybe I need to find someone that will make me happy.

Later, When I tell Raff my plans to start dating, they laugh so much, they hold on to each other. I roll my eyes. "Fuck off. I can do this; it can't be that hard."

"You realise you have to stay faithful, you can't be having orgies or other dates," says Raff.

"And the dating app he signed up to was used purely for hook ups," JP reminds him.

"If she's the right one I won't want to cheat, will I?"

JP nods. "That's true, I don't want to cheat on Aria." Raff throws a dish towel at him.

"That's because you're scared of the nutter," I laugh, and Raff high fives me.

Bella

It's official, I hate pregnancy. I'm seven months gone, and already I'm finding it hard. I can't sleep, and I constantly feel like my insides are being shoved out of my vagina. I'm grumpy and fed up, and the only bonus to it all, is that the winter weather is so cold I'm not overheating.

The middle of the night is when the baby dino always likes to play, and so I find myself taking a short walk through the empty village to try and wear myself out. It's two in the morning and the only sounds I can hear in the street are animals that surround us in the fields.

After ten minutes I decide to turn back. The dino is much calmer.

I get to my gate when I hear my name. I notice Grant sticking his head out of his bedroom window and smile.

I head over to his gate. "What are you doing, you crazy woman?"

"I can't sleep again; I thought a walk would help."

"Must be something in the air, me either. Come in, I'll make us some cocoa."

I wait at the door, and he eventually opens it, pulling me inside. "Mrs. Bennett will be gossiping if she sees you sneaking into the doctors house in the wee hours," he grins mischievously.

"They'll think you got me in this state," I tease pointing to my swollen stomach.

He unbuttons my coat, hanging it next to the door. "That beats the rumours that I'm gay."

"Yeah, I heard that one, it makes no difference to me though."

Grant looks at me blankly. "Bella, you know I'm not gay right?" he asks, and I shrug, "I'm not gay. Not that there's anything wrong with it, but it's not for me. A man can't possibly just be single these days," he says with a huff.

"Well in a small village like this people will wonder. A good-looking doctor with no interest in the local women, it raises questions," I say. I sit at his breakfast bar whilst he pours milk into a saucepan.

"I was married. She died," he says quietly.

"Oh, crap Grant, I am so sorry. It's none of my business."

He turns the gas on the stove up and places the pan down. "We married at eighteen. She was my childhood sweetheart. She died five years ago after a short illness. I came here to be alone. I don't want to find love because she was it for me, so I found this small village that needed a GP." He pours the milk over the cocoa and gives it a stir. "What about you?" he asks sitting down.

"I met Aiden through my dad. I fell in love, and he hurt me. He isn't ready for babies or settling down and I didn't want him to feel obliged, so I came here. He doesn't know about the baby, and I don't plan on telling him. Single parents raise babies all of the time."

He nods. "That they do Bella, that they do. Don't you ever get lonely though?"

I think over his question, before shaking my head. "No, never. This village is the best. I've got you and Blair. Brook. All of the locals really. And even if you were all busy, I know I could just go into the local pub and find someone to chat to." I take a sip and close my eyes in delight as the smooth chocolate warms my insides. "Do you get lonely?"

He nods. "All of the time. I miss her so much. And I miss the little things we did together like lying in bed on a Sunday morning reading the newspapers. Enjoying a glass of wine in the garden together and debriefing about our day."

I never really had that with Aiden. We argued and had sex, and I can only recall a few times when we lay in bed chatting. It makes me feel sad that we never really got that far. I won't have any good tales to tell my child about his or her father. "Well, I can drink wine in the garden once this dinosaur is born," I say with a smile, "And I'm always free to chat, Grant, don't be alone. I know it's not the same."

Aiden

Dating has been interesting. And using the app was not the best idea. Firstly, I discovered there are a lot of liars out there catfishing people. Secondly, there are way too many unstable people in the world and that damn app gives them the perfect opportunity to meet unsuspecting people. So, when JP suggested I meet his old college friend, Jenifer, I was a little wary. But it turns out, she's normal. And to my relief, she's exactly my type looks wise too.

We've been on four dates, and I've managed to keep my hands to myself and be the perfect gentleman. A first for me if you don't count Bella. We've even been to the cinema, something I haven't done since school. And I'm enjoying it. I don't know why I didn't try it before. She also confided that she's looking for a career change after working years in a sandwich deli, and rather than ignore it, I took action, offering her a non-existent position at the bakery.

So, on Monday morning, I drop by to find Aria whipping up something in a large bowl. She sighs when she spots me. "What?"

"What time does he turn up to open?" I ask.

"He's coming in late today, why?"

It irritates me that he's not open like Aria. "I've hired an apprentice. Get him to call me when he decides to show up." I head for the door.

"What? You can't just hire someone, that's a joint decision for you and Bella to make," she argues.

I round on her, irritated she's questioning me. "Does Bella know he's not opening up on time?" I snap.

"Does she know about your apprentice?"

"She doesn't need to know because I own half of the shop, Aria," I shout. "But I could always have a drive up to Scotland to ask her face to face if you like?" I know this will shut her up because for some reason, she doesn't want me to know about Bella's new life all of a sudden.

"Who is this person anyway, how do you know them and do they have experience at all?"

I check my watch, "She's almost here, you can ask her yourself."

"A woman?" she says with a sigh.

Guy and Jenifer arrive together a few minutes later. "Guy, just in time. Meet your new apprentice, Jenifer." I say with a grin.

He looks at Aria confused. Jenifer comes straight to me, and I wrap an arm around her shoulders and kiss her on the side of her head.

"Oh my god, is this your latest fuck?" Aria asks.

"You're being rude," I snap. "And for the record, this has nothing to do with you."

"This isn't going to happen," she snaps. "No offence Jenifer," she adds, "But I know him, and he'll get bored. Where will that leave Guy?"

I tug Jen closer, trying to reassure her. "Ignore her, she's bitter and twisted," I tell her.

"Is Bella okay with this?" asks Guy.

"I'll smooth things with Bella but as part owner, this is my decision. And it's final."

♥

I spend the rest of the day in meetings, and so I don't get the chance to call Bella. I don't feel bad about it. It's been months and I've herd nothing from her. She's clearly happy in Scotland and we've all moved on. I just need to convince Aria to back off.

When I arrive at the shop to pick Jen up, there's an atmosphere. Guy avoids my eye, as he packs cakes away into boxes. Aria is resting her hip against the counter with her arms crossed and her eyes narrowed. And Jen looks ready to burst into tears.

"What's wrong?" I ask, as Jen slips her coat on and heads towards me.

"It's not going to work out for me here, Aiden. But thanks for the chance," she says quietly. Aria gives me a smug smile.

"Don't you like the baking side of things?" I push.

"It's not that," she mutters.

"Guy, what happened?" I demand.

"I guess it's just awkward for the girls," he says, shrugging.

"Did you have a problem with Jen working with you today?" I ask, and he shakes his head. I turn to Aria, "So you have the problem?"

"Yes Aiden, yes, I do have a problem. You screwed over my best friend and now you bring your fuck of the week to work in her shop," she snaps.

I grab her by the top of her arm, and she starts yelling abuse at me. My large frame maneuver's hers without a problem, and I shove her through to her own shop. "If you carry on with these antics, I'll brick this door up. This business is nothing to do with you. Stay the fuck out my shop." I slam the door in her face.

I turn to Guy, "I'm the boss. Jen is staying. If there are any more problems, the door goes. Understand?"

Guy nods and gives Jen a smile, "See you tomorrow."

Jen is quiet on the journey back to mine. I take her hand. "Sorry for losing it back there. Aria drives me insane sometimes," I explain.

"Are you doing this to upset your ex?" she asks.

I take a minute to think about her question. "No," I reply honestly. "I just wanted to help you out. If you don't want to be there you don't have to stay."

"I do, it's just Aria doesn't like me."

"Aria doesn't like anyone."

"She said you treated your ex really badly and that you're going to hurt me."

"Aria needs to keep her nose out. Bella lied to me, and I dumped her, end of. Aria's only pissed because Bella moved away and she blames me for that, when in actual fact, it was her own decision."

I stop the car outside the club. I can feel Jen watching me closely, I turn to her, and she sighs, "It's just you haven't made any move on me yet, I was wondering if it's because you still love her?"

"I didn't love her in the first place. It was just sex. I don't want that with you, I want to get to know you properly. Do things right." The lie burns my chest, but I don't want Jen to worry about me and Bella when that's not the issue.

Jen leans in for a kiss and I happily oblige. She wraps her hands around the back of my neck and deepens it, flitting her tongue against mine, teasing me. She climbs over to me, not breaking the kiss, and sits in my lap before I can pull away. "Fuck getting it right," she whispers with a smile, rubbing against me.

My chest tightens and I feel enclosed, like it's all too much. Her rubbing against me and kissing me like I'm her last meal, doesn't feel right and this isn't the first time it's happened. My cock stays in its sleepy state and I pull back slightly, gently placing my hands on her shoulders and offering a weak smile. She sighs in defeat, already knowing this will end in rejection. "Slow down," I say, keeping my tone light so I don't offend her. I brush a thumb over her cheek and smile, "I need to do this right." She rolls her eyes, falling back into her seat beside me.

I'm saved when my mobile begins to vibrate in my pocket. "Sorry," I mutter, as I pull it out, "I need to take this."

I don't even check the caller display before I answer, happy for the excuse to escape this awkwardness. "How dare you make decisions like hiring a fucking apprentice without speaking to me," Bella yells.

I pull it away from my ear, wincing. "Bella," I say with a false enthusiasm. "I was going to call."

"But as usual you decided to go into cunt mode and make all your own decisions without thinking about the business."

"I think you'll find I was thinking completely about the business. An extra pair of hands is going to help us make more orders. You left leaving us a person down."

"Bullshit," she cries, "I managed the shop completely alone and I was doing just fine. For once in your selfish life admit the truth. You do this shit to get a rise from me."

"Believe it or not, Bella, this isn't about you."

"We don't need an apprentice. Especially not one that you'll dump in a week because you've found a prettier one."

I look over at Jenifer, who's staring straight ahead, clearly able to hear every word. "Jen is different," I say, and Jenifer glances at me, "I'm doing it right with her." She gives me a small smile.

"What?" Bella snaps, and I'm not sure if she didn't hear me or she's just shocked.

"Me and Jen are serious."

There's silence from Bella's end, and then she scoffs. "Well, congratulations, Aiden. Congratu-fuck-ing-lations!" she says sarcastically before disconnecting the call.

CHAPTER THIRTY

Bella

I'm furious. The second Aria called me, I was raging and even though Grant warned me not to call Aiden whilst I was so angry, I couldn't help myself.

Grant places a herbal tea on the table for me and sits beside me. "You okay?"

I burst into tears, and he wraps an arm around me. "I don't know why I'm so upset," I say between sobs, "It's hormones."

"It's natural you're going to feel upset, Bella. He's messing with the business and making decisions without informing you. But at this late stage, you could do without the stress. Maybe now would be a good time to tell him the truth?"

I shake my head, wiping my tears on the sleeve of my jumper. "No. He's happy, I can tell by his voice. If I go wading in there to tell him about this baby, he'll accuse me of just trying to ruin his new relationship." I bury my face in my hands, I just feel like he's replaced me so easily. What does she have that I don't?" I sob some more, and Grant gently rubs my back.

"He's a fool, Bella. Some guys don't know what they have right in front of them."

I stare at him, my mind racing with thoughts. Aiden moving on. Being a single parent. And Grant. What would it feel like to kiss someone that isn't Aiden? Is Grant a gentle lover or will he take control? I tilt my head slightly, not registering the confused look on his face as I press my lips to his. I cup his face, then realise he's not responding to me. I pull back and his eyes find mine. They're not full of heat like I imagined, but of fear, a stone-cold fear.

"Oh shit," I whisper, "I'm so sorry."

"It's fine," he mutters, standing.

"No, it's not. I just got confused, I'm an emotional mess," I mutter, my face burning with embarrassment.

My mobile begins to ring and we both stare at it. I snatch it up, seeing my dad's name.

"Hello."

"Hi Isabella, It's Claire, your dad's friend."

I frown in confusion. "Oh, hi Claire. Is everything Okay?"

"Not really sweetie. I have some bad news. Your Dad has deteriorated. He's in hospital but the Doctors have asked me to contact you because they aren't sure if he's going to get through this."

I let her words sink in, "Oh god, I didn't realise he was sick."

"He didn't want to tell you, Bella. He thought it would make you stick around, and he knew you needed to get away."

"I'll get the train as soon as I can. Tell him I'm on my way."

I disconnect with a heavy heart. I know we've been estranged lately but I still love him. Grant is watching me with concern. "It's my dad," I tell him, shrugging, "He's taken ill."

"The train is a long ride; I can take you?" It's sweet of him to offer, especially after what just happened between us.

I begin to gather things I'll need and Grant follows. "No, it's too far, and you have your duties here. How will Mrs. Brown cope with her blisters," I joke. "Besides, the train gives me a chance to move around, you know how uncomfortable I'm getting now I'm closer to the end, it's the reason I'm not driving myself."

I begin to grab clothes from my closet and Grant taps away on his mobile. "The next train to London is in one hour," he says, "I'll drop you at the station."

"Thank you," I say, "And I'm sorry about-"

"It's already forgotten about," he says, smiling. "And for the record, it's not you-"

I groan, burying my face in my hands, "Please don't say that line."

He laughs, tugging my hands away, "But it's true. It really is me. I can't move on, I'm not ready. But if I was, you'd totally be the one for me."

I feel my cheeks burning with embarrassment. "Thanks for not making it awkward."

"Friends?" he asks.

I nod, "Friends."

"Good. Finish packing, we need to go."

The train stops in St Pancras, and I drag my case off with a heavy heart. I called Aria during the journey, and she insisted I stay with her. I spot her waiting by the entrance and as I approach, she rushes over, wrapping me in a big hug and taking my case from me. "Oh wow, you look amazing," she says, holding me at arm's length. "And the bump is bumping," she adds, gently placing her hand there. "What do you want to do first, sleep, eat or visit your dad?" she asks, leading the way to her car.

"Hospital," I reply, "Claire has been updating me over text message and it's not looking good."

Aria gives me a sympathetic smile, "I'm so sorry, Bells."

She drops me at the hospital where Claire greets me with a hug. It's comforting and I sense relief pouring from her. "he's been asking for you," she whispers, taking me by the hand and leading me into the intensive care ward. "And your mum." My heart twists. "He's confused but they say that's normal. He's sleeping a lot but he'll be so happy to see you." She stops by a closed curtain, "Don't be alarmed. There are a lot of machines and wires but they're there to help him." I hold my breath as she pulls the curtain back. My eyes fill with tears at seeing the man I love, so small and vulnerable. A sob escapes and I slap my hand over my mouth. Claire gently rubs my back. "It's a lot to take," she whispers.

I move to the side of his bed, carefully taking his hand in mine. It feels so cold and thin. I watch as Claire places a kiss on his head, "Guess who came to see you," she tells him, even though he doesn't respond. "Isabella." His eyes flutter open, and she smiles, running a hand over his cheek. "And look at that bump," she adds.

He turns his head slowly, until his eyes find me, and he offers a weak smile. There are dark circles under his eyes, they even look a little sunken that I remember. I return the smile, "Hey you."

"You came," he croaks.

"Of course I came, you're my dad."

"Sorry. I know it's hassle," he murmurs.

Before I can respond, his eyes flutter closed again and Claire gives a sad smile, "He keeps drifting off mid conversation. It's normal at this stage."

"What stage?" I ask, frowning. "I didn't know he was sick."

Claire lowers into a seat, "It's cancer, Bella."

I inhale sharply, my world tilting slightly. I feel behind me until my hands find the chair and I also sit. "It was in his liver, and we thought he was beating it, but then they found it in other places."

Tears slip down my cheeks. "He didn't say anything." Suddenly the months of not speaking hit me hard. If only I hadn't walked out and cut him off.

"It's not your fault, Bella. He didn't want you to know and he was so certain he'd beat it, he didn't want to worry you."

"So can they treat it? Will he recover?"

I see by her expression that he won't, and more sobs escape me. "I'm so sorry, Bella but the doctors don't think he's going to make the week."

I cry hard, until my chest aches and my throat's sore. And when I begin to settle, Claire moves closer and we sit hand in hand, watching him sleep.

Aiden

"What do you mean you need a night off?" I ask as JP sits opposite me.

I came into the office to catch up on some paperwork but if JP takes the night off, I may end up pulling in a shift if I can't find cover.

"Aria's busy for a few nights so I thought I could get a night off from the club whilst she's busy. I need some alone time."

I frown, "Alone time. What are you going to do on your own?"

"Just chill probably, I haven't had a night to myself in so long."

"Do I detect trouble in paradise. Is the relationship thing a bit too full on?" I joke, "What's Aria doing anyway?"

He shrugs. "I don't know, she's being secretive to be honest. I'm starting to wonder what's going on." He looks sheepish and I narrow my eyes.

"You're going to spy on her, see what she's up to?" I guess. JP shifts uncomfortably, not quite meeting my eye. "Oh shit, you really are." I howl with laughter. "You know she'll kill you if she finds out."

"She's acting crazy," he argues, "She kicked me out of her apartment at the crack of dawn and said she can't see me for a few days. I asked her why, but she wouldn't say. I have to know; it's driving me mad."

"Do you think she's seeing someone else?"

He shrugs, looking miserable. "I just don't understand why she's being so secretive. Anyway, she's booked a restaurant tonight, I saw it scribbled on her notepad. So, I thought I'd show up there."

I rub my hands together with a huge grin on my face. "I'm in, what time are we going?"

JP shakes his head, "No way. You're not coming to stir shit up."

"Me, stir shit?" I ask, innocently. "I'm being a good friend. What if she's with another man, you'll need my support."

"I don't need your kind of support, Aiden. It'll just piss her off more."

"More than you showing up out the blue?" I ask, scoffing. "Look, at least if we all go, you can make it look like a coincidence."

"All?"

I grin, "What time shall we be there?"

He groans, "I can't believe I'm agreeing to this. Eight o'clock."

♥

Luckily, I know the owner of said restaurant, so when JP told me he couldn't get a table, I managed to get us one. Not only that, but I made sure it was right next to Aria's. I don't want to risk not seeing exactly what she's up to, and a small part of me can't wait to see her reaction.

So, when we arrive at exactly eight o'clock, and we're shown to our table, I'm more than shocked to see that Aria isn't with another man, like I expected. Instead, she's sitting opposite Bella.

"Oh shit," mutters JP, glancing at me.

"Well this backfired," I hiss as the waiter pulls out our seats.

Aria glances our way, doing a double take before glaring angrily at JP. He shifts uncomfortably in his chair, taking the offered menu. Once the waiter has left, she leans closer, "What the hell are you doing here?"

JP squares his shoulders, ready for battle. "I'm having dinner with Aiden, what does it look like?"

I risk a quick glance at Bella over my menu. She looks great, glowing in fact. But she refuses to look in my direction, instead, fixing her eyes to her own menu.

"You're spying on me," Aria accuses.

JP scoffs, rolling his eyes. "As if."

"I'm not stupid, JP," she snaps.

"He was worried when you were behaving suspiciously," I cut in. "I booked this table to cheer him up."

She narrows her eyes, "Since when have you ever bothered about anyone but yourself?"

I fain hurt, placing my hand over my chest. "How were we supposed to know you'd be here?"

"Maybe we should all just calm down," Bella cuts in, glancing around. "People are looking at us."

"This isn't over," Aria snaps, turning back to her menu.

I pull out my mobile, hoping to text Jenifer to cancel, but as I pull up her name, I see her entering the restaurant.

JP's eyes widen and he leans across the table, "You invited Jenifer?" he whisper hisses.

"I didn't know Bella would be here," I mutter.

I stand, smiling as Jenifer approaches and kiss her on the cheek. "You look amazing," I say, pulling out the seat beside me.

She spots Aria and smiles, "Aria," she greets, "You didn't say you were coming here tonight."

"Yes," she says stiffly, "There was a good reason for that. Jen meet Bella."

Jen glances at me, her eyes filled with panic. I offer a reassuring smile as she sits down. "Hi."

Bella looks up, "Hi, Jenifer, nice to finally meet you. How are you finding the job?"

"Oh my god, I love it," she gushes, suddenly relaxing. "It's my dream job."

I lean back, trying to focus on my menu as my current girlfriend, and my ex, chat like they're best friends.

The waiter returns and notices the conversation across the two tables. "Would you like to join? We can move the tables together," he suggests.

I'm already shaking my head in protest but JP grins, "Yeah, great idea," he says, standing so the waiter can drag the table across. Jen slides into the booth, sitting right next to Bella, and I tag onto the end.

"Bella, tell Jen about the doctor," Aria suggests, her smug smile aimed in my direction.

Bella blushes, "I got the phone call about my dad before anything could happen."

"Your dad?" I ask, changing the subject cos I don't want to know about the fucking doctor.

Bella smiles sadly, "He's not well. He's the reason I'm back here."

"Sorry to hear that, I didn't realise," I mutter, frowning.

"Why should you?" asks Aria, "It's none of your business."

I ignore her. "Will he be okay?"

Bella shakes her head, "No. He doesn't have long left."

Jen places her hand over Bella's, "Oh gosh, that's awful. If there's anything we can do?"

And suddenly, I want Jen to leave. We're not a 'we'. Me and Bella, we were a 'we', but not me and Jen.

I spend the rest of the meal in silence, thinking up ways to let Jen down easily, and when the bill arrives, I place my card on top of it. Bella adds some cash, and I glance her way. She shrugs, "I can cover my own food."

"It was just a gesture," I say. "Can't a guy buy his ex some dinner?" I joke. Nobody laughs.

Bella smiles tightly, "To be an ex, we would have had to have been in a relationship."

I give a stiff nod. "I'll just pay this on the way out," I mutter, grabbing the bill and my card. Bella slides the cash closer, and I sigh, taking it. Bella and Aria remain seated whilst the rest of us stand. JP waits a beat before frowning, "Aren't you coming?"

"No, we'll have another coffee for the road," Aria says.

"Seriously, what's going on?" he pushes.

"Christ, JP, stop suffocating me," Aria snaps and he sighs heavily, before shrugging and heading for the exit.

"It was nice to see you," I tell Bella. She gives a small smile that doesn't quite reach her eyes, and I follow after JP with Jen right behind.

CHAPTER THIRTY-ONE

Aiden

I stare hard at the applications in front of me. The sound of Jenifer's phone irritates me as she concentrates on the screen. It's another reminder that she's younger than me with an addiction to social media.

It's been two weeks since I last saw Bella, which is two weeks since I decided to break up with Jen. It's harder than I thought, and no amount of hinting is giving Jen the message. Because like the coward I am, I thought it would be better all-round if Jen dumped me. That way I could avoid Aria giving me the whole, *'I told you so'* speech, and I wouldn't have the guys on my back, laughing because I've failed at dating.

"How come you're not at the shop today?" I inquire.

"They closed for today, its Bella's dad's funeral," she mutters, not bothering to look up from her phone.

"He died. Since when?" I ask.

"Don't know," she shrugs. "Jenifer, put the damn phone down. I'm trying to have a conversation with you."

She sighs, dragging her attention to me. "I don't know when he died, all I know is they told me the shop would be closed today because they were all going to the funeral to support Bella. JP and Raff went too," she tells me, shrugging. I hate that everyone knew except for me. It's another reminder I'm not a part of Bella's life anymore.

"Did anyone happen to mention when Bella's going back to Scotland?" Maybe I can arrange to meet her for dinner so we can clear the air properly.

"Straight after the funeral. Not surprising really, now she's on countdown."

"Countdown?"

She meets my eye. "Well, it can't be long, can it? My sister looked like that right before she dropped it."

I frown, "Dropped what?"

"The baby," she says with a laugh, like I'm stupid.

"Baby?" I repeat, "What baby? Who's having a baby."

"Bella."

I scoff, "Don't be ridiculous. My ex, Bella? She's not pregnant."

"Aiden, I sat next to her in the restaurant, she's pregnant. She had a perfectly round bump." She laughs, "How didn't you notice?"

I grip the arms on the chair, trying to focus on Jen's words. *There's no fucking way Bella could be pregnant.* Aria would have jumped at the chance to rub my face in it, *unless* . . . I stand abruptly and Jen raises a brow. "Are you okay?"

Questions race through my mind as I pull on my jacket. *Is that why she ran? Did she know all along she was having my child again?*

I grab my car keys. "I have to see for myself," I mutter, heading for the door.

Bella

I stare at my reflection in Arias long mirror. I don't look like a girl with no parents. Tears prickle my eyes again and I'm unsure if they're for dad, or for myself. Maybe a little of both.

I got the call right after I left the restaurant after seeing Aiden. And I've spent the last two weeks making calls and sorting out the funeral. So today feels bittersweet because

I'm sad to say goodbye to my dad, but I also can't wait to leave London and go home.

I open my clutch to check my train ticket is there. I plan on leaving right from the church. I take a deep breath before heading downstairs. The sooner this is over with, the sooner I can head back and put London behind me.

***

I stand beside Claire outside the same church my mum is buried at. It was dad's wishes to rest here too.

The car slows outside, and Claire takes my hand. "Are you ready?" she asks, with a sad smile. I give a nod, and we slide from the vehicle together.

We move along the line of guests, each of them offering well wishes, and then we stand by the door, waiting for dad to be taken from the back of the car. The guests begin to filter into the church, and we follow the coffin down the aisle.

We sit through the service together, both sniffling into tissues as the vicar talks about my dad's early life, his marriage to my mum, and brief stories of happier times. I didn't want to say any words, mainly because I didn't have any to say. Our happy memories were few and far between and I couldn't bring myself to lie. But when Claire stands to speak, my heart swells with happiness. Her tales of their short time together gives me peace that at least when he passed, he was happy.

We hold on to one another as they lower him into the ground. It's the final goodbye and somehow this hurts more than the service.

We lie roses on top of the coffin, and once everyone has slowly wandered off, we stand in silence. Both lost in our own thoughts.

I eventually say my goodbyes to Claire, promising to keep in touch. I owe her for making my dad's final months, happy. And she's been a fantastic support to me, I like her.

Aria and Cal are waiting by the church. "Are you sure you have to go back?" asks Aria, pulling me into a hug.

"I know you can't believe it," I say with a laugh, "But there are way better places than London."

I hug Cal. "Call the second you get back. Have a safe journey."

"And we want news the second this baby arrives," adds Aria, rubbing her hand over my stomach.

My taxi pulls in and I feel relieved. Cal puts my bags in the boot, and I get another hug. "Take care," I say, rubbing a hand over my swollen stomach. It feels so heavy today after being on my feet for so long.

I turn to slide in the taxi, my eyes catching sight of a figure by the trees. Aiden. I gasp, immediately dropping my hand from my bump. But it's too late, I can tell by his shocked expression that he's seen me in all my pregnant glory. I get into the car, slamming the door. "Quick," I mutter, "My train is due."

The cab drives past Aiden, and our eyes lock for the briefest second before he calls out my name, running towards me. His hand catches the window, and I jump in fright. "Don't stop," I tell the driver. "Keep going."

I lean my head back, slowly releasing a nervous breath. "Can you drop me at the tube," I tell the driver. I'll need to head to a different station further away, so Aiden doesn't turn up and make a scene.

It's not until I'm on the train pulling out of the station that I begin to relax. I pull out my mobile, cancelling the tenth call from Aiden. After today, we'll never see each other again. I open the text messages he's sent and read them again.

> *Aiden: Please don't run, Bella. Talk to me.*

> *Aiden: I just need to know if it's mine.*

I delete them both and sigh when my phone alerts me to a new voicemail. I reluctantly press play. "Please, I get why you ran. But just talk to me, Bella."

I press delete and drop the phone in my bag. It was hard enough when Aiden rejected me, I can't stand the thought of him rejecting our child. It's the only family I have and I'll protect it no matter what.

Aiden

> **Me: Meet me at Tremos now and bring Aria and Raff.**

I hit send and wait for JP to turn up as I pour myself a double whiskey. The second they arrive, they look guilty. Raff speaks first, "What's up?"

"Did you all know or just that lying bitch?" I ask, pointing at Aria.

"Know what?" asks JP.

I dive from the chair, heading right for him but Raff intercepts, holding me back. "What's going on?" he asks.

"You all fucking knew and said nothing," I yell accusingly.

"Knew what?" he demands, and I realise he looks confused.

"JP?" I ask, and he glances at Aria who sighs.

"They don't know," she admits. "I haven't told them."

"Told us what?" asks JP.

"How did you find out?" she asks me, ignoring him.

"Jen told me." I groan out loud, "Fuck. It all makes sense now. That's why you were sneaking around. That's why she wouldn't stand up at the restaurant."

"She didn't want you to know, Aiden, not after how you treated her before. What was I supposed to do?"

"What are we missing?" asks Raff.

"Is it mine?" I snap.

Aria gives a sarcastic laugh. "Of course it's yours," she yells. "She threw up after you forced her to take the morning after pill." She narrows her eyes, "You treated her so badly, you made her vomit."

"Bella's pregnant?" asks JP, looking at Aria in shock. "Why didn't you say anything?"

"Bigger problems right now, JP," she hisses.

I pace, pulling at my hair in frustration. "I need her address," I say, and Aria shakes her head.

"No chance. No way. Just leave her alone, Aiden. You've done enough damage. She chose to have this baby knowing she was alone. She doesn't need you."

"And what if I need her, Aria?" I snap. They all exchange looks that almost look pitying. "What if it was her all along?" I add.

Aria breaks eye contact, still shaking her head. "It's not your choice, Aiden. You made her so sad and finally, she's happy."

"Does the doctor think it's his?" I demand.

"No. But he's been there for her. He checks on her all the time and takes care of her when she's sick." A tear slides down her cheek and she swipes it away. "He's sad too and I know they can be happy together. Just let them be." She turns on her heel, leaving. JP gives me a sad smile and a sympathetic pat on the shoulder before heading after her.

Raff takes my whiskey off the bar and downs it. "Fuck, Aid. What are you gonna do?"

"Tell her I know," I say. "And then it's her choice."

I head for the office, closing the door and leaning against it to gather my thoughts. I take a deep breath before dialling her number, knowing she won't answer. I wait for the voicemail to kick in and close my eyes. "Hey," I almost whisper. "I don't know what to do, Bella," I admit. "I want to chase you to Scotland. I want to hear you say the words out loud, that you're having our child. And I'm ready for that. I am. I know you don't think it, but I've spent the months we've been apart, growing up. But Aria said you're happier without me, that I just make you sad. So, tell me, Bella, what should I do? Pretend I don't know, and we go on with our lives? Or come and find you?" I disconnect the call, surprised when a minute later, I get a text from her.

> **Bella: Walk away. Pretend we don't exist. Please.**

Bella

I lean over the couch for support as another pain rips through me. I reach for my phone, grabbing it from the cushion and I dial Grant's number. It's the middle of the night but he's usually awake so I'm not surprised when the call connects.

"Baby," I pant, "Coming." And I disconnect, throwing the device on the couch as a second pain hits me.

Grant comes barreling the door minutes later, "It's not time," he says, his eyes wide as he takes in my ruffled state.

"I'm aware," I grit out impatiently. "I thought it was Braxton hicks again but it's not going."

He places his bag down and reaches inside, retrieving a stethoscope. "Did you call the hospital?"

"No, I called you," I snap. "My doctor."

He presses it to my stomach and listens for a moment. "Heartbeat is nice and strong." He stands again. "I'll call the hospital. They may ask you to come in to be monitored seeing as you're a few weeks early."

"Does it matter?" I ask, grabbing his wrist, "That it's early?"

He smiles, "No. It's just two weeks." He goes into the kitchen to make the call. I stand straighter, trying to grab my phone to text Aria, when there's a warmth between my legs. I look down as wetness soaks my pyjamas.

Grant comes back, "I need to examine you. The hospital wants to know how dilated you are."

I stare in horror. "Absolutely not."

He smirks, "Bells, I'm a doctor."

"That has yet to see my vagina," I remind him.

He laughs. "If you're not dilated, there's no point in us going all the way to the hospital. They'll just send you home."

He helps me to lie on the couch before putting on some gloves. I lift my backside, and he tugs my pyjama bottoms down, frowning. "Did your waters break?"

I feel myself blush. "I thought I peed."

"Jesus, Bella, how long have you been having pains?"

"Hours," I say with a groan as my stomach tightens.

Grant waits for it to pass before placing a sheet over me and removing my underwear. "I need to feel," he says, wincing slightly.

"Knock yourself out," I mutter, "although this isn't how I imagined our first time to go," I tease, and he laughs.

After a few silent minutes he arches a brow. "You're almost ten centimeters."

"That's good, right?"

"It means you've done all the hard work, and your baby is almost here."

"No," I say, trying to sit up. Another pain forces me to lie back. "But what about the pain relief?"

"You've done the hard work, Bella, didn't you hear me?" He laughs again, "When you feel the urge to push, go for it."

I stare wide eyed. "What? Here, on the couch?"

He looks around, "Um, good point. Maybe we should lay sheets on the floor and move to an area we can clean easily?"

"You're missing my point," I cry. "I'm having the baby here in the cottage?"

He smiles wide, "Yep. It'll be my tenth delivery," he announces proudly. "Now, shall we move to the floor? Maybe all fours might feel more comfortable?"

"So you can see my backside to," I hiss, holding out my hand so he can help me up. "Not a chance."

I waddle through to the kitchen and Grant lays out some sheets and towels. Pain rips through me again and this time, there's a pressure between my legs, telling me I need to push. I grab onto Grant's hands and follow my body's instinct, pushing down until the urge passes.

"That's it," Grant says, "Now pant between pushes."

Aiden

I sit in the booth watching the after-party chaos, wondering when this all stopped being so much fun. I lived for these nights and yet, here I am, bored and eager to close up so I can fall into bed to enjoy another sleepless night.

Jenifer drops down beside me, "What's wrong with you?" I shrug and she groans. "You're so boring these days." Her comment makes me laugh and she narrows her eyes. "I'm serious. Like, what is the point in even being together when you spend all your time working or mooching around like your life is about to end."

"You're right," I agree, nodding. I take a breath; I've been waiting for this moment for weeks and she's handing it to me on a plate. "You deserve better."

She begins to shake her head and fury fills her expression. "Don't you fucking dare," she whispers in a low, angry voice.

"I don't make you happy," I reason.

"My god, you've been waiting for this haven't you." I stay quiet, admitting it will only send her nuts. "I saw it coming," she says, scoffing. "But I thought you were just depressed over the whole Bella thing, but now I see it's because you're a selfish, self-absorbed, prick."

"That I am," I mutter.

"No wonder Bella left."

"Exactly," I agree.

"She's better off without you. That baby boy deserves better."

My head whips up in her direction and I stare wide-eyed. "Baby boy?"

Her expression softens slightly. "Yeah, a few days ago." She pulls out her mobile and opens Bella's social media account. I frown, wondering when they became friends, especially since I'd blocked Bella's account to stop me searching her up. She turns the screen towards me, and I inhale sharply. A blue eyed, tiny baby boy fills my heart, and suddenly, it's too hard to breathe. I tug at my collar, taking the mobile from her and peering closer.

"A boy, she had a boy," I whisper.

"You miss her don't you?" she asks.

I could lie, it might make her feel better, but for once in my life, I want to be honest, so I nod. "More than anything."

"You've wasted all this time," she says sadly. "You could have been making things right with her."

"Aren't you mad?"

She shrugs, "It's not like you were ever really mine, Aiden. We haven't even had sex, I was beginning to wonder if it was me."

I shake my head, taking her hand. "I'm sorry. I shouldn't have dragged you into any of this. I just wanted to move on, and I thought dating you would help with that."

"Well, for the record, it just makes things messier," she says, "But, I get it." She takes her mobile back, even though I resist because I want to stare some more at my son. "I can give you Bella's address," she mutters. I release the handset immediately and she laughs. "But if you tell anyone it came from me, I'll gut you like a fish."

I grin, "You've been spending way too much time with Aria."

"At least now we can bitch about you at work, and maybe she'll like me." My phone beeps and I open the screenshot she's sent me. "It was on an invoice. I don't know why I took the picture," she admits, "I guess I knew you'd need it eventually."

"Thank you, Jen. This means so much to me."

"You'd better not fire me," she adds, standing.

I smirk, "Wouldn't dream of it."

CHAPTER THIRTY-TWO

Aiden

Arriving in the little town, I drive slowly. I admire the little cottages, lined up evenly on each side of the road. People are chatting in the streets, laughing and smiling. It's a quaint little place and I see why Bella loves it so much.

I stop the car outside her pretty little cottage, taking a moment to examine its beauty. The garden is overflowing with bright flowers, and I can almost picture Bella out there enjoying the fruits of her labour.

I take a deep breath before getting out the car. It feels good to stretch my legs after such a long journey but as I look around, I notice the neighbours staring at me with curiosity. It's almost like they can sense I'm a stranger, and I wonder how Bella managed to fit herself in to such a tight community.

I get the gift bags from the back seat. Also retrieving the huge balloon that's spent the entire journey bobbing up and down and driving me insane.

I head up the garden path, knocking gently on the door in case the baby is sleeping. I'm nervous, and I try to recall a time when I felt like this . . . there isn't one.

The door swings open, taking me by surprise as I watch Bella's retreating form. She didn't even look up to see me.

"Why are you knocking?" she asks. "Thank God you're here. I need a shower, and I can't put him down because he screams. I stink of milk and baby sick," she's saying as she walks away. I step inside, quickly glancing around outside before gently closing the door and placing my gifts down. I drop the latch, just to avoid any interruptions from whoever she was expecting, and then I follow her. "I am so tired; please tell me you're staying over tonight."

I ignore the sting to my heart at the thought of someone else spending the night here with my newborn. I clear my throat, "I was hoping to, if there's room." Her head whips round to look at me and I offer a little smile. "It was a long journey."

"Aiden," she whispers, her eyes wide with shock.

"Sorry, I should have announced it was me, but you seemed so harassed . . ." I trail off, my eyes falling to the bundle wrapped in blankets as she gently rocks side to side.

She stops swaying. "What are you doing here?"

I nod at the bundle. "I saw a picture," I reply. "He has my eyes."

"Most babies are born with blue eyes," she mutters.

"I couldn't stay away, Bella. I'm sorry. I tried," I tell her, shrugging. "Just, knowing he's here is different. He's real now."

"Yeah, it does hit different seeing him," she whispers, her lip lifting slightly in a smile. She takes a step closer, then pauses, her expression hesitant. "I can't stop you seeing him, I wouldn't because I want what's best for him. But understand this, you can't abandon him," she says, her voice breaking slightly. "If you meet him and you hold him, you can't then just leave and pretend he's not here."

I'm already shaking my head before her sentence is finished. "I wouldn't ever . . . I won't. I swear."

"Because I can't watch you leave him, Aiden. It would hurt too much. I can't have you coming and going from his life and making him feel like he's not enough for you." A tear slips from her eye and guilt floods me. "So, if I let you meet him properly, you have to promise to be a dad to him."

"I promise."

"I know he won't remember this, but I will, and my heart can't take anymore crap from you, not when it comes to my son."

"Our son," I correct, closing the gap between us.

We both look down at the bundle and a gasp escapes me. He's asleep, snuggled in against Bella, looking peaceful. "He's perfect," I whisper, carefully moving the blanket further from his face. "Absolutely gorgeous."

"Isn't he?" she says quietly, "I just . . . I haven't ever felt anything like it. The love . . . it's just so overwhelming." She let's out a happy sigh and brings her eyes to mine. "Would you like to hold him?" I nod, unable to speak through the emotion that's currently lodged in my throat. "Have you held a baby before?" she asks and I shake my head, giving a nervous laugh. "Maybe sit down?" she suggests, nodding to the couch.

I lower, getting comfortable. She places the baby in my arms, and I hold my breath, terrified that I might wake him, and he'll scream, and I'll have to hand him back. Bella smiles, brushing a hand over his tiny head. "Breathe, Aiden," she whispers. "He won't break."

"He's so small," I remark, staring in wonderment. I raise him slightly, inhaling the mix of baby and Bella. I close my eyes, it's the best scent in the world.

"Do you want to know his name?"

My eyes open and she's still smiling. I hadn't even thought about his name or what she might have chosen so I nod, bracing myself in case I hate it. "Braiden Jake," she says, another tear slipping down her cheek. "I've spelt Braiden to include your name," she adds, swiping the tear away. "I wanted him to have a piece of you even though he wouldn't know you."

I was certain I couldn't feel any happier in this moment, until those words left her mouth. My own eyes glisten as I stare down at my son. "Braiden Jake," I repeat, a smile forming, "It's perfect." I raise my head, meeting her eye. "After everything I did to you, I didn't deserve you to be so kind and thoughtful." Shame washes over me. "You're amazing, do you know that?"

"We both made mistakes," she says, "We both did things we regret."

"I don't even know where to start making it right," I admit.

She places a hand on my knee, gently squeezing. "Just being here for him is a great start." She inhales, releasing it slowly, "You have no idea how badly I wanted to call you to tell you about him. I hated that you were missing out on him."

"I was stupid to ever think I could exist in this world without being in his life."

"I'm glad you're here, Aiden."

"I thought you'd send me packing," I say with a small laugh, "It's what I deserved."

"We're parents now," she says, "Whatever we did or whatever happened, is in the past. Our future is all about him. We both have to grow up and be there as parents."

"Together or apart?" I ask, risking another glance at her.

She runs her lower lip through her teeth, "One step at a time, Aiden. I'm emotional and full of hormones. I can't trust my judgement right now."

I give a nod. "I understand."

"Do you plan on sticking around for a few days?"

"I'll stay around as long as you need me to," I say firmly. "I'll call JP and have him and Raff run things."

"I'd like . . . I mean, that's great . . . for Braiden." She stands, "I can show you his room?"

I nod, holding Braiden towards her to take. She laughs, "You can walk around with him."

I wince. "I'm terrified I'll drop him."

She shakes her head, laughing again, "You won't." And she heads out the room.

Bella

I step from the shower and breathe a sigh of relief. The shock is finally starting to wear off that Aiden is here, in my home, holding our son. It took me a good ten minutes to convince him he'd be fine alone with Braiden whilst I took a quick shower.

I rub my hair, a thousand thoughts running through my head while I contemplate where we go from here. I can't deny I wasn't pleased when Aiden promised not to leave Braiden. The thought of him playing dad whenever it suits, is far from the life I want for our son. And ideally, I want to be a family. But deep down, I don't know if I can ever trust him again after everything that's happened.

When I return to my bedroom, Aiden is sitting on the bed, still clutching Braiden to his chest. He smiles, "He opened his eyes," he whispers excitedly.

I grin, "Yeah, he tends to do that."

"But he looked at me and didn't cry. It's like he knew."

I smirk, "Maybe." It's at that point Braiden wakes again, this time squawking in that way I've come to love. "He's hungry," I add, reaching for him.

Aiden reluctantly hands him over. I know how he feels, it's weird having someone to share him with.

I take a seat in the rocking chair by the window and loosen the top of my towel, uncovering one breast. Braiden roots around, his mouth frantic until he latches on. Aiden watches in amazement. "You're breast feeding," he says.

"Apparently, it's best, but I think that's a lie to make new mums feel bad. I've seen perfectly healthy babies on formula." I sigh, "But it's not as bad as I thought it would be and I'm actually quite enjoying it. But don't tell Grant that." The words tumble out and I instantly regret them, even though I have nothing to feel bad about, I just don't want to ruin this moment of truce.

"Grant . . . the doctor?" Aiden asks. I give a nod. "And what's his . . . role in your life?"

"He's my friend," I tell him. "A really good friend, but there's nothing romantic between us."

Aiden looks relieved. "Do you want there to be?"

I shake my head, laughing. "No. I thought I did, but as time's past, I realise he's almost like a brother to me. Besides," I add with a shrug, "He's seen way too much for him to be anything else."

"What do you mean?"

I smile, "Grant delivered Braiden." His eyes widen. "I know, shocking, right. I gave birth right on the kitchen floor."

"Jesus, without pain relief?"

I nod, feeling proud. "He just came right out after a few pushes."

"Wow." Aiden's smile fades, "I hate I missed it."

"Trust me, that's a good thing," I say, keeping my tone light. "There's no point dwelling." I take a breath, then add, "What's going to happen?"

"With what?"

"This. Contact. Us? Not that there is an us," I say, flustering over my words. "Sorry, I just can't think straight. You turning up like this is unexpected."

"Let's take a few days to settle," he suggests. "I don't have all the answers and like you rightly pointed out, things are still up in the air for you. Let's just enjoy this, right now."

"I'm talking about after, Aiden. When this bubble of joy fades away and it's back to reality. You living in London and us here, how will we arrange contact?"

"We'll cross that bridge when we come to it, but honestly, Bells, right now whilst I'm still in this bubble, I want to be wherever he is."

We're interrupted by a knock on the door. "It'll be Grant," I say and Aiden's smile fades. "Why is the door locked?" I add as an afterthought.

"You're alone with a newborn, it's dangerous to leave it open."

I grin, "We're not in London anymore, Aiden. Everyone leaves their doors unlocked here."

He visibly shudders then stands, "I better go and meet your doctor friend."

"Be nice," I warn as he disappears to let Grant in.

I hear Aiden introduce himself, and Grant makes a remark about it being a long time coming. "I'm in here," I call out, trying to avoid any conflict between the pair.

Grant appears in the doorway with Aiden hot on his heels protesting. Grant ignores him, coming close and gently brushing his hand over Braiden's silky hair. "How is the wee man?" he asks.

"She's feeding," says Aiden, his eyes wide with disbelief. "Bella, you're feeding."

I smile, "Grant's a doctor, and like I said, he's seen way more than me feed."

"Well let's not think about that right now," says Aiden stiffly.

Grant smirks, taking a few steps back. "I'll call back tomorrow if you don't need anything?"

I shake my head. "We're good, thanks."

Aiden waits for him to leave before sitting on the bed. "I didn't like it," he mutters, and I frown. "Him being here like he knows you better than me."

"He does," I say simply. "He's been here for me, Aiden and I can tell you right now, that isn't going to change. He brought Braiden into the world so you can either get on with him, or not, but he's a part of our lives and he's staying."

He thinks over my words before giving a nod. "Okay." He pushes to stand again. "Are you hungry? I'll make us something."

I scoff, "You'll make us food?"

"Hey," he says, faking hurt, "I can cook. I just choose not to."

"Well, luckily for you, there's at least six meals in the fridge just waiting to be eaten."

He frowns, "You were prepared."

"Not at all. But I have fantastic neighbours that keep cooking for me."

CHAPTER THIRTY-THREE

Aiden

I get it. I get exactly why Bella settled so easily here and as we walk through the village, being greeted by friendly faces, I can almost picture myself here . . . with Bella and Braiden.

I take control of the pushchair whilst Bella pops into the bakery to get freshly made bread, it's becoming our morning routine. A walk. Fresh produce. Breakfast in the garden.

"Well, well, well, that's a sight I never thought I'd see in this lifetime." I turn to the sound of JP's voice, smiling as he approaches with Aria by his side. We shake hands and when I turn to Aria she scowls. "Don't even think about touching me."

I smirk. "Still as prickly I see."

Bella rushes from the shop. "Oh my god, what are you guys doing here?" she cries, wrapping each one in her arms in greeting.

"We thought we'd come and visit before this one turned into a teenager," Aria jokes, peering into the pushchair. "Oh, Bella, he's gorgeous."

Bella smiles proudly, "I know. I make the cutest kids." I clear my throat, and she laughs, "With your help of course."

"You're just in time for brunch," I announce, turning the pushchair around. "I'm about to cook my famous poached eggs."

I feel JP fall into step beside me, "Famous cos you killed someone from food poisoning?"

I grin. "I don't know why everyone thinks I can't cook."

"You're looking good, brother. Really good," he says, glancing at me. "Time away is doing you good."

I nod in agreement. "I feel good, JP. This place . . . it's exactly what I need."

"We had bets you'd be home within a week," he says, smirking. "But here you are, almost a month later. Are you ever coming home?"

I shrug. "Home," I repeat. "I don't even know where that is anymore."

"Serious?" he asks, staring at me through wide eyes.

"Home is where she is, JP. I don't know if I can be away from either of them now, and she won't move back to London. I mean, look at this place, why would she?" He grins wide and I narrow my eyes, "What?" I ask.

"It's what Jake wanted all along, isn't it. You and Bella together."

"That bastard always knew what I needed, more than I ever did."

"And does Bella feel the same?"

My smile fades. "I don't know. We haven't talked about it."

"You've been here a month, man, and you're telling me you've not even spoke about the future?"

"We sort of broached it when I first got here, and we agreed it was too soon to talk that deep when we were both emotional and riding high on the fact we just had a kid. Since then, there's not been a right time."

"Aiden, you have to talk to her. If she's not on the same page, then what?"

"How can I expect her to forgive me for everything?" I ask. The thought's been playing on my mind way too much and I still don't have the right answers. We've fallen into a nice routine of being Braiden's parents, but there's been no hint of anything else.

"What are you two talking about?" Bella calls from behind. I stop, waiting for her and Aria to catch up. "It looks serious," she adds.

I smile, "Nothing important," I lie. "Just business talk."

Her smile falters and she gives a slight nod. "Have you come to drag him home?" she asks JP.

He laughs. "Since when has anyone been able to make Aiden do anything he doesn't want to do?"

Her eyes find mine again. "You don't want to go home?" I detect a note of hope in her voice, and I take my chance, slipping my hand in hers.

"I am home, Bella. I told you; I'll be wherever you and Braiden are."

"Jesus, pass me a bucket," mutters Aria. Bella shoots her a glare and we walk the rest of the way home in silence.

※

I make us all some poached egg on fresh toasted bread, and we talk about the bakery and how well things are going for Aria. JP briefly discusses the bar and then Bella fills everyone in on what it's like to be a parent, and even when she talks about the sleepless nights, she smiles. Secretly, I love that time the best. The second I hear Braiden wake, I get up and change his bottom before Bella feeds him. But the most special part of that, is how we sit in bed together and just talk. I hate it when he drifts back off to sleep and I have to go back to the spare room.

"Why don't you go sit in the garden and catch up," JP suggests. "Me and Aiden can watch the baby."

We wait for them to leave before JP turns to me, "I've got an idea."

"That's never good."

"Bella's seen you're a good dad, right?" I nod. "So now you need to show her you're a good boyfriend."

"That's the problem," I remind him, "I did too much damage there."

"But you've changed. Show her."

"How?"

"Put down roots here, so she knows you're sticking around."

"Like rent my own place?"

He nods, "Or buy. I mean, that screams settled."

"Or it screams crazy. What if she doesn't want me to stick around forever? It might scare her off. I have to play it cool, let her lead."

"I saw her face, man, when she asked if I'd come back to drag you home, she was anxious."

"She's just had a baby and I'm here helping, she probably panicked at the thought of doing it alone." Braiden begins to stir and I go over to the pushchair and lift him out. "I'll talk to her, see what she's thinking. But even if she doesn't want to be with me, I'm still staying here, JP. I can't leave my son."

"You know the one person you really need on your side in this . . . Aria." I scoff. "I'm serious, Aiden. Sort shit with her and that's the way to Bella's heart.

♥

Aria eyes me suspiciously. "What are you doing here?"

It was JP's idea for me to meet Aria in the local bar. I'd announced I was nipping out to get supplies, JP and Aria were meant to be going for a drink tonight, but he sent her ahead with the promise to catch up.

"I wanted to talk to you."

She lowers into the chair opposite me, "You should make it quick, JP is on his way."

"I know you hate me," I begin and she arches a brow. "And I get it. You should hate me. I've been a complete wanker to Bella and I don't deserve her time."

"You got that right."

"But, we have Braiden now. And so, I want to make things right."

"What's that got to do with me?"

"You're Bella's best friend. She loves you. It's important we get along."

"You didn't care about that before?"

"I didn't care about a lot of things before," I admit. "I'm making the effort to change, Aria. I want to be good enough for her and Braiden. Your blessing means a lot to me."

"So you want to get back with her?"

"I'd like to, if it's what she wants."

Aria sighs heavily, "She does."

I sit straighter, "She said that?"

She shakes her head. "I can tell. Besties, remember."

"And how do you feel about that?"

She scoffs, "What does it matter?"

"It matters," I say firmly. "To me. To Bella."

"I don't think you're good enough for her." She's blunt but it's what I expected. "And I don't know why she's even giving you the time of day." She takes a breath. "But it's not up to me what Bella does. She told me how great you've been with Braiden."

"He's got me wrapped around his finger and he doesn't even realise," I say with a small smile.

"I thought you'd give up after a week," she admits. "But you've proved me wrong so far."

"And I will continue to. I want this, Aria. I want Bella and Braiden in my life. And I'll take whatever she gives me. I can't even begin to apologise for everything I've done. And if she gives me a chance, I'll put it all right."

"How?"

"I'm gonna marry her."

Aria sits up, leaning closer. "Marry her?" she repeats.

"Tomorrow if she'd let me. I'm serious, Aria. I love her."

Aria smiles. It's the first genuine smile she's offered me in a long time. "Then we have some plans to make."

CHAPTER THIRTY-FOUR

Bella

It's Aria's last day and I'll be sad to see them both leave. But they've been here a week already and they have to get back to the businesses. I wish I could bring my London life to here, because I miss them so much.

"You have to look perfect," Aria says, brining me back into the room.

"Huh?"

"For lunch today, you have to look perfect."

I frown, "Why? I don't think Bob and Sheila will care what I look like." The local bar owners aren't really fussy about attire when the place is always full with the farm lads.

"Because it's my last day and I want it to be amazing." She holds up a white summer dress and I narrow my eyes.

"It's just the local."

"Please," she begs, "For me."

I sigh. "Fine, whatever."

"And I'm doing your makeup, no arguments."

I groan dramatically. "I'll stand out like a sore thumb."

"When was the last time you bothered with makeup?" she asks.

I laugh, "I don't even remember."

"Exactly. Plus, I want some nice pictures of you, Aiden and the baby to take home."

My frown deepens. "You want Aiden on the pictures?"

She gives a small shrug, "Well, he's trying hard."

I smirk. "Wow, Aria, are you warming to Aiden?"

"We've reached an understanding," she says, pulling out her makeup bag. "I won't kill him if he doesn't hurt you."

I scoff, "Fat chance of that happening, Ari, he's not interested in me like that."

"Say's who?" she asks, dabbing foundation on my skin with a beauty blender.

"We both know Aiden, if he wanted to be with me, he'd have made it clear."

"Perhaps he's doing things differently this time."

"I don't know," I mutter. "I should speak to him about it, see how he feels. But it scares me."

"Why?" she asks.

"I don't want to remind him that he's got a life back in London. I'm not ready for him to leave."

"I thought he told you he's staying wherever Braiden is."

"How long can he do that realistically? His life is in London. His businesses. He fought so hard to keep that club, he isn't going to let it go."

"The club practically runs itself," she says, shrugging. "Besides, he can hire a manager. And he can't parent Braiden whilst being back in London. That's not practical."

"Shared parenting is a thing," I tell her. "I looked online. He could have Braiden in the holidays." I sigh heavily. "Although I hate that thought."

"You could just tell him how you really feel."

I shake my head. "No way. If Aiden wants to be with me, he's got to come to me. I can't put myself out there again."

"Let's go for lunch and then I can watch the baby and you two can talk."

Half an hour later, I stare at my reflection. "Wow, I look ... pretty," I say.

Aria grins beside me. "Stunning," she agrees.

"It's a little much for lunch."

"Nonsense. You just had a baby; you deserve to feel nice. And, I had a message from JP, Braiden took the bottle no problem." It's our second attempt at offering Braiden breast milk from a bottle, I wanted to give Aiden a chance to help with feeds.

"Those two were acting odd this morning," I comment, "Don't you think?"

"They're always up to something," she mutters, grabbing my hand. "Now, let's head over and meet them for lunch."

We step out into the sunshine, and as I turn to head up the path, my step falters at the sight of Aiden standing in the gateway. He's dressed in a suit, which confuses me momentarily, although before I can question it, he pulls out a bouquet of flowers. My frown deepens as I head towards him, gently encouraged by Aria who offers me a reassuring smile.

I take the flowers and he kisses me on the cheek and offers me his arm to hold. I take it, smiling. "What's going on?"

"All in good time," he says, and I can see the mischief in his expression.

"You're up to something."

"I wanted to show you how much you mean to me."

My heart rate picks up with excitement. "Now I know you love the cottage, it's perfect. So I approached the owner, Mr. Limes. And guess what, he agreed to sell it to me."

I gasp, "You didn't bully him, did you?"

He laughs, "No. I simply asked, and he practically bit my hand off. Apparently, he didn't have a clue how to sell up and I offered well over the asking price." We begin to walk slowly towards the village. "And because I'm still on probation, it's all in your name." He smirks, "Now, I know that doesn't hold much weight given my past behaviour, but I have all the paperwork, all the legal stuff, and it's completely yours. But, if I prove myself to you, I hope we can eventually own a place together." I'm lost for words and when I look behind to see where Aria is, she's nowhere to be found. "I sorted things with Aria," he adds, noticing my confusion. "We're all good."

"I thought it was odd when she was so reasonable earlier. Usually when I mention you, she gives me an eyeroll."

He laughs, "I've still got to prove myself to her, but these last few days, we've been working together, and I don't want to tempt fate, but so far, I think I'm winning." He stops, turning to face me and taking both my hands. "I know how much Aria means to you, so I know I have to show her how much I love you too."

I bite my lower lip, trying to stop the smile that's taking over my face. "You love me?"

He grins, "More than life itself."

"Did you know that the owners of The Dog and Sheep are retiring?" He takes me gently by the shoulders and turns me so I'm facing the local.

"I did not know that," I confirm, unable to stop the smile now. "But you seem to know so much about the locals."

"We got chatting and I mentioned I run a very impressive bar myself."

"And what did they say?"

He wraps his arms around me and rests his chin on my shoulder. "They said if I was to stick around, they'd be happy to take the asking price. They wanted to sell to someone they trust."

I gasp again, turning in his arms. "Are you serious?"

"It's an investment for Braiden, and a place I can hang out if you'll let me stay."

"You want to stay?" He nods and I cup his cheeks. "I've been wanting to ask for so long but I was scared you'd tell me you were leaving."

"I love you, Bella. I fucked up so many times and I hate myself for letting you down time and time again. I'm sorry.

So fucking sorry. But, if you'll have me, I'd like to make things up to you."

"Aiden, you've been great since you came here. I don't know how I'd have gotten by. But it's not just your help with Braiden that's been nice, but the fact we talk, and we watch movies together. I love the routine of our night feeds and how we sit and chat utter bollocks until he goes back to sleep."

Relief washes over his expression. "Thank God, cos I feel the exact same. It kills me leaving your bedroom when he goes back to sleep. I just want to be with you all the time."

"Me too," I cry, laughing whilst my eyes glisten with happy tears.

He takes a breath, "Okay, so this next bit is going to either send you crazy with happiness or I'm gonna undo everything I just did."

I brace myself as he takes my shoulders again, this time turning me towards the church where all of my friends are standing dressed nice and smiling back at me. I slam my hands over my mouth, "oh my god, what are they all doing here?" I whisper. I turn back to Aiden, to find him on one knee. My eyes widen. "Oh my god," I repeat.

He smiles, opening a box and presenting me with a ring that glistens in the sun. "I know we've got a long way to go and me just saying the words isn't enough. I hope that in time, you'll learn to trust me completely, because Bella, you're it for me. Jake was right, we're the perfect match. It took me too long to see that, and I don't want to waste another second of our lives apart." He takes a breath, and I dab away the tears that are slipping down my cheeks. "From changing dirty nappies, to sleepless nights, to walks in the village and watching you plant flowers. You're it. I am in love with you Bella. And I would be honoured if you'd marry me."

I nod, my hands shaking badly as I hold my left hand towards him. "Yes," I whisper.

He grins, standing and wrapping me in his arms, spinning me round. "She said yes," he yells and our friends whoop in delight. He steps back and places the diamond ring on my finger. "The church is booked," he tells me, giving me an unsure look.

"For now?" I cry, my mouth falling open in shock.

He nods. "I didn't want to risk you changing your mind."

"We're getting married ... now?"

"If you'll agree."

"Weddings take months to plan, years even."

Aria rushes over, "Stop overthinking," she demands, turning me to her and straightening my hair. "Everyone is going inside, and Aiden is going to be at the altar," she glances at him, "Go." He places a kiss on my head and rushes off. Aria turns back to me. "I took care of everything, and I think I've given you the perfect wedding. But you have to change. Josey has your actual dress in the pub," she says, grabbing my hand and dragging me off.

"I'm so overwhelmed," I mutter.

"You're so in love," she says over her shoulder. "So why wait."

We get into the pub that's completely empty now everyone is at the church. It's been decorated with cream and silver balloons. "This is your reception," Aria explains with a laugh. "And that . . ." she points to the dress hanging up. "Is your dress."

"Oh my god, it's perfect," I whisper.

"I paid attention when you talked about your perfect wedding," she says with a smile.

EPILOGUE

♡

Bella

I watch as Aiden rushes after Braiden. I wished for the toddler years to come quickly because I was so excited to see him up and walking. But now it's here, I take it back. Because with the walking, comes tantrums. Real tantrums that are like no other, and as Aiden sweeps our eighteen-month-old son into his arms, another one hits, and he looks over to me with helplessness. I laugh, "I have no idea," I say, gently rubbing my hand over my swollen stomach. In less than two weeks, we'll be a family of four. And this time around, feels extra special because Aiden has been a part of it. He's been to every scan, every appointment and even signed us up to antenatal classes because he's determined to be the best birthing partner. It's a real testament to how much we've both grown as parents, and as husband and wife.

We couldn't be happier.

And with all the businesses running well, it's given us a chance to enjoy Braiden. We have more time for each other, and running The Dog and Sheep is fun, it doesn't feel like work when we're surrounded by the locals who have become our friends.

In the beginning, we might have got it all wrong, but we're getting it right now, and that's all that matters. With our future mapped out, I have no regrets.

Well, maybe just one . . . ***that it took us so long to sort our shit out.***

THE END

A NOTE BEFORE YOU GO

♡

I wrote this book back in 2019. It was the first book I'd ever written and it was never meant to be published. But I stumbled across a small publishing company, and decided to go for it. When they agreed to publish it, I was over the moon. Of course, it flopped. I was a brand new author and I had no idea how to market or grow my audience.

I went on to publish many more books, and when my contract ended with the publishing company and they gave me the rights back to this book, it sat unpublished for a few years.

ABOUT THE AUTHOR

Nicola Jane, a native of Nottinghamshire, England, has always harboured a deep passion for literature. From her formative years, she found solace and excitement within the pages of books, often allowing her imagination to roam freely. As a teenager, she would weave her own narratives through short stories, a practice that ignited her creative spirit.

After a hiatus, Nicola returned to writing as a means to liberate the stories swirling within her mind. It wasn't until approximately five years ago that she summoned the courage to share her work with the world. Since then,

Nicola has dedicated herself tirelessly to crafting poignant, drama-infused romance tales. Her stories are imbued with a sense of realism, tackling challenging themes with a deft touch.

Outside of her literary pursuits, Nicola finds joy in the company of her husband and two teenage children. They share moments of laughter and bonding that enrich her life beyond the realm of words.

Nicola Jane has many books from motorcycle romance to mafia romance, all can be found on Amazon and in Kindle Unlimited.

Social Media

I love to hear from my readers and if you'd like to get in touch, you can find me here...

My Facebook Page

My Facebook Readers Group

Bookbub

Instagram

Goodreads

Amazon

I'm also on Tiktok

Printed in Dunstable, United Kingdom